ANATOMY
of
A MEET
CUTE

OTHER TITLES BY ADDIE WOOLRIDGE

The Checklist

The Bounce Back

ANATOMY
of
A MEET
CUTE

ADDIE WOOLRIDGE

 Montlake

This is a work of fiction. Names, characters, organizations, places, events, and incidents are either products of the author's imagination or are used fictitiously. Otherwise, any resemblance to actual persons, living or dead, is purely coincidental.

Published by Montlake, Seattle

www.apub.com

Amazon, the Amazon logo, and Montlake are trademarks of Amazon.com, Inc., or its affiliates.

ISBN-13: 9781662504570 (paperback)
ISBN-13: 9781662504587 (digital)

Cover design by Caroline Teagle Johnson
Cover image: © Malte Mueller / Getty; © nadia bormotova / Getty

Printed in the United States of America

To the messy ones. I love you.

Chapter One

"If there is a doctor or a nurse on board, will you please ring the call button?"

The soothing voice of the flight attendant glided across Sam's consciousness, jolting her out of her early-flight stupor. Pushing her sleep mask to the top of her head, she sat upright in her chair, stretching to her full height so she could look around the plane. No one else was ringing the call button. Shit.

Taking a deep breath, she raised a shaky hand and pressed the dreaded button above her seat. Nervous energy coursed through her as she tried to recall what her professors and any doctor she had ever encountered said about medical emergencies and aviation. She'd been warned that this could happen to her one day. Sam had just thought she'd have a lot more actual doctoring under her belt when it did.

"Ma'am, are you a medical professional?" the flight attendant asked, his voice low and calm, as if someone weren't somewhere on the plane experiencing a trauma.

"I'm an ob-gyn. Will that work?"

The flight attendant's flinch was almost imperceptible. "I think it'll have to. Would you come with me, please?"

Sam tried not to let the fear creeping through her skin make its way to her face as she mumbled apologies to her seatmates, both of whom smiled at her in the vaguely uninterested but encouraging way that only a plane full of Los Angelenos making their way to the freezing wasteland that was San Francisco could. This was probably an average Tuesday to the Hollywood set.

Snatching her sleep mask off her head, she looked at the flight attendant, who began to walk down the aisle. "Can you tell me anything about the individual?"

"We have a gentleman in first class, wearing dark sunglasses, who started behaving strangely just after departure. He keeps trying to take off his clothes, saying he is melting, then saying he needs help. We're about twenty minutes to San Francisco; the captain has already called ahead, so medical attention will be waiting for him at the gate. We just need to make sure we can get him there in one piece."

"Right," Sam said, taking a deep breath. What she really wanted to say was *oh shit*. The flight attendant's description wasn't much for her to go on, but it would have to be enough, since she'd decided to take her Hippocratic oath seriously.

"Excuse me," a passenger said, stopping the flight attendant as they neared the front of the plane. The attendant motioned for Sam to continue as he leaned in to listen to the passenger's request.

Pushing aside the thin curtain that separated the economy cabin from first class, Sam spotted the man almost immediately. Even as he wrestled with his jacket, it was impossible not to notice how good looking he was. He was probably four years older than her. His fine face twisted as he fussed with a zipper, the tawny color of his East Asian features slightly flushed from exertion, the muscles in his sculpted shoulders flexing as he shook his arm free from one sleeve.

Pursing her lips, Sam reminded herself that this was someone in need. Ogling was wasting valuable seconds that might save his life. Filling her lungs with air, Sam bent down next to the man, gently setting a hand on his arm. Twisting around in his seat, the man snatched a pair of designer headphones off his head and lifted his Wayfarer sunglasses to look down at her. "Can I help you?"

Sam fought the urge to squirm and reminded herself that the flight attendants had put out this call because the individual in need was acting strangely. "Hi. I'm just here to check on you. The flight attendants thought you may need some medical attention?"

"Excuse me?"

Sam shifted uncomfortably under the intensity of his gaze. His eyes were just-woke-up puffy but not bloodshot. She registered this as a good sign, trying to ignore the fact that his eyes were so dark they seemed more black than brown. That information wasn't, strictly speaking, medically relevant.

"How are you feeling?" Sam asked, cursing her hair puffs. Of course, this man didn't recognize her as a doctor. She was wearing pigtails, not scrubs, and thanks to God and a sprinkling of melanin, people often mistook her for younger than thirty-two.

"I'm fine. I work in medicine. Why would I need a doctor?"

Sam took a deep breath, giving the man a once-over. If she had to guess, he was on a bad trip. The question was, What had he taken? Fake Ambien? Maybe a party drug?

"I see. Did you, by chance, consume anything before you boarded the plane? You're not in trouble."

"No. You're mistaken. I'm not in need of medical—"

"He took something right when we boarded. I saw it," the elderly man next to him chimed in, causing the man's head to whip around. Not helpful. She was trying to establish trust with the patient, which she couldn't do if the older man was going to tattle on Mr. Sexy Ambien.

Rolling his eyes, the man said, "It was Advil. I have a headache."

Doing her best to look sympathetic, Sam nodded. "It is possible to have an unusual reaction to—"

"What reaction do you think I'm having?" the man asked, squinting at her, wrinkling the fine smattering of freckles across his nose.

"You were—"

"Oh, no," the flight attendant said, placing a hand on her shoulder. "Doctor, the—"

"I'm dying!"

Sam's head jerked up just in time to catch a blond man with a bun scratching at the sleeve of his blazer and jerking around in his seat two rows up.

"Oh. The attendant said a man in sunglasses needed help." The heat in her body kicked up a notch, and no amount of additional poolside tan was going to save her from the visible humiliation flooding her face.

"And you thought it was me?" Mr. Sexy Not Ambien looked incredulous.

"Well, you were struggling with your—"

"It's here," Man Bun whispered to the terrified-looking woman across from him.

Taking a deep breath, Sam stood abruptly as Mr. Sexy Not Ambien leaned into the aisle to get a good look at the guy, then looked up at her as if she were less useful than a box of weasels. Whatever—the good-looking dude could be offended. Right now she had an actual patient. Giving the man a curt wave, she said, "My apologies."

Taking two quick strides toward Man Bun, who had started buckling and unbuckling his belt, Sam dredged up her very best calming voice, again, and said, "Hello, how are you feeling?"

The man looked up at her wildly, pushing his mirrored aviator sunglasses onto the top of his head. "Do you see it?"

"Can you tell me what you're seeing?" Sam asked, hoping to get a sense of what the man was experiencing so she could start calming him down.

"My face is pixelated. My whole body is." He had the nerve to look at her as if she were completely stupid for not seeing it. And Sam did feel a little stupid. Hallucinations could be caused by anything, and she was no closer to soothing the man than she had been when she was talking to Mr. Sexy Not Ambien.

"Can you tell me if you ate or drank anything out of the ordinary before boarding the plane?"

The man looked up at her and winked. "Why should I tell you?"

Gross. Sam sighed, placing her hand on the back of the man's chair and giving his gold-and-black brocade blazer a once-over. He looked like the kind of nightclub promoter who lied about having a private jet to impress bumpkins from out of state.

"I want to help you, but . . ." Sam paused as a seat belt unbuckled. The man wiggled his eyebrows, then seemed to remember that his skin was loading slowly and began pressing on either elbow in short, jerky bursts.

"Sir. Can you please tell us what you ingested? You're not in trouble." A voice rang out, causing Sam to jump. She turned to see Mr. Sexy Not Ambien standing directly over her shoulder, looking put upon in one of those magical black T-shirts that managed to hug the chest but not look tight.

"What are you doing?" Sam asked. It was one thing for Mr. Sexy Not Ambien to observe a medical emergency. It was another thing for him to steal her line and impersonate a care provider. She was already not an emergency medicine doctor; the last thing she needed was someone who wanted to play one on TV jumping in to try to be "helpful."

"My job."

Just my luck. She would have two delusional people on one flight. "Could you please sit down?" Sam hissed, running out of patience. This guy was not helping. If anything, he was making the patient more antsy, and she'd just been starting to establish . . . well, nothing, but he was still in her way.

"I'm a doc-tor," the guy said like she was dense.

"Then why didn't you ring the call button?"

"Noise-canceling headphones," Mr. Sexy Not Ambien said, pointing to where the headphones hung around his neck.

"Is he a Fed?" Man Bun interrupted their conversation, loudly addressing his question to Sam. This was not how she'd imagined helping someone in need on a plane.

"Ladies and gentlemen, we have begun our descent into San Francisco. The flight attendants will be coming through the cabin shortly to collect any remaining service items. If you could please help us out by . . ." Sam, Mr.—no, Dr.—Sexy Not Ambien, and Man Bun all stopped to listen to the announcement, as if someone had hit pause on the entire bizarre scenario.

"Is that God?" Man Bun asked as soon as the attendant uttered their final thank-you.

"No, sir," both Sam and Dr. Sexy Not Ambien said at the same time. Sam sighed, looking down at the man and over at the new doctor. What was she doing here? Maybe her mother was right and she had no business becoming a doctor, let alone a researcher. Almost any other doctor was more qualified to deal with the hallucinating club kid. Looking back at the other doctor, Sam watched as he scrubbed his hand down the back of his close-cropped black hair, and she prepared to come clean about being a researcher. Better to admit that she spent more time behind a desk, hunched over journal articles, than in the emergency room.

"You know what—" Sam began at the same time Dr. Sexy Not Ambien began to speak.

"I'm sorry."

For a moment, the pair blinked at one another. Sam watched as the guy exhaled, a half smile tracing the left side of his face. "I interrupted you just now. I'm sorry for that and for butting in. This guy is all yours. Let me know if I can help."

With that, Dr. Sexy Not Ambien rolled his shoulders and turned to go back to his seat, leaving Sam slightly stunned.

"I just need my face to load," Man Bun whispered, snapping Sam out of her trance and back into the very real present.

Looking from the man to Dr. Sexy Not Ambien, Sam made a snap judgment. "Uh, Doctor?" Watching him turn around, Sam tried to ignore the tired expression on his face.

"Yeah?" he said, a barely masked irritation riding his tone. Sam almost changed her mind. Almost. The Hippocratic oath said *do no harm*, didn't it? She couldn't lose her nerve, even if this doctor was a jerk. She'd made a promise.

"I could use your help. I'm not a doctor." Sam flailed her hands and rushed to finish as his eyebrows shot toward his hairline as if she might be as high as the man they were trying to help. "I mean, I'm a doctor, but I'm a community health research fellow. I recently finished my residency, and I haven't spent time in emergency since med school."

Dr. Sexy Not Ambien took a deep and seriously overtaxed breath before exhaling an "Oh." Rubbing his eyes, he straightened up again and walked back toward her. Giving her a once-over, he gestured to the man and said, "Proceed."

Somehow, Sam had expected him to be less professorial and more, you know, helpful. Sam nodded, looking from him to Man Bun, who was loudly patting his cheeks.

"Can you tell me your name?"

"Mark von Erik." He wiggled his eyebrows at her like his name should mean something to her. It didn't.

"Well, Mark. Can you tell me when your face started to . . ." She looked over at Dr. Sexy, who quirked an eyebrow but said nothing. *Thanks, Doc.* "Pixelate?"

Wrong question. Mark's eyes got wide as saucers. Filling up his lungs with good old-fashioned plane air, he shouted, "Is it still doing that?"

"No. No. It's stopped," Sam said, holding her hand out to try to stave off another round of shouting and pulling at his clothes. Dr. Sexy pursed his lips but said nothing.

"I'm not sure you're telling the truth." Mark looked down at his hands.

"Can you tell me what medications you are taking?" Sam asked, trying a change of subject.

"I don't take pharmaceuticals," Mark burst out before pulling on his belt buckle.

Sam looked at the not-so-good doctor and shrugged, telegraphing *What do I do?* with her eyes. For his part, Dr. Sexy smirked before breaking down and asking, "Have you mentioned nonpharmaceutical substances to him?"

Whipping her attention back to the man, she asked, "What about anything plant based?"

At this, Mark looked up, giggled, and said, "You don't strike me as into mushrooms."

Bingo! Sam smiled as her ears popped. Judging from the tiny window to the outside, she had about seven minutes of flight time to keep this guy calm. She could do that. It was unlikely he was going to die in the next seven minutes, but it might be helpful to have a sample of what he'd taken, or at least the name of what he thought he'd taken, once he was off the plane.

"Do you have mushrooms on you still?" Sam said.

"Oh, you're *that* kind." A lewd smile cropped up on Mark's face. Next to her, Dr. Sexy snorted but turned it into a cough when Sam shot him a dirty look. "I guess I'd share with you."

"I want to know what it's called," Sam said, forcing a smile on her face.

"God's tea."

In hindsight, expecting him to use the plant's formal name might have been asking too much. Sam looked over at the other doctor, who shook his head as if to signal that he wasn't familiar with it, either, before asking her, "How else could you find out the name?"

Sam almost strangled him. The last thing she felt like doing was playing twenty questions with a distracting and obtuse doctor when they had a man they needed to keep calm and ten thousand feet to go before their wheels blessedly touched the ground.

Sighing, she turned back to the man and asked, "Where were you when you got God's tea?"

Mark opened his mouth, and Sam prayed he wouldn't answer *Mars*. "Cows, dude. Canadian cows."

The synapses in her brain fired, connecting the dots, her grin spreading with them. She knew what this was. Turning to Dr. Sexy, she whispered, "*Psilocybe fimetaria*."

"You know mushrooms?" he said, his smooth forehead wrinkling with surprise. Daggers shot out of Sam's eyes—just because she had a hard time figuring out which indoor-sunglasses guy needed help didn't mean she was totally useless. Dr. Sexy must have read her irritation, forcing him to attempt a botched recovery with, "Surprised is all. Good work."

Good work, no thanks to him. Sam opened her mouth to say as much when a flight attendant interrupted them. "Doctors, we are going to be landing shortly, if you could brace yourselves."

"Why don't you sit in my seat? I'll stay with him and function as the attending for the medical team when we land." Dr. Sexy put a gentle hand on her upper arm, and Sam almost jumped out of her skin. It was a brotherly gesture, but her body did not respond to it in a brotherly way. Sam looked down at his hand, checking to see if the tingling feeling in her arm meant he was actually melting her skin away. Nope, still there. Taking a deep breath, she looked up at him. Dr. Sexy's gaze mirrored her movements, and heat crept into his cheekbones as he let his hand drop away.

Swallowing the lump in her throat, Sam stuffed her bodily response in the "To Understand Later" file and nodded as if her head were filled with cement. "I'll do that."

Without another word, Sam walked past him down the aisle. Reaching his seat, she picked up his sweatshirt, then buckled herself in. Still reeling from whatever inexplicable reaction her body had decided to have to Dr. Sexy, Sam looked down at the sweatshirt in her hands and back up at the man who owned it. He had tucked himself against the galley barrier wall and the man's chair and bent down so he was eye to eye with Mark the Man Bun, holding on to his wrist.

Sam chastised herself. Why hadn't she checked for an erratic pulse? No wonder he was surprised she could identify a mushroom. She had failed to do the most basic of crisis-management procedures. They literally taught that to fifth graders in babysitting classes. Her face rapidly cooled as all the blood rushed out of it to make way for ashen humiliation as the wheels of the plane bumped along the tarmac. Dr. Sexy hadn't offered her his seat to be nice. He'd offered her his seat to get her out of the way while he did the real medical stuff. At least he'd done it nicely. Looking down at the sweatshirt in her lap, she picked up the item and began carefully folding it. If she couldn't do a good job doctoring, at least she could fold with military precision.

As people on the plane began to shift, Sam risked a glance up to where the doctor was still wall sitting and talking to Mark in a low whisper, probably checking for pupil dilation, because she hadn't. The corner of her mind where she had stuffed her ill-advised physical reaction noted that it was particularly difficult to maintain a wall sit for the length of time he was managing. The rest of her mind began to wonder how she was going to disembark when all her stuff was in the back of the plane, where the budgetiest of the budget seats were located.

Ears popping as the cabin depressurized, Sam watched Dr. Sexy help Mark out of his chair and into the arms of the first responders. At least she could relax now, knowing she would never see Mark or Dr. Sexy again. As soon as she could get back to 30A, she was off this disastermobile and free to forget her experiment in emergency medicine and heroics.

As the flow of passenger traffic slowed, Sam gently placed the sweat-shirt on the doctor's seat and began the arduous process of making her way to the back of the plane to get her things. As Sam row hopped her way to the back of the plane—ducking into row 10, then 17, then 25—passersby congratulated her on helping. Sam felt every inch a fraud. She hadn't helped anyone.

Retrieving her bag from the overhead bin, Sam began her trudge back toward the front of the plane, grateful only the flight attendants were left to see her gracelessly knock her rolling suitcase into the arm-rest of nearly every row. Frowning down at her uncooperative suitcase, she had just enough time to wonder why she couldn't wheel the stupid thing in a straight line when a voice caught her attention.

"No big deal. Happy to help," Dr. Sexy told an airline attendant as he stepped back onto the plane.

For a brief moment, Sam thought about diving into the row she was standing near and hiding until he deplaned. She was taller than normal thanks to the stupid platform sneakers her mother had insisted she buy, but she could crouch and maybe—

"Hello," Dr. Sexy said, picking up his sweatshirt. Waving the crisply folded garment at her, he added, "Thanks for this."

Grasping at words through the pit of her humiliation, Sam cleared her throat and let what she hoped was a gracious smile cross her face. "Well, I can't remember to take someone's vitals, but I can fold, so at least there is that. Thank you for your help."

The guy shrugged. The half smile was back, showing off a faint dimple in his cheek that Sam promptly ignored. She didn't need another misguided physical reaction right now. "It was more important to keep him calm so we could land. It was clear he wasn't dying, and the para-medics would have done the vitals again anyway."

Turning to face the exit, he started walking, and Sam followed, still knocking her bag into every armrest, despite the aisle being wider in first class. Reaching the jet bridge, he turned with a sort of casual

11

economy that reminded Sam of celebrities on a red carpet. Not at all like he was in a hurry but rather like he had a sort of graceful schedule to keep. Passing the sweatshirt to his left hand, he held out his free hand to her and said, "I'm Grant."

"Sam. Nice to meet you, Grant."

"Nice to meet you too." He smiled, then added, "Little tip for your fellowship: You're a doctor now. If someone like me barges in on your patient, you can tell them to back off."

The attraction Sam had been fighting died in the middle of the frigid San Francisco jet bridge. "I did."

Grant raised an eyebrow at her, and the familiar sensation of being on unsure footing returned, as if he were her professor. A better-looking professor than anyone she'd had at Case Western but still distinctly professorial.

"I mean, I didn't know you were a doctor when I asked you why you weren't in your seat, but I most definitely did tell you to go away."

"Did you? Because I heard a barrage of questions about a call button," Grant asked, his half smile turning into a smirk.

Sam tried not to sound indignant as she snapped back, "It's not my fault you failed to read the room."

"No. I guess it isn't." Grant shrugged, amusement still written on his face. He was laughing at her. This was officially the worst career experience ever. "Do you live in San Francisco?"

"I do," Sam said, grateful for the subject change as she began walking again, bumping her way through the entrance to the boarding gate.

"So do I. Do you need a ride to the city? We could split a car."

Sam marveled at Grant's delivery, so friendly, as if he weren't offering to share a cab with someone he had just insulted only moments before. Nothing could be less desirable than a twenty-five-minute ride back to the city in which she had to hear about her numerous failures as delivered by Dr. Grant. That was a hard pass from her, thanks.

"That's nice of you to offer. I have a friend coming to pick me up." Sam watched his face fall, and a small corner of her heart twinged with guilt. But not enough guilt to make her offer him a seat in her imaginary friend's car. "I'd offer you a ride, but he drives a two-seater from 1987. You don't want to ride in that thing."

Guilt averted. Her midwestern-white-lady mother would be so proud of the brush-off she'd just delivered. Besides, if he could afford to fly first class, he could afford a forty-five-dollar ride home. In fact, he was probably offering her a ride because she'd admitted to being a lowly, overworked and underpaid, newly minted fellow.

"You're right; I choose life." Grant smiled at her joke, and the guilty twinge kicked back up a notch. "Get home safe."

"You too," Sam called as he began walking toward the SFO ride-share pickup spot, a fancy new phone in his hand. She waited a beat before wheeling her bag over toward the BART entrance. Sure, it would take her twice as long and be three times as unpleasant as sharing a car, but at least public transit wouldn't judge her performance today. Wrestling her suitcase through the ticket barrier, Sam was convinced her pride was worth the hassle.

Chapter Two

Sam tumbled through the door of her third-floor walk-up, sweaty. Why had she let her stupid pride get in the way of sharing a ride with Grant? He could have berated her for twenty-five straight minutes, and it would have made the absurd BART-to-Muni-to-hiking-up-the-Potrero-Hill-of-doom trek home seem like the foxtrot. Really, the two flights of stairs up to her shared apartment were just salt in a very open judgment wound.

"Look who's back," Duke's low voice called from the living room, where he and their other roommate, Jehan, were sprawled on the couches, his beloved Louisiana State University Tigers baseball game on at top volume.

"Hey," Sam called, closing the front door with her sneaker. After shoving her suitcase down the narrow hallway that led to their bedrooms and the shared bathroom, she turned and marched toward the couch, then flopped onto the empty space next to her roommate with a muffled thud.

"How was LA? And your mom? Was she still"—Jehan paused, wiggling her perfectly shaped eyebrows—"weird about the move?"

"Not as weird as I expected. Mom just sort of pretended that she hasn't stopped speaking to me, which was strange because then she'd do things like pass Isaiah the salt to give to me when I asked for it. But whatever. On the upside, my brother seems happy," Sam said, letting her eyes come to rest on the TV remote just as Duke picked it up to turn down the volume. Her brother had left for Los Angeles about six months before she'd moved. To say her mother took the news of his departure poorly would have been generous. When Sam moved to the Bay Area to start her fellowship, her mother had gone nuclear. Starting with a fit of tears that rapidly turned into a series of but-you-can't-even-make-a-frittata-how-will-you-survive-on-your-own phone calls, and when that didn't work, the silent treatment.

Sam would be lying if she said the cold shoulder hadn't broken her heart. In the past, she would have even given in to her mother's demands, but she couldn't be in two places at once. She would figure out how to make it in the Bay Area, and her mother would adjust sooner or later. Maybe.

"Okay, but she didn't freak out on you again?" Duke asked. There was less wiggle in his eyebrows but just as much curiosity in his tone.

"No. I think the tantrum-throwing phase is officially over. Now it's just the awkward let's-talk-at-Christmas phase." Sam laughed, mostly to cover up the sting. Diana Holbrook had basically put her daughter on ice once Sam accepted a highly coveted spot as a research fellow with San Francisco Central Hospital. She'd done the first phase of her residency in a public hospital back in Ohio before applying for the fellowship. At SF Central she would learn how to run her own research program focusing on pregnancy and public policy interventions. This wasn't training that she could get just anywhere, but as far as her mother was concerned, she could deliver babies in Akron just the same as she could in San Francisco.

"Did your mom actually say *let's talk at Christmas*?" Jehan asked. If Sam hadn't known the shock on her face was sincere, she would have laughed. Jehan genuinely thought the best of everyone, including the semiferal cats outside their apartment that tried to claw her face off if she got within ten feet.

"Not in so many words," Sam said, kicking her legs out in front of her. Her roommates knew that as fickle as her mother sounded, Sam missed her. Sure, her mom had a list of expectations a mile long that Sam never seemed to meet, but she was also loving when she wanted to be. After all, this was the same woman who'd read Sam one children's book about thirty-five times a day without complaint for six months. Never mind that Sam had the book memorized. It was the sound of her mother's voice that was comforting, especially when her dad was away and her brother had the nerve to go to big-kid school without her.

Sam scratched at a fray in the fabric of the couch, trying to decide how to explain their complicated relationship. "I think my brother hoped we'd all eat tacos and hug it out, but Mom's not there yet."

"Do you think she'll ever come around?" A crease formed along either side of Jehan's mouth as she frowned.

"Maybe." Sam stopped pulling at the fabric, then said, "But in my experience, it's better to just let her come to you. Mom's a fine line you have to walk. If I ask her for anything, she thinks I'm incompetent. But if I don't ask for enough, she thinks I've forgotten she exists. Better to just let sleeping dogs lie."

"That's blood, Sam. You'll have to work it out, eventually." Duke's southern drawl wrapped around her. The guy managed to be both relentlessly pragmatic and good humored at all times. It was part of the reason why Sam had agreed to room with him and Jehan after exactly three seconds of talking to them during the hospital's informal New Fellows Weekend.

"*Eventually* being the key word." Sam smiled and eyed her friend, who scratched a day's worth of fine stubble clinging to his chin before stretching up.

"Sounds like you're just bein' stubborn, but have it your way." He grinned, the deep lines of his smile stretching across the dark skin of his otherwise ageless face.

"I will, thank you." Sam smiled. Noticing the papers spread out in front of Jehan, she asked, "What's all that?"

Jehan lit up like the Bat-Signal, a massive grin crossing her face. "They are marriage license applications." She paused for dramatic effect, and Sam could have sworn she saw Duke flinch. "Because Travis asked me to marry him!"

"Oh. Wow," Sam said, forcing brightness into her tone. Her roommate's engagement was the exact opposite of what she'd hoped would happen. Travis had come with Jehan to the New Fellows Weekend, and he left Sam and Duke with a sour taste in their mouths. After spending six minutes with the guy, Sam decided he was clingy and controlling. He spent three-quarters of the weekend asking Jehan why she couldn't stay in Washington, DC, where he worked as an analyst for a bank, and the last quarter glaring at anyone who didn't recognize him as the sole reason Jehan was matched with such a prestigious program. This last part was nearly impossible to give him credit for, since Jehan was an actual badass.

"That is so exciting. Can I hug you?" Sam asked, standing up and forcing Duke to take his feet off the ottoman so she could reach her friend, who bounced off the couch like she was a rubber ball.

"Yes! Thank you. I didn't expect it at all," Jehan said, hugging Sam as if her excitement were transferable.

"How did it happen?" Sam asked, pulling back and reaching for Jehan's left hand.

"Oh, I don't have a ring yet. He asked me over Zoom." Sam could almost hear Duke's eyes rolling from across the room, but that didn't slow Jehan's joy. "I guess he was just so excited about the idea that he couldn't wait until he saw me next."

"Smart man," Duke said, a good-natured look scrawled across his face as if he were reminding Sam to act ecstatic, before standing up and shuffling toward the kitchen, the top of his six-foot-four frame nearly grazing a low-hanging light fixture as he went.

"Well, that is fantastic." Sam took a step back so she could see Jehan's face. "I know it just happened, but have you thought about a date at all?"

Jehan's smile faltered slightly, but she picked it up so fast Sam hardly had time to notice. "Well, that's being discussed. He wants to get married ASAP. I believe his exact words were 'let's wait just long enough to prove you are not pregnant.'" She laughed, shaking her long hair over her shoulder. "But I want something more traditional, the whole big Egyptian engagement party, and then set a date."

Sam smiled. "Obviously it's up to you two, but—"

"I'd throw the party," Duke shouted from his room, interrupting Sam as she searched for nicer words to say the same thing.

Rolling her eyes, Sam called back, "You already had your chance to weigh in last week." From somewhere down the hall, Duke chuckled as she turned her attention back to her friend. "But Duke is right. Take your time with this. Planning a wedding during the first year of your fellowship seems like a lot . . . unless you're secretly pregnant?"

Jehan laughed at Sam's half-assed attempt at a joke. "No. Although throwing a big engagement party is probably just as much work as my fellowship."

"Yeah, but it's work you want to do," Sam said, releasing her hands. "Besides, didn't you, like, triple major while working two jobs in undergrad?"

"It was a double major," Jehan snorted as if the adjustment made her less impressive.

"But one was in nanorobotics," Duke said, walking out of his bedroom. "Sam, didn't you read the *Meet the Hospital* guide?"

"No. Why would I read that? I am going to meet everyone at orientation and then get stuck asking about their hobbies anyway. Easier to honestly not know than to act like I don't while people repeat themselves."

Duke gave Jehan a sideways look. "Twenty bucks says she is gonna ask to borrow your face flash cards."

"You made flash cards? Who are you?"

"Someone who majored in nanorobotics and worked in a remote village to improve emergency medical outcomes using cell phone technology from 1995," Duke answered for their roommate.

"The old-tech part wasn't in the guide," Jehan said, giving Duke a quizzical look.

"Some people make flash cards; I LinkedIn stalk." Duke shrugged over the sound of Sam's laughter.

Turning to look at her, Duke said, "So, Mini Martha Stewart, you gonna clean the bathroom today, or was all that sparkle-tape chore chart for fun?"

"It's called washi tape, and it is both fun and functional," Sam said, glancing lovingly at her chore chart. "Besides, the schedule was Jehan's idea. I just made it appealing."

"Don't blame that pink-glitter chart on her. And if that glitter ends up in my hair or anywhere on my face, you better let me know," Duke said, eyeing the thing hanging on the fridge with mistrust.

"Do you really think I'd have you out here looking like a Christmas tree?" Sam joked before hooking her hand on her hip and adding, "Yes, I'm gonna clean the shower. Why, do you want to get in first?"

"If he isn't showering, I want to shower," Jehan piped up.

"Now hang on." Duke held up a hand. "Are you washing your hair, 'cause if that takes you four hours—"

"I'll clean the shower, but y'all have to keep me company while I do it, 'cause I need to tell someone about the ridiculous plane ride I just had. It involved magic mushrooms and a fight with another doctor."

"Wait. What? How did you not lead with that?" Jehan asked, her incredulous tone filling the cracks between the floorboards in the living room.

"Honestly, I was so tired from coming up that hill that it sort of slipped my mind." Sam shrugged, making her way toward the hallway closet.

"Well, I wish you had remembered, because now we have to try and squeeze all three of us into that tiny bathroom," Jehan sighed.

"I second that. Get out your little toothbrush, your rubber gloves, and your homemade cleaning products, Dr. Holbrook." Duke could joke, but Sam had never met anyone who loved to be tidy more than him. He would put her father's naval precision to shame.

Sam smiled at her two new roommates. Sure, she still had a week's worth of Los Angeles dirt to wash off her clothes and a full day of New Staff Orientation to think about, but before she could stress about the future, she had at least an hour's worth of laughing to do with two people she wished had entered her life much sooner.

~

"See ya," Jehan called over her shoulder as they walked into the shiny hospital building. Her research would focus on examining the efficacy of low-cost nanotechnologies to help patients in emergency medicine, while Sam and Duke had the same obstetrics and gynecology focus. Duke would be spending his time looking at data on former cancer patients who were pregnant and receiving care in public-hospital settings. Meanwhile, Sam was hoping to develop and analyze direct intervention methods to improve outcomes for marginalized pregnant people. It was wild to think of tiny, lovely Jehan tracking how robots could help with gruesome gunshot wounds and kitchen accidents. Then again, Jehan seemed thrilled, so who was Sam to judge?

The three of them had spent the morning huddling in the general New Staff Orientation and learning about the basics of time cards, which didn't really apply to them, and how to blow the whistle on HR concerns, which would apply to them, although Sam hoped she wouldn't need the information. Now, facing down the doors of her specialty orientation, Sam felt the butterflies return in full force.

"I'll be right back. I'm just gonna run to the bathroom. Save me a seat, yeah?" Sam said to Duke, not really waiting for an answer before dashing to the blue door marked **RESTROOM**.

Walking into the first available stall, she sat down. Feeling green around the gills, Sam closed her eyes, forcing herself to take three deep breaths to try to get a handle on the butterfly rampage inside herself. God, she wanted this to go better than the plane. This was a chance to redeem herself and prove she wasn't nearly as helpless as Mark the Mushroom Man had made her feel. All she had ever wanted was to help people, and in a few minutes, she would be one step closer to her own panel of patients.

Opening her eyes, she walked out of the stall and began washing her hands. Even though she was half-Black, anxiety had robbed her skin of enough color that she looked gray. Using a damp paper towel, she wiped a bit of stray mascara out from under her brown eyes, fussed with the tight curls in her ponytail, then pinched some life back into her cheeks. Taking one more deep breath, she pulled the bathroom door open and dashed across the hall to the conference room the new fellows and residents were gathering in.

Spotting Duke, Sam slunk past a few semifamiliar faces until she reached the chair he'd saved for her and dropped into it with a noisy exhale.

"Doing okay?" Duke whispered. "You look pale."

"Fine. Just nerves. Gotta make up for the—"

The conference room door whooshed open, halting Sam mid-speech. Her mouth went dry. Somewhere in her chest, the butterflies she had recently caught began pummeling her heart, causing it to beat erratically against the lump in her throat.

"Shit."

"What's wrong?" Duke hissed, eyeing her with concern.

"Hi, everyone, let's get started."

For a moment, Sam almost let herself believe that he wasn't there. That the clipboard in his hands wasn't actually happening to her. At least, until she heard his voice. That same velvety tenor. It had no sharp edges but gave no ground either.

"Hi, I'm Dr. Grant Gao, a senior fellow and an attending here at SF Central Hospital completing my specialist training in maternal-fetal medicine and emergency surgery. A little later today you will also hear from the head of our residency and fellowship programs, chief attending physician Dr. Howie Franklin." Grant looked up from his clipboard briefly, and Sam felt herself sink to the bottom of her chair. Why did Duke have to pick seats so close to the front of the room?

"We're just gonna get through a quick roll call to make sure no one is lost; then we will get down to business. Is Sophia Beck here?"

As Sophia raised her hand, Duke leaned over, oblivious to how much attention he was drawing to them, and whispered, "What are you doing? Are you all right?"

"Faith Choi?"

Sam fought the urge to shove him back toward his seat as she hissed, "That's the guy from the plane."

"You got in a fight with the senior fellow?" Duke said, his voice creeping above a whisper as his body started shaking with silent laughter.

"Michael Gordon?"

"Don't laugh. I have to get out of here. Do you think it is too late to be assigned to the emergency—"

"Michael? There you are. Welcome, Michael."

"This is too good. I gotta text Jehan."

"Samantha Holbrook."

Sam wasn't sure that she had ever prayed so hard for a sinkhole to magically appear and swallow her whole. As the silence stretched around the room, Sam sat up and raised her hand, silently cursing any god she could think of for failing to strike the building with lightning so powerful they would be left in complete darkness.

"Ah." The single syllable hung in the air between them for what felt like one hundred seconds, making the lump in her throat turn over a few times, as a lazy smile crossed Grant's face. "Hello again, Sam. Or should I say, Dr. Holbrook. Nice to see you."

"Hello," Sam croaked. Next to her, Duke was nearly falling out of his chair with the effort it took not to cackle.

"It looks like we'll have plenty of time to work through all of the tools that can be helpful if anyone ever needs you on a plane again." Dr. Gao chuckled, then said, "Right, moving on."

Sam tried to swallow her humiliation and started coughing instead. Duke reached over to thump her back, still grinning and holding his phone. Risking a glance upward, she almost kicked herself. Of course Grant had the nerve to stand there looking dapper in scrubs, as if they suited him better than any tuxedo could. And of course he and his stupidly perfect bone structure would mention her failing in front of all her new coworkers.

Duke slid his phone in front of her, pulling her out of her mortification-induced trance, right as Grant called, "Duke Washington?"

Looking down at the phone, Sam read Jehan's response to Duke's text:

So, we are stopping on the way home for shame ice cream tonight, yes?

Sam nodded her head at Duke so hard that her ponytail shook. If nothing else, at least she had some friends to help her pick up the pieces of her dignity. The thought almost made her smile. In fact, she was halfway there when Grant said, "All right. We're all here, so if you'll just stick close to me, I'll give you a tour."

Pushing back from the chair, Sam stood up and gathered what was left of her pride. She was not going to let Grant make her feel useless. She had her mother for that. And she hadn't spent the last few months calling her father only when she knew her mother was out just to let Grant scare her into failing now. Nope. Instead, she would prove both of them wrong. Trudging to the door, careful to look Grant in the eye and smile as she crossed the threshold. It should have been an act of defiance, but the smile he sent back made her face heat up all over again.

As soon as she was out of earshot, Sam turned toward Duke and said, "You better tell Jehan we'll need to add wine to the list."

Without missing a beat, Duke's laugh rumbled behind her. "Already taken care of. Hang in there."

Chapter Three

"Doctor?"

Sam turned around, smiling more at being called *Doctor* than anything else. The sensation never got old for her, and she loved it every bit as much as she'd dreamed she would. She knew she still had more patients to see, but Sam hadn't mastered the art of the swift exit yet, and besides, Monica was six months pregnant, had higher blood pressure than Sam would like, and had missed several appointments leading up to this one. She could find an extra three minutes for her.

"Yes?"

"You asked if I was taking any classes." SF Central was not rich, and neither were its clients. Sam hadn't expected her patients to have gone to every birthing specialist in the country or anything, but she was surprised by the number of people she saw who hadn't been informed that the local YMCA offered parenting-and-delivery classes.

"Yes. The nurse has some great resources about programs in the area." Sam nodded.

Monica twisted her hands in her lap for a moment, eyes shifting from side to side. "There is a woman who comes into my salon—she is the one who insisted I come in here to ask about my blood pressure. She isn't a doctor, but she helps deliver babies. She said she'd help me. Does that count?"

"Oh," Sam said, blinking rapidly as she tried to suppress her panic. There were so many charlatans attempting to profit off pregnant people with limited resources. If this woman had tried to sell Monica magic herbs for stretch marks, Sam might have to find her and wring her neck. Then again, she'd managed to get Monica to come in for a checkup, so she didn't sound like a total menace. "Is she a nurse? A midwife?" When Monica shook her head, Sam let her brain stretch to the outer fringes of the obstetric-health world. "A doula?"

"Yes! That is the word."

"That can be a good thing," Sam said, searching for a diplomatic answer. Doulas had been a part of nearly every culture on the planet until recent history. Western medicine had spent the last seventy years mocking them as backwoods mystics encouraging people to give birth in kiddie-pool death traps. Or the domain of overindulged, rich white women with too much money and not enough sense. But in many parts of the world, doulas were the only care a pregnant person was likely to receive. The question was whether this woman was an actual doula or someone sketchy.

"Tell me more about her. What's her name? How does she help you?"

Monica took a deep breath, adjusting her posture on the examination table, which had to be getting uncomfortable for her, not that there was much that was comfortable at this stage in her pregnancy. "Kaiya . . . Owens. I think it's Owens. Anyway, she mostly just checks on my stress level, suggests stuff I can do to make myself more comfortable, because I'm feeling so hot and slow, Dr. Holbrook. It takes me forever to get anywhere. My job does not have maternity parking, so I have to hike into the salon," Monica said, dropping her hands noisily onto the table in exasperation.

"It sounds like Kaiya knows a lot about being a new parent. I'll have to look her up. And she is right. I know time off can be hard to come by, but please listen to her and continue to see us." Sam smiled.

"Think of me, the nurse-midwife, and Kaiya like your team. Between the three of us, we got you."

"I can do that." Monica nodded.

"Good. And don't feel so bad if you have to miss an appointment that you skip the next one. We want to see you, even if you're a little late."

"I'll be better about coming in, I promise." Her face didn't hold any of the fear or reservation that Sam's other patients had had earlier in the morning.

"In that case, I'll see you soon. If you have any questions in the interim, you can always call the nurse, and they will track me down. Sound good?"

"Thank you, Dr. Holbrook. It was nice to meet you."

"Nice to meet you too, Monica. Take care." Sam smiled as she backed out of the shoebox of an exam room.

She waited for exactly three seconds before looking over her shoulder to find the hallway empty, then hopped from one foot to the other, grinning so hard her eyes were nearly closed as she whispered, "Yes!"

For the first time since she'd started her research fellowship, she felt like she knew what she was doing. Not once today had she had to utter the words *I don't know* or *let me check* before dashing out of the room to find literally any other medical professional within fifty yards of her. The only upside to the last few weeks of feeling stupid was that Grant—or Dr. Gao, as she should really be calling him—wasn't around to see her panic and ask questions. That honor belonged to the forever-patient if extremely old-school Dr. Franklin.

Shuffling toward the sky bridge that connected the clinic side of the building, where she saw patients, to the hospital side, where she would help deliver their babies, Sam began turning her visit with Monica over in her head. She wasn't the only person Sam had met with this morning whose primary form of preparation during pregnancy had come from someone they knew. This week alone she had not one but two patients who had been asked to stay in the hospital overnight for monitoring due to abnormalities developed between their long-delayed visits. At least with Monica, the doula had enough knowledge to encourage her to see a doctor.

Sam knew it was unreasonable to expect people without sick leave, transit money, or childcare to come into the clinic anywhere between once a month and once a week. If her patients had been wealthy, they would've just hired midwives who made house calls or gotten fancy telehealth supplemental medical plans. As it stood, her patients were in no such position. If she could just call a meeting of the doulas, aunties, coworkers with horror stories, birth coaches, and other advice dispensers in the area, so many potential disasters could be avoided. Everyone around the person giving birth would know what problems to look for.

A community meeting would help with the Dr. Google problem too. The literature Sam was reviewing for her still-to-be-decided research agenda made it clear that people were more likely to search the internet and attempt bizarre home remedies to avoid paying to feel stupid in front of a doctor. Which explained the woman Duke had seen in clinic last week with garlic shoved up her—

Sam's mind hiccuped. Maybe there was a way . . . in med school, she'd had an interprofessional where she'd followed around a social worker to understand how they interacted with a client. It had helped her gain a new perspective on patient care. Doulas weren't doctors or nurses, but they could make house calls, and their sole job was to build trust with the person giving birth, so if she could—

"Yo, Sam, wait up!" Duke called, rounding a corner and jogging toward her, the same exhausted look on his face that she wore. Fellow schedules were notoriously brutal. Going into her fellowship, Sam had thought this was an exaggeration. Turned out generations of doctors were not lying. Even fellows, who in theory should spend less time seeing patients so they could conduct their research, got wrung out to the max.

"Hey, Duke. What's up?"

"I've been looking for you. Got a proposition I think you'll like."

"If it is trading chores again because you want to fall asleep before you finish half your beer, the answer is a hard pass," Sam snarked. Last week she and Jehan had pitched in to cover his chores because Duke had been assigned his first twenty-four-hour shift. The guy was so beat afterward that he barely said thanks before the sounds of ESPN and snoring tried to wake up their downstairs neighbors.

"Ha. Ha. Ha." Duke's laugh was flat, although he was still smiling. Twelve-hour days hadn't broken either of them yet. "I was gonna ask if you would like to join the prestigious SF Central Hoopers. How 'bout it?"

"What?" Sam asked, absently setting a file into the proper slot on the nurses' station wall.

"The hospital has an entire basketball rec league. I was recently asked to join the Hoopers. Also known as last year's league champions."

"If someone wants you on their team, they must be desperate." Sam snorted. "What are they doing, asking all the Black staff to join just in case one of us is good at basketball?"

"Both of us *are* good at basketball."

"Don't tell anyone that; otherwise it'll justify the behavior."

Duke cackled. "Under any other circumstances, I'd say yes, that is what the teams are doing. But in this one case, no. They asked me because Raphael knew I rode the pine pony in the D-League. Did you ever read the orientation booklet?" he asked, somewhat skeptical.

"I skimmed it," Sam lied and choked back a laugh once she saw Duke's face.

"I hope you read charts better than you read about our peers. So you want to join the league or not?"

Sam sighed. "Look, Duke. These days are long, and I already have a ton on my plate. I'm gonna pass. But maybe next season."

"Please," Duke said, drawing out the *e* sound to impossibly long lengths. In another life, he must have been a singer. "We need at least one woman on our team to play in the league."

Sam scoffed. "Thank you for your honesty. Did you ask Jehan?"

"Jehan would bring down the team's average height by like five inches." Duke rolled his eyes like Sam had asked a silly question. "I told Raphael I'd convince you to join the team before our rivals figure out there is a five-foot-eight woman in the building."

"Jehan already said no, didn't she?"

"Yeah, but she has a big party to plan and all that," Duke said on an exhale. "Seriously, I know you made your high school state playoffs, so you are at least a half-decent point guard."

"I know I didn't put that in the orientation bio."

"The internet is forever, Samantha. I know how to google, and I watched the clip of that last game. That was a tough loss, but you had a nice jumper in there."

"A little tip: if you are trying to get me to join your team, maybe don't bring up the most traumatic moments from my childhood." Sam cringed. In some ways she'd been trying to live down that loss for over ten years.

Duke chuckled. "So will you please join us?"

"It's been a long time since I've played."

"It's like riding a bike." Duke shrugged at this profoundly bad lie, which Sam let slide for the sake of her living arrangement. Admittedly, she didn't have as much time for exercise as she would like, so playing basketball with Duke would be a good forcing function. Now she could feel less guilty about all the runs she wasn't going on. If she never made it out to the gym again, at least she'd have this.

"Fine."

"Thank you!" Duke shouted as they rounded the corner into the staff area to pick up their bags. "First game is tonight. You won't regret it."

"Tonight? Bruh, we just finished a twelve-hour day. You couldn't have mentioned that?"

"No takebacks," Duke said, not looking the least bit sorry. "The good news is we have time to get home and get our stuff before we meet at the middle school."

"You owe me." Sam narrowed her eyes at him.

"I'll do double chores next week."

"You already owed me that."

"Fine, double chores, and I'll get you some of that washing tape, but not the kind with glitter."

"Washi tape." Sam smirked. "Anyone else play semipro ball or anything I should know about?"

"Nah. Between you and me, the SF Central Hoopers are gonna crush these other teams."

Sam wasn't sure if she was still in shape enough to make a layup, let alone crush anything. Duke might be confident, but she would settle for bench time and not pulling a hamstring tonight.

~

The giant gym bag knocked against Sam's thigh as she tried to climb out of the heap of metal that was Duke's car. Why on earth had she agreed to play basketball in her very limited time off when it was so painfully evident that every single bone in her body would rather be sleeping?

"Who are we playing again?" Sam called to Duke as he jogged toward the dingy gym, trying to outrun the pernicious San Francisco cold. It would never work, but that didn't stop Duke from plodding away.

"The Central Flyers," Duke said, yanking the door open and then waiting for her, tapping his toe in chilly impatience as she sauntered through it.

"Thank you." Sam grinned up at him. It wasn't Sam's fault he was raised well enough to hold a door but not well enough to remember his own jacket. "Central Flyers. What kind of name is that? Were all the good names taken?"

"There are only four teams in the league, so I doubt it." Duke chuckled, stomping his sock-and-sandal-clad feet as the smell of old chlorine and sweat wafted down the hallway.

"There are only four teams?"

"Yup! Basically, we play each other once a week for four months, have a championship tournament, and call it a day."

Sam snorted. "At least it won't be much of a time commitment."

"That's the spirit," Duke said as they approached another large set of double doors, the sound of basketballs already pounding the wood floor. Sam waited for Duke to open the door, the muscles in her body beginning to vibrate with the echoes of dribble drills, the swish of nets, and the familiar sounds of people joking over the chaos. As she walked through the doors, the fluorescent lighting of the gym strained her vision and caused Sam to blink a few times at the guy shooting from the top of the key. His mechanics were excellent. If this was the Flyers point guard, she had her work cut out for her. A teammate fed him the ball as he jogged to the two spot, and Sam stopped short, causing Duke to swivel around so they wouldn't crash into one another.

"Ugh."

Of course the guy with excellent form had to be Grant. For the last few weeks, Sam had been congratulating herself on not having to ask him a single question. Mostly because they had not been scheduled for the same shifts, but still. And yes, she had checked the schedule for him. She needed to know when and where to avoid him.

"Why'd you stop in the mid—oh." Duke looked down at her and began laughing before giving her a shove out of the doorway. "You still holding that grudge?"

"There is no grudge. I just don't feel like reliving my most recent lowlights or asking for any more help from him." Sam's lip began to curl like a preteen's, and she snatched the look off her face before Duke could register it.

"You are so stubborn. You have got to find a way to get over that," Duke said as they shuffled to a set of partially extended bleachers. Sam was careful to keep herself in line with Duke's frame. He was wiry and didn't provide nearly as much cover as she would like, which, in this case, was a giant tent to hide under until after the game.

"Easy for you to say. The first person who thought you were a medical professional wasn't high off of some ill-advised mushrooms at forty thousand feet in the air."

"Technically the first person who thought you were a medical professional was Grant. Who wasn't high at all."

"Who wears sunglasses on a plane?" Sam hissed, pulling her basketball shoes out of her bag and slipping off her old-school Adidas slides.

"Apparently, senior fellows." Duke shrugged, mirroring her motions as they tied their shoes.

Standing up, Sam unzipped her jacket and stuffed it in her bag before adding, "Honestly, that is the flight attendant's fault. He should have been more specific."

Duke shook his head. "Well, here's your chance to beat him at something." Looking over her head, he winced at the sound of another shot falling. "I hope you like playing defense. Come on, Raphael isn't here yet. Let's warm up."

"I never should have agreed to this," Sam said, reaching for the ball in her bag before following him to the opposite end of the court, where two other people were already warming up. She recognized one of them as a nurse named Theo from the NICU. After introducing herself, she learned the other man was a surgery tech called Alan. Both men seemed to think they would be playing post, but Sam suspected she'd have a floor full of power forwards and Duke as her only actual post. Unless

Raphael had a strong three-point game, she would have to put in serious work to negate Grant's jumper.

Sam felt her eyes flick to his side of the court. He had moved to practicing midrange jump shots, his motions fluid, as if the ball were an extension of himself. The muscles in his back rippled as he bounded off the floor, releasing the ball in a perfect arc. She tried not to stare at the flex of his shoulder blades through the practice jersey he wore. It was like staring at a perfect diagram of back muscles in motion. If she were forced to admit it, and luckily no one was forcing her, Sam could see how some people would consider him beautiful. Graceful, even.

The sound of a ball smashing into the board behind her caused Sam to jump and broke Grant's concentration enough that he actually turned around to see what was happening. For a fleeting second their eyes met, and he smiled. Sam wanted to dive into the six inches of space between the bleachers and the floor. Did he know she'd been staring? Had he been experiencing that someone-is-watching-me sensation the whole time she was appreciating—no, scratch that—appraising his well-developed rhomboids? She was a doctor. It was basically hardwired into her to appreciate a well-defined anatomy.

The smile she offered in return was more of a baring of teeth than a friendly gesture. Adding a dramatic look left, then right, for good measure to cover her tracks, Sam turned her back on Grant just in time to catch the rest of her teammates taking turns at a running slam dunk.

Shaking her head, Sam called, "Y'all are gonna hurt yourselves with that."

"He might." Alan pointed at Theo before firing off a wild shot from the far corner of the court.

Sam smiled to herself, letting the ball spin in her hand for the first time. Her fingers adjusting to the feel of the leather whirling in her palms, the familiar motion intensifying her focus. Who cared if Grant was there? Duke was right: sooner or later she'd have to let the plane go. And what better way to do that than crushing a man's pride over some good-natured intramural basketball. Sam stepped to her favorite spot just outside the free throw line and fired away. The sound of the net swishing was so satisfying that she almost wanted to turn around and yell *Ha!* at Grant.

Luckily, she didn't need to, because Theo shouted, "Sweet!" then jogged over to retrieve her ball, like Sam's personal hype man. She let off another few carefully placed shots, sinking each specifically because they were the shots she knew she could make. The kind of baskets most likely to intimidate an opponent. Not that she was trying to intimidate anyone.

"Sorry I'm late." Raphael jogged over to where the rest of the team had gathered, including Kyle and Evan from pediatrics. "Are we ready to do this?"

"Sam's ready. She is fire," Theo said, smiling so big that she could see his perfectly even bottom teeth.

"Don't believe him." Sam smiled, shaking Raphael's hand.

"Duke said you can play. And that's good. We lost our point when she took a job in North Carolina at the end of last season."

"I wouldn't trust Duke, but I'll try and make y'all proud." Sam rolled her neck as the team stripped off their sweatshirts and walked toward the center of the court. On the other side, Grant stood huddled with his team, which managed to have three women, two of whom she planned to track down for coffee on a slow night, once she learned their names. The only people she recognized, besides Grant—who she wished she didn't recognize—were a guy named Danny, an RN in the ob-gyn department, and a woman named Kelly from emergency. Giving Danny a genuine smile, Sam found her spot, a little way outside center court, farther into Flyer territory.

She was just beginning to visualize the first play she would set up when Grant walked into her space. Sam shifted a few feet away, trying to give herself a little extra room to think, but he followed. Not close enough to be guarding her tight, just close enough to talk.

"So you're the new point guard?"

"Sure looks like it," Sam grumbled.

Grant snorted a laugh, an odd sound for someone who looked like the TV version of a doctor. It was just dorky enough to make him seem approachable. "I guess you're right. I should have figured it was you."

"What does that mean?"

"You're like six feet tall. I should've asked you to join our team first."

"I'm five foot eight."

"You're as tall as I am," Grant needled.

Sam threw him a sideways look and got into ready position, holding her response until the ref bent his knees to release the ball. "Then you're not six feet tall. It's okay. Men lie about their height all the time."

Grant took his eyes off the ball to look at her, incredulous, and Sam took off. She snatched the ball out of the air and locked it. Then she grinned at Grant, who was just realizing that she'd timed the perfect distraction. Shaking his head, he laughed it off and jogged down the court with the rest of the players.

Sam began a lazy dribble down the court, scanning the faces of her teammates. Sure, she needed to crush Grant, but she also needed to do it with style. No need to let her competitive streak get the best of her in front of her new coworkers.

Theo shoved off his defender and swung up the wing to signal that he was open. Sam read the movement but didn't pass. Grant had stationed himself at the top of the key, hanging back with the smirk still firmly attached to his face. He looked relaxed, but the move was calculated. He would step in to fill the gap in defense if she was foolish enough to pass to Theo. No. It was better to draw Grant out of the swing spot. Crossing over, Sam took two steps to the right, forcing Grant to shift toward her as she dribbled, careful to keep herself out of arm's reach.

"Little slow at tip-off." Sam mumbled the words in Grant's direction. As a rule, she wasn't much of a trash-talker, but this was too good to pass up. Besides, her brother was a mediocre player but a professional shit-talker. Surely that was a genetic trait she could call on in times of desperation.

"Trying to distract me?" Grant's smile spread as he sank lower into a defense stance, the muscles in his thighs flexing as he followed her across the floor. "It's not gonna work."

"I think it already did." Sam smiled as her eyes flicked toward the basket while Duke cut across the key, his hand up to signal that he was open. Twisting around, she bounce passed the ball under her arm and back to Theo, who managed to catch it. Grant rotated around just in time to watch Theo lob the ball over to Duke for an easy layup.

"Good pass, Sam," Kyle shouted from the bench.

"Ah. Lucky play," Grant said over his shoulder as he jogged toward the sidelines to throw the ball in.

"Get ready. You're gonna watch me get lucky *all night*." Sam punctuated the last two words, letting her neck work for extra emphasis. She laughed as she jogged down the court.

Sinking into a self-satisfied defensive stance, Sam glanced over her shoulder quickly to read the court. Duke appeared to be chatting affably with Kelly, and Sam felt the urge to clap at him and yell *Focus*. Unless small talk was his form of defense, Duke's chitchat was going to allow the Flyers to score.

The sounds of a basketball hitting the wood close to her brought Sam back to attention. She looked up just in time to catch Grant grinning at her. He bounced the ball through his legs to avoid Sam's reach. "Get lucky all night?" he asked, tilting his head and raising an eyebrow.

"Yup." Sam maintained her smile. Grant's movements were precise but unhurried. He could try to wait her out, but she refused to lose focus. She sank her hips deeper into her stance and shifted her weight toward her toes so she could be ready to move.

"You are terrible at trash-talking." Grant's dark eyes scanned the court.

"I thought that was pretty good," Sam said, scowling.

"It sounded less like trash and more like B movie dirty talk." Grant's smile lines deepened as he laughed, the sound mingling with the thump-thump of his dribble. "Are you gonna break out a riding crop and a feather duster next?"

Images of Grant in a leather halter, body glistening with oil and cracking a riding crop, flooded Sam's imagination. It wasn't a fantasy she'd known she had, but on him it was hot. He probably used flavored oil, too, but not the gross kind that tasted like chemicals. Given his attention to detail, he'd absolutely buy the good stuff for whatever he was going to do to her—

Not that he was going to do anything to her. Sam gave her head a little shake, trying to brush off the sizzling mental picture. Grant's nose wrinkled with his mischievous smile, and Sam recognized the distraction just a fraction of a second too late as he stopped short and lobbed the ball over her head. The woman Duke had been chatting with caught it and got an easy shot off, tying the game at 2–2.

Sam turned around just in time to watch Grant backpedal down the court. Making eye contact with her, he called, "Lucky. All. Night," his tone closer to a phone sex operator's than an NBA trash-talker's.

Sam waved him off and turned to retrieve the ball as a smile crept across her face. She was not going to be seen laughing at her nemesis if she could help it. No matter how well he mimicked rap-video vixens of the early nineties. If that was how Grant wanted to play, he would have to deal with the burners. Crossing the half-court line, Sam let herself get close to Grant at the top of the key. Keeping her dribble low, she leaned forward and felt the front of her baggy tank top peel away from her skin, and she said, "Okay, so my trash talk is a little rusty. But my game ain't."

Sam popped up out of the dribble with surgical accuracy and fired a three. If LeBron James himself had staged this play, he could not have managed a better shot. The ball rotated perfectly in the air, the spinning

Wilson logo winking at her. The entire court stopped moving to follow the ball as it rocketed toward the basket with the cleanest swish Sam had ever sunk.

"Oh!" Duke yelled, holding a fist up to his mouth and rocking back and forth. "Told ya. You don't even need me."

From the bleachers, Evan popped up and started clapping and nodding like the revered coach Pat Summitt following a close game in a D1 playoff.

Grant's jaw dropped as the ball bounced off the padded wall, waiting for someone to retrieve it. Eventually, he turned back to face her, surprise still scrawled across his face.

"Guess I don't need trash talk." Sam let a slow smile creep over her face.

By the time Grant checked the ball, the mood on the court had changed. Everything up to that point had been a warm-up, but Sam's three-pointer was a warning volley, and it did not go unanswered. Grant was quick and precise, and if Sam let up for even a millisecond, his sharp instincts took advantage of her slack. Like three seconds ago, when he'd sunk a jumper and tied the score.

"Nice shot," Sam called, in spite of her competitive streak, as she brought the ball down the court.

"Thanks." The muscles in Grant's cheeks twitched toward a smile, and then he focused again. Apparently, she had fooled him one too many times with small talk today.

Sam kept her dribble close to the ground and pivoted quickly, using her ass to back Grant closer to the hoop. Stutter-stepping three inches back, Sam could feel his sweat on her shoulder as she pressed into him and tried not to notice the smell of him. The mix of salty skin and spicy deodorant coming off a good-looking man was almost intoxicating.

Not that she was enjoying Grant. Or the way he smelled. She shoved the thoughts out of her head, focusing on Duke as he swung wide and clapped for the ball. They were four points away from winning the game. Sam stuttered back another inch, hoping Grant would give her a little more room to execute the pass. She wasn't a tiny girl, and most guys got out of the way if she put even a quarter of her body weight on them. Unfortunately, Grant must have been into squats, because he didn't back up. Tossing a glance over her shoulder, Sam caught him smiling at her like she could rest her weight on him all day. She growled in frustration, which seemed to heighten his enjoyment of the situation. He was laughing at her. She was going to have to fight dirty.

He was leaning over her so close that she could feel him breathing on her neck. This could work for her. Without warning, she stood up suddenly, her shoulder catching Grant in the chest and knocking him off balance. She passed the ball to Duke, who pulled up for a midrange jumper that circled the rim exactly twice before it sank with a satisfying swish.

"Ugh." Grant let his head drop to his chest, and she felt the sheer joy of having backed him into a corner start to well inside her.

If ever there was a time to reprise trash talk, it was now. Waiting until he had the ball, she said, "Don't feel bad, Grant. Everyone loses sometimes. Maybe you should have been more assertive?" Her tone was innocent enough, but the look on Grant's face sagged as he remembered his crappy advice to her. On either side of them, Grant's teammates ran up and called for the ball. Grant smirked and looked over like he was going to pass the ball to Kelly. Instinctively, Sam moved toward her, trying to fill the gap and intercept the pass. She was halfway through the movement when she realized her error. Grant hadn't telegraphed a pass; he had faked her out and thrown a no-look pass at Danny.

Sam scrambled to get back into position as the ball whizzed toward Danny. In that moment, time seemed to stand still. Grant came to a halt as Sam ran toward him, and . . . Danny was not paying attention to the ball.

"Yo—" Grant's face froze in horror as soon as he realized what Sam and half the court already saw. Danny turned just in time for the pass to hit him directly in the face with enough force to dent a car.

A collective yelp went around the group as Danny hit the ground with a thud, his limbs splayed like in one of da Vinci's anatomy drawings from the fifteenth century.

"Ow," Danny moaned from the floor as the entire court jogged over to check on him.

"Don't move," Theo and Kelly shouted at the same time. Sam was torn between running over to help and trying not to crowd the people in the room with actual emergency medical training.

"I'm pretty sure I'm just rattled," Danny said. To his credit, he did obey the roomful of doctors, who were all watching him like a hawk. He wiggled his ankles but didn't try to get up, and Sam's neck muscles started to relax. Gratitude that someone else was there to handle the emergency flooded her senses. No repeat of the plane for her.

"Maybe. But I didn't like the sound of that fall," Kelly said, leaning over him. "Can you look at me?"

Sam felt Grant stand next to her before she saw him. Looking over at him, she felt instantly guilty for mocking him all night. The poor guy looked like he had accidentally punched both of his grandmothers as Kelly helped Danny sit up.

Without thinking, Sam leaned into Grant and whispered, "You all right?"

"Better than Danny. Jeez." Grant scrubbed his hand over his face. "I hope he doesn't have a concussion. He is supposed to work tomorrow."

"I'm sure he'll be fine. He clearly remembers getting hit by the ball, which is a good sign," Sam said as Danny reenacted getting socked with his hands. That knowledge did not seem to have any effect on Grant's mood. Sam sighed. "For what it's worth. That was a really good pass."

Grant blinked at her for a few moments, the corners of his mouth lifting. "Thanks."

"Maybe you were a touch too assertive for poor Danny," Sam said, watching Grant's smile broaden as he shook his head.

"I earned that," Grant said, shrugging at her. Something stretched between them, and she wasn't entirely sure what to do with it. She'd liked it better when she'd just wanted to avoid speaking to him ever again.

"We went to elementary school together, and I gave that guy a concussion when we were like ten. Apparently, he is still holding a grudge," Danny shouted, getting slowly to his feet and drawing Grant's attention.

"I waited twenty-four years to pay you back," Grant called, making his way through the group of people to get to Danny's side. "Sorry, man."

"I'm all right, really. We could finish the game."

"I wouldn't go that far. I said you could probably get up, not *you can get your head knocked again*." Kelly chuckled.

"It's their possession anyway. I think they won this one. I'm not trying to let Duke dunk on you again." Grant laughed.

"I'm willing to call it a draw, given the loss of one of your star players," Raphael said, with a magnanimous bow.

"You're too kind," Kelly said, rolling her eyes.

"Draw it is," Grant said, nodding to Raphael. "Good game, everyone."

"Good game," Sam said, shaking hands and nudging shoulders with different players as she ambled off the court toward the bench. She could already feel her thighs starting to scream from all the defensive squats.

"For someone who had to be dragged here, you sure played like you cared," Duke said, sidling up beside her and taking in her sweat-soaked jersey.

"Ha. Ha. For someone who said they wanted to play, you sure spent a lot of time chitchatting."

Duke snorted and grabbed his bag. "Fine. But if I see you chatting and jogging at the next game, then I know that you are on some petty hustle shit."

"Oh. That hustle was absolutely about being petty." Sam laughed as she slipped into her sandals. "You don't even need to wait for next week. I just had to put Grant on notice."

"You played that game like it was the 1996 Bulls versus the Sonics playoffs. 'Back That Azz Up' was basically your theme music," Duke said, hoisting his bag to his shoulder and waiting for her to stand up.

Sam chuckled and shoved herself off the bench, feeling her muscles whine. "That's just a hazard of playing close defense. Grant knew."

"Grant knew something," Duke said, smirking.

"What are you saying?" Sam asked, arching an eyebrow at him as she scooped up her bag.

"All I'm saying is y'all were awful close."

"How far away am I supposed to be when you have Evan playing clown defense and Theo shooting moon balls?"

"I don't know, but what I do know is—"

"Hey, Sam." Grant's voice cut down the hallway, echoing off the concrete floors.

Sam was irritated with herself for not feeling more irritation over being interrupted by him. This person was not her friend. No matter how pained he'd looked over knocking Danny out. "Hey, Grant. What's up?"

Grant pulled even with them, and keeping one hand wrapped around the strap of his gym bag, he extended the other to Duke. "Good game."

"You're pretty good," Duke said, shaking his hand.

"Not as good as her." Grant nodded at Sam, and Duke laughed.

"Sam didn't even want to play. I had to beg her to join. Next thing you know, she is all competitive. I played with guys in the D-League who had less hustle." Duke snorted.

"I don't see the point in playing unless I'm gonna play to win," Sam said, glancing over at Grant as they began walking to the parking lot.

"Fun," Duke deadpanned.

"Winning is fun." The laughter in her tone betrayed her. It was hard to be petty when Duke was cracking jokes and Grant had just nailed a guy in the face like a stunt in a Three Stooges movie.

"Intense much?" Duke asked.

"Says the guy who lives and dies by our cleaning schedule." Sam rolled her eyes.

"Housemate rules are a different thing. You gotta be intense about those."

Grant laughed at the pair of them as they reached Duke's busted car. Belatedly, Sam remembered her lie about the car being a two-seater, then decided to tuck her shame into her pocket. For all Grant knew, Jehan had an equally shitty car that only held two. At least, he would think that until he saw Jehan in the hospital parking lot with her bicycle.

"Anyway, I just wanted to say good game to you." Grant held out his hand to Sam and smiled. San Francisco was absolutely frigid that evening, but his smile could have warmed up half the parking lot. It was the kind of smile that made her feel like he meant the gesture just for her . . . which Sam knew was absolutely not true. Exhaling a chilly breath, Sam shook his hand, the sureness of his grip matching the confidence he exuded. His hands were warm but not clammy with sweat like she would expect from someone who'd just played a basketball game. It was funny: she had brushed, pushed, and even once elbowed him all night, and she had never noticed the static that buzzed off his smooth skin. It was disarming but not altogether unpleasant. Sam released his hand before she could think any more about it.

"If you care for your patients with as much heart as you play pickup basketball, you are gonna be a great addition to SF Central."

"Oh. Thanks," Sam said, wishing her surprise hadn't rendered her so ineloquent. It wasn't that she had expected a repeat of the plane incident or anything. But she hadn't expected to give someone the full-court press and walk away with a new friend. Not that this was friendship. Grant's eyebrow twitched up, and Sam remembered to smile. "I'm sure you're at least as good a doctor as you are a basketball player."

"Let's hope. Seeing as I concussed a guy tonight." Grant half smiled at her, then pulled out a set of keys from his sweatshirt pocket. "See you both tomorrow."

Sam watched Grant slide into a sleek luxury SUV while Duke reached across to unlock the passenger-side door. Sliding into the car seat, she looked over at Duke as she buckled her seat belt and caught him grinning at her.

"What?" she asked, trying to tighten the overused belt strap. Duke continued to smirk, raised an eyebrow, and said nothing, so Sam made a face at him.

"I don't think he got the message about your petty revenge." Duke chuckled as he began easing out of the parking lot.

"I mean, I caused him to concuss someone, so I think he knows I'm not a fan," Sam said, tilting her head against the headrest as much in exasperation as in exhaustion.

"You sure about that?" Duke said, nodding his head toward her window and lifting his steering wheel hand in a classic driver's salute. Sam looked over in time to catch Grant waving at them with a big goofy gesture. "Like I said, I'm not sure he got your message."

Holding her posture ramrod straight, she looked back at Duke. "That was just unfortunate timing. He hasn't had a moment to reflect on how I destroyed his midrange game. It'll hit him later tonight. The grief will probably wake him up."

"I'll let you keep believing that," Duke said, still grinning as he turned left out of the parking lot.

Chapter Four

"I promise. It'll be like ten minutes max," Duke said as he unlocked the front door.

"I've lived with you for two months. You've never taken a ten-minute shower in your life." Sam chuckled, following him in. By the time they reached the house, Duke and Sam had broken down their entire day at the hospital, laughed at Raphael's lucky game socks, and rock-paper-scissors battled for the shower. Sam lost. And now it would be a good forty-five minutes before she could get near the shower. Probably longer if Duke used up all the hot water.

"You always act like I'm—" He stopped short just a few feet into the hallway. "Hey, Jehan, what's going on?"

Duke sounded like someone trying to talk a child into handing them a kitchen knife instead of running over and sticking it in an electrical socket. Peeking around him, Sam saw why. Jehan had situated herself on the couch, face splotchy with tears, surrounded by bits and pieces from magazines, a few legal documents, and a laptop and tablet, both of which were open to Pinterest.

"I'm just a little overwhelmed. Trav doesn't really get the engagement party thing, so I'm trying to move fast, but now my mom and my aunts have opinions . . ." Jehan's lip quivered as she forced a shuddering breath into her lungs. "It's a lot to handle."

"It's okay. We'll get through this," Sam said as Jehan picked up a magazine and halfheartedly stacked it on top of another. Sam pointed to a semicleared spot on the floor next to her. "Can I sit down?"

"Of course. I didn't expect you all to be home for another twenty minutes. I thought I had time to clean up." She sniffed, grabbing another fistful of papers and shuffling them around.

"Don't worry about it. We'll help." Sam caught Duke's eye. He shrugged at Jehan and shook his head as she continued to rearrange papers, oblivious to the both of them. Sam widened her eyes and jerked her head at him to come sit down. He shook his head again, right as Jehan looked up.

Stopping midmotion, Duke tried to turn his vigorous headshake into some sort of sniffing gesture, then said, "I really smell after that game. Let me hit up the shower, and then we can all"—he pointed vaguely in the direction of Jehan's piles and shrugged—"organize things."

"Thanks," Jehan hiccuped, looking back down at the piles around her and missing the pointed look he gave Sam before disappearing in the direction of the shower.

"So what happened?" Sam asked, gingerly peering at her friend.

"I started talking to my mom about the party, and it exploded."

"Exploded how?" Sam asked, then immediately wished she hadn't.

Great soggy tears started rolling down Jehan's face as she pointed to the magazines. "My mother started sending me all this. Then she told my aunts, who got involved. Now there are multiple Pinterest boards, and everyone has expectations, but no one is helping."

"Okay, so we want to work on managing expectations. After all, it's just a small party—"

"Not anymore." Jehan's voice wobbled as she dropped her head into her hands. "My mom is insisting I invite everyone from my parents' social circle. She wants half her office here."

"It's okay. We can get through this," Sam said, pulling Jehan's hands away from her face so she could look her in the eye.

"Mom wants a proper wedding; Travis wants a fast wedding in DC. I just want to practice medicine and be left alone," Jehan continued as if she hadn't heard anything Sam had said.

"I'm here. Duke's here. You don't have to do this by yourself." The sentiment that Jehan just wanted to be alone during what should be a happy time struck Sam as odd, but she decided to poke at it later. Right now, she needed to calm her friend down, not help her spin out faster.

"This whole fellowship thing is so much harder than they told us it would be."

"Ain't that the truth," Sam laughed. "Honestly, how long was your last shift?"

"Sixteen hours. The doctor taking over for me was late and—"

"Girl, after a sixteen-hour shift is not the time to look at your auntie's Pinterest board. You're tired."

"You're right," Jehan sniffed, looking around with a critical eye for possibly the first time in hours. "And Travis and I haven't ever been separated like this since we started dating six years ago. I know it's a sensitive time for him. We've never had to negotiate our relationship from a distance. He likely thinks dismissing my family's expectations is helpful."

"See. Everyone's processing right now." Sam picked up a pile and stacked it carelessly on top of another, trying to think. Jabs at Travis would not help anyone right now. Looking for an encouraging way to reframe her friend's struggle, she said, "I'm sure Travis can learn to respect the role your family plays in important events. Your mom and aunts can wait forty-eight hours, and tomorrow, we can space out after work, look at the pretty pictures, decide which ones to keep and which ones to throw out. Sound good?"

"When you say it like that, I feel ridiculous."

"Don't worry about it." Smiling at her, Sam shook her head and laughed. "After all, you talked me out of flipping out over seeing my mom in LA. Roomies are good for perspective."

~

"Honestly, anxiety is really normal," Sam said, smiling up at the woman in front of her. Sheila was relatively new to the clinic, which meant that her baby and Sam would get to go through her first year at SF Central together. The thought was fun for Sam, but she didn't voice that to her patient, who was already looking a little nauseous while Sam walked her through an outline of the next six months pre- and postpartum.

"This is a lot," Sheila said, fidgeting on the exam table. "How does anyone remember all this?"

"A lot of it, your body will likely do for you." Sam laughed. "And what it doesn't do, anyone in your life who has been pregnant in the last few years will remember for you."

Sheila giggled. "Advice from strangers. Every pregnant person's worst nightmare."

"I'm not sure I'd take it from them. At least not without vetting it first," Sam laughed, then began to write down a list of a few things Sheila should keep in the house as her pregnancy progressed. "Does your family live locally?"

"No. It's just me and my partner. They drive a short-haul truck route, so right now it is just me. We're originally from Utah."

"Oh," Sam said. Suddenly her nerves made a lot more sense. "In that case, I might recommend taking a few classes to help you make a few other pregnant friends, and if you are so inclined, you might want to speak with a birthing specialist."

"Birthing specialist?"

"Commonly called a doula." Sam made a mental note to cut down on the jargon next time she had this conversation.

"Where can I find those? Classes and the birthing . . . whatever you called it." Sam felt her heartbeat pick up. Not three seconds ago she'd been riding high on her ability to suggest resources. Now she was crashing under the weight of where to actually get them. Sheila must have sensed her hesitance, because she started, "I can google—"

"No worries!" While Sam was a fan of learning to change a headlight from YouTube, googling pregnancy plus anything had an equal likelihood of getting her ripped off as solving her problem. "It's just that I'm still new here, so I am not sure which services are reputable in the area. But you have another appointment in a few weeks, so why don't I ask around, and we can talk about your options then?"

Sheila nodded, the corners of her mouth turning up slowly. "Sounds good."

"Okay then. Any other questions I can answer for you?" Sam asked, praying that if she had questions, they were medical in nature. Last week someone had asked where the nearest coffee place was, and it had nearly killed Sam to admit she didn't know that either.

"No, I think I'm all set. Thank you, Doctor."

"All right. Take care. And call that number or send me an email if you have any questions before your next appointment." Sam handed her the page she had been writing on and stepped out of the room, careful to gently close the door behind her.

Sam walked down the hallway, sighing heavily as she made her way to the nurses' station. She felt Sheila's question rattling around in her head and winced. Much to her chagrin, the charge nurse was not at the desk. Sam wanted to be able to email her patient the information as soon as possible. She also wanted to get the answers to her questions from anyone other than Grant.

She'd seen him at the short convening he held for the fellows and residents he was supervising that day. The meeting was only fifteen minutes and entirely patient focused, but Sam could almost feel Grant's mind assessing her every word, looking for some new way to retrieve the upper hand the entire time. By the end of the morning, she decided that avoiding him was the best possible outcome. Duke pointed out that it would be physically impossible for her to avoid the man for the next three years, but Sam had to disagree. Where there was a will, there was a way. And she had a lot of will. Except . . .

She also had a lot of questions. Loath as she was to admit it, Grant would have the answers. If it was between maintaining a petty grudge and providing patient care, Sam could suck it up for twenty minutes.

Rounding the corner toward the graying staff lounge, Sam spotted him through the webbed window in the door. Perched on the end of a couch, he was huddled over some paper spread out over a coffee table. His dark hair was perfectly in place, held together by the same kind of alchemy that also made his scrubs wrinkle-free despite being six hours into a shift. The muscles in his left arm flexed as his pen hovered over the page, preparing to write down notes on whatever was causing the crease in his brow.

Does he have to be hot? It was one thing to have to work with someone who you didn't really like. It was another thing to work with someone who was so good looking it was difficult to make eye contact with them. Why couldn't he just be disheveled like everyone else?

Taking a deep breath, Sam reminded herself that she'd watched the guy peg someone with a basketball. Whether or not he was perfectly put together, she didn't need to be intimidated by him. Grant's gaze flicked briefly to the door as Sam did her best to glide through it, willing her heartbeat to slow down as she entered the room.

"Hey," Grant said, the muscles in his face twitching toward a smile before he looked back down at whatever he was writing.

"Hello," Sam said, with a small wave that instantaneously felt absurd. He wasn't looking at her. Why was she waving? Looking for something to do with her hands, she went over to the coffee machine and stared at its buttons for a moment. She just needed to be cool. Colleagues bounced ideas off each other all the time. Fumbling with a puny-looking paper cup, Sam poked at a button promising a latte before turning to face the couch and its occupant again.

"Hey, Grant. I've been meaning to ask—" The sound of the machine wheezing and grinding coffee beans interrupted her right as he looked up, a hint of his earlier concentration still furrowing his brow. The machine let out a puff of steam and seemed to quiet down as it began to fill her cup, and Sam took another deep breath. "Wow, that is loud. How does anyone have a conversation over that?"

"Fair warning—it tastes how it sounds. Most of us get coffee from the cafeteria." Grant half smiled, and the lines on his forehead disappeared. "What's up?"

"I just saw a patient and—" The machine began to beep like a construction truck backing up, causing Sam to jump three inches. She clutched her collarbone and tried to identify the source of the sound.

"It means it's done. You've never used this before?"

"How is this done? There is like two tablespoons of weird sludge in there." Sam frowned at the machine, which continued to squawk. "And no. Jehan makes us all a big thermos of coffee every shift. Now I know why."

"You have to take the cup out, or it'll just keep beeping," Grant said, sounding tired.

"Talk about a design flaw," Sam mumbled, snatching the cup out of the machine. In her mind, this conversation had gone a lot smoother. Still holding the weird cup of foam, she turned to face Grant. "Right. So where was I?"

"You had a question." He raised an eyebrow at her from over his shoulder.

"Yeah . . ." How could one eyebrow make someone feel so stupid? Struggling to reform her question, she said, "I'm wondering what resources or coaching we have available for pregnant individuals?"

"Oh. Good question . . . ," Grant said, leaning away from the coffee table and drawing his shoulders back in a subconscious stretch as he thought. "Do you mean in the hospital?"

"Yes." Sam felt the tension in her face return and rubbed her forehead as she made her way over to the shabby chair next to the couch. Dropping herself into it, she added, "Typically, hospitals often have community programs. I know I should know these things by now—"

"You have been a doctor here for exactly two months. Why would you know that?" Grant chuckled, then grinned at her. There was that disarming smile again. The one that felt like sunshine. "I can guarantee you half the staff here don't have a sense of any community programs besides the one for smoking cessation."

"Yeah, but—"

"Don't beat yourself up over this one. There will be plenty of other stuff to be upset about. Trust me," Grant said. His tone was more kind than the dismissive shrug that accompanied his words, and Sam found herself smiling in spite of her best efforts.

"As long as there is an avenue for guilt somewhere. Wouldn't want to miss out on the self-flagellation."

Grant smirked at her joke, then leaned forward again. "To answer your question. It wasn't covered in orientation because we don't have any community programs for it."

"What?"

"You came to SF Central because you wanted to work with some of the city's most underserved people, didn't you?" Grant asked. It wasn't an accusation, but it wasn't warm and fuzzy either.

Sam's unease returned as she nodded her affirmation, deciding that words would likely get her in trouble.

"I did too. The reality is that public hospitals and clinics don't have that kind of money, even with our research partnership with Stanford. This hospital barely has money to keep the lights on. We don't have staff for community groups."

Sam inhaled sharply in an effort not to bite Grant's head off. She understood the budget situation. It was evident in everything she saw all day, from the dated exam rooms in the clinic to the fact that she didn't have a laptop for charting. She knew what a lack of funding looked like, and she didn't need him to explain it. If the hospital didn't receive funds from the government to hire young doctors like her, she wouldn't be here.

"I know the hospital has limited resources. I'm not completely stupid, contrary to my efforts on the plane." Grant's eyes went wide, his eyebrows inching toward his hairline. "Using my own powers of observation and a shred of common sense, I figured out the funding thing pretty quickly. I just thought maybe someone here might have started—"

"I'm sorry. Of course you understand hospital budgets. You're a community health researcher." Grant twisted the pen in his hand and let out a nervous chuckle. "You have a master's in public policy."

"How do you know that?"

"Orientation booklet." Grant shrugged, managing to look both contrite and charming. "Anyway, I don't think you are stupid, and implying that was not my intention."

"Oh." Sam blinked a few times. She had steeled herself for a fight, and now she was sitting in her battle armor with no enemy in sight. The whole interaction had caught her off guard. She wanted to hold a grudge, but a small voice in the back of her head registered Grant's tone. He wasn't trying to be rude. If anything, he seemed to be attempting to relate. Albeit poorly. Still bristling, she said, "It happens."

Grant's expression hovered somewhere between charming repentance and a grimace. "Anyway, before I interrupted you, you were saying?"

Sam looked down at her coffee cup, less with the intention of drinking whatever was in there and more to help herself focus. Better to block out Grant's presence while she tried to formulate her question. "I was just thinking that maybe some of the staff might have gotten something off the ground. Maybe partnered with a local birthing center or something?"

Sam looked up in time to catch Grant exhaling slowly. Letting his eyes flick to the door of the room, he shifted his posture, leaning toward her. "It's a little trickier than just funding limitations. There is a generation gap at play. I think you'll find that some doctors here are excited about community programming and the idea of a community hospital as more than a triage center for people who are underinsured."

"And?" Sam felt herself leaning forward, too, as if being pulled into his secretive observations by a magnet and abandoning whatever effort she might have made to be cool.

"Then we have some who are . . ." Grant looked back toward the door again, dropping his voice to just above a whisper. "They are just more comfortable with how things have always been done."

"Oh." Sam's heart sank as Grant's meaning dawned on her. "Let me guess—the people who are 'traditional' also happen to be making program decisions?" Sam asked, putting *traditional* in air quotes.

Grant nodded at her, as if he had just conveyed some sort of conspiracy theory, then leaned back against the couch, his lips pressed into a thin line.

"And no one has tried to find a way around this?"

"Well"—Grant used his hands to heighten his shrug—"not since I've been here. It's kind of a lot for a new fellow to take on, and there is already such high burnout among physicians. Starting something like that is a big ask, even if you could get the support or funding."

"Right. So you don't know of anyone who has actually tried, then?" Sam asked, attempting to soften her words. She didn't want to make it sound like Grant or any of her other colleagues hadn't been doing their jobs. Still, it nagged at her. How did an entire hospital full of people just decide to ignore an obvious problem?

"I don't think I do," Grant said, glancing back down at the journal article he was reading, clearly signaling that Sam's line of questioning should wrap up before he needed to get to wherever it was that senior fellows went next.

Hint taken. Reaching for her coffee cup, Sam sighed. "Okay then, I guess it is up to me to try. One more question, then I'll leave you alone. Who is the best person for me to approach about getting a program off the ground?"

"Try to start a program?" Grant's head tilted in surprise, as if Sam had just told him that she wanted to parachute off the roof.

"Yup. Someone has to push the old guard. It's clear the program is needed. Why not me?"

"Being a research fellow is hard. You're working like seventy hours a week," Grant said. The incredulity on his face was almost funny. "I don't want to tell you how to live, but I might suggest scaling back your ambition. It takes most researchers a decade to get a single initiative off the ground. Doing it in your first year of fellowship is a stretch."

"I can't just let my patients get half the care they deserve," Sam said, ignoring the fact that Grant's eyebrows were dangerously close to his hairline. Clearly, he hadn't expected pushback from her. "I assume I should start with Dr. Franklin?"

"Well, yes. He would be the one to start with." Grant tilted his head and stared at her as if she were a journal article that he didn't totally understand. "But like I said, why not give yourself more than a few years in the job before you try to get community programming off the ground? The other research fellows are just doing small studies for their projects. Blood analysis, patient-attitude surveys, and that kind of stuff. This is really swinging for the fences."

Her mother had been trying to control her for years. Waiting for Sam to fail so she could pick at her. But this time she wasn't going to fail. Nope. She'd give up breathing long before she went back to Ohio as a failure. She might be biting off more than most people could chew, but she could do it. Grant would have to do better than a stern talking-to if he wanted her to be less ambitious.

Sam put her free hand on her hip and looked him right in the eye. "And like I said, the patient I just saw deserves support. It's not like I can ask her to let her baby bake for the next three years because it is convenient for my schedule."

Grant's laugh filled the room, lighting up all four graying corners with his tenor. "I appreciate the sense of urgency. And if anyone could do it, I'm sure you could."

"Can and will." Sam felt her jaw set. He had a warm, rich laugh. A laugh she probably would have enjoyed under other circumstances. She liked it a lot less when he was trying to talk her out of something.

"Right." Grant nodded, the humor still playing around his eyes as he looked her over like her dream was too adorable for him to crush. A man who looked like that probably hadn't failed at anything in his life. Perfect people never did. She hated that look almost as much as she hated people doubting her. "Well, they say advice is worth what you pay for it. And mine's free, so do what you want. But if I were you, I'd focus on securing funding for a simple research question for your fellowship."

"Duly noted. Where is Dr. Franklin's office?"

"Up on the fifth floor, near the men's room," Grant sighed, the tired expression returning to his face as he watched her walk her untouched coffee over to the trash can.

"Wonderful. I'll have a chat with him," Sam said, her words a little too perky to be believable.

"Hey, Sam." Grant's words floated over her shoulder, stopping her as she pushed on the door.

Turning slowly to face him again, Sam schooled her features into a neutral expression as best she could. "Yes?"

"Dr. Franklin can be sticky, but he'll usually meet you halfway. I hope it works out."

"I'll keep that in mind." Sam felt a half smile creep across her face as he extended her an olive branch. "Thank you for your help."

"Anytime." Grant flashed a hundred-watt smile, making eye contact. It should have been a simple glance, a gesture that was easy for Sam to return. Then their eyes met, and something in the air changed along with Grant's expression. It was as if electricity ran hot and buzzing between them, and Sam felt like she was one half of a magnet helpless against the pull of his other half. Sam felt the heat returning to her cheeks. Grant licked his lips, and she bit down on hers to keep from gasping.

It hit her that she was dangerously close to crossing over into meaningful-eye-contact territory. If she didn't move soon, either she was going to melt with unexpected sexual tension or things would get hot enough in the little lounge that the papers in front of Grant ignited. She could not dissolve into a quivering mass in front of this man, first because that would be extremely unsanitary in a hospital and second because not ten seconds ago he'd been actively trying to dissuade her from pursuing her research idea. Clearing her throat, Sam blinked and looked down at the floor, causing Grant to clear his throat and look at his papers, effectively halting the pull between them.

"Gonna get back to work," Grant said, gesturing vaguely over the papers at the same time Sam spoke.

"Okay, bye."

Nodding once, Sam turned and walked through the door without a word. Safely in the hallway, she exhaled. She was lucky that smile came attached to someone so difficult, or she would have much bigger problems to solve than starting a community program.

Chapter Five

Sam dropped the mail on the kitchen counter for her roommates and opened the fridge, feeling exhaustion creep into her every movement. She had gone looking for Dr. Franklin right after talking to Grant. And then she went looking for him again after seeing a few more patients, and again after filing some paperwork. She even went looking after their outpatient-report meeting. By about the fifth pass through, the head of general surgery finally took pity on her and let her know that Dr. Franklin was most likely gone for the day. Not to be deterred—or let Grant say *I told you so*—Sam broke down and sent Dr. Franklin an email asking when he'd be around. So far, she hadn't heard anything, but she had only been relentlessly checking her email for two hours, so there was still time.

Grabbing an apple off one of the shelves, Sam was in the middle of cursing herself for whatever wild notion had made her decide not to get snack food at the grocery store when her phone rang. She exhaled as Mom scrolled across the screen, accompanied by a photo of a woman wearing too much hair spray and blue eye shadow in a hospital bed, holding baby Sam and smiling next to her father, whose dark skin made her mother look even more pale than her freckles implied. Her father wore his favorite old T-shirt from the navy and had a hand on her older brother's chest, ostensibly to keep the mischievous-looking toddler from bolting around the room long enough to take Sam's first family photo.

The picture made her smile. Her mom hadn't called since Los Angeles, and Sam had started to wonder if she would ever speak to her again. As controlling as her mom could be, Sam missed her laugh, the text messages with the beautiful photos she took of their garden back home, and the regular report on their cat-obsessed neighbor, which was only complete with her mother's color commentary. Their relationship was rocky, but Sam knew her mom's forgiveness and love could be earned with the right combination of humor and deference to her judgment.

"Hi, Mom, what's going on?"

"Hi, Sammy. How are you?"

"Good. I just got home and am trying to figure out whether I want to snack or shower first." Sam chuckled as she pulled a knife from the drawer. Putting her mother on speaker, she began slicing her apple as she spoke. "How are things on your end?"

"Things are fantastic. Your father mentioned he got a text from you, and I knew I had to call."

"Uh-huh," Sam murmured, still focusing on the apple. For years, her dad had played the family-moderator role. He kept up with both her and her brother and tried to curb some of her mom's more extreme impulses. It never really worked, but Sam appreciated that he tried.

"He said you were asking for a status report on one of Mrs. Morrow's cats. Pretty sure you wanted an update about the latest antics of Precious, a.k.a. the wicked beast that has started breaking into our garage to steal our canned food."

"Better or worse than when he peed in the shed?" Sam asked, imagining the smush-faced cat howling at their Costco stash of soup.

"Is it possible for it to be worse?" Diana laughed. "Anyway, I just got off the phone with your brother. You know he is helping me organize a little reunion for our retired navy friends in Southern California? We are even going to blow up my photos from our time there and put them on display." Sam hadn't known that. She and Isaiah generally avoided talking about their mom, unless it was to share tips from their respective therapists, friends, or memes.

"So exciting."

"Well, it gave me an idea. Why shouldn't we do the same thing in Northern California? Wouldn't want our friends on the other end of the state to feel left out, would we."

"It could be a good idea," Sam hedged as she opened the freezer, praying to find some forgotten ice cream in there. No such luck. "Or you could always invite them to LA, make a big weekend of it."

There was silence on the other end, and regret filled Sam's lungs. She knew better than to make suggestions when her mother clearly had a plan. Bracing for a potential storm, she added, "But yeah, a party in the Bay could be fun too."

"I'm so glad you agree, because I was thinking it could be a fun project for you and me to work on together." Her words sounded tight, as if Sam not jumping up and down over the prospect annoyed her.

"What did you have in mind?" Sam stopped hunting around for food, giving her mother her full attention. She didn't have much time, but a joint project always made her mother happy. It was how Sam had ended up painting her bedroom lavender when she was sixteen. Did Sam like the color? No. But her mother did, and the trade-off meant that Sam could get her driver's license, so it was worth it. Kind of.

"Nothing big. Isaiah is helping me find a venue in LA since I don't live there. I was thinking you could do the same thing in San Francisco. Then just a bit of help with planning and such. But only the easy stuff."

Sam's mind began spinning as her mother listed every retired navy member within three hundred miles of San Francisco who should be invited to the party. This reunion didn't sound small. And of course Isaiah was doing all this for her. He always cracked under family pressure. All Mom had to do was pack for the shortest of guilt trips, and off he went. If Sam didn't help, she'd be in the doghouse again, and who knew how long it would be before her mother spoke to her this time.

"I really want to help, but I just don't think I can plan a big thing. My fellowship is really starting to get busy, and I have this program I want to start. The hospital—"

"Oh no, Sammy. This wouldn't be a big ask. Really, I am thinking something low key."

"I know you think it's low key. But—"

"I get it, Sam." Her mother's voice went cold with disappointment, and she could almost feel the relationship door slamming in her face. "You're too busy. You have your own life to focus on."

"Mom, I want to do it. I just can't take on too much."

"No, no, no. Really, Sammy, don't worry about it. You moved out to California to focus on your career, and you're on track with your personal goals. My little party isn't your work. I get it. Truly, I do."

Her mother always did this—say something stunningly passive aggressive in a soothing tone so that it was hard to argue.

Sam's mind began to spin and crack. She didn't really want to do this, but Diana's demands were clear. The party was her one chance to get back into her mother's good graces. Admittedly, Sam wished that her mother's forgiveness could be purchased with a pedicure and some girl talk, but after more than two months of silence, she would take what she could get.

"Mom, you can still have the party, and I can help. I just can't handle every logistical detail." Sam heard herself begin to break. Hadn't she just said she didn't have time to help? She needed to get off the phone before her arm was fully twisted and tied behind her back. Duke had called her stubborn, but clearly he'd never seen her with her mother.

"I appreciate that, sweetheart; I really do. But I just don't see the point in having a party when I don't know the area like someone who lives there."

"I have been here for all of two months. I hardly think that qualifies—"

"It's a shame. But you're right. Your work has to come first. I was being selfish."

Sam flinched. Diana Holbrook had spent the majority of her time propping up the family, packing and unpacking the house. She hadn't even had a chance to have a career until after Sam's dad retired and they settled in Ohio when Sam was in the seventh grade. Even then, her mom went back and got her teaching credential and became a high school biology teacher, helping pay the bills while Sam's dad retooled his résumé. Then she continued to work, putting Sam and Isaiah through college. Her mother was difficult, but she wasn't selfish.

"No, Mom. You really aren't being selfish. I'm just so slammed." Sam gritted her teeth over the sound of her mother's resigned sigh.

"Forget I even said anything." The enthusiasm had completely deflated from her mother's tone.

Closing her eyes, Sam left her apple on the counter and dropped herself onto the couch. "Honestly, Mom, I can help. It's no big deal. I'll do it."

"Are you sure? Because I wouldn't want you to feel put out."

Too late for that. "I'll make it work. I'm sure Isaiah has some pointers too."

"Well, if you are sure . . ."

"One hundred percent," Sam said, sinking lower onto the couch. Sure, she'd fudged the decimal point on that number a bit. But really, 10 percent and 100 percent were not *that* far apart.

"Oh, Sammy. Thank you. This is going to be so much fun! I'll send you what I am thinking, and we can go from there. Sound good?"

"Sure does." She was lucky her mother didn't pick up on anything other than a sentence that had her name in front of it, or Diana would have realized that she was as excited about this party as she was about eating the apple she had sliced up.

"All right, sweetheart. Well, I need to run, but take care of yourself."

"Love you."

"Bye!"

Her mother breezed off the phone just in time to miss Sam sighing like a duchess in a novel from the 1800s. So much for avoiding the guilt trip. If anything, her mother would ask her to buy a whole new wardrobe for it. Pushing herself off the couch, Sam shuffled back into the kitchen and yanked open a cupboard. Spotting Duke's peanut butter, she felt her heart lift as she reached for the jar with only a little remorse and a silent promise to buy him some more Jif before he noticed it was gone. Sure, she was stuck with the adult equivalent of a lavender room, but at least she had something to make her apple worthwhile.

Chapter Six

Sam hesitated just down the hallway from Dr. Franklin's office. It had taken him a few days to get back to her, which gave Sam plenty of time to think through what she was asking for. If Grant was right, then Dr. Franklin wasn't likely to be over the moon about her idea, which was why she had come prepared with stats of every sort. It was harder to argue with numbers.

Giving herself a shake, she pushed her nerves aside, pulled her shoulders back, and strutted toward Dr. Franklin's office. Stopping just outside the door, Sam saw Dr. Franklin staring at a computer, his glasses pushed way down his nose and his head tilted back as he scowled at whatever was on the screen. Taking a deep breath, Sam raised her hand and knocked on the doorframe, instantaneously pulling his laser focus away from the computer.

"Hi, Dr. Franklin. I'm Sam Holbrook; we were going to chat about birthing-and-parental programs at the hospital."

"Oh yes. Hello, Dr. Holbrook, have a seat." Dr. Franklin's blue eyes sparkled as he pushed his chair away from his monitor and stood to beckon her in. Sam felt like she was being welcomed by a fit Santa Claus, minus the beard.

"Thank you." Sam walked into the room, doing her best to maintain her confidence as she shook his hand. The office was the sort of place that wasn't intentionally intimidating but ended up feeling that way just the same. It was full of faux-cherrywood furniture, complete with the particleboard desk and half a dozen bookshelves lining the room. Dr. Franklin had only managed to fill half the shelves, but he had done it with a perfectly calculated balance of books, knickknacks, photos of kids, degrees, certifications, and finger paintings that made Sam wonder if his office moonlighted as a movie set.

"So what can I do for you?" Dr. Franklin asked, his voice gently easing her mind away from the sundry items on his shelves.

"I talked to Dr. Gao, and he mentioned that the hospital hasn't developed a comprehensive birthing program. Did I understand him correctly?"

Dr. Franklin's eyes flicked to the screen in front of him, then returned to Sam. "Yes, that is correct. It's just not something our hospital has the resources for." His tone sounded like he was mentally composing an email and was just waiting for Sam to leave so he could get started on it.

Not that it mattered. She was determined to see this through, no matter how intimidating his particleboard office was. "I'm curious—if I could identify a funding source for a program, would it be possible for us to start one?"

The shift in Dr. Franklin's attention was palpable. Looking directly at her, he said, "What kind of program did you have in mind?"

"Well, I have been doing some research, and I think a partnership with local doulas would benefit us. According to the *Journal of Perinatal Medicine*, pre- and postpartum care is crucial to—"

Dr. Franklin's burst of laughter sliced through her sentence, cutting off her prepared display of research. "I'm sorry. Doulas?"

"Yes. When you think about it, a well-trained doula has seen hundreds of pregnant people in all different settings. In fact, Medi-Cal is considering covering doula services for Californians with state insurance as we speak. SF Central could be on the cutting edge of understanding how doulas impact care in populations like ours."

"That is some very hippie-dippie stuff there." Sam watched as Dr. Franklin's eyebrows crept up his forehead, his brow wrinkled as he concentrated on not laughing.

"I know it sounds that way. But I think you'll find that the practice of being a doula is very different from the sort of 1960s 'have a baby in the woods while praying to a tree' that people imagine." Dr. Franklin laughed at this, and Sam was relieved that he was finally laughing with her, as opposed to at her. She tried to keep her smile light as she doubled back to the topic at hand. "For many cultures, doulas have always been part of pregnancy. This is just incorporating historical and cultural practices into modern care. Over the centuries, doulas have provided the sort of pre- and postpregnancy care that helps fill the gap between patients and medical-care providers."

Dr. Franklin snorted and leaned back in his chair, studying Sam. "You're a community health research fellow, aren't you? What study did you read that brought this idea on?"

"Okay, yes. You are correct. I'm a community health research fellow." Sam laughed. She had to hand it to Dr. Franklin: at least he knew his fellows and residents well. "I did my master's in public health policy, looking at successful mentorship programs for pregnant teens, so I know community programs can work. Why shouldn't they work for our pregnant population? It's widely understood that the risk of birth complications for trans people, people with disabilities, lesbians, and people of color is much higher. But the risk of complications decreases when people have access to doulas, which is often the exclusive domain of rich people. If my hypothesis is correct and we design a thoughtful program—and don't worry; I plan to study this—then we could help improve the experience of and outcomes for marginalized pregnant people tremendously."

"By using a doula? Why not additional training for staff? A training day is much cheaper than a new program." Dr. Franklin steepled his fingers and squinted at Sam, his gaze making her nervous all over again.

"I would argue that we could do both. My interest is in community programs. But if we have another fellow on staff who is interested in researching physician education, then let's include them." Sam shrugged.

Dr. Franklin shook his head as if he was trying to come up with a nice way to say no. Sam couldn't let that happen. Jumping in, she added, "Think about it. Only fifty percent of the people who deliver here received care at SF Central prior to having a baby. But our hospital could be a place where people who typically avoid medical care or whose outcomes are poor actually want to come and give birth. Doulas can help bridge the gap between the medical experience and everyday life. Not to mention help provide care for people whose pregnancies may not come to term for whatever reason. Right now, we don't offer them any real support to speak of, and that is a shame."

"Dr. Holbrook, I appreciate your enthusiasm, and you certainly make a good point about patient experience affecting the bottom line. However, I know you are new here. Do you have any idea how many of these fly-by-night, fad community health programs have come and gone?"

Sam felt her stomach drop. She should have anticipated this question. Hell, Grant had warned her that this wouldn't be an easy sell. "Well, no. But that's the thing—"

"Our midwives do a great job with the postcare checkup after someone has given birth. I fail to see how using a doula for that would be any different. If anything, it is just inviting someone without any formal medical training to do a clinician's job, despite the fact that we are already paying to have a nurse there."

Ouch. That was blunt. A small voice in the back of Sam's head pointed out that although it was harsh, Dr. Franklin had tipped his hand. She was thinking about this the wrong way. Patient centric might be her goal, but it wasn't his. Money and the old guard were what mattered here. Sam smiled.

"Not everyone who comes here has a baby when they leave. Nurses aren't much help there, but a doula could be. And for those who do, are we paying nurses to make house calls or scheduling them for more than ten minutes for each patient?" Sam asked, letting her eyes go wide in the hopes that it would sound more naive than judgmental. Dr. Franklin smirked as if he bought her act about as much as he believed in leprechauns, but she continued. "Bringing in a doula allows the nurses to focus on patient care, while someone else handles the aspects that don't require medical attention so much as managing patient and familial comfort and anxiety. Not to mention the basics of changing and swaddling postbirth and the general reassuring everyone that they are normal." Sam steadied her breathing as Dr. Franklin shifted his attention away from his watch and back toward her, his focus becoming more intent as she spoke.

"I can see where you have a point." Dr. Franklin nodded, his expression looking like someone who is trying to decide between a Big Mac and a Quarter Pounder.

"And," Sam added, pushing her luck just a little further, "if we do this right, the doula will have a relationship with the patient, so they can help with lactation support, finding life balance, and any number of questions that come up in the first few months after the baby is born. It would cut down on calls to the clinic for things that really don't require a nurse or a doctor's attention."

Dr. Franklin's sigh was heavy, as if Sam's line of thinking was wearing him out. He leaned back in his chair, letting his eyes flick toward his screen again. "These are all very appealing reasons to consider a community program. But that still doesn't change the hospital's financial situation. We just don't have the cash on hand for something like that."

"Dr. Gao said as much. But I have done some thinking about this." Sam refused to let his exhaustion deter her. Not when she was this close to getting her way. "Part of a fellowship is learning how to apply for grants. I know this isn't likely to get NIH funding, but if I could find us philanthropic support for a pilot program, would you be willing to give my research idea your blessing?"

Standing up, Dr. Franklin looked down at Sam, cueing her to stand without so much as a word. Exhaling so his cheeks puffed out like a bath toy, he said, "Physicians always think their ideas are surefire, easy grant money, and they never are. And doulas? Talk about a tricky sell." Dr. Franklin snorted as he said the word *doula*, and Sam held her breath, refusing to walk toward the door until she had a firm yes or no. He eyed her, waiting for a response.

"I suspect you are right. But what could it hurt to try?"

Dr. Franklin shook his head and walked around the desk, effectively herding her toward the door. "Well, if you are determined to try it. Sure. Go ahead and look for grants. If you can find someone to fund it and a senior physician to advise you since you're in your first year, then by all means. I'll let you give it a go."

"Thank you, Dr. Franklin," Sam gushed. When she'd envisioned this part of the conversation, she'd thought she'd be chill. It turned out she had zero chill when it came to patient care. "I look forward to updating you as I develop the program."

The older man walked to the door, the humor returning to his face. Laughing lightly, he said, "Right. Good luck getting doulas in my hospital."

"I know the idea is unorthodox, but I think it might just work out in everyone's favor." Stepping through the door, Sam forced herself to smile. He could underestimate her all he wanted. Sooner or later, Dr. Franklin would eat his words, and then she would be laughing all the way to better patient outcomes and an article published in the *American Journal of Medicine* or something. "Thank you again for making time to see me. You won't regret it."

Sam saw him shaking his head. His expression was the sort of amused look that adults usually reserved for small children telling bizarre stories. She waited until she rounded the corner and heard his door shut before busting out a small happy dance, complete with a shimmy and a few hops.

To think Grant thought it couldn't be done. Sam grinned as she got in the elevator and pressed the button to the third floor. She wasn't planning to track down Grant and tell him he was wrong or anything . . . but if she happened to see him in the staff lounge, she couldn't promise she wouldn't mention it. She could do that without sounding too smug . . . or at least she would try.

~

"How'd it go?" Duke asked as soon as she opened the front door.

For a moment, Sam's tired mind went empty as she sifted through her shift until it hit on her meeting with Dr. Franklin. "I got the green light."

"I told you!" Jehan's voice rushed down the hall, with the sound of her footsteps.

"I see you." Duke spread out his arms and pulled the two of them into his massive wingspan for a group hug.

"This is the gangliest group hug." Jehan giggled as she tried to navigate two taller people's arms. "Seriously. I'm rooming with people who should be in a professional basketball league."

Sam laughed as the three of them let go. "Maybe it'll rub off and you won't need a step stool to reach the kitchen counter."

Jehan snorted and followed Sam over to the couch, flopping down next to her with the same exhausted sigh. "So what happened? Was Grant right? Details, please."

"I mean, he was kinda right." Sam wrinkled her nose. "But also wrong in several ways, which I am choosing to focus on because I'm petty."

"Attagirl," Duke snarked, his head in the fridge as he dug around for something to eat.

"Obviously, you are superior in every way." Jehan nodded. "But how exactly was he wrong? We need these details in order to silently gloat through our next hell shifts."

"Basically, Dr. Franklin tried to laugh me out of there as soon as the words *community program* and *doula* were uttered. He started saying all kinds of things about the budget. And when I wouldn't give up on that, he tried to ask why nurses couldn't just do the work—"

"Did you say, *'Cause they have other jobs?*" Jehan jumped in, slapping the back of the couch as she got into the story.

"I did just that," Sam said, shaking her head. "Then, get this, he basically said that every physician is a narcissist and that no one cares about our ideas as much as us."

"What?" Duke shouted, popping his head out of the fridge. "That is rich coming from a man who insists on introducing himself as *Doctor* to all the other doctors he knows."

"I know. I know. I could understand if I was asking for them to build me a space medicine laboratory or something. But honestly, I'm not that original," Sam cackled.

"No, your program idea is way better than that," Jehan said, shaking her head and missing the joke.

"Yeah, but you know what I mean. This ain't exactly brand-new stuff. Rich women have had birthing coaches for years."

"Okay, yeah. But don't sell yourself short," Jehan said, tapping the couch again. "Keep going. How did it end?"

"Right, right. Well, anyway. I could tell that making it all about patient outcomes wasn't getting me anywhere, so then I shifted. Made it about saving money and staff time."

"I'll bet he was into that," Duke said.

"He tried to play it off, like, whatever. But he was listening. So then I thought, *Okay, maybe we compromise.* So—"

"Wait. I thought we were being petty and focusing on where Grant was wrong. Didn't he say to compromise?" Duke asked, coming out of the kitchen with something that looked suspiciously like a protein shake with coffee in it.

"Well, yes . . . ," Sam said, shifting in her divot in the couch. "But this is different."

"Different how? I thought this was about proving Grant wrong, not taking his advice and pretending you didn't." Duke sipped his glass of whatever and looked smug for all of three seconds, until the taste of what he was drinking started to burn his throat and he coughed. He deserved that. With the way he was raining on her superiority parade, Sam hoped the drink tasted like the dirt on a hubcap. "What's the deal with you and him? Why do you hate him?"

"I don't hate him."

"You said you loathed his smug face last week," Jehan said, narrowing her eyes at Sam.

Avoiding the weight of her roommates' gazes, Sam wrinkled her nose and said, "Loathing a smug face isn't hating."

Jehan snorted and rolled her eyes before dramatically flopping onto the side of the couch just to drive her point home in case she wasn't clear about how affronted she was by Sam's logic.

"It's just . . . I feel like he is too perfect. There is something untrustworthy about good-looking people who are smart."

"So you hate him because of his face?" Jehan asked.

"You don't hate me, and I'm basically a god," Duke said.

Both she and Jehan stopped to stare at Duke, who started cackling like the joke was the best one he'd told all day. When no one joined him, he straightened up and said, "Anyway. Carry on. You don't trust his extremely symmetrical face because why?"

Why didn't she trust him? She could admit it wasn't just the plane thing, although that didn't help. If she was honest with herself, Grant just felt too good. People like him weren't interested in people like her—the messy kind, with broken family relationships and something to prove. They dated people who didn't keep their phones in airplane mode to avoid hard phone calls and emergency ice cream in the fridge to survive hard days. No. She didn't hate him. It was more that she was afraid of him. Of what he'd see if he looked too close. All the cracks in her life on display like that . . .

She didn't even want to think about it. Looking at her friends, she pasted a smile on and said, "Because I just don't."

"Duke, don't pester poor Sam. Can't you see she is basically melting under the pressure of explaining the unexplainable?" Jehan said, cutting Duke off before he could try to reason with Sam.

"Make fun all you want. I don't see Grant Gao running a doula-and-doctor community program."

"Technically you aren't either," Duke said, wincing through another sip of his drink.

"Okay, pipe down before you catch a knuckle sandwich," Jehan said, coming to Sam's defense with more sincerity this time.

"Knuckle sandwich? Is this 1972? Who says that?" Duke rasped, shaking his head and glaring at his drink. For a fraction of a second, Sam wondered why he was so dedicated to finishing that thing when it clearly tasted like rubber cement smelled.

"Just saying—our girl is on a roll with this."

"My bad. You are right. Sam is definitely far superior to a certain doctor that we all dislike because reasons."

"Thank you, Duke." Sam gestured to her heart. "Besides, I will be leading the clinic shortly, because Dr. Howie Franklin said that if I can find the funding and a senior adviser, I can have my program."

"That is so exciting. Seriously, Sam, congratulations on clearing the first hurdle."

"Now, I just gotta find me some funding." Sam sighed, leaning back into the couch and fighting the urge to close her eyes.

"We got you. English major right here," Duke said, tapping his chest and grinning.

"And I have grant-writing experience from my days with the international medical charity. I'm happy to chip in," Jehan said, pulling out the hair tie that was supporting her ponytail and giving her hair a shake.

"Y'all are sweet. But you don't have to do that." A small part of Sam's chest twinged with fear. Her friends weren't wrong about how much work writing grants could take, especially without Dr. Franklin's full blessing. But if she allowed her friends to help and she still failed . . . letting her friends down and not getting her program funded was too much. Shaking her head, she said, "I'm good. You both have enough work to do without me."

Duke looked like he was happy to leave it at that when Jehan said, "You are doing something important. Of course we will help."

For a moment, Sam was quiet. What had she done to deserve such wonderful roommates? It wasn't like either of them had a ton of free time. She certainly hadn't done anything this big and time consuming for them. Yet here they were, pitching in to make her community program a reality. She'd find a way to pay them back, even if it meant doing Duke's chores for the next six months.

"It's no trouble at all," Duke added, interpreting the silence caused by Sam's emotional vortex as hesitation.

"Thank you both. I'm lucky to have you two around."

"We know." Duke laughed, giving up and placing his drink back in the fridge. "Sam, we're gonna have to help you at a different time, though, or we'll be late."

"What?" Sam asked.

"We got a game tonight. Remember? Are you gonna play in your scrubs or what?"

Sam really looked at Duke for the first time. He was dressed in his basketball gear, which explained the protein shake from hell. "Ugh. Jehan, you sure you don't want to play? You can have my spot."

"Nope. That is the one thing I can't help you with." Her friend laughed, pushing herself off the couch.

"Who are we playing?"

"Not Dr. Too-Perfect Face, so you don't have to see someone you don't like." Duke smirked as he added extra emphasis to the words *don't like* just to hammer home how much he didn't believe Sam, even if Jehan had made him let it go.

"That just means I'll have to wait to rub my success in Grant's face." Sam shrugged, then took Jehan's hand and let herself be yanked off the perfectly fluffy couch with a groan. Turning back to Duke, she asked, "How did I let you talk me into this?"

"I don't know, but you can't quit now. You got a reputation to uphold, point guard." Duke chuckled as Sam shuffled down the hallway.

"I regret our friendship. I could be sleeping right now," Sam called as she reached her bedroom door.

"Don't lie. You regret nothing," Duke shouted from somewhere in the living room.

Sam smiled as she dug out a pair of shorts from a drawer. He was right; she loved having her roommates around, so sleep would just have to wait.

Chapter Seven

Sam eyed the email suspiciously. It had been a month since she had started applying for grants to support what she had termed the official-sounding San Francisco Central Hospital Birthing Program, and the rejections had been stacking up ever since. Jehan swore this was normal, but Sam wasn't convinced. Honestly, she had started asking Duke to read the emails first so that she could ease herself into the heartbreak of rejection. But Duke wasn't scheduled to come in today, and outside of a very exhausted-looking emergency pharmacist, no one else was in the staff lounge. The little blue new-email dot glared at her, and Sam cursed whoever had drafted the email for failing to indicate whether this was good news or bad news in the subject line.

Tapping the phone in her hand twice, Sam held her breath. She needed to make up her mind. At any moment, she could be called over to the hospital to check on patients. Either she was going to be brave now, or she was going to wait roughly six hours until she got home.

"Just do it," Sam said to herself, exhaling. The pharmacist looked up from his cup of sludge, and Sam nodded apologetically before closing her eyes all but a crack as she tapped the email.

Dear Dr. Holbrook:

Thank you for your application for funding from the Anjo Group Foundation. The Anjo Group is committed to funding projects that display visionary leadership and deploy unique solutions to some of our community's most challenging problems. We believe—

Seriously? Talk about burying the lede. Sam's eyes skipped over the paragraph, looking for the salient information. If she got the grant, she could go back and read more about whatever world-class, innovative nonsense Anjo was investing in. A few paragraphs down, her eyes snagged on something.

It is the application review committee's belief that the San Francisco Central Hospital Birthing Program has the high potential to offer tremendous community good. We would very much like the opportunity to speak with you in person regarding the finer details of the proposed Birthing Program and your accompanying Obstetric Outcomes Improvement Pilot Study.

"Holy shit," Sam said, blinking at her phone. Then she reread the paragraph again just to make sure she wasn't hallucinating.

Still there.

"Oh my God," she said, looking around the room for someone to tell and catching the pharmacist just as he was trying to look like he was minding his own business. Rotating to face him, Sam said, "Hey. Want to hear some good news?"

"Uh. Sure," the guy said, after looking around the room like there could be someone else she was talking to.

"I got a grant," Sam shouted, the couch beneath her wheezing as she bounced up and down.

"A grant?" The pharmacist blinked at her a few times, and Sam suppressed the urge to holler again or roll her eyes. This guy must be having a really long day.

"Yes. You know, like for funding a project. At the hospital." Sam waved around the room, waiting for the guy's mind to catch up.

"That's great." The guy practically yawned at her.

"It is, isn't it!" Fine. If this guy couldn't get excited about it, she would just have to be excited enough for the both of them. "And they said it couldn't be done. Just goes to show—"

Sam halted that thought midsentence as another idea crossed her mind. Turning abruptly back around, she looked down at her phone.

> At your earliest convenience, please fill out the attached preliminary grant agreement. Upon receipt of the form, we will schedule a meeting for you and any other program administrators at our offices.

"Shit."

"What happened?" The pharmacist's voice floated over her shoulder. Of course he wanted to be engaged now that she had a problem.

"They want to meet the other program supervisor." Sam turned to face the guy again.

"Is that bad?"

"It wouldn't be. Except I don't have one."

"Why did you apply for the grant, then?" the guy asked, looking skeptical.

"Because Dr. Franklin and Grant didn't think I could do it. But I did, and—" Sam stopped herself as the pharmacist's pale eyebrows crept toward his hairline. Why was she defending her decisions to this guy? What did he know about obstetric care? He was drinking sludge from the coffee machine, for Pete's sake. Sam shook her head. "Actually, ignore that. I'll figure it out."

"It just seems like you didn't really think this through."

"Mind your own business." Sam squinted at the name on his coat, then added, "Phil."

"You are the one who started talking to me." Phil shrugged.

"I was talking to myself first, so what does that say about you?" Sam stood up and offered him her best cutesy smile to soften the blow. "See you at the program's grand opening, Phil."

She made it all the way out the door grinning before the problem came back to her. Maybe she'd text Jehan and Duke? They'd know what to do. Hell, maybe one of them could tell her which of them had applied for this grant in the first place.

Firing off a quick text, Sam began walking toward the elevators. Just because she'd received funding didn't mean that she could just stop doing her job. Right as she neared the elevator, a text came.

AH! I knew we'd get one! Congratulations!!! How much is it for?

Jehan's excitement nearly jumped off the screen at her. Sam hopped in the elevator and was halfway through a reply when Duke chimed in:

Congrats! Which one is it?

Sam grinned at the closing elevator doors. Telling her friends over text was so much better than telling Phil in person.

Anjo. Don't know how much yet. Have to meet with their founder or something first. Who wrote that one?

There was a moment's pause when the elevator doors opened before Jehan shot back,

I did! It is on our tracking spreadsheet, remember?

Sam laughed. Jehan had insisted that they be systematic about the application process, setting up a spreadsheet to track who was the primary person on each grant, how much money they asked for, the date they had turned in the application, etc. She and Duke thought the spreadsheet was almost as difficult to fill out as a grant application, so Jehan was the only one who ever actually used the thing. Apparently, it worked, because Jehan had written the winning grant for Sam's program.

One problem. We need to find an adviser.

What about Dr. Schwartz? Isn't he the head of obstetrics?

Leave it to Jehan to go straight to the top. Sam smiled as she replied.

Dr. Schwartz is Dr. Franklin's cousin. I feel like birds of a feather. Blah blah . . .

Ask Grant?

Sam felt herself flinch at Duke's idea. It was harder to gloat when you needed someone's help. And gloating over the fact that Dr. Franklin had said she could run the program with caveats wasn't nearly as satisfying as the idea of gloating while running the program without Grant.

Dr. Franklin said it has to be a Sr. Adviser.

She typed back quickly as she slowed her walking pace, trying to finish the conversation before she started rounding on patients.

Pretty sure Sr. is in his title. Just sayin'.

It's not a bad idea.

Of course Duke would point out the loophole in Dr. Franklin's requirement. And of course Jehan would agree with him. Why did she think she had nice friends again?

Don't think that's what Dr. Franklin meant. LOL!

I have to go round. Talk later?

Sam nodded at the phone in her hand as if her friends could see her putting a lid on the discussion. Why did the funder need to meet the other program administrator as well? She was about to tap back over to reread the email when another text from Duke came in.

Don't be stubborn. Ask Grant. Then we can have ice cream to celebrate.

Deciding to answer the text later, she dropped her phone in her pocket. It occurred to her that Jehan was right. Dr. Schwartz was the most appropriate person. But from what little she'd seen of Dr. Schwartz, a pregnancy-care program under him would look almost exactly like the program they already had.

Sam bit down on her bottom lip. Maybe her best option was Grant? The thought made the muscles in the back of her neck bunch. Asking

Grant to be her adviser was like suggesting that she put all the holes in her knowledge and personal imperfections on a billboard and post it outside his house. She was trying to do something new on her own, not get bogged down by his judgment and stern glances.

Then again, she had learned a lot in the last three months alone. June Sam wouldn't even recognize August Sam, and not just because she hadn't found a good place to get her eyebrows done then. She was a better doctor now. Asking Grant didn't have to be a big deal. Sam could swallow her pride and ask for help. After all, he'd be swallowing his pride once he found out she'd secured funding. No one here was losing, per se. They were both making compromises . . . kind of.

~

Sam had thought she was out of good reasons to stop stalling and ask Grant for help. Then she'd remembered that she had patients. And then the day had sort of slipped away from her. Or at least that was what she'd told her roommates when she'd shuffled home last night.

But now that she was standing in the middle school gym with Duke's eyes burning a hole into her, she was pretty sure she had managed to stall without fooling anyone except herself. It was just that she really didn't feel like having this conversation with Grant.

PHTHUNK. The sound of a ball being slammed into the floor jolted her out of her thoughts. Sam looked over to find Duke clutching the ball. Arching an eyebrow at her still-half-tied basketball shoe, he asked, "You gonna go over there or not? 'Cause I didn't research all those foundations so that your stubborn ass could mess up this program."

"I'm goin'. Let me tie my shoe."

"You've been tying that shoe for twenty minutes, and the game is going to start in five, so . . ." Duke trailed off, bouncing the ball again and giving her a sideways look. "You scared or something?"

"I'm not scared," Sam said, rolling her eyes and tying off the loop of her shoelace.

"If you're scared, I can go talk to him. I mean, I want this program for my patients too."

"I'm not scared. I'm just tryna figure out exactly how to suggest he involve himself."

"Right. And that is different from scared how?" Duke asked, humor softening the edges of his accusation as Sam stood up.

"It's different because I'm going over there right now. Happy?" Sam said, throwing her arms wide and sauntering backward. The slow walk gave her a chance to glower at Duke and had the added benefit of offering her a moment to steel her nerves. Not that they needed steeling. Maybe just a little reinforcement.

Duke smirked and slammed the ball into the ground a few more times before turning toward the basket to attempt a jump shot—which he missed, much to Sam's personal enjoyment.

Dropping her arms, Sam turned around and forced herself to slow-jog toward Grant's end of the court, where he was going through his meticulous midrange-jumper routine. Sam watched as his calf muscles flexed with the effort of lifting himself off the ground. It was the only part of him that even looked like he was working. The rest of his shot was the same graceful movement she had observed before. Watching him was almost like watching a dancer. A very good-looking dancer . . . who was also a colleague.

Grant's back was to her, giving her a moment to compose herself. This didn't have to feel like she was waxing her eyebrows with duct tape. She could just say, *Hey, Grant. Remember that program we talked about—yes, the one you told me not to bother with* . . .

Okay, no. If she was going to be petty, this partnership wouldn't work. Sam flinched as a teammate noticed her hovering and nodded in her general vicinity, redirecting Grant's focus from the basket to whoever was lurking just over his shoulder. When he turned to face her, his expression shifted from laser intense to something softer. Passing the ball off to his teammate, he jogged the few feet between them.

"Hey. What's up?"

"Hi," Sam said, suddenly wishing that she had spent less time dragging her feet and more time preparing for this conversation. After all, he was smiling that smile. The one that felt like the sun warming her up after too much time in an air-conditioned building. She wished she could say that she had gotten used to it, but as Grant stood there waiting for her to say anything, she knew she still had work to do in that department. "Got a minute?"

Grant glanced up at the clock above the gym door and smirked. "I have four minutes, in fact."

The joke was so corny it cut through the awkwardness she was feeling, forcing a snort-laugh out of her. That smile might be a magnet, but his jokes were a repelling force. "I'm not giving you credit for that joke."

"Okay, but you laughed at it."

"I laughed because it was bad."

"No takebacks. I need to be able to tell my mom someone other than her thinks I'm funny."

"I'll let you have it." This time Sam did laugh against her better judgment. Whatever, she needed to butter him up anyway. "But only because your mother deserves happiness."

"Thank you." Grant nodded. "So what can I help you with? Please tell me you aren't thinking of leaving medicine."

"What? God, no. I just got here. Why would you think that?"

"Let's just say it would be in keeping with the theme of new hires after a few months of long shifts." Grant shook his head.

"Good news. I'm not quitting. Just the opposite, in fact." Sam watched as Grant wrapped the hem of his jersey around his hand, making an informal armrest for himself. "So remember when Dr. Franklin said that I could start a birthing program if I could find funding and a senior adviser to take on the institutional risk?"

"Not really." Grant's smile tightened, echoing the suspicion in his eyes.

"Well, I managed to find myself some funding. Now, I just need a senior adviser, since I'm still in my first year of training to run my own research program." Sam drew out the last sentence. A small part of her hoped that he would leap up and volunteer for the position. Instead, he looked like he was about two seconds away from forfeiting the game and running for the door. Forcing herself not to pull at the hem of her shirt, she finished her ask. "Anyhoo . . . I thought about it, and you seem like the best-qualified person for the job. So what do you say?"

Grant's eyebrows shot up his forehead. "That is a big ask. What did you envision this adviser doing for the program?"

"Honestly, Dr. Franklin told me I had to have one since I'm in training to run a program and not, you know, actually running one yet." Sam shrugged. The corners of Grant's mouth turned southward. Sam checked herself. No matter how she felt, her goal was not to scare off the only viable adviser she could think of. "I sort of envisioned me and the doulas just coming up with a model to test and you as our figurehead in meetings or if we get into trouble. I mean, you'd have to participate in some meetings too. I think. I've never set up a research program before. But I figure that's what I'm at SF Central to learn."

"And you think I have time to teach you because . . ." Grant let the end of his question fall off.

Sam looked around the gym, searching for so much as a hint for how to answer him. He seemed to expect her to approach this request in a different manner. As if he were operating under some sort of code that only people who had attained perfection knew. That he expected this from Sam, who had a hole in the armpit of her sweatshirt clearly indicating that she had not reached that level of personal excellence, was almost unreasonable. In fact, it irked her. If she had her druthers, she wouldn't have to ask for anyone's help, let alone someone who had apparently attained some state of faultless existence.

Sam waited one more beat for some magical, flawless explanation for why she wanted him to help to pop into her brain other than the truth. When it didn't come, she broke down and said, "Candidly, you were the only senior adviser I could think of who wasn't likely to shoot the idea down on sight."

"Flattering," Grant deadpanned.

Sam floundered. "Well, if we are going to be partners, I figure it is good to reinforce honesty in our relationship."

Grant didn't look nearly so amused. "It's just that I have limited time. If you drop the ball on something, the burden ultimately falls on your senior adviser."

"You mentioned the workload thing before. I know it's a lot of work, but I managed to find funding, so obviously, this idea is viable. Why do you think I'm going to fail?" Sam's spine stiffened. She wasn't totally oblivious to the fact that she had limited time, but clearly Anjo believed she could manage it, so why couldn't Grant? She'd find a way not to let him and her patients down even if it meant giving up sleep—and *Housewives*.

"I don't mean fail like a crash and burn," Grant said, his expression softening slightly. "More that research and community programs are a full-time job. Not a five-hour-a-week thing, so you are going to need help from time to time, and with my fellowship wrapping—"

"Y'all about ready to go?" Duke called from center court, making both of them jump. Sam had never been so happy to be interrupted in her life. Duke must have psychically sensed that things were not going her way and stepped in to save the day. Okay, maybe that was giving him too much credit. It was a few minutes past six thirty, so it was more than likely he was just trying to get the game going before they all starved to death.

"Yup," Grant called, waving to him. Turning his attention back to Sam, he squinted. "How about this? I'll play you for it."

"What?"

Sam's face must have looked like her voice sounded, because Grant started laughing almost immediately. "You look like I asked you if you wanted to commit a bank heist."

"I mean, this is the future of a community program and the success of my research initiative, and you want to bet it on a basketball game?"

"Sounds about right." He shrugged and started walking slowly toward the center of the court, forcing Sam to jog to catch up with him. "Besides, you said it yourself: Who else might say yes?"

"If this is how you are going to make a decision, why not just flip a coin?"

"Makes the game more fun," Grant said, stopping just outside the knot of players who were gathered for the tip-off. "Deal?"

Sam sputtered. This was not how responsible people made career decisions. This wasn't even how irresponsible people made career decisions. Why couldn't he just give her a straight answer? What was the point in making her guess? This was why she said that he was too perfect. Only people who never failed would bet on something like this, because they thought they were going to win. Cocky much?

She wanted time to think, or at least a second to reason with Grant, but Duke and the Central Flyers' center were already shaking hands. She was out of time. Holding her breath for three seconds, she looked over to find Grant staring at her, a smirk glued to his face. A face she sort of hoped got hit by a rogue no-look pass.

"Fine." She exhaled, watching as Grant's smirk turned into a full-blown mischievous grin.

"May the best team win."

"You mean my team," Sam said with more bravado than she felt before sinking into a defensive stance.

~

Her tank top stuck to her like a rumor clinging to a celebrity. And Sam was sure she'd managed to sweat off her extra-strength deodorant. She didn't care. In high school, she'd been convinced that the state championship game was the single most important game she would ever play. She thought she knew what it meant to want to win so bad it hurt. But that was before she spent a full hour in a horse stance chasing Grant Gao around the court while Duke missed every possible shot that was more than two feet away from the basket with her precious program on the line.

With two minutes to go, Sam's thighs were practically screaming as she sank her dribble a little lower to shield the ball from Grant's reach. They were down four points. She could make that up with a couple of smart plays. Duke was having a bad night, but both Theo and Raphael were playing solid if she could get them the ball. But that was a big if because Grant seemed to predict her every move. She'd barely think of a play, and he'd be standing in her way, ready to block a pass. His defense was so close that some of the sweat she was wearing was probably his. At least he smelled good.

Sam wrinkled her nose at the thought. Now was not the time or place for a scent analysis of the person who was making her life difficult. Praying Theo was watching her closely, Sam threw her shoulder into Grant's body and bounce passed the ball to her teammate.

"Oof. That's a charge," Grant said, rubbing the spot on his chest where Sam had treated him like a human battering ram.

"No one else called it." She smiled as Theo sank a midrange two-pointer. All she had to do was make sure Grant didn't score, and she could win this thing.

"I see you don't deny it." Grant laughed, jogging to retrieve the ball from beneath the basket, his hair stuck to his forehead with sweat.

"All's fair in community programs and basketball." Sam shrugged. "But you could give up and join the program. Then you wouldn't have to take a shoulder to the chest."

"Where is the fun in that?" Grant said, carefully keeping a forearm between her and the ball as he began to dribble down the court.

"You have a strange idea of fun."

"Watching you lose, after all the trash you talked during the last game? I've never had such a good time." Grant's voice was barely above a whisper, sending tingles down Sam's spine that had nothing to do with their wager.

Nope. She forced herself to focus on the sound of Grant's teammates around her clapping for the ball. Pulling herself back together, Sam said, "This won't be nearly as much fun for you when you lose."

"Making you sweat is always fun."

Sam's heart stopped as heat flooded her face. Endorphins, adrenaline, serotonin, dopamine, and every other hormone and neurotransmitter known to science went to war in her brain, causing everything to pause. Surely he didn't mean that kind of sweat. She was vaguely aware that her jaw might have dropped. Grant's smile was as mischievous as ever.

Everything happened at once. Sam had only stopped for what felt like a fraction of a second to try to blink her thoughts into coherence when Grant backed up, dropping his forearm, leaving just enough space to pull off one of his perfectly executed jump shots. Sam stopped stock still as she watched the ball soar overhead in a perfect arc. It was as if she could hear the clean swooshing sound of the net before it even approached the basket. She had just enough time to close her eyes before the sound actually came and with it the *oh*s of both teams celebrating a perfect shot.

The agony and irony of the moment sank in as the muscles in Sam's throat closed almost immediately. She had used the exact same distraction technique on Grant a few weeks ago. All he'd done was throw a new package on it, and she'd fallen for it hook, line, and sinker. How could she be that stupid?

Tears threatened to glass over her eyes as soon as she opened them. No matter what, she refused to cry in a middle school gym over a stupid basketball game. Honestly, what kind of program adviser would bet their involvement on a game anyway? Instead of just saying no, he'd toyed with her, setting her up to fail before the center had even gotten off the ground. Worse, it was a humiliating defeat. The kind perfect people like him—whose greatest failure was probably having to try parallel parking in a tight spot twice—couldn't possibly understand.

Pulling her shoulders back, Sam breathed in for the count of three before opening her eyes and pasting on her very best I'm-not-bitter smile. Running her palm down her shorts so that her hand wasn't sweaty, she turned to face Grant. "Disappointing for me. But I expect you're relieved to be off the hook. Good game." Sam mentally awarded herself a consolation prize for not adding *you asshole* to her concession speech.

Grant's forehead wrinkled in surprise, and for a heartbeat, Sam wondered if he might refuse to shake her hand. Then he smiled. "Oh. I forgot about that. Good game."

"Sure. You just happened to save that mean jumper until things were desperate." Sam had to dig deep to make that joke. Looking around the court, she prayed for someone to come and interrupt the conversation. Hell, she would take a freak tornado warning to get out of this without another word.

"Just lucky, I guess." Grant shrugged. "So listen—"

"That was an amazing shot!" Raphael popped up over Sam's shoulder, causing Grant to jump in surprise.

"Thanks," Grant said, holding out a hand to Raphael.

"Seriously, it was a thing of beauty, man."

"I'll let y'all discuss it," Sam broke in, sensing a chance to get out of the gym before things got more awkward and she was forced to talk to Grant about what she would do for a program adviser in place of him.

Better to leave with at least some of her dignity intact. Waving over her shoulder, she called, "Good game," before jogging over to her gym bag.

Anger and hurt threatened to overwhelm whatever rational thoughts she had. How could she lose this game? She'd basically beaten Grant before—it was tough, but she'd done it. Instead, she'd let Grant in all his perfect smiling glory take a thing she cared about and turn it into a game. A game she'd lost, no less. She never should have asked for his help. Help always had strings attached. Really, this disaster was as much her fault as Grant's. More, even.

Throwing her holey sweatshirt over her head, Sam waved to Duke, who was happily chatting with Theo. Nodding his acknowledgment, Duke said something to Theo, who laughed, before he shuffled over to her. "What's up?"

"We gotta get outa here," Sam whispered, trying to get her sweats on right side out.

"Okay, okay," Duke said, giving her side-eye as he slowly began to unlace his sneakers.

Giving up and leaving her pants fuzzy side out, Sam threw her shoes in her bag and chucked her slides on the ground with a thud. "Like, now, dude. I bet Grant that if we won he'd be our program adviser. But we didn't win and—"

"You what?" Duke asked at a volume that could've been heard all the way back in Akron. Worse, he stopped taking off his shoes to look at her.

"That was the only way he would consider it," Sam said, moving her hand in a circular hurry-it-up gesture. "And now he doesn't have to consider it. So let's go before I lose my mind."

"Shit. Why didn't you say something?"

"So—what? You could miss more shots than you were already missing? I don't think the added pressure would have helped."

"Ouch. You're a sore loser," Duke mumbled.

"If he didn't want to help, he could have just said no. Instead, he's gonna be all smug and rub it in my face; I can just feel it."

"I don't think he's gonna do that." Duke dropped his sandals onto the floor and stood up, leisurely sliding his feet into them.

Sam could have punched his casual demeanor. She needed to get her own car so he wasn't her only means of escape in awkward situations. Grabbing her bag off the bleachers, she said, "I'm not fixing to wait around and find out. Let's go."

"Fine," Duke said, fishing his keys out of his bag pocket. "You're bossy. You know that?"

"Of course I do." Hustling Duke out of the gym doors, she added, "How do you think I got this program thing going in the first place?"

"Jehan's organization and grant-writing skills." Duke snickered as they crossed the parking lot toward the sad hunk of metal they were calling a car.

"Ha. Ha," Sam said, the tension in her shoulders beginning to thaw as she let her hand rest on the passenger-side door. Soon this would all be over. Once she got home, she could hop in a nice long shower—maybe even deep condition her hair—and put this whole stupid game behind her. That was, if Duke would hurry up and reach across the damn car to unlock her door.

"Sam?"

No. No, no, no. This was not happening. Sam refused to acknowledge that voice or even turn around as her blood instantly acquired the same frosty texture as the car's windshield. This wasn't happening. Not when she was this close to a shower, perfectly hydrated curls, and—you know what? Hell, why not? She'd even have a glass of wine. All these things were still a likely and enjoyable part of her future, as long as she didn't turn around.

"Hey, Sam."

She pulled on the door handle, glaring at Duke's form through the foggy glass as he coaxed the car to life while the voice got closer.

"Hey. I'm glad I caught you."

Shit. Grant was standing next to her. There went her perfect night. Maybe she'd still have the wine . . .

"Hey, Grant." Sam finally looked up from the door handle. Compelling herself to smile took superhuman strength, and if she was honest, she was shocked she had it in her after tonight's disappointment. "What's up?"

"You left so fast." Grant laughed as he ran his hand over the back of his hair, the sweat making the ends of it stick together. "I wanted to talk to you about the program."

"Uh-huh," Sam said, feeling her smile go rigid.

Grant must have sensed her trepidation, and his own smile faltered in response. She watched as he stood up a fraction of an inch straighter, as if the act alone would make whatever it was he was trying to do less awkward. "You seriously want to start the doula thing?" Sam opened her mouth to correct him, but Grant caught himself. "Program. The birthing program?"

"Yup. That's why I got funding for it." Sam dropped the smile in favor of something closer to a dubious baring of teeth.

"Of course. That is why you found funding. And who wouldn't find funding? 'Cause it's a good idea." He said the last sentence more to the lines delineating the parking spaces than to her. His voice sounded stretched, as if he had run out of helium to talk with.

What was happening here? It didn't seem like he was making fun of her. Whatever this rambling was, it seemed sincere. Was Grant nervous? For the life of her, Sam couldn't imagine why. It wasn't like he had just lost a program adviser betting on a basketball game, then run from the gym so no one would see him sob over it in public.

"Right. So I was—man, it's cold out here. Aren't you cold?" He gestured at her with his free hand, before wrapping it around his biceps, as if giving himself a hug. "No, you're probably not. You're from a cold place." Sam felt her eyebrow tick up, despite her best efforts to school her expression. Where was he going with this discussion of the weather? Grant was succinct. His wordy meandering made no sense, and she was getting colder. Not that she would admit it, being from Ohio and all.

Grant's eyes seemed to follow the trail of his words toward the moon, as if its glow somehow held his train of thought. Giving himself a shake, he said, "Let me start again."

"Yes." Sam nodded.

"I'm struggling here."

"I can see that," Sam said, forgetting to hold her tongue.

Grant's yelp of laughter echoed around the parking lot, drawing looks from a knot of players as they walked to their cars. "Leave it to you to point out my faults when I am trying to admit I was wrong. Wow, my sister is right. I am not great at apologies."

"Oh." Sam could feel the surprise lines wrinkling her forehead. She opened her mouth to say something, but Grant was faster.

"Or I wasn't really wrong. I was more flippant," Grant said, tilting his head as if pondering the precise usage of his vocabulary.

"I'm confused. What are you apologizing for?"

"For betting on being the senior adviser of your program. Obviously, that is a serious job, and you take it as such. And I should have treated it with the seriousness it was due, but I didn't. And now I messed that up . . . ," Grant said, bringing his meandering apology to an end with a shrug. "I guess what I am trying to say is that . . . if you still need an adviser, I'd be willing to do it . . . or whatever you need."

"I . . ." Roughly sixty emotions ran through Sam. Irritation. Anger. And relief. Sam wanted to block that emotion out. She wanted to stay angry. Really, what kind of jerk left someone guessing about their research? Then again, she didn't want to have to deal with Dr. Schwartz. She wanted Grant to be the program's senior adviser. He was open to the idea, and at least he had a sense of humor, sometimes. Not that she would admit that to him after what he'd just put her through.

"I see. Just to be clear—you put me through the workout from hell so that you could change your mind and help out after all?"

Grant's expression relaxed into his easy smile, its wattage rivaling the moon overhead. "You have to admit that was a really good game."

"I don't have to admit that. You could have just said yes." Sam shook her head. "My thighs will be screaming for a week."

"Fine. Pretend you don't like a side of healthy competition to go with your physical activity." Grant smirked, then let his expression relax into something more serious, the angles of his cheekbones highlighted by the moon's glow. "So would you still like help?"

"You know there is no extra money in your paycheck for this, right?" Sam asked, placing a hand on her hip. Whatever had brought about this change of heart, she didn't trust it.

"I know. I genuinely think it is a good idea. Honestly, I'm flattered you even asked."

Against her better judgment, Sam found herself softening. Maybe it was the gentle glow of the moon, but there was something oddly endearing about the way he'd stammered through his apology. As if he was genuinely worried she might not accept it. The fact that he was nervous talking to her was almost adorable.

Almost. Sam gave herself a shake, grateful that the cold provided her with a way to clear her wandering thoughts. His being adorable was neither here nor there. Really, even if his apology hadn't felt sincere, what choice did she have? No one else was going to do this.

Exhaling like a put-upon horse, Sam said, "Fine. If you still want to be the senior adviser, I'd be delighted to have you, but—" Sam held up a hand as Grant's smile spread, his features softening as his shoulders melted away from his ears. "No more funny business. And no more basketball games. Just tell me what you think and what you want. I don't have time to keep playing guessing games with you."

"I'm mysterious and I like it that way." Grant smirked and Sam rolled her eyes. Straightening up, he nodded. "Deal."

"Seriously. My thighs cannot take that level of defense every time we have to make a decision about intake forms or something."

Grant snorted. "Your thighs? Pretty sure I'm gonna have a bruise from where you charged me."

"No call, no foul." Sam shook her head, smiling despite her misgivings. "It's getting cold, and I need a shower. I'll send you all of the funder details tomorrow. Sound good?"

"Can't wait."

"You say that, but the funder wants to meet with us in person."

"I'll clear my schedule." Grant lifted one shoulder, then dropped it as if he didn't care, like he hadn't just made a big speech about how precious his time was. "Seriously, thank you for thinking of me. I have a feeling you are going to do something great with this program."

"I sure hope so . . . ," Sam said, suddenly unsure of what direction to take the conversation. "I guess—"

"It looks—"

She and Grant started to speak at the same time, then laughed. Sam felt as awkward as Grant looked.

"Sorry," he said.

"I was just going to say we should probably head out."

"Yeah, Duke is looking mighty bored on his phone." Grant nodded toward the car and waved. Sam turned just in time to see Duke wave back, the glow of his cell phone confirming that he was texting Jehan every word of her and Grant's conversation, complete with GIFs.

"See you tomorrow."

"Looking forward to it." Grant began walking slowly backward across the parking lot. "Night."

"Night," Sam called, making sure to tone down her smile before opening the passenger-side door.

"Took you long enough," Duke said as soon as she settled into the somewhat warm car. "So what did he have to say?"

Sam rubbed her hands in front of a heating vent and shot Duke a look. "Please. I know you were listening."

"Yes, but the engine on this thing is too loud for me to get every word. You two seemed to be smiling a lot. You still not interested in him?"

Sam's face flushed, and she was grateful for the darkness. "You know what. Mind your own and drive."

Duke cackled. "Okay. You don't have to tell me everything. As long as we have our program adviser, I'm happy. It's just . . . Jehan is gonna wanna know."

"Right. I'm sure that's who wants to know." Sam rolled her eyes. "It's too bad she is also gonna have to mind her own business because I want to deep condition my hair, and I need a glass of wine."

Chapter Eight

"Thank you," Sam said to the driver as she pushed her way out of the rideshare to stand in front of a large, boxy-looking three-story office building in the Fillmore District. Literally every spare moment of the last four days had been spent trying to find a doula to help start this program. Indeed, it felt like she had called every birthing professional on the internet in between seeing patients, ordering diagnostics, and poring over medical histories. Part of the problem was that what Sam wanted to do was big. Most of the people she talked to had no desire to run a full-on birthing center in addition to the private practices they maintained. When Monica had mentioned the name Kaiya Owens, Sam hadn't thought much about it. However, after speaking to what felt like every birth worker west of the Mississippi, she kept hearing the same thing: the only doula that anyone knew with the audacity to take on something like this was Kaiya. Who, unsurprisingly, every doula and their mother made out to be an unreachable legend.

Based on everyone's glowing recommendations, Sam spent two evenings falling down the internet rabbit hole researching the renowned doula. Early in her career, Kaiya had refused to ever bifurcate her identity as a trans woman and a birth worker, and she brought a level of energy and advocacy to her practice that had Sam nodding and yesing while watching talks Kaiya had given at random doula conferences on YouTube. The more Sam read and watched, the more she was convinced that Kaiya was the sort of woman Sam wanted to be when she grew up. Plus, the internet said she was an expert quilter. Some of her pieces had even been displayed in the Oakland Museum of California.

After nearly selling her soul for Kaiya's direct contact information, Sam was shocked when the legend agreed to meet with her. Feeling starstruck, she checked her blouse to make sure she hadn't spilled any mustard on it, then pulled her shoulders back and walked toward the building's door with all the confidence she could dredge up.

Finding the correct office door, Sam knocked. For a moment there was silence and then a loud crash before someone on the other side of the door yelled, "Just one minute."

If Sam hadn't read the plaque on the door, she would have been shocked that this was Kaiya's office. The voice on the other side of the door let out a string of curses that managed to be as blasphemous as it was creative, and Sam started to laugh. The words were so incongruous with the statuesque woman she had seen on the internet. She was just starting to feel like maybe she didn't need to be intimidated when the door swung open and silenced all the courage her laughter had summoned.

"May I help you?" Kaiya asked. Even if Sam hadn't googled her, she'd know this woman was Kaiya. As promised, everything about her screamed gravitas even as she clutched a rag soaked in coffee. She was a few inches taller than Sam, with her immaculately kept long beaded braids piled half-up in an intricate knot and a sweater set that was likely marketed to CPAs but looked better on her than it would have on any accountant. Giving Sam a once-over, Kaiya adopted an I'll-wait expression while Sam pulled herself together.

"Hi. I'm Dr. Sam Holbrook, fellow and researcher at SF Central. Nice to meet you." She stuck out her hand as she delivered the same opening spiel she gave to a new patient, then kicked herself as confusion washed over Kaiya's face. How had she managed to practice her pitch but not plan a cool way to introduce herself? Instead, she must look like a silly nervous wreck. It took everything in her not to say, *So what brings you in here today?*

For a moment, Kaiya just stared at her, and then something clicked and she took Sam's hand. "Oh, am I meeting with you today? I completely forgot." Giving her hand a shake, she said, "Nice to meet you, Sam. I'm Kaiya Owens, founder of this practice."

"Nice to meet you, Kaiya. I have to say, everyone I spoke to about you said you were the absolute best in the business." Sam was grinning so hard she hoped she didn't come off as a total fangirl.

"Would you like to come in?" Kaiya didn't actually wait for her response. Instead, she turned and chucked the coffee-laden towel in a nearby bin, then walked toward a small couch and chair situated at the end of the office, across from a massive paper-strewed desk. "Would you like some water?"

"That would be lovely, thank you," Sam said, making her way over to one corner of the couch to take a seat. On the coffee table next to her were a few books titled things like *The First Year*, *A New Dad's Guide to Parenting*, and *Baby's Brain*, as well as one ominously titled *It's Okay*.

Sam was about to reach for the questionable book when a blue glass bottle appeared in front of her. With her own bottle in hand, Kaiya made her way to the chair across from Sam and settled in, her air managing to be both warm and no nonsense as she said, "So, Sam, tell me why you are here again?"

Be cool, Sam thought as she took a sip of water, followed by what she hoped was a calming breath. "Sure. So I might have mentioned over the phone that I'm a new research fellow examining community engagement with public health programs at San Francisco Central Hospital, and in just my short time there, I've noticed that there is a disconnect between the pregnant people we serve and what care the hospital and clinicians offer."

"Right," Kaiya said. The word was simple, but it packed a punch, as if she could have predicted what Sam would find but was trying not to show how not surprised she was for the sake of expediency.

"I'm sure you could have told me that; given all of your experience, you've probably seen everything under the sun. I mean, I read your article on the prevalence of the expectation in the medical field that new parents, particularly minorities, should magically be able to intuit the needs of their bodies and their babies, when we have spent—in some cases—literal centuries denying them access to their cultural frameworks for intuition and . . ."

Sam let her voice trail off as Kaiya's eyebrows shot toward her hairline. So much for a better second impression. For a moment, she debated trying to come up with a third fresh start, until the tilt of Kaiya's head changed and Sam decided to just be honest. "Sorry. I get excited about this."

"I can tell," Kaiya said. Her eyebrows had retreated from her hairline, but her gaze was still laser focused on Sam.

"It's just . . . I know I'm new to the field, but SF Central is a good hospital. The care patients receive is top notch, if a little rushed. It's not person-centered birth. It's kind of transactional, but there are many of us who believe that our patients deserve the same kind of care that their rich counterparts can afford. Not just the one-hour visit to a lactation consultant that insurance will fight them tooth and nail over paying the fifty dollars for, or a quick tutorial from an excellent but busy nurse, or whatever they can google."

"Of course they do. I've made a career working with these patients," Kaiya said, gently cutting off Sam's burgeoning rant.

"That is why I had to talk to you. I sought a grant from the Anjo Foundation to start a real, more holistic birthing program at the hospital. So that I don't have to worry that my patients are getting questionable nutrition information from a social media influencer. Instead, they could have access to home visits and check-ins when they aren't able to get childcare. They'd know that SF Central had their back. Everyone I spoke with said you were the only woman up to this job."

"And what exactly is this job?" Kaiya asked, giving Sam a once-over that made her feel like maybe she did have mustard on her top.

"Good question. From a patient standpoint, you'd be doing what you do best. I don't have any intention of interfering in your work. From a partnership standpoint, it would be recruiting and managing additional doulas. Working with me to get doulas and patients appropriately matched based on their needs, ranging from early pregnancy, abortion, miscarriage, birth, and postpartum, helping me gather and assess doula and patient feedback and getting it submitted to the funder as needed."

Kaiya whistled low. "That's a big job. You want me to help you establish this thing? Why on God's earth would I do that when I have a block full of pregnant individuals who need me?"

Sam closed her mouth, trying to gather her thoughts. She wasn't exactly surprised by the question. Three minutes with Kaiya had already taught her that while her words were never unkind, the term *no bullshit* perfectly described her.

"Everything about me has long been unwelcome in the formal medical establishment. I and my fellow birth workers who share this philosophy have built a world without your constraints, quietly helping people as unwelcome as ourselves without the crushing weight of bureaucracy hanging over our heads. We get to choose our clients, and the human being giving birth is already at the center of our work." Kaiya took a breath, smiled, and then added, "Plus, I'm my own boss. I leave the office when I like."

"I think . . . ," Sam started slowly, then stopped. She wanted to make sure her next words were the exact ones she wanted to say. Kaiya was right, and Sam would be a fool not to heed her wisdom. Taking a breath, she started again. "Everything you have said is the reason I hoped you'd do this. You *have* built a community. You did your work in spite of so many people—confident in the righteousness of your charge. I can't tell you how many birthing professionals talked about you as a mentor and the person who taught them what community-centered birthing really means. With a partnership at SF Central, you could triple your impact."

"Confident in the righteousness of my charge?" Kaiya smirked at her.

"Okay, I admit the phrasing is a little dramatic, but where is the lie? You made a home for the clients who no one else was making room for. People in recovery, those in poverty, sex workers, families struggling to find care during the early AIDS crisis—the list goes on. Before I was born, you were the kind of caring professional I want to be."

"Okay, youngun, don't rub it in." Kaiya laughed. "You made your point. The face of medicine is changing. Blah, blah, blah."

"I know I sound corny. But I think this could be a new model for community care. It would be hard work, but if we pull it off, this center could be the one that hospitals around the country try to emulate." Sam sighed, then threw out her final pitch: "So yes. You could stay under the radar, doing the amazing work you are doing. Or you could make your legacy even bigger."

Silence hung between them as Kaiya uncrossed and then recrossed her legs and looked out her office window, the act of thinking written in fine lines between her eyebrows. Sam ran her finger along the edge of her water bottle and held her breath in an attempt to keep her fidgeting small. She could feel nervous energy pulsing through her, and she was almost certain the anxiety would cause her to pass out when Kaiya turned to face her.

"I wanted to open a center when I was young. I had big dreams." Kaiya shook her head. "I was naive back then, and the red tape alone was crushing. I could barely get a community center to rent me a gym. Do you know how hard it is to run programs for an underserved community when you can't even tell them where they will be meeting next week?"

Sam shook her head but didn't dare interrupt.

"No, I don't suppose you would know that. You're too young." Kaiya looked out the window again. Her voice sounded like she was talking to herself more than to Sam as she said, "But you are right; things have changed."

"I can't promise there won't be red tape. But you have a set space, a group of people who are committed, and a community who needs you."

The sound of Sam's voice brought Kaiya's attention back from the window. She pulled her shoulders back, and her expression was wistful as she said, "I was just too far ahead for my time."

"But you aren't now."

"No, I'm not." Kaiya's tone was matter of fact. Looking Sam dead in the eyes, she said, "If I do this—don't grin like that; I haven't said yes."

"Not grinning," Sam said, doing her best to press her lips into a flat line. She was absolutely positive that she still looked excited.

"No one gets turned away unless we're at capacity. This stays a community-centered approach. None of this private-party, rent-out-the-room-for-mimosas-and-swaddling-class stuff."

"I wouldn't dream of that. Can you even have liquor in a hospital?"

Kaiya raised an eyebrow and shook her head as if Sam was so inexperienced she couldn't even be bothered with the statement. "And other early parenting skills. I want that on the menu from the start."

"Yes. Yes. Yes." Sam was nodding her head so hard that it almost hurt.

"And this Anjo Foundation is not gonna be underpaying any of our practitioners. I won't be calling my colleagues and begging them to volunteer, will I?"

"No. We have stipends built into the ask." Sam was starting to feel light headed. She was this close to having the final partner in place.

"All right then. One more thing. I'm gonna need you one hundred and ten percent in on this. No distractions, no shortchanging. I've worked with enough doctors to know that this program is a big time commitment."

"Everyone says that," Sam laughed. "But I made it this far, and I've got help from some of the other young doctors as well."

"I'll just say this: If you feel like you are coming up short, you need to tell me. I won't be able to coddle you, but I can help you if I know you need it. You don't have to be perfect; you just have to be honest with me. Cool?"

"Understood. I know I tend to overcommit, but I really don't want to let you, the hospital, or any of our patients down," Sam said, looking Kaiya in the eye. She couldn't bring herself to play down her flaws, so she just had to hope Kaiya would take her self-awareness as a positive trait.

"As long as you remember that when you are being pulled in fifteen different directions, this is the priority. We both commit to this, so we both agree that whatever else is going on, every heartbeat that we spend in that center is focused on the families. Got it?"

"Got it." Sam nodded. If Kaiya hadn't been as serious as a heart attack, Sam would have laughed. Somehow she'd started the program, but as far as Kaiya was concerned, Sam was brand new and only a little in charge.

"Then I'm in."

"Yes!" Sam's whole face split into the smile she'd been fighting. Trying to calm herself, she bounced up and down on the couch a few times.

Kaiya leaned back in her chair a fraction of an inch, but joy was written on her face. "All right, all right. Calm down. I'll come by in a week or so, and then we can start thinking about classes and referrals."

"Yes. I'm very excited about all of this," Sam said, jumping up when Kaiya stood up. She wanted to hug her, but now seemed a little early in their relationship, so instead, she wrapped her arms around herself.

"I can tell," Kaiya said, kindly. "All right, well, you enjoy your afternoon, and keep a watch for an email from me. We have work to do."

"Of course. I won't miss it," Sam rambled as Kaiya walked the short distance to the office door. As she reached for the handle, Sam added, "Thank you very much for seeing me. I promise you're not going to regret this. It's gonna be amazing."

"All right. But one more thing. 'My legacy'?" Kaiya asked, holding the door open for her and repeating Sam's words back to her again.

"Yes. This program is going to be your legacy," Sam said, feeling more confident than she had felt since she'd walked through the clinic door. With Kaiya on board, the center would be the jewel in SF Central's crown. A program that would be celebrated for generations.

Kaiya looked at her and smirked. "Little girl, I have a long time before my legacy is set. I'm fifty-four and just getting started."

~

The sound of her phone buzzing against the nightstand made Sam jump. Squashing an errant curl back into her conditioner-slicked cap, she squinted at the screen just long enough to see Mom scroll across the top. Sam's heartbeat picked up, and she debated not answering. She was so happy to have her mom calling her again. But she'd had a patient complication this morning that had made today so much longer than she had anticipated. If her mom was in one of her moods, Sam wasn't sure that she could deal with it in a kind way. Plus, she had a glass of wine waiting for her in the kitchen and the latest episode of a deeply boring British reality show about home gardens to stream.

Then again, she was deep conditioning her hair, so it wasn't like she had much else to do for the next three hours. Reaching the side table just in time to pick up before the last buzz, Sam swiped the answer toggle and held the phone a half inch from her ear so that she wouldn't get conditioner gunk on it.

"Hi, Mom."

"Hi, Sammy." Her mother's tone was positively chipper for it being so late. Tapping the speakerphone button, Sam's gaze flicked toward the clock to confirm. It was almost midnight for her mother.

"What's up?"

"Nothing much. Just wanted to update you on the reunion."

"At eleven thirty p.m.?" Sam laughed, but her mother did not follow suit, so she attempted to mask the sound by clearing her throat. "Must be big news to be calling now."

"Oh, it is." Her mother paused, and Sam could almost feel her holding her breath for dramatic effect. As the silence began to pull at Sam's attention span, her mom exhaled, "I picked a date for San Francisco!"

"What?" Sam asked on autopilot.

"A date. You know, for my shindig in the city?" Her mother sounded exasperated, and Sam wished she'd thought to get her wine before she'd answered the call. "And I've found a design for an invitation that I love."

"Yes. Of course." Sam retreated hastily.

"Now we just have to find somewhere really special, Sammy. Did Isaiah tell you? For the LA reunion he found an amazing venue. It's in one of those 1920s hotels. We've got to be sure whatever we do in San Francisco is just as special. You sure you don't want to come down for the LA party as well?"

"Wish I could. But the rotation schedule isn't out that far in advance, and I want to be able to swap shifts for your party in the Bay if needed." Sam did not wish that she could attend. In fact, the last thing she needed was the added pressure of comparison to her sainted older brother.

"Right. Well, we can talk about it later," her mother said, as if brushing the inconvenient truth about maternal care aside. "I texted you a link to the invite. Did you get it?"

"Not yet," Sam half truthed. The text had come in, but she hadn't opened it. Pursing her lips, Sam tapped the link to see a mint-green invitation pop up. Looking closely at the detailed flourishes, she realized they were leaves drawn into the corners where swoops and curlicues would usually be. It was completely perfect for a woman who photographed macrobiology for fun. "Mom. This is gorgeous."

"I know, right! Now you see why I had to call you, Sammy."

Sam wasn't sure that the invitation warranted a midnight phone call, but she let the reasoning slide. "It is perfect for you."

"Well, thank you. In the end, I decided to just pony up and pay for the custom graphics. This is a big-deal party, and I thought the invite went nicely with all the photos I'll be shipping out."

"It's money well spent." Sam smiled. This was the real reason her mother had called. She was excited about the party and sharing her memories with her friends. In fact, this was the first time in many, many years that her interests and hobbies could take center stage. If that wasn't a good-enough reason to be excited and call your daughter after midnight, Sam wasn't sure what was.

"Anyway. Now that I have the invites all done, you can find me a venue, send out the invitations, and we'll be off to the races."

"Uh-huh," Sam said, eyeing her phone. She remembered agreeing to help out with the venue. Had she also put invitations on the list? Not that it mattered—her mother clearly wasn't planning on sending out the invitations herself. Sam had known when she'd agreed to help that her duties would swell. If this was the last of it, she'd be lucky.

"Have you started thinking about venues at all? Hopefully my date won't conflict with the ones you like. I already set up a Facebook invite," her mother said, sounding nonplussed about the idea of further inconveniencing her.

"I, um . . ." Sam shrugged, looking longingly at her computer. She'd had every intention of looking for venues, but then she'd managed to get a meeting with Kaiya, and she'd needed to prep for the interview with Anjo, and the time had just gotten away from her. Letting her eyes flick toward the clock, Sam decided to skip the explanation. Her mother wouldn't understand it anyway. And really, she only had a few more minutes before she could reasonably extricate herself from this conversation, hopefully before her mother added *hire a skywriter* to her to-do list. "I plan to go on my next day off."

"Oh, good. When is that?"

"Six days from now," Sam said, cringing at the brutality of her schedule.

"I know that is the best you can do." Her mother did not sound like she knew it. "In the meantime, I'll send you the email list and the file so you can just tell people to hold the date."

"Right. Sounds good, Mom," Sam said, attempting not to get short as her mother added more to her list. Deciding now was the perfect time to end the call, she added, "I need to head to bed soon. Early start tomorrow. Talk later?"

"All righty, Sammy. Love you."

"Love you. Bye."

Sam's breath caught as she processed hearing her mother say that she loved her. She didn't really care that her mother hadn't asked a single question about her day or that her list had gotten longer in spite of Diana's reassurances. The party was bringing them closer together just like Sam had hoped it would. And now, she could get her wine and turn her attention to an overgrown hedge and a snide TV presenter.

Chapter Nine

Sam pushed her way off BART and readjusted her skirt. She was already sweating buckets and her thighs were beginning to chafe, and it wasn't even 10:00 a.m. yet. Not for the first time today, she wondered how anyone went to work in something so uncomfortable as a pencil skirt and suit jacket. If she hadn't already decided on medicine, the whole banker uniform would have scared her out of the profession entirely.

Tapping her metro card on the way out of the train station turnstile, Sam took a moment to orient herself. According to Google Maps, she just needed to walk five blocks from the Civic Center Station, and she would see the Anjo building. According to Sherilynn, the assistant to Duesa Azevedo, who'd helped set up her meeting, the building was easy to find in between a massive social media company and some sort of rideshare start-up. But Sherilynn had also promised her that BART was a "super easy" way to get to the meeting, so Sam had her doubts.

Doing her best to speed walk in the most restrictive skirt ever invented, Sam ran through the list of program points she had developed. When she and Grant had talked about him agreeing to be the program's adviser during their small group huddle, he reiterated that this meeting was hers to run since his free time was limited. In his cranky way, he even admitted that he had only skimmed the application materials she had painstakingly gathered for him.

Rounding the corner, Sam caught sight of the imposing stone building, Grant standing underneath it and looking striking in a gray, carefully tailored suit, his forehead creased as he looked at his watch. Holding her breath, Sam glanced down at her phone to make sure she wasn't late.

9:43 a.m. Exhaling with the relief that comes with being two minutes early, Sam said, "Hi, Grant. Sorry I'm cutting it close. I took the BART here, and that was an experience."

Grant's attention snapped from his watch to Sam's eyes, the tension melting from his face. "No worries. We still have time." Readjusting the strap on his bag, he gave her an appraising look before asking, "Where were you coming from?"

"Dogpatch," Sam said, fighting the urge to fan her face.

"That's a schlep," Grant said, frowning slightly before adding, "Why didn't you just take Muni the whole way?"

"You can do that?" Sam asked, surprised that Sherilynn hadn't mentioned that the train change was entirely unnecessary.

"Yup. That's why it took so long. You don't have to change trains." Grant smirked. "You clearly haven't explored much of the city yet."

"On a fellow's schedule with Duke's rust bucket as my ride? Of course not." Sam laughed.

"Remind me after the meeting, and I'll give you the local rundown on the city. Starting with public transit." Grant smiled at her, and Sam felt her heartbeat tick up in a way that she couldn't attribute to her brisk walking pace. Before she had a chance to interrogate the feeling, Grant turned to face the building's industrial metal-and-glass doors before asking, "You ready for this?"

"As I'll ever be," Sam said, pulling her shoulders back. Grant made an indignant snorting sound. It should have been unattractive, and yet she did not find it the least bit problematic. In fact, it was kind of adora—Sam stopped and redirected her focus. "What? Not all of us can be born ready," she said, using her best Grant tone for the words *born ready*.

"I would never say 'I was born ready.' Do I look like I wear neon tank tops to the gym?" Grant asked, wrinkling his nose.

Starting to walk toward the door, Sam said, "I bet you have a pair of mirror aviators and some hot-pink workout gear stashed in a drawer, just waiting for the day that it is acceptable to be *That Guy* again."

Reaching to hold the door open for Sam with one hand, Grant threw his other hand over his heart and looked pained. "You wound me."

"Somehow I think your ego will survive." Sam snickered as she walked through the door toward the reception desk. Turning to face the person behind the desk, she said, "Hello. We have a meeting with the Anjo Group."

"Oh. Ms. Azevedo. Good luck," the man behind the desk said, with a tone that implied that she would actually need luck.

Sam glanced up at Grant, who frowned at her before returning his focus to the guard. "Are they doing a lot of interviews?"

"Not a lot. But everyone who goes up comes down looking . . ." The guard stopped to make eye contact with them, his brown eyes going wide to match the overwhelmed expression on his face before continuing, "They look like they survived a bull run."

"I see." Grant's voice was light as the crease returned to his brow. Sam had the unreasonable urge to smooth a hand over it.

She immediately checked that sensation and chalked it up to skipping breakfast. The lack of nutrients plus her nerves were doing weird things to her common sense. Focusing her attention back on the guard, she said, "Thanks for the warning. Can you scan us up to the fifteenth floor?"

"Of course." The guard moved from behind the grand marble counter, fumbling with a badge as he said, "One piece of advice: Ms. Azevedo loves high energy. Make sure you smile as you talk about your project."

Sam opened her mouth to protest being told to smile when she realized the comment was aimed at Grant. He opened his mouth to respond right as the elevator doors slid open. Nudging him into the elevator before his grumpy demeanor got them in trouble, Sam made sure to smile before she said, "Thanks for the tip."

Grant jabbed a finger on the button marked "15" as the doors closed, then said, "Did that man just tell me to smile? I smile all the time."

"Do you, though?" Sam tried to make the question sound genuine and failed.

"I mean, yes. I'm a very jovial person," Grant said, his tone flat as he turned the full force of his gaze on her. His expression would have been deadpan, but now that she was getting to know him, she could see the corners of his eyes crinkle just a little. So Mr. Serious was capable of a self-deprecating joke after all.

"I don't think jovial people need to tell people they are fun." Sam smiled, then swallowed it almost immediately as Grant lit up.

"Oh, come on. You can smile at that. It was a good joke. Would a guy who wears neon make that joke?"

"Neon guy would make that joke." Sam wrinkled her nose. The last thing she wanted to do was give Grant too much credit, lest the airplane ego reappear. "And again, if you have to tell people you are joking—"

"It's okay; you don't have to laugh at my jokes. I'll make you feel good. Just wait."

"Right. Sure, buddy. Way to dream big." Sam snorted gracelessly at his awkward phrasing. "Make me feel good?"

Grant blinked as if he was just putting together his words and her response. Sam expected him to cackle or blush or something. Instead, a sly smile slid across his face as he said, "Deny it if you want. It's just a matter of time."

Sam's thoughts hopped in about a million directions at once. *Did he . . . was he . . . surely he didn't mean it like . . .*

The elevator announced that they had arrived at the fifteenth floor, startling Sam. Without missing a beat, Grant held his arm out and said, "After you."

"Oh."

It wasn't graceful, but it was the only syllable her mind could manage to form as she stared at him. Looking at his full lips, Sam was lucky to think any words at all. At least, she thought she was lucky until Grant said, "Are you going to get out?"

And with that, the spell was broken. Sam waited until she was off the elevator before she took a deep breath to clear her thoughts. It wouldn't help her focus if the air around her smelled like Grant. Not that she knew the smell of whatever spicy cologne he wore or anything. Because she hadn't noticed it before. And she certainly couldn't call that smell up now. So really it wasn't that she—

"Welcome to the Anjo Group. How may I help you?"

The voice of an exquisitely dressed person interrupted Sam's thoughts. Before Sam could pull herself together, Grant appeared by her side and said, "Hello. We are here from SF Central Hospital to meet with Ms. Azevedo."

"Ah yes. Welcome! Duesa is so excited to hear your pitch. I'm Sherilynn, she/they pronouns. Which of you is Sam?" Sherilynn said all this in one fast-moving stream of consciousness that felt both friendly and somewhat intimidating all at once.

"I am," Sam said as a wave of nervous energy washed over her. Extending her hand, she said, "Nice to meet you. Dr. Samantha Holbrook. I use she/her pronouns, and I'm a research fellow at SF Central specializing in obstetrics and—"

"Dr. Grant Gao. I use he/him pronouns. But I think 'Grant' and 'Sam' are fine. No need to keep the 'Doctor' in front of our names today," Grant cut in, saving Sam from embarrassing herself with her nervous spiel.

"So nice to finally have a face to put to the name, Sam." Sherilynn extended her hand without missing a beat. Turning to shake Grant's hand, she said, "Let me grab you two some coffees and tell Duesa you're here. Hold on just a minute."

Before Sam could really register what was happening, Sherilynn disappeared behind a frosted-glass wall. Sam turned to look at Grant, who eyed her with humor.

"You gonna calm down, or should I be prepared for you to treat everyone like a new patient?"

"Don't make fun. I'm on nervous autopilot."

"I can tell." Grant laughed.

"Not comforting," Sam said, wondering where that relaxing elevator presence of his had run off to. Searching for a way to change the subject, she asked under her breath, "Do you drink coffee?"

"If we didn't, does it matter? She seemed pretty intent on us having one," Grant said, shrugging as he looked down at his watch.

"True," Sam said.

"All right, Duesa is ready for you two, if you will just follow me," Sherilynn said, popping their head around the edge of the glass wall and causing both of them to jump. She shook what appeared to be two small milk cartons at them, then disappeared back around the wall without another word.

The hallway was lined with the sort of white carpet that looked like whoever worked there never fumbled their coffee while they rushed to get into the office on time. Reaching the end of the hall, Sherilynn expertly shifted the milk cartons and opened the door. Sam blinked. Duesa's office was all chrome, white, glass, and clean lines. It felt like the intimidating laboratory that the bad guy had on a TV show.

Sam was just starting to wonder what she had gotten herself into when Sherilynn set the coffees down and said, "Please make yourself comfortable." Before Sam and Grant could even be seated, she was gone, having closed the door with a gentle click.

"I don't think comfortable is possible," Sam said, eyeing the chrome-and-glass chair dubiously as Grant came around to sit.

"I don't think coffee is possible," Grant said, giving the carton a sniff. Wrinkling his nose, he took a sip and winced. "Woof."

Sam dropped into the surprisingly sturdy chair and picked up her carton, then took a sip. The process of forcing herself to swallow was almost painful, and she put her drink down. "Whatever is in there may have once been coffee, but—"

"Hello, welcome to Anjo!" Sam and Grant whipped their heads around to face the door right as it flew open, revealing who the internet said was Duesa Azevedo, number seven on *Forbes*'s list of "Top 50 Female Dealmakers." And while *Forbes* might have gotten her résumé right, what it failed to accurately convey was that Duesa Azevedo was a ball of electricity in human form. Clad in white pants and the sort of bright-green blouse that made Sam wonder exactly what color she was wearing, Duesa had fawn-colored skin, a dusting of freckles, and thick, tight red curls that screamed *I use products that cost more than you make in a month.*

"Thank you for having us," Grant said, standing and extending a hand, prompting Sam to do the same.

"Of course, of course," Duesa said, shaking both of their hands and gesturing for them to sit again. "So how do you like the coffee?"

Grant looked down at the carton in front of him, and Sam could see his brain looking for a way to be nice without having to lie. That was going to be hard for him. Perhaps it was better for her to redirect the question.

"I've never had coffee in a carton before."

"It's unique," Grant added. Sam wanted to punch him in the arm. Saying *it's unique* in this case was very clearly not a compliment.

Duesa's laugh floated around them. "It's okay. You can say it tastes terrible. I didn't invest in the company because of the taste of their coffee; I invested in it for the technology. The carton is self-heating. You open the spout, and it heats up. The possibilities on that one . . ." Duesa shook her head, then redirected her focus. Pointing to the cartons, she said, "I've asked Sherilynn to get you a real cup of coffee, but that carton. It's gonna make us a lot of money, which I will then be giving to people like you!"

"Thank you," Sam said, hating the note of hesitance in her voice. She wasn't sure how she'd thought this conversation would go, but it definitely wasn't like this.

"So I have to say, my partners and I loved your proposal. What I want to do today is get a sense of who *you* two are. It's clear you understand the technicalities of the thing you are trying to build, but I like to say that I'm not investing in the idea; I am investing in the founder. So who are you? Why this project?"

Sam looked at Grant, who nodded at her, suggesting she should start. Likely so he could try to figure out why this felt more like a venture capital funding round than a foundation interview.

Taking a calming breath, Sam said, "Well, this started because I was talking to a patient who had missed a few appointments. She mentioned that she had a client at her salon who is a doula that encouraged her to go to the doctor to have her blood pressure checked. From there I started thinking about traditional and cultural ways of knowing, birthing, and medicine. For many communities—particularly lower income and communities of color—traditionally, a doula would have been who cared for parents pre- and postbirth. Modern medicine in the United States tends to shun this, but increasingly we are seeing wealthy white women hiring doulas or birthing coaches to work in conjunction with their doctors.

"Then I thought, If we can treat wealthy women's doulas as a welcome thing, why not make the tradition available in other communities? We would better serve the needs of our patients by working within a culturally familiar framework. And here we are."

"It's weird, and I love it." Duesa had placed her elbows on the glass desk and steepled her fingers. Her eyes were closed as she nodded. Before Sam could decide if she was offended or flattered, Duesa abruptly opened her eyes and said, "Your why is sound. Anjo Foundation wants to know the story we will tell the world. Not schools and résumés. I have that on paper. Who are you? What is your backstory? Who . . . are . . . *you*?"

The question made Sam think of the caterpillar in *Alice in Wonderland*, and she bit back the urge to laugh at the image of Duesa blowing smoke rings and surrounded by psychedelic colors. Sam looked at Grant, who looked at her, the two of them silently doing the you-want-to-go-first dance.

Clearly remembering her stubborn streak, Grant exhaled and said, "I'm a fourth-generation Bay Area resident on my mother's side. My mother is an opera singer, and my father is the director at one of the local Chinese community centers. I think my parents would have loved for me to be a musician so we could be like a family act, but I can't carry a tune, and I hated piano lessons. They finally gave up and let me join the science club and become a doctor. It's okay; both of my sisters are musicians, so they got over it." Grant paused his story to add a casual shrug, then said, "Eventually."

Charm rolled off Grant as he laughed at his own story, and Sam had to remind herself that she was sitting next to the same man who she'd nearly had to physically pummel with a basketball to make him help her. Who was this easygoing son of a musician? And was he related to the flirty guy in the elevator? What else didn't she know about Grant?

Duesa's laugh floated around the room. "You know what I love about this story? Usually, we get these guys coming in here, and they want to tell me about their degrees from Harvard and Wharton and how they won this cutthroat competition and beat out that guy over there. But you"—Duesa stopped to gesture at Grant with an outstretched hand—"you tell me about piano lessons. I love it. And you? Who are you?"

Sticking with Grant's theme of radical candor, Sam threw out a moon shot. "I am a military kid. My dad retired from the navy when I was in the seventh grade, and we settled down in the glorious city of Akron, Ohio, where my mom became a biology teacher. I have an older brother who is a saint that works in marketing. I'm not a saint. But I am highly competitive, and I recently beat this guy playing basketball. A thing I'll never let him forget, even if he is my senior adviser."

Grant snorted, and Sam turned to watch him shake his head. "Okay, what she isn't saying is that she played in college on a good team on TV and stuff, as did one other guy on her team. It wasn't like it was a super fair game."

"It wasn't college." Sam laughed and shook her head. "It was high school. They only televised the state playoffs."

"Oh, my bad," Grant chuckled. "She just played on a high school team that was good enough to make it to the state playoffs."

"You two are so adorable," Duesa said, grinning at them like she had found a treasure. "I love this energy. Great for video. It's perfect. Sam, I do have one question for you. I know new doctors' schedules are miserable. Why do this now?"

Grant swiveled in his chair to watch her more closely, as if he was also wondering about this. Looking down, she ran her palms across the front of her skirt to hide her nerves, then said, "For me, it's both personal and professional. I broke my foot playing basketball in high school. Anyway, since I couldn't attend PE, my mom arranged for me to do community service tutoring young people working on their GEDs. They were mostly girls, really, who had stopped out of school when they became mothers. I think my mom didn't like my boyfriend, so she was trying to scare me."

Sam paused as Duesa shook her head and laughed at her mother. When her laughter died down, Sam continued. "Anyway, it didn't scare me, but it did make me think about public policy as I watched them struggle with basic questions about their health and their babies' health. They needed someone who had been in their shoes to help them navigate their new lives—a task my very ill-equipped high school self was not qualified for. It made me recognize the power of mentors."

"That must have been difficult to watch." Duesa nodded, her energy level dipping slightly.

"I didn't have the skills or power to fix the system then, but I do now. My plan is to make a career as an ob-gyn at SF Central. Why would I wait to make my workplace the kind of environment I want to spend my days in? Waiting doesn't benefit me or the people who walk through my door, so I may as well put in the extra work now instead of delaying until it is convenient for my schedule."

For a moment, Duesa squinted at her as if the sheer force of her look were some sort of barometer for Sam's sincerity. Fighting the childish urge to squint back, Sam waited for a heartbeat. Then two. Grant was just starting to fidget when Duesa yelled, "See! This is why I asked. True innovation does not wait for convenient timing. Heart of steel, this one. And a good story about why she became a doctor too."

Sam exhaled slowly and smiled as Duesa pointed her finger at her. "I knew I had to meet the woman just wild enough to launch something like this only a few months after starting a job. What you two are doing is truly the heart of social problem-solving."

Mentally, Sam broke into a happy dance. Duesa liked what she had to say. Better yet, she'd managed to say just the right thing without having to think about it for hours. Sam had been in the Bay Area for no time at all, and already she was feeling the crunch of tech culture on her life. If she wasn't careful, pretty soon she'd be saying nonsense buzz phrases like *world-class solutions* and *hub for innovation* too. Sure, Duesa using *social problem-solving* seemed a little grandiose for starting a birthing program at a public hospital. But it was peak Silicon Valley jargon, and Sam had earned it.

Clapping her hands together, Duesa said, "I love it! We have got to get this going now. Is four weeks enough time to stand up a prototype?"

"I'm sorry?" Grant asked.

At the same time Sam choked out, "A month?"

"You know. Big announcement. Splashy launch event. New company. Move fast and smash items or whatever the stupid saying is," Duesa said with a dismissive wave, as if health care were the same as coming up with a mock-up for a new designer-shoe app. Reading their faces, she said, "What? Do you need six weeks? Eight weeks?"

"Launch event?" Grant asked.

"Eight weeks is the max we could do before we need to start seeing progress reports anyway. Don't worry; Sherilynn will put it in the email." Duesa stopped talking just long enough to wave her hand dismissively, then plowed on. "Since the reports trigger each funding payment, this works out nicely. You get the program running, and you have good news from the progress report to celebrate at the launch. Yes. I can make that work, but no later because then I am off to visit my mother in Brazil, and then I go straight to Mykonos, and I want to present our involvement in this, so that is as far out as we can push the launch event."

"Does this mean we got the funding?" Sam asked, still trying to make sense of Duesa's stream of consciousness.

"I mean, yes. How long have you been in this room?" Duesa asked, leaning forward to look at Grant's watch. "Twenty minutes. If you hadn't gotten the funding, you would have been out of here in five minutes. My time is extremely valuable. And I don't give money to people I don't like. Now, about promo materials—"

Sam stopped listening as she turned to face Grant. She could feel herself grinning, but she couldn't stop it. This was happening. Her plan was working. Attempting to force her grin under wraps, Sam tuned back in right as Duesa said, "I'm thinking video. You two have such great chemistry. Very videogenic. I can already see it. I'll play it before my talk—the venture-summit people are going to eat this up."

Duesa popped the *p* sound in *up*, forcing Sam's mind back to reality. Clearing her throat gently, Sam said, "I assume we will need our two legal teams to work together on some sort of agreement?"

"Hmmm . . . ," Duesa said, giving her head a little shake as if Sam's real-world question had disrupted her visions of venture-summit success. "Ah! Yes, yes, yes. I'm getting ahead of myself. Sherilynn will work out all of the details. They will send you a draft of the grant agreement, which I'm sure the hospital will want to take a look at. After that, she will be in touch with a promo schedule and to work out the details of the launch event before my trip to Brazil. Let's say sometime in the afternoon on the . . ." Duesa stopped and poked at her own smart watch before saying, "October twenty-second. Does that work for you?"

"I'll make it work," Grant said, nodding first at Duesa and then at Sam.

A not-insubstantial voice in the front of Sam's mind pointed out that this was the same date her mother wanted for her party. But her mother's party wouldn't be until like 6:00 p.m.—and that was on the early side, Sam reasoned. She could absolutely do both. "Works for me. I just want to thank you for meeting with us today—"

"The pleasure is all mine," Duesa interrupted with a dismissive wave; then, taking a massive breath, she yelled, "Sherilynn."

Grant jumped, then looked at the phone on the desk before glancing sideways at Sam, who realized that she was clutching a stitch in her chest. Grant seemed to be in the process of stifling a laugh when Sherilynn burst into the room with as much energy. "All done?"

"Yes! So excited about this one. I said you'd be back in touch with all of the paperwork, monthly reporting requirements, and to sort out the details for the launch."

Sherilynn nodded as if all of this made sense to them, and Sam took that as a sign to go. Nodding at Duesa, she stood up and extended her hand. "Thank you again for your support. We look forward to working with you."

"I think this is going to be great fun," Duesa said, releasing Sam's hand and turning to shake Grant's, who managed to rebutton his coat jacket with one hand while shaking Duesa's with the other. Releasing his hand, she said, "See you soon!"

Chapter Ten

Sam barely heard a word Sherilynn said as she walked them toward the elevators. In fact, she hardly noticed when she took their coffee cartons from them and replaced them with real coffee. She knew Grant said something to her before they got in the elevator, but it wasn't until the doors shut that everything began to sink in.

"Oh my God! This is happening." Sam started to bounce on the balls of her feet until she realized that her coffee was sloshing precariously close to the edge of the cup.

"Congratulations," Grant said, his voice as even as the smooth elevator ride.

"We really have to get going on this. I need to tell Kaiya. We need to start recruiting additional doulas. I just hope we can find enough people who want to work for us."

"That'll be challenging. Have you given any thought to the administrative end of this program? Like who will keep track of the budget or the monthly grant report she just mentioned?"

"Well, no . . . but that will go on the list too," Sam said, refusing to let Grant's reality-based questions bring her down. Taking a big sip of her coffee, she looked back up at Grant, who was smiling at her in the way that someone smiled at a friend who'd just shown them the wonky holiday cookies they'd made—one part humoring and one part trepidation over having to eat a questionable cookie.

Whatever. It wasn't like she could expect the charming man from the interview to last forever. Grant likely still thought this idea would fail. He was probably just being nice to soften the anticipated blow. How magnanimous, Sam thought, suppressing an eye roll.

Grant had opened his mouth to say something else when the elevator doors opened and the security guard looked up. The mischievous glint returned to Grant's eye, and he pasted the most outrageous and oversize grin on his face. It was so absurd that it took everything in her not to crack up as the guard said, "Well, you look happy."

"Sure am! I just have so much energy," Grant said, putting his hands in the pockets of his slacks and sauntering out of the elevator. By now, his face muscles had to be hurting.

"Have a good one," Sam managed to say. Giving Grant a shove out the door, she stumbled away from the giant glass window before laughing.

Grant maintained his weird smile and said, "Do you think I smiled big enough? I mean . . ." Whatever Grant was going to say got lost in a fit of laughter as he slowly broke character.

"What was that face?" Sam said, straightening up.

"What face?" Grant said, making the absurd V shape with his mouth again. "This is just how I smile at men who tell me to smile."

Sam guffawed, then looked down at her much-improved cup of coffee. "Well—"

"Do you want a ride home?" Grant asked, then added, "Sorry to interrupt you. You can finish."

"No worries. I was actually just thinking about locating the train station."

"I'd be happy to give you a ride."

"It isn't out of your way? I still don't know the city, but I feel like Potrero is out of everyone's way."

"It's not that far," Grant laughed. "I live toward Golden Gate Park, in the Outer Sunset."

"That means nothing to me yet. But I'll take your word for it," Sam laughed.

"You haven't been to the park?" Grant looked stunned.

"Don't look at me like that. I've driven by it, and I went as a kid."

Grant threw a hand over his chest and slumped dramatically. "This pains me."

"Oh, please. That is extremely dramatic of you. Then again, your mother is an opera singer. How has this not come up?"

"It's really not that interesting." Grant half smiled over at her as he started to walk down the block. "Coming?"

"Your mother is, like, the woman with the blonde braids and Viking helmet? How is that not interesting?" Sam asked, trailing behind him.

Grant shrugged. "The Viking-helmet lady is a Wagnerian soprano, which is actually just a dramatic soprano. My mother is a coloratura, so it's different." Grant digressed as he tried to navigate the complexity of however many types of opera singers there were. Giving his head a little shake, he said, "Not that it matters. For most people: Yes, sure. She is the Viking-helmet lady."

"What do you mean, it doesn't matter? You are, like, the only person I know who knows things about opera."

"I mean, it matters, but it isn't like I am going to convince you to start watching and listening to opera based on this."

"Okay, Mr. Epicurean Tastes. You don't know me. Just because I've never been exposed to something doesn't mean I wouldn't like it. I would totally listen to opera," Sam said, feeling the pull of a challenge tug at her. Not that Grant thinking she wouldn't like opera should matter. It totally didn't. Except that it did, a little. Drawing herself up to her full height, she said, "Where should I start?"

Grant raised an eyebrow at her as if testing her sincerity. "Most people like Mozart. It's very accessible," he said, and Sam got the distinct impression that *accessible* was somehow a bad thing. After a minute, he added, "If you are serious, I'll text you a podcast that is a good intro to opera and a link to a good recording to start with."

"I am dead serious. Is your mom in this one?"

Grant snorted and shook his head. "No."

"That's okay. What's your mom's name? I'll track a recording down."

"Maybe just start with Mozart. Then you can watch my mom's entire career if you like it," Grant said, his laugh sounding skeptical as he stopped in front of a newer-model Audi SUV. "This is me."

Sam waited until Grant shoved a stack of papers onto the passenger-side floor before opening the car door. As much as she didn't want to admit it, his car was much more comfortable than public transport. Looking down at the floor mat, she caught a glimpse of the papers he had shoved off the seat. They were the documents she had prepared for him about the Anjo Group and the project, and they were covered in highlights with little notes in the margin. If this was Grant's idea of skimming, she wondered what it looked like when he really studied.

Grant pressed the start button, and the car hummed to life as he said, "I'm just gonna head in the general direction. You can put your address in the GPS if you want."

"Ooh, nav system and flying first class. You're a fancy senior fellow," Sam laughed.

"Not really. This was my graduation gift from my biological father. He's a banker. I don't think either of us has much interest in a relationship at this point, but I do enjoy using his airline status for upgrades and driving this car. Okay, and the occasional nice watch."

"I hadn't noticed the watch."

"I figured I'd better confess or you'd think I was a liar as well as a snob," Grant said, checking his mirror before pulling away from the curb.

For a moment Sam was quiet, unsure of what to do with Grant's honesty. She did think he was a snob. She just hadn't expected him to call her on it. Recovering a beat too slowly, Sam felt her cheeks heat up as she said, "I don't think you're a snob."

"I think you're a bad liar." Grant smirked as he layered on the sarcasm.

"You know what?" Sam laughed. "I was going to say thank you for trusting me, but now I don't think I will."

"Trusting you with what? My car's origin story?" Grant laughed low and smiled at her like she was amusing.

"Sure, that too. But more that you could have backed out of being the program's supervisor. I know you weren't that excited about it. But you trusted me to try, so if I were going to say thank you, I would say it for that. But I'm not."

"If you were thanking me, I'd say it wasn't like a big thing. Really, all I had to do is show up."

"Right . . . only yesterday, you said you hadn't read the materials, but the funding paperwork on your floor is covered in highlights and notes. That doesn't look like you just showed up."

Grant frowned slightly as if having been caught making an obvious effort to help was deeply uncomfortable to him. "I had extra time this morning."

"What? At four thirty a.m.?" Sam arched an eyebrow and looked over at Grant, who was suddenly very engaged in checking his rearview mirror.

"It's not a big thing."

"Sure." Sam's heart squeezed as Grant attempted to play off his hard work. Try as he might to be aloof, there was no way around the fact that he had done something totally sweet for her. At best, Sam had expected a power read. He'd even made it sound like that was all he would do. Maybe he didn't want to make a big deal out of it, but Sam could totally hug him right now . . . if he was open to it. She didn't know why he would be. Except for what he'd said in the elevator . . .

A pothole in the road rocked Sam back into the moment. Catching sight of Grant's apprehension, she decided to let him off the hook. "Have it your way, Grant. I totally believe that you expended zero energy on this despite the highlights and the neon-green sticky note on the front."

Grant snorted. "Are you calling me stubborn?"

"Yes. And a snob."

"What happened to thank-you Sam? I liked her."

Sam was opening her mouth to say something as Grant made a right when a sign on a gray building with stained glass windows and friendly-looking planter boxes caught her eye.

HOST YOUR PARTY HERE

"Hey, do you know that place?" Sam asked, changing subjects abruptly enough that Grant did a double take at her before following her finger to where she was pointing.

"The Bishop? Yes."

"It's called the Bishop. That feels on the nose."

"It makes sense for the clientele." Grant shrugged. "Why?"

"My mom is determined to throw a reunion party in San Francisco. On October twenty-second, in fact. It's mostly for friends that my parents made when my dad was stationed in the Bay Area like twenty-five years ago. But because it's my mom, she wants me to plan it. Anyway, is the Bishop a good spot?"

"Meh. It's fine. A favorite for the kind of tech bro who wears sneakers made of supposedly thermodynamic plastics and is super into optimizing his diet based on whatever that six-hour-workday guy says."

"That is an extremely specific and deeply unpleasant-sounding archetype of a person," Sam laughed. "I'm guessing you are not a fan of him?"

"Just wait until you end up dealing with one when the ER is understaffed. At least one of those guys comes in there a day, typically with a shattered wrist from ignoring traffic signs on their motorized skateboard."

"Noted. So much for the Bishop. I guess it's back to scouring the internet," Sam sighed, watching out the window as Grant made a right turn onto a street so steep the incline forced her to lean back into the plush car seats.

It took Sam a moment to notice the silence between them. It was unexpected . . . and comfortable. She should not feel so comfortable around someone who was effectively judging her career choices and medical knowledge every day. The thought shook Sam, and she felt her mind race to find a topic of conversation to try to fill the silence.

Sam was taking a deep breath, determined to say something banal about the big hills, when Grant spoke. "You know, if you are looking for venues, I could show you a couple that I like." She looked over at Grant to find him watching her out of the corner of his eye. Haltingly, he added, "You know. Just so you can check something off your list and focus on opening the center."

"Oh . . . I—"

Catching her eye, he turned his attention back to the road, focusing intently on the stop sign near her house. "That is, if you want help."

"I would . . ." The offer caught Sam off guard, and she was surprised at the answer that rolled off her tongue. ". . . like that."

"Okay. I'll come up with some ideas," Grant said, sounding almost as surprised by her answer as they pulled up to the front of her apartment.

An idea hit Sam a minute too late, and she felt her face begin to flush.

"Are you asking me out?" Sam blurted, feeling the heat in her cheeks come to a boil as soon as the words came out of her mouth. She hadn't intended this to be a date or anything, but then the way it was phrased left some room for ambiguity. Not that there was much that she could do about it if it was a date—it wasn't like the idea of dating Grant was so terrible that she'd throw herself from a moving vehicle to avoid it or anything. And help plus a date wouldn't be so bad, but still, a little clarity here would be good.

"Do you want to be asked out?" Grant asked, his expression giving away almost nothing as he eyed her before returning his attention to the road, where exactly no cars were driving toward them.

How was she supposed to answer that? If he wasn't asking her out and she said yes, then she'd sound like she'd been picturing him in the shower and biding her time until she could trap him into some kind of good-guy sneaky date. If she said no, was she closing a door to something? Did she even want that door open?

"Um." Better to just stay in the middle until he gave her a hint. Before she could think too hard about her body's reaction, she reached for the car door and her seat belt simultaneously, tangling herself up in her limbs as she stammered, "I'll see you at work, and we can talk about all this."

"Sure," Grant said, amusement tingeing his voice as he watched her twist around in her seat.

"Great," she said. The inward cringe at her own inability to articulate her thoughts was only cut short when she finally managed to escape the hostage situation that was his passenger seat. Pushing the door open and jumping out, she said, "Thanks for the ride," before closing the door just as quickly. With a short, jerky wave, she turned and began speed walking up the steep driveway to her front door as she fumbled around her bag for her keys.

Unlocking the front door, Sam forced herself to take deep, calming breaths before looking over her shoulder. Grant was still there, apparently making sure she made it inside despite the fact that it was broad daylight. She smiled, then closed the door.

Walking just far enough down the hallway that she could watch Grant pull away, Sam leaned against the cool wall to think. She wasn't sure what was going on or what he was thinking, but Sam was sure of two things. Grant Gao was not who she thought he was. And she liked that about him a little too much.

~

"How'd it go?" Jehan's voice floated through the hallway as soon as Sam closed the apartment door.

"Hey," Sam called, stepping out of her shoes and setting her bag down.

"Don't 'hey' me. How was it?" Jehan stuck her head out of the kitchen and narrowed her eyes at Sam.

"Oh, you know, as well as these things can." Sam could swear that taking the MCAT had been easier than keeping the excitement out of her voice.

Jehan wrinkled her nose and shook her salad fork at Sam. "What does that mean? *Well* like good-feeling well? Or *well* like you are going to get a rejection email in a week?" Originally, Sam had thought she would keep the good news to herself until she, Jehan, and Duke were all home tomorrow night. But given the way Jehan was looking at her, she'd be lucky if the tiny woman didn't pry it from her in the next thirty-three seconds.

"Well, I don't think we'll be getting a rejection email . . ." Sighing, Sam looked at the floor, then back at her friend, savoring the suspense for a moment longer before saying, "Because they gave us a yes today!"

Jehan shrieked and dropped her fork on the counter as she launched a hug at Sam. "This is amazing!"

"I know. I wanted to surprise you and Duke, but now we'll just have to surprise him when he gets home," Sam said, marveling at how tight Jehan was squeezing.

"I want to know every detail. Who did you meet with? What kind of questions did they ask? Did they like my proposal? Was Grant nice?" Jehan asked all these questions in rapid succession as she released Sam.

Letting the air flow back into her lungs, Sam started answering the first question, which prompted Jehan to ask about fifteen more as she carried her lunch to the table by the big window, forcing Sam to follow her so she could eat while they spoke.

"It sounds like a success, all things considered."

"I'd say so," Sam said, still buzzing with excitement as she tried to read upside down the papers that Jehan had strewed all over the table.

"And Grant gave you a ride home, even though he lives in the Outer Sunset?" Jehan asked, swallowing a final bite of salad as Sam stopped to take a breath.

"Yeah, he said it is close by."

"I don't think that's true. Pretty sure my eyebrow stylist is out there. It's like on the exact opposite side of town," Jehan said, raising one perfectly manicured eyebrow.

Sam was halfway through marveling at the fact that Jehan even had an eyebrow stylist when she processed what her friend was implying. "Maybe he had an errand to run?"

"Right." Jehan nodded, drawing the *r* sound in the word out a little too much for Sam's liking.

"What? I don't know why he said what he said. But I very much doubt he would go that far out of his way for me," Sam said, trying not to taste the fib in that sentence. This morning, she would've been able to deny that sentence with confidence. Now she wasn't so sure. But Jehan didn't need to know that.

Looking around the table for a subject change, Sam reexamined the handful of paper spread out in front of her friend. She realized that it was lists and samples of engagement party save-the-dates. Glancing back up at Jehan, Sam saw the puffiness around her eyes in a new light. This wasn't just standard long-shift tired; this was something else. After waiting for Jehan to finish chewing, Sam asked, "So how's the party planning going?"

"It's, um . . . it's going. Kind of." Jehan looked at the paper on either side of her and sagged.

"Is it going? Because it doesn't sound like it is," Sam said, readjusting in her seat to try to catch her friend's eye.

Jehan scowled and poked at the last few bites of her salad for a moment before exhaling like someone had punched her in the stomach. "Okay, it's not going well at all. In fact, I would say that it is going terrible, and if I hadn't just woken up from a nap, I'd likely be crying over it. As it stands, I'm just sort of wallowing in avoidance mode."

"Okay, well, maybe don't do that." Sam suppressed a chuckle as her friend set her salad bowl down and put her head in her hands. "Can you tell me what happened? I thought you decided not to stress about your mom, the aunts, and Travis."

"I did. And it was going really great until we actually set a date for the party. Now I'm being bombarded by opinions on the invitations and the catering for the thing, which is ridiculous. My family has a zillion opinions about the color; meanwhile Travis just wants to send an e-vite, which is basically causing my father to have a meltdown. And I just—"

"Can't you do both?" Sam asked, gently reaching across the table and pulling on one of her roommate's arms so that she had to look up.

"I could, but then there is my mom and the guest list to contend with, and I . . . I just don't know. I wish I could elope and throw a big party all at the same time." Jehan sighed and frowned over at her salad bowl again, looking exhausted.

Sam's heart broke for her friend. Jehan was constantly helping others, and it always seemed like she had no one in her corner.

The thought that her roommate needed help poked at Sam's conscience. Jehan had written the Anjo grant report for Sam—money that typically took an inexperienced grant writer years to get. With Jehan's help Sam had gotten a grant within two months. Just last week, she'd done Duke's chores after he had a rough night shift and picked up some new beauty product for Sam because she knew she was looking for it. Sam couldn't not help her. If anything, this was her chance to pay her friend back for the myriad kindnesses she'd shown Sam since they moved in together.

"Jehan, what if I took care of the invites and all that for you? Tell me which invite you like best, give me the list of names, and I'll mail them out. Then you can tell your family and Travis that it's handled and be done with it."

"I can't ask you to do that," Jehan said, looking up from her salad bowl in surprise. "Seriously, invites are time consuming, and you have your research program to get off the ground."

"A program I wouldn't have without your help. Just saying." Sam shrugged.

"I don't know . . ." Jehan wrinkled her nose as she processed.

"Really. Happy to help with all that. Plus, I love invitations and decor and guest lists and all that stuff. And I'm doing them for my mom's party anyway, so my helping you is really just more efficient," Sam said, lying ever so slightly to her friend. In reality, she knew almost nothing about that stuff outside what her high school best friend's mother, Dr. Victoria Blake, housekeeping and party planner extraordinaire, had taught her.

Jehan blinked at her for a minute, then grinned big enough to show all her teeth before saying, "Oh, thank you!"

"Anytime." Sam counted her blessings. Jehan was clearly exhausted. Otherwise, she would have known that Sam was lying. "Just send me what you need, and I'll let you know when it is done."

"Of course. I'll send it over as soon as I finish forcing vegetables down my throat." Jehan giggled, looking lighter than Sam had seen her all week.

"Excellent," Sam said, standing up and walking toward her room. "I'm gonna go change outa this suit and then email Kaiya about the funding."

"Good luck. Let me know if you need help shouting the good news," Jehan called as Sam walked down the hall.

"Don't worry about me. Just worry about sending me your lists." Sam smiled over her shoulder as she hustled into her room.

She had just shed the uncomfortable waistband of her skirt and pulled her laptop out from its cubby by her bed when her phone buzzed. When she looked down, Sam's heart flipped around in her chest as Grant's name scrolled across the screen.

> Dr. Franklin is looking for volunteers to chart records this afternoon. If you offer to help, he might be nicer when you ask him for a room for the program.

Sam felt herself smile as the little ... that implied he was still typing blinked at her. This was a Grant she recognized. Before she would have seen this text as the frosty work of a man who was a little too perfect for his own good. Now she wasn't so sure. He'd downplayed the way he'd prepared for their meeting, instead trying to guide her in his own quiet way. Sam pursed her lips and was trying to think of how best to respond when his texts arrived one after the other.

> Just a tip. Of course, you do not have to work on your day off.

> And congratulations, again. :-)

Sam almost laughed. She could practically see him grimacing as he typed the most uncharacteristically Grant thing in the world—a smiley face. He must really want her to know that he was trying to help. Still smiling, she typed back.

Couldn't have done it without you.

After hitting send, she quickly added a :-) to the chain, just so that he wouldn't be left feeling foolish for sharing a small emotion. Sam held her phone in her hands for just a moment, fighting the urge to reread his text like it was a precious message, but the time caught her eye. *1:42 p.m.* If she was going to catch Dr. Franklin in order to volunteer, she needed to get a move on.

Chapter Eleven

If this doula program was successful, Sam decided her next fundraising effort would focus on helping the hospital update its software so that no one ever had to manually enter another patient chart into the system again. As soon as she'd received her assignment, Sam had tried to get a moment of Dr. Franklin's time to no avail: he'd rushed off to a meeting and then taken a seemingly endless number of phone calls—which Sam knew because she casually walked by his office every forty-five minutes just to see if he was available.

Rounding the corner, she paused just outside the door to listen for Dr. Franklin on the phone and instead heard the promising sounds of furious typing. This was a good sign. Shaking out her hands as if that would also shake out her nerves, she leaned around the half-open door and knocked.

"Hi, Dr. Franklin. Got a minute?"

Dr. Franklin's head jerked up in surprise, and he blinked at her three times, as if he were getting his bearings. Reaching under his blue-light-reflecting computer glasses, he rubbed his eyes and said, "Yes. Hello, Samantha. Come in. How can I help?"

"Thanks." Sam took a tentative step in and reminded herself that she did not need to feel bad for interrupting him. In fact, she'd just gotten the hospital almost a quarter of a million dollars in grant money. If it were her on the receiving end of that news, she'd be jumping for joy. "I know you got my email with the good news about the funding for the birthing program."

"Uh-huh." Dr. Franklin nodded. He didn't look like he remembered this email at all.

Undeterred, Sam powered through. "Anyway, it looks like this program can officially take off. We just need a space—"

"Oh, I remember. This is the thing with the woo-woo birthing people."

"You mean the program to make pregnancy support available to all people in our community?" She was trying to keep the irritation from her voice. She was also aware that she was failing. There were plenty of charlatans in the medical field, but what Sam was proposing wasn't quackery. There was no need for Dr. Franklin to act like she was shilling $1,000 magnets to desperate people.

"Sure." Dr. Franklin shrugged as if the details were irrelevant to his analysis, then said, "Isn't today your day off? Why are you here?"

"Grant—I mean Dr. Gao—mentioned that you were looking for volunteers, and I thought, *Well, I care about this place, and I need to talk to Dr. Franklin, so why not?*" Sam shrugged, trying not to be taken aback that the attending even looked at the schedule, let alone knew when she was supposed to be in the hospital.

"All right, I get it. You care." Dr. Franklin rolled his eyes and waved her off, but his expression had gone from exhausted to amused. "Enough blowing smoke. You came here to ask me to help you cut through all the red tape and find the program a room?"

"More or less." Sam laughed. "We can share the room with another office; it just needs to be one that can transition into a classroom space or offer a bit of privacy for the doulas."

"Such an easy ask," Dr. Franklin mumbled.

"I know, but I've thought long and hard about this, and do we really want our future parents meeting in the covered parking lot?"

Dr. Franklin smirked at her joke. "If I recall correctly, the chaplains have been asking to fix up the space behind the chapel for some time. If you all would be willing to use some of your funds to fix it up, I think I could convince them to share."

"We can do that." Sam practically bounced to the end of her chair, she was so eager to make this work.

"Don't get excited. The chapel is located in the old hospital wing, and I don't think it has seen a renovation since I was in med school—"

"So ten years ago?" Sam grinned.

"Don't push it. You are already getting what you want." Dr. Franklin smiled, then let his expression grow serious. "Anyway, it is going to need some work. And I want to be clear that I'm holding you and Dr. Gao responsible for the program from start to finish. If so much as a speck of paint seems out of place, I will put a stop to this. The last thing this hospital needs is some new It Program nonsense to ding our reputation. Got it?"

"I completely understand, and I won't let you down," Sam said, feeling joy bubble up inside herself, despite his stern warning.

"All right then. Send me an email with your needs so I can forward it to our director of operations."

"Yes, sir. Thank you, Dr. Franklin," Sam said, jumping up from her chair before the attending had the chance to change his mind.

"After you send that email, head home, Dr. Holbrook. Tomorrow looks to be a busy one," Dr. Franklin called after her.

Sam paused at the door and waved. "Of course, sir. Thank you for this opportunity. I won't let you down."

"Good night." Dr. Franklin shook his head and half smiled before turning his attention back to his email.

Grinning like a cat that caught a mouse, Sam walked three steps away from the office door before bouncing up and down in a half dance, half skip. The interaction with Dr. Franklin hadn't been nearly as bad as she had anticipated. In fact, if she had to grade it, she would give it a six out of ten. Not good but still above average. She should celebrate. She rounded the corner to the fellows' office, trying to figure out what kind of takeout she could afford that also felt special. Whatever it was, she should probably order enough for Jehan and Duke. Remembering that she should text Grant, she reached into her pocket and pulled out her cell phone. Looking down, she quickly typed out,

It worked!

After hitting send, she tapped over to the group text to ask her roommates what they wanted for dinner.

"What worked?"

Sam jumped halfway out of her very practical running sneakers, clutching her phone with one hand and a stitch in her chest with the other. Standing halfway down the hall was Grant, holding his phone, the corners of his mouth turned up.

"This is the second time you have sent my heart racing. Are you trying to do this to me?" Sam asked, feeling her shoulders relax as she laughed.

"Not in this precise way, no." Grant shrugged, his expression hovering somewhere between mischievous and matter of fact.

The image of him sweaty and shirtless rocked Sam's consciousness so hard she had to close her eyes. She could imagine the feel of his breath on her neck, the feel of his skin against her own, electricity pulsing between them.

"Sam?"

The sound of his voice shot her back to reality. Forcing her eyes open wide, she looked at him and bit down hard on her lower lip to make herself focus. Until this moment, Sam had thought that a steamy fantasy flashing before someone's eyes was only the stuff of TV shows. It was just unfortunate timing that she only learned the truth right now.

"You okay?"

"Ha. Yeah." Sam's laugh sounded as dazed as she felt. Clearing her throat, she tried again. "Sorry, just spaced out."

Spaced out? Sam kicked herself. As if she could space out with a walking sex dream in front of her.

"You just texted me that something worked?" Grant said, rolling his shoulders forward ever so slightly. For a brief moment, Sam wondered if he was also trying to find his footing with her and whatever their new, potentially less antagonistic relationship was at the moment.

"Yes! Your advice for managing Dr. Franklin worked. He is going to help with the room." Sam was pleased with herself for sounding less breathless than she felt. Inside, it felt like she had sprinted a three-hour marathon.

"Oh. Good." Grant's eyebrows shot up with surprise, as if he hadn't expected her to text over something so trivial, but he quickly masked the expression with his usual no-nonsense demeanor. Clearing his throat, he said, "So I actually hoped I'd run into you."

"Why's that? Trying to scare me to death so you won't have to work with me on this project?"

"Not quite. At this rate, I think Duesa would make me do it without you, and that wouldn't be any fun." Grant laughed and shook his head. "I've been thinking about places that might work for your mom's party. And I've got a couple in mind. If you want to go check them out, I think we both have next Thursday off."

The word *great* was on the tip of Sam's tongue when Jehan's voice giving her a hard time echoed in her head. Given the unexpected energy that had passed between them, Sam couldn't help but feel that her friend might have had a point. Perhaps Grant was going out of his way for her? She shouldn't inconvenience him when he was already helping her with the program. "I think that—"

"We could also get ice cream to celebrate." Grant was halfway through his rush to fill the silence when he winced, slowed down, and added, "Sorry. I'm from a family that talks over each other when we get excited. What were you going to say?"

Sam's heart squeezed. She couldn't bring herself to listen to Jehan. And really, what did her roommate know anyway? "Just that I think that sounds fun. And I love ice cream. And my family talks over each other too."

"Oh . . ." Grant gave Sam a shy smile as if he hadn't expected the answer to be a straightforward yes, then remembered himself. Pulling his shoulders back, he said, "Well . . . then I'll pick you up on Thursday."

"You know where I live."

"That I do. See you around, Dr. Holbrook." Although he used her formal title, his tone was soft.

"See you, Dr. Gao." Sam felt heat rush into her cheeks. Giving him a small smile, she forced herself to walk down the hall without looking back, although she was almost sure that if she had, she would have caught him looking back too.

~

Sam dragged herself up the stairs behind Duke, who was happily bab-bling about the early results of his research on pregnancy post–cancer diagnosis. She had to appreciate how easily he shook off defeat, as if they hadn't just lost a game to the SF Central Swishers, a team so bad that fourth graders could have beaten them.

"I promise, this time, I'll be quick," Duke said, as he unlocked the door and sauntered toward the shower like he'd never met the word *hurry* in his life.

"Yeah, right," Sam mumbled as her phone buzzed. When she looked down, a text from her brother popped up.

Heads up. Mom's probably gonna call you in 20 minutes about sending the save the dates.

Sam winced as she walked into her room and dropped her gym bag on the floor. She really should have done this weeks ago, but she'd been so busy prepping for the interview and trying to get her research off the ground that it had slipped her mind. Now the activity that was supposed to help her fix things with her mom was making Diana more upset. Sighing down at the screen, she typed out,

Thanks for the warning. I'll get on it.

I'm on the phone with her now. I'll stall for you. Either send them now or put your phone in do not disturb.

Sam snickered at her brother's joke.

I'll do it now. Thanks for stalling. Love you!

Dropping onto her bed, Sam reached for her computer and tried to push her guilt aside. Sure, she was slow to send out her mom's save-the-dates, but there was still plenty of time before the event, and at least now she could send Jehan's and her mom's at the same time.

Tossing her phone to the side, she pulled up the Glam Party Invites website and clicked over to Jehan's save-the-dates. Pulling up her email, she downloaded the spreadsheet of guests' addresses for her roommate's party and dropped it on the desktop. Clicking back over to the invites, she uploaded the mailing info from the spreadsheet on her desktop as quickly as she could. Keeping one eye on her phone, she prayed she could at least tell the company to mail them before her mother called. Fishing around for her credit card, Sam absently clicked the various approvals while also scanning her work email for messages from Kaiya. Several are-you-sure-this-is-right clicks later, the save-the-dates were approved, and her mother still hadn't called. Isaiah really was a peach of an older brother.

Bouncing out of her room, Sam checked to see if Duke was out of the shower—of course he was not—then spotted Jehan poking around the kitchen. Wandering over, she said, "Hey, just letting you know that I mailed out the save-the-dates. I'll send a formal invitation in a couple of weeks once you and my mom have settled on venues."

"You are the absolute best," Jehan said, closing a mostly empty cupboard and bounding over to give Sam a hug.

"I wouldn't go that far. Glam Party Invites is doing most of the work," Sam said, laughing as her friend tried to squeeze the life out of her.

"You still did the hard part so I didn't have to second-guess myself. Therefore both you and Glam Party are my heroes." Releasing Sam, Jehan sniffed in her general direction. "Don't get me wrong; I'm super grateful for your help. But you are damp, and you smell like a gym bag."

"Well, I wouldn't, if Duke would get out of the shower," Sam called down the hallway right as Duke wrenched open the bathroom door and strolled back toward his room.

Without missing a beat, he chuckled and yelled back, "We're running out of hot water. Shower fast."

Chapter Twelve

Sam smoothed down the front of her bright-yellow dress and peeked out the window. The trick was to get out the front door without arousing any of Duke's suspicions. It was just her luck that he'd asked why she wasn't playing in tonight's game while she was doing battle with an iron and a linen sundress. That man noticed details like no one's business, and she was almost sure he hadn't bought the excuse about wanting to wear something fun on a sunny day.

Okay, even she could admit that her excuse was a bit of a stretch. But what was she supposed to say? *I want to look nice for a not-date with our senior fellow, who I may not hate as much as I thought I did* seemed like a more detailed conversation than she wanted to have with either of her nosy roommates just now.

The shower shut off, and Sam's eyes flitted to the bathroom door. Maybe she should just wait in her bedroom. Really, wouldn't it look weird to—

She cut the thought off as Grant's car pulled up in front of the apartment. Snatching her purse and sweater from the kitchen table, she bolted for the door, only stopping long enough to yell, "Headed out. See you later!"

Sam made a conscious effort to slow her pace just a few steps before the front entrance to her apartment so that she wouldn't appear overeager. She wasn't sure why she was so jittery. They were literally going to physically look at a couple of buildings. That was it.

Exhaling out her nerves, she opened the front door to the apartment and bounced down the driveway as Grant rolled down the window and said, "You look nice."

"Sunny dress for a sunny day," Sam said, smiling as she opened the car door. Sunny dress? Internally, she hoped she didn't sound like a grade-schooler. Who even thought things like that?

Pulling herself together, Sam took a good look at Grant as she was getting into the car, and her brain capacity plummeted. She might look nice, but he . . . wow.

Grant had managed to pull off tousled sexy while still being entirely too clothed. His dark hair, usually so carefully styled, was just sort of pushed around his head like someone had only recently run both hands through it. The lightweight tan cotton sweater he wore complemented the same rich undertones in his skin and might have actually been sewn around his torso. It was the only way Sam could imagine making a sweater that managed to hug every muscle without looking like he'd squeezed into the thing.

Sam was begging her brain to get back in gear and stop staring when Grant leaned forward and squinted up at her apartment. Something about the motion snapped Sam back into reality, and she turned to see Duke standing in the living room window in his towel, waving and grinning like he was enjoying a fantastic joke. Mortified, she turned away from the window just in time to catch Grant waving and looking baffled.

Humiliation nearly forced Sam to melt into the passenger seat as Grant silently rolled up the window. She felt his eyes on her, and it took everything inside her not to cover her face with her sweater and hope that she disappeared. Reaching to take the car out of park, he said, "What's with Duke—"

"Sorry. My roommates are extremely nosy." Sam winced, finally making eye contact with Grant.

"I know he's nosy. I was just gonna ask why he's wearing a towel." Grant laughed out the last half of the sentence.

"I tried to sneak out of the apartment before he got out of the shower. I didn't want him asking too many questions."

"Questions? What kind of questions?"

If it hadn't been obvious that Sam was embarrassed before, the flush she was rocking now had to be a dead giveaway. Pushing her thick curls to one side so she could get some air on her neck, Sam tried to sound nonchalant as she said, "They are too stupid to repeat."

Grant arched an eyebrow, and she realized that she was going to have to force a conversational about-face or risk having him grill her. Clearing her throat, she asked, "So where are we going first?"

For a moment, Grant just looked at her, and then he shook his head as if he had decided against pressing for details. "I thought we'd start with the Lost Key in SoMa."

"I've never heard of that place."

"That's kind of the point. It's one of those places that you have to know about to find," Grant said, easing the car away from the curb.

"How did you find it?"

"My sister played a charity recital there a few years ago." Anticipating her next question, Grant added, "Mandy, the cellist."

"I'm excited to see where rich people have their supersecret charity events," Sam said, letting go of her hair as she started to cool off.

"Did Dr. Franklin tell you that the chaplains agreed to share the room with us as long as we spruce it up?" Grant said, tossing a brief smile over at her before he made a careful right-hand turn, guiding them past the freeway.

"They did?" Sam twisted around in her seat to look directly at him. "I emailed him several times about it, and he didn't respond. I figured he was still waiting for the slow-ass legal team to sign off on the Anjo agreement before he even bothered to ask."

Grant laughed. "Be nice to the team. There are like two lawyers for the whole hospital."

"Well, there could be more if we start bringing in money with our fancy birthing program," Sam mumbled, crossing her arms. "And before you say anything else, yes, I know our little public hospital is not about to turn into the next Cleveland Clinic or anything. I dream big, but I'm not delusional."

"Hey, even Cleveland had to start somewhere." Grant shrugged, then slowly cocked a smile. "You may be a little delusional, but this particular nonreality wouldn't be the biggest red flag."

Sam eyed Grant, checking to see if he was truly joking or if he was judging her and covering his tracks. She was never entirely sure what foot she was standing on with him. After the Anjo group meeting and what she had dubbed the Hallway Incident, Sam had thought they'd come to an agreement. Then she'd had seventy-two hours' worth of hospital shifts with him questioning her every move, and suddenly, she was right back on the plane failing to take Man Bun's pulse all over again.

"Ha. Ha," Sam said, as a block of warehouses whizzed by. "Very funny."

"I am funny. Thank you for noticing," Grant said, looking pleased with himself.

"If you were actually funny, I feel like you would have—" Sam cut herself off as Grant turned down a sketchy-looking alleyway, complete with the horror-movie harbinger of doom—wet cement on a conspicuously sunny day. Hoping she didn't sound totally freaked out, she asked, "Where are you going?"

"The Lost Key. Listen, I couldn't get us in to see the place properly, so we're gonna gate-crash. Just play along."

"Wait. What?" Panic shot through Sam's veins. He had to be joking. What kind of doctor gate-crashed parties?

"Don't worry. I got this," Grant said, grinning as he turned in to a random garage. Putting the car in park, he pressed the ignition button and looked over at her. Something in her expression must have read as terrified, because he added, "This is the most murdery part. I promise," before unbuckling his seat belt and getting out of the car.

Sam couldn't imagine where this fancy place was among all the eerie warehouse vibes, but she got out of the car anyway, mostly because the prospect of staying alone in it was more terrifying. She caught up with Grant right as a parking attendant crept out of the shadows, sending her heart into her throat.

"We are closed today. Unless you are the Johnson party," the bored-sounding parking attendant with a patchy beard said.

"We're with the Johnsons," Grant replied, with all the confidence of a man who was actually with the Johnsons. Never mind that the attendant had asked if they *were* the Johnsons.

The attendant looked at them for a moment, then shrugged, taking Grant's keys. "Lot closes at eleven p.m."

"Right. We won't be more than an hour or so," Grant said, his solemn demeanor never cracking.

Handing Grant a ticket, the attendant said, "Entrance is through that black door on the left. Hope you find what you are looking for."

"Thanks," Grant said, taking the ticket. He waited until the attendant was in the car before turning and mouthing to Sam, "Hope you find what you are looking for."

"What does that even mean?" Sam whispered, the apprehension she'd felt in the car continuing to build.

"That they have a catchphrase that the poor people who work here are forced to say." Grant winced, then added, "I'm sure we can ask them not to do that for your mom's event, though."

"Or you brought me to some kind of twisted sex club turned murder room," Sam said as they watched the car disappear into an elevator lit by none other than red lights.

"First, I wouldn't bring you to a murder-themed sex club. I'd bring you to a way nicer one. Second, 'sex club turned murder room' sounds like a B horror movie." Grant shook his head as if the idea were offensive. "And finally, what sex club would murder its patrons? They'd be out of business within weeks."

"That's what they want you to believe," Sam shot back. "Tell me this doesn't look like a murder dungeon."

"It's supposed to. Trust me, the inside is well worth it."

"You better not murder me."

"I wouldn't dream of it," Grant said, gently taking her elbow and steering her toward the shadowy black door. Every bit of skin he touched tingled with his closeness. It was one of those small, intimate gestures that people who were comfortable with each other's bodies used every day without thinking. It shouldn't have been a big deal. But it stole the attention of every one of her senses. Lost in the sensation of his touch, she didn't have time to think of anything clever to respond with before someone in black slacks, suspenders, and a white shirt with the sleeves rolled up opened the door and said, "You've found the Lost Key. Can I get you anything to drink?"

"I'm sorry?" Sam asked, right as Grant said, "Sparkling water for me."

"And for you? We have water, soda, or wine. Red, white, or sparkling."

"I—"

"Actually, could I have sparkling wine?" Grant asked like he should be drinking the Johnsons' liquor.

"Of course. And you?" the server asked again with the most practiced patience Sam had seen in years.

"I'll have the same."

"Wonderful. If you'll just step this way to the front of the house, I'll bring your beverages shortly."

"Thank you," Grant said, stepping through the door and turning to face Sam. He whispered, "Whoever the Johnsons are, their party is getting top-notch service."

"Let's just hope, whoever the Johnsons are, they don't realize that we aren't one of them," Sam said, shaking her head.

"Oh, we'll only be a second; I doubt they'll even notice." Grant smirked, then walked into the dark hallway and pushed aside a heavy red velvet curtain. Taking a deep breath, Sam stepped into the hallway and then into what was possibly the most exquisite room she had ever been in. Big frosted gallery windows lined one wall and bathed the entire place in a delicate light, while black-and-white tiles checked the floor. Strategically placed around the room were massive palms, ferns, and an array of lilies, their bright colors highlighting the clean, unadorned white walls, while an octagonal fountain in the middle of the room ran playfully over the sound of a piped-in string quartet.

"Wow," Sam whispered as she turned to look at the lighting. Out of the corner of her eye, she could see Grant standing at a simple check-in desk, his hands tucked into his pockets and a small, satisfied expression on his face.

"Was I right?"

"This is—"

"Sorry, we are closed to street traffic." A deeply uninterested-sounding woman with a long blonde ponytail stepped out from behind one of the curtained-off hallways and glared down at them.

"Ah yes. We're part of the Johnson party," Grant said, matching her bored tone as if it were his natural state.

"You're the son of Irish shipping magnate Carlyle Johnson?" she asked, raising a very well-groomed eyebrow and stepping behind the check-in desk.

"Cousin," Grant said, without flinching. This, Sam decided, was the upside of Grant's imperious nature. She would have given up on the whole shenanigan by now, but he was sticking to it as if he had every right to call himself an heir to a shipping empire.

"Right." The ponytail person's expression did not change, and she was opening her mouth to say something more when they were interrupted by a harried-looking person in an immaculate maroon suit.

"You're with the Johnsons? The wedding planner just called like twenty minutes ago to say that you had decided to cancel the engagement party."

"My cousin did, but we have a last-minute event that we thought we would check out the venue for. My admin called you a day or two ago to confirm the venue was available, I believe." Turning to Sam, he scowled and said, "If Sherilynn messed up again, I swear—"

"Not to worry, sir," the person in the suit jumped in. Extending a hand to Grant, they said, "My name is Yesenia."

"Grant, and this is Sam," Grant said, releasing Yesenia's hand and gesturing to her.

"Nice to meet you," Sam said, shaking Yesenia's hand and fighting the feeling of schadenfreude as Ponytail glared at them.

"Aren't you lovely? I assume you'll want the same sort of bridal amenities as the former future Mrs. Johnson?" Sam's mind had only just processed Yesenia's assumption when they added, "If so, I can show you our smaller wedding staging rooms and our exclusive pregathering spaces."

"Oh, I . . . we—" Sam stumbled, trying to find a way to explain that while the Johnsons might have wanted a wedding, she and her coworker wanted no such thing.

"She is lovely," Grant jumped in, his mischievous streak firing back up as he looked between Sam and Yesenia. "Well, would you like to see them, honey?"

Sam looked over at Grant, and their eyes met. In that look, it was like the two of them had an entire conversation—Grant raised an eyebrow, Sam blinked, and both of them smiled. Sam's apprehension melted. If they were going to be in the Johnson family, they were going to do this all the way. No need to discuss it. Their understanding of one another just clicked.

Turning to Yesenia, Sam said, "Thank you for the compliment. We would love to see the preparation rooms and the prewedding space."

"All right. Let's get started," Yesenia said, turning to walk into the venue.

Looking over at her, Grant tried to press a grin into a straight face before extending his arm to her. It was such a casual movement that Sam didn't think about it until she touched the fabric of his sweater. The material was thin enough that she could feel the warmth of his skin and the muscles of his forearm flex just slightly under her palm. Such a small gesture shouldn't have sent her mind reeling—she had basically clobbered the guy playing basketball—but for some reason this was different. It felt more intimate in a way she hadn't prepared for. Heat and craving swept over her in waves so intense that she wondered if she would be able to focus on anything other than the feel of him so close to her.

"Ready?" Grant asked.

Sam nodded and hoped that Grant would be more interested in the decor than whatever shade of pink had to have appeared on her face by now. Clearing her throat, she said, "Lead the way, future husband."

Grant snort-laughed, and Sam considered kicking herself. *Future husband . . . could I be any less chill right now?*

Letting Grant guide her up a few stairs into the room, she started to pay attention right as Yesenia said, "And the space is fully ADA compliant, so if you have guests who need ramp access, we are happy to work with you and them to make sure their needs are met."

"Uncle Yíchén will be delighted by that," Grant said, maintaining the bored-rich-boy manner. Sam snickered, and Grant looked over at her, simultaneously trying to give her the get-it-together look and fighting a smile himself. Sam made a mental note to ask him if he even had an Uncle Yichén.

While Yesenia rattled off facts about other well-heeled individuals who had recently used the space, Grant gently guided them around the room. With each step, Sam became more aware of their closeness. The feel of his sweater against her upper arm. The brush of his thigh against hers if they didn't walk in a perfectly straight line. His smell—

"I bet they have easels you could rent for the pictures your mom wants to display. That way she wouldn't have to ship or buy them." Grant's whisper interrupted her thoughts.

"Good idea." Sam realized that she needed to put some space between the two of them. He hadn't brought her here so she could think about his forearm. They were two not-enemies on a mission to find her mother a party venue so she could dedicate all her energy to opening the center; therefore, she needed to pay attention to the task at hand.

Taking a deep, mostly thought-cleansing breath, Sam released Grant's arm quickly, as if she were ripping off a bandage to avoid prolonging the pain. He looked down at the place she had been, then back at her with a question in his eyes. Ignoring how cold her arm felt without him next to her, she focused on Yesenia. "Do you by chance have easels available? I think we would like to have photos from our engagement shoot and our travels on display."

"Yes. We have some, as does the vendor we rent from . . ."

"Travels?" Grant quirked an eyebrow. Putting his hands in his pockets, he leaned close to her so they couldn't be heard, his shoulder brushing hers and triggering a cascade of sensation as he whispered, "Good one."

"Just playing my part." Sam tossed her hair playfully over her shoulder. Attempting to disregard the tingling of her skin where they'd just touched, she wondered how they had gotten so close to one another again. When she'd set out to create space to focus, this intimate huddle was not what she'd envisioned.

Out of the corner of her eye, she saw the server with the suspenders walking toward them with two glasses of sparkling wine. Breaking the spell Grant's nearness had on her, she backed away and flashed him her best this-is-acting smile, before turning to Suspenders with the drinks and saying, "Are those for us?"

"They are. Here you go, Miss . . ." Suspenders echoed her playful tone as they held out a glass to Sam, who passed it to Grant. Turning back to take her glass, she offered Suspenders a smile and opened her mouth to answer the question.

"Doctor."

"I'm sorry?" Suspenders said, blinking as if they'd just remembered Grant was there.

"She's a doctor." Irritation tinged Grant's voice, and Sam wondered what on earth could have prompted him to serve a death glare to poor Suspenders for the grand error of failing to anticipate her medical degree.

"Oh, I'm sorry."

"No worries. Sam is fine. Thank you for this," Sam said, holding up her glass.

"You're welcome, Dr. Sam," Suspenders said, maintaining the playful tone as they walked away.

Sam turned her attention back to Grant just in time to catch him rolling his eyes. "What?"

"'Miss'? That seems a little fishy when you know someone is getting married," Grant said, under his breath.

"Okay, Mr. Rules"—Sam held up her free hand and smirked—"excuse me, Dr. Rules. The thing is, we aren't actually getting married."

"They don't know that." Grant frowned into his glass of bubbles as he took a drink.

It took Sam everything in her not to laugh at his offended sense of propriety. "If this were anywhere else, you would have blown our cover. Lucky for you, rich people love getting angry over silly slights."

"And threatening to fire people." Grant chuckled, his scowl relaxing. "My apologies to Sherilynn."

"Come on. Let's catch up to Yesenia." Sam laughed, taking a sip of her drink and walking through an archway into the next room, where their guide was already rattling off facts.

The room was equally beautiful, with the same hidden-garden feel, but softer than the first room. The lighting had an almost pink feel to it, and the wrought iron fixtures had been swapped out for dainty gold sconces and chandeliers.

"This is one of our more intimate spaces. As you can see, if you want additional room, we can connect the two rooms, or this one does have its own entrance if you wanted a smaller gathering."

"A separate entrance is nice," Sam said, absently circling around the room. She stopped to touch what looked like a bamboo palm—to figure out if it was fake or just the best-cared-for plant in the world—and noticed Grant a few paces behind her.

Catching her eye, he smiled briefly before turning away to look at Yesenia. Sam couldn't put her finger on what she felt. It was like the room got a little colder without that smile, although she knew that was objectively not what was happening. If she was cold, she could put on her sweater. Medically speaking, that smile had nothing to do with regulating her body temperature. Or at least it shouldn't.

"Is there storage on site? For example, if we wanted to have photos or goodies shipped to the venue ahead of time?" Grant asked.

"Typically, we are able to store things for a week prior to the event, depending on the size of the items. We couldn't keep an elephant or anything, but framed images and gift bags should be fine."

"I see," Grant said, nodding at Yesenia. He turned back to Sam, an eyebrow raised as if to check in with her to see if the storage capacity met her approval, and her heart squeezed. For all the jokes and sneaking around, he was taking her mom's party seriously. He didn't even know her mom. There was no reason for him to be this thoughtful. He turned back to Yesenia and asked, "And what about venue prep? Would we be able to get into the space early, say, to arrange the photos?"

"Sure. Or if you have a diagram, we would be happy to do our best to get everything lined up; that way you are only approving things on the day of. Save you both time."

"It's really more of her mother's approval," Grant said, wrinkling his nose and trying not to laugh at his own joke.

Yesenia laughed at the first layer of the joke, then started chatting about different event caterers they had used in this space. Sam wandered over to another practically perfect plant, still smiling at the second layer of Grant's joke.

Reaching out to touch the shiny green leaf of a small banana plant, Sam determined that it was, in fact, a real plant. She was just about to ask Yesenia how they cared for all these beautiful palms when she noticed Grant slowly meandering in her direction again, as if the paint on the wall five feet from her were the most interesting paint he had ever run across. It dawned on her that maybe he wasn't all that interested in looking around. After all, he had been here before. He might be in this corner of the room because she was in this corner of the room.

Something about having Grant as a shadow made her smile in spite of herself. Yes, he was hard to read and inaccessibly put together. But under all those layers he might like her company. It was sweet and unexpected.

She certainly hadn't meant to, but somehow, Sam found herself smiling over at him. Waiting for him to stop pretending the paint was fascinating and look at her. Her heart thudded in her chest. One beat. Two beats. Then three. She was just about to come to her senses and move on when he finally looked over at her . . . and smiled. It wasn't the big brash smile he usually wore. This was a quiet smile. The kind of smile that meant everything but communicated nothing. That smile was intoxicating.

"Hey," Sam said, doing her best to seem casual as she released the banana plant and wandered toward him.

"Hey. Do you want to see the private suites next?" Grant asked, looking over their shoulder at Yesenia, who was conspicuously giving them space to discuss who-knew-what.

"I mean, we can do that." Sam shrugged, feeling tongue tied all of a sudden. Why hadn't she come up with some kind of cool thing to say? Instead, she was going to tour the part of the building that she had entirely forgotten about somewhere between getting her glass of bubbles and Grant's smile.

"Right." His expression transitioned back into Business Grant, and Sam suddenly hated the look. She wasn't in a rush to see anything. He turned to face Yesenia, and instinctively, Sam placed a hand on his upper arm to get his attention. Grant looked down at her hand, then back at her, questions written on his face.

Letting her hand drop, Sam said, "Actually, I was wondering. How was this place set up when your sister played here?"

Grant's expression melted into another warm, gentle smile, and Sam almost melted right along with it. "They used this side room as more of a food area. The show was in the main room. She was playing as part of a youth-orchestra fundraising event. You know, where these programs trot out their best three players and have them show off for the donors."

"Peak big-brother-duty event," Sam joked.

"Oh, totally."

"Did you ever feel bad about not being a musician?" Sam asked, partly out of curiosity and partly because she couldn't imagine what it was like to sit through his sister's concerts knowing his parents wanted that for him too. The pressure alone would have kept Sam playing the piano until judgment day. "How did your parents take it when you told them no?"

"It's funny. I used to feel so bad about not being a musician. I was so worried about letting my parents down. The truth was, I'd been mediocre at it for so long they saw it coming a mile off. I feel like my mom gave me a hug and delivered this slightly dramatic monologue about me finding my true path. I think my dad just made a joke about not having to pay for lessons anymore."

"Must have been nice." Sam's heart squeezed. She and Grant had family expectations in common. But where she couldn't seem to make her mother understand, he felt loved.

"You know, it was. Not feeling the comparison between my sisters and me also helped our relationship tremendously."

"I can imagine. I mean, not the part where my parents would ever be cool about me not doing what they want. But the part where you and your sisters get along better." Sam laughed, hoping to cover the gaping hole in her own family story with a joke. The idea that someone could disappoint their parents and still want to see their family felt like the cognitive equivalent of putting a shoe on the wrong foot. Instinctively, she knew it was possible for people to do this, but she couldn't figure out how to make the same happen for herself.

"I got lucky in the parent department." Grant paused and looked up at the ceiling, as if the rest of his thoughts were up there. After a moment, he turned his gaze back to her and added, "In the end, I was the one beating myself up over not being a musician. I mean, don't get me wrong—there was definitely an adjustment period, and they still make me play at holidays and things, but I don't mind that. I think my being honest made everyone happier in the end."

"I want to be invited to a holiday party so I can hear you play." Sam smiled over at him. A small piece of her hoped that if she hung around Grant long enough, whatever magic made telling your family a difficult truth and reaching an understanding would rub off on her. Maybe family could become easy and less messy for her too.

"Trust me. Time has not made me better. You don't want to hear me play." Grant laughed.

"Agree to disagree." Sam shrugged and Grant shook his head. "Finish telling me about your sister and the staff."

"Oh, right. So it was a big deal for my sister to be selected for the showcase so young, and my parents had bought a special dress for the occasion. The food was amazing, and they offered it to her, but she was afraid of getting even a crumb on her dress, so she wouldn't eat anything. Spent the whole night gazing at the buffet longingly. My dad told the caterers, and they actually boxed up all the fancy stuff so she could try it once she got home."

"That is adorable," Sam said, watching him light up as he talked about his family. She was simply enjoying the glow of the nostalgia he was basking in.

Grant turned and began guiding them back into the main room. Gesturing toward the fountain area, he kept his voice low as he said, "They had her set up right over there. Obviously, they want the donors sitting up front, so my dad and I just kind of hovered back here. At one point, I went over to get a drink—I'd just turned twenty-one, so basically I had to show off—and I come back, and my dad is all choked up watching her play. The staff actually brought him a cocktail napkin so he could wipe his eyes. He was so proud of her."

For a moment, Sam didn't say anything, afraid that she would break the spell. Instead, she just watched him, his gaze directed at the floor where his father would have stood, a smile playing with one side of his mouth. This memory was personal and quiet. It still had Grant's pride attached to it, but this was a soft satisfaction. There was no bravado connected to this, just an older brother who was proud of his little sister and found joy in having a tenderhearted father.

The sound of Yesenia's dress shoes clicking across the floor broke Grant's reverie, and he looked up suddenly, forcing Sam to look away.

"Anyway, they have good staff here," Grant said, the gentle version of him evaporating in an instant. "Should we go look at those dressing rooms?"

"I mean, we should. They were the selling point, after all," Sam said, pointedly ignoring the ache she felt as the moment passed.

"Shall we?" Grant's lips quirked into a half smile as he extended his elbow to her again.

Sam glanced at the elbow, then up at him. Taking a deep breath, she looped her arm through his and said, "Lead the way."

Chapter Thirteen

It took everything in Sam not to bounce up and down as the ice cream attendant handed her a cone full of green-chili ice cream. She even managed to wait until Grant accepted a deeply standard-sounding mango ice cream, and they made it out of the store before taking a lick. Closing her eyes, she let the surprising sweetness wash over her tongue, getting just a tiny kick of spice on the back end of her first taste. Opening her eyes, she sighed, as people Hula-Hooped in the park up the street.

"Is the ice cream weird?" Grant asked, watching her with a mix of apprehension and skepticism. "It sounded weird to me."

"It is not weird. It is delicious." Sam took another swipe at her ice cream before asking, "Is yours boring? It sounded boring."

"Who thinks mango is boring?" Grant laughed, and the small knot in Sam's chest loosened. When Grant had suggested they get ice cream, she was worried that the spell cast by the Lost Key would be broken. But his sense of humor seemed to want to stick around.

"It's boring when you have flavors like green chili, avocado, and black sesame to try," Sam continued to needle. Half grinning over at him, she watched as he shook his head and tucked into his cone.

"I had no idea you had such strong feelings about ice cream."

"Oh, but I do. Jehan and I are using ice cream as a reason to get out and see the city. I don't have a lot of time off, but the time I do have is spent trying different ice cream spots around the Bay."

"I saw Jehan at the coffee cart a while back, and she mentioned that you two went to a place in Oakland," Grant said, absentmindedly steering them toward the park.

Sam felt heat creep into her cheeks. That trip had been a month ago. Grant had retained that little bit of information about her just so that he could recall it if the opportunity to make her happy ever magically presented itself. She was making a mental note to add it to the astonishingly fast-growing list of nice traits about Grant when she checked herself. How did she know he was listening for details about her? For all she knew, her overly enthusiastic roommate shipped them so hard that she'd cornered him and drilled it into his brain.

Clearing his throat, Grant asked, "So how did you get roped into throwing a party for your mom?"

"Oof. Long story," Sam sighed.

"We've got time. Unless you don't want to talk about it."

She rarely wanted to talk about her mother, but something in the way Grant said it made Sam want to be honest with him. After all, their situations were different, but if anyone could understand struggling with family expectations, it was him. Taking a deep breath, she said, "I love my mom. I have to start with that, because otherwise the rest of this sounds kind of . . ." Pausing for a moment, she nodded her head a fraction of an inch from side to side until the right words came to her. "It just sounds mean."

"Okay," Grant said, stopping with his ice cream about six inches from his face to look at her. "Mean how?"

"She wouldn't admit it, but my mom thinks of her kids as extensions of herself. She is proud of us, but she doesn't actually want us living separate lives away from her. Our lives are her hobby and, in some ways, her personality. She gets super worked up if we deviate from her plan."

"What do you mean by *deviate*?"

"She was convinced I should be a biology teacher like her and stay close to home. Even when I was accepted to medical school, she just kind of pretended I wasn't becoming a doctor. Then when I left Ohio . . ."

Sam paused, and Grant looked over at her. Grimacing, he asked, "Was it yikes?"

"Worse. She refused to speak to me for two months. That would have been fine. But with her it isn't just silence. She does passive-aggressive stuff like getting my dad to encourage me to 'see her side,' like I'm the one being ridiculous."

"All this because you moved?" Grant said, doing his best to keep his shock under wraps.

"It gets weirder. She started leaving me off the group chat, so my brother had to screenshot or call with important updates. For example, when their basement flooded and they needed to stay in a hotel for a couple days. Or when Mom needed to get a mole checked out. According to my father, hearing my voice was too painful. But like all things with my mom, eventually she gets tired of whatever punishment she has imposed and comes up with a reason to reengage with us. It's weird, but stuff like helping her throw a party puts her at the center of attention and reminds her that we love her. The parties are my and Isaiah's way of compromising with her."

"I think being starved for attention happens to a lot of moms. In my case, my mom just has a job that gives it to her, so our family isn't her only source of specialness." Grant's voice was gentle, as if he were holding a delicate idea on the tip of his tongue and speaking too plainly would cause it to break. In some ways, her and her mother's relationship was as fragile as he made it feel. Realistically, Sam had nearly shattered it just by moving to the Bay Area.

Trying to laugh off the uneasy feeling, Sam said, "Grant, we may not always agree, but when we do, it's because of our mothers."

"Probably." Grant shrugged. "What do you think caused her to behave this way?"

Sam took a big chunk out of her ice cream to buy herself thinking time. Eventually, she said, "My parents married young, and my dad was in the navy, so we moved a lot. Her kids were her social life, which I kind of understand. Creating rich friend connections is hard when you move around a bunch, so she has tons of casual friends but can't really call anyone to dish about her life. I think that by the time we settled down, she'd forgotten how to develop hobbies or deep friendships, so she just kept leaning on Isaiah and me."

"Where is your dad in all of this?"

"Possibly willfully oblivious but stepping in with the occasional reality check when her demands get too outlandish. Since she hasn't asked for an animatronic elephant for the party, he isn't required to speak up yet."

Grant looked over at her to judge how serious she was about the elephant, so Sam did what anyone with a deadly serious friend would do—kept a straight face for exactly five seconds, then burst into laughter.

"So I take it the elephant isn't an actual demand then?"

"Not yet." Sam shook her head and crunched down on her cone.

"Good, because I was gonna say that the Lost Key was very clear about not being able to do that."

"But wouldn't you love to see that person at the front desk's face if we tried," Sam chuckled.

"Talk about a catastrophic request." Grant laughed. "We'd probably stop her heart."

"Which is fine, because you told everyone that I'm a doctor."

Grant tilted his head back and let out a big rumbling laugh. "I won't apologize for that."

"I would never ask you to." Sam smirked, then looked over at him.

Grant's features had softened again, as if he was thinking about something he held close. After a moment he said, "It's not my place to tell you how to manage your relationship with your mom. But if you want a boundary, it seems like you may need to set it yourself."

Sam knew objectively that she hadn't stopped walking, yet it felt like Grant had hit pause on all her thoughts in the most painful way. As much as she didn't want to admit it, he had a point. There was absolutely no evidence to suggest that if she managed to pull off all her mother's requests, then she would magically be okay with Sam making her own choices. But how could she just stop doing all this? What would happen to their relationship if she tried to renegotiate the terms? She wasn't ready to give up on her mother. The compromises were still better than letting her parents down and getting cut off again. She'd rather be spread too thin than not know if her dad went to the hospital or force Isaiah to speak on her behalf. The strain was just too much when a solution was at hand. A boundary might have helped Grant with his family, but Sam would have to take baby steps.

The feel of uneven pavement underneath her feet pulled Sam out of her reflective moment. She could sense Grant monitoring her. He wasn't watching her, more reading her energy and giving her space to process his words and respond. She just wasn't sure she was ready to be quite that vulnerable with him. After all, one ice cream didn't make him a trusted confidant or anything. And like he'd said after the Anjo interview, he had a vested interest in her resolving things with her mother so she could focus on opening the center and keep crises off his desk.

"You are probably right." Sam took another crunchy bite of ice cream cone to break the tension. "On the upside, Isaiah may be the favorite, but with the Lost Key, I'm gonna give him a run for his money."

Grant chuckled under his breath, as if he could appreciate the joke but wasn't quite ready to let his line of questioning go. As he took a bite out of his sugar cone, Sam focused on their surroundings. They were at the edge of a grassy park dotted with people lying on blankets, enjoying bottles of wine and lying out to catch a bit of sun. She heard kids shrieking as they rolled down the hill, sweaty from running as their parents pestered them about sunscreen and drinking water. A vendor was dragging a cooler and a basket of baked goods that Sam strongly suspected contained more than just flour and sugar in them, occasionally stopping to offer people a cold drink or a cookie.

"Is that a weed man?" Sam asked the first question that came to her mind.

Grant's laugh was full as he shook his head. "It's Dolores Park. You have to have a weed man. Otherwise, you don't know if you are in the right place."

"Go figure. Dolores Park is good for weed."

"It's really more edibles. They run articles about the best ones in a couple of the alt newspapers," Grant said, offhandedly, as if "The Best Edibles in the Park" were a normal newspaper story. After a beat, he grinned and added, "They also do movies in the park. I took my little cousins to watch *Finding Nemo* a couple of years ago. It was actually delightful."

"Was it delightful because you ate an edible?" Sam teased.

"I'm a medical professional and won't confirm or deny anything." Grant snorted at his own joke. "Really, I was thinking more about how uncommonly warm it was. Usually, the little ones get cold, and you end up giving them all of your layers and carrying them to the car halfway through the movie when they pass out."

"Well, that's adorable," Sam said, fighting to keep the look that accompanied cartoon hearts off her face. "I've always wanted to go to a movie in the park, but my friends and I could never get it together back in Ohio. The only time we managed to plan something, a freak summer storm rolled through and crushed the dream."

"Whomp whomp." Grant's tone gently mocked.

"It was whomp whomp," Sam said, laughter seeping into the edge of her voice. "Thank you for acknowledging that."

"You'll just have to go to movies in the park in California. The parks department is running them now, I think. I'll text you the schedule. So not to change the subject, but Duke waving from the window," Grant said, reaching out toward a trash can to throw out the napkin that had once been wrapped around his ice cream cone. "You said he had questions. Are you going to tell me what they were now?"

Sam's panic alarm sprang to life as she tried to come up with an answer that wasn't *my roommates will think this sounds suspiciously like a date.* Although now that she thought about it, she could see how walking slowly around a park and eating ice cream might seem like she was on a date . . .

Nope. Sam checked herself. They had independently paid for their own ice creams, for crying out loud. There was no earthly way she was going to tell Grant that her friends—and apparently her myth-based, completely fabricated, scientifically nonexistent lizard brain—thought they might be dating. She might be willing to be honest about her mother, but there was not a snowball's chance in hell she would be honest about why Duke had been in the window.

"Ah, well, Duke wanted to know what kind of car you drove because I said it was nice, and he and Jehan said that only drug dealers or trust fund babies have fancy cars as fellows. I said your parents worked in the arts and nonprofits, so a trust seemed unlikely. I guess Duke wanted to see the car for himself."

For a moment, Grant just blinked at her, a stunned look glued to his face. And then he started to laugh, that same glowing look from the Lost Key flooding over him. Sam felt her pulse slow down and her own smile return as she watched him grin.

"Sam, I hope you didn't put money on me."

"Why?" She narrowed her eyes. Using her best suspicious voice, she asked, "Are you the Dolores Park weed man?"

Grant laughed even harder and shook his head. "No. I do have a trust fund, though."

"What?" Sam balked. Maybe she misunderstood how much money opera singers made. Google could be misleading.

"My biological father—his name is Gary—is a banker based in New York and Hong Kong. He is where the trust comes from."

"Oh," Sam said, letting silence fall between them for a minute before echoing Grant's words from earlier. "You don't have to talk about it if you don't want to."

"I actually don't mind." Grant smiled over at her, then said, "My mom got pregnant when they were both in college. At the time Gary didn't want to be a father. My mom met my dad, Wei, not long after I was born. They married when I was two, and he legally adopted me. As far as I am concerned, I only have one dad—Wei. He read me bedtime stories, came to my soccer games, took me to some god-awful piano lessons, and saw me graduate from medical school. My dad did the emotional work that dads do, so that title remains his."

"Makes sense," Sam said, watching Grant's face soften again as he listed all the things his dad did for him.

"Anyhow, I guess when I was around ten, Gary got in touch with my mom. She doesn't like to talk about it, but as far as I can tell, she worked it out so that whatever he would have wanted to pay in child support, he would put into a trust. To be honest, I don't think she thought about how much money was actually on the table. I think she thought maybe a year or two of college and then he'd get over it and move on." Grant laughed, then added, "To her credit, she never lied to me. When Gary was in town, she would give me the option to see him. Sometimes I did; sometimes I didn't. Anyway, when I turned eighteen, Gary actually made good on his promise. I didn't need all the money to get me through school, so my trust turned into my car and house fund."

"That is better than college. Those car seats feel like a hug."

"I know, right? I love those things. They make traffic a luxury experience." Grant beamed over at her as they walked back toward where they had parked.

For a moment, Sam let herself war over whether to ask Grant any questions about his story. Part of her was afraid that if she asked the wrong thing, he might close up again, and she would get Business Grant back. But another part of her wanted to know more about him. How he spent his time outside of the hospital, basketball, and apparently, having the time of his life in traffic.

"Do you still see Gary?" she asked, carefully watching his face for any signs that he might be done with the subject.

"If it's convenient for me, we might grab coffee, but I don't go out of my way." Grant shrugged one shoulder, then scowled slightly. "I don't typically tell people about Gary. Does that sound cold?"

"Not any colder than me saying my mom is controlling." Sam chuckled and watched the lines on Grant's face relax. Somewhere in the back of her mind, she registered that he might be nervous about what she thought of him, and it made her heart squeeze just a little. For good measure, she threw in, "But I'm coldhearted. Hence why I like ice cream so much."

"In that case, I guess we'll just be coldhearted together. Must be why we are engaged," Grant said, beaming at her corny joke as they approached the block where the car was parked. Pulling his keys from his pocket, he said, "What do you say, fiancée? Want to check out another venue? Or do you need more weird-flavored ice cream?"

"Is both an option?" Sam laughed.

"I think I can arrange for that." Grant winked at her as he unlocked the car, and Sam was almost positive that if she hadn't been holding so tightly to her heart, it might have floated away.

Chapter Fourteen

"No wonder the chaplains were so willing to share."

Duke's voice bounced off the sad beige walls and shook Sam out of her horror-induced stupor. When Dr. Franklin had said the space needed work, she'd thought he meant it needed paint or something. This room didn't just need paint; it needed an act of God.

On one side of the room, decrepit-looking benches were piled high. Dust and spiderwebs that looked too costumey to be real hung off them. On the other side of the room was a series of scattered folding chairs, ancient desks, a tipped-over garbage bin, and one half-deflated BOSU ball. The one bright spot was a stained glass window depicting a peaceful garden scene, which was mysteriously mounted on a wall with no windows.

"The head of the chaplains and therapy services swore that the window works if we change the light bulb," Grant said helpfully. Taking in Duke's look of skepticism, he added, "I don't think an imam would lie."

"There is a first time for everything," Theo said under his breath. Jehan snickered at the joke, which she quickly turned into a cough when Kaiya glared at her.

Turning her attention to Sam and Grant, Kaiya asked, "This is what we've got?"

"Yes," Sam said, feeling disappointment set in. It wasn't really the grand unveiling she had wanted to give Kaiya and the team. She had hoped to at least run down here and look at the room before everyone else, but of course, a doctor's schedule was never that simple. Instead, she'd been called in to observe the birth of triplets, an experience that was great for her continued education but terrible for her preparation.

"And this is who is going to help us get the room together?" Kaiya sniffed at the stale air, then looked at the group of helpers Sam had cobbled together.

"That's right." Sam tried to sound upbeat. When she'd recruited everyone, it seemed like enough people; three players from her and Grant's respective basketball teams, plus Duke, Jehan, and two other emergency doctors Jehan had managed to guilt into helping. Of course, now that she was taking the mess in, Sam wished she'd recruited the entire hospital basketball league.

Finally, Kaiya shrugged and said, "We'll make it work."

Next to her, Sam heard Grant's audible sigh and looked over just in time to see his shoulders relax. After Kaiya had agreed to be part of the project, Sam had sent Grant literally everything she'd written. He hadn't said much about her at the time, but given the way he was acting, Sam suspected she wasn't the only one who was a little starstruck.

Nodding at Kaiya, Grant said, "All right. While Kaiya works on a new layout for the room, why don't we get busy cleaning up? Theo, Raphael, and Kelly, would you all be up for carrying the benches and old furniture down to storage? Jehan and the emergency team, maybe you all could be in charge of clearing up the dust and dirt. And Duke, I'm sorry, but you are the tallest, and before we can get this room painted professionally, someone has to take the cobwebs off the walls."

"Well, what are you and Sam gonna do?" Duke asked, frowning at the walls like they might bite him. Sam almost laughed. Grant had no way of knowing that he had literally just assigned the biggest neat freak in the entire hospital to lean up against dirt.

"We're going to take on the most emotionally taxing job of all." Grant half smiled and paused a beat for dramatic effect before saying, "Putting together IKEA furniture."

"Woof. Good luck with that," someone from the emergency team laughed.

"If you want to sit on the dirty floor and wonder where the hell I9 is, you're welcome to join us." Sam smiled sweetly at Duke while the rest of the room started to shuffle toward their assignments.

Duke looked down at the floor, then back at the walls before saying, "I'll stay standing, thanks."

For a moment, Sam and Grant watched Duke shuffle toward the wall in silence as if he were about to face a firing squad. Turning to look at Sam, Grant said, "Do you think he is gonna pass out before he gets to the wall, or . . ."

"He might. You never really know with Duke."

Grant smirked and shook his head, then looked over his shoulder at the small mountain of filing cabinets, desks, and storage crates that needed constructing. Kaiya had rightly suggested that they get the chaplains and doulas furniture on casters so the room could be rearranged as needed. At the time, Sam had thought this was a great idea, but now, staring down at about a zillion wheels she needed to attach, she wished they had the budget for something preassembled. Sighing, she said, "You ready to feel deeply inadequate and fight with a tiny wrench?"

When Grant didn't immediately respond, Sam looked up to find him staring at her hard. Locking eyes with her, he said, "I was born ready."

Sam's memory flashed back to their interview at Anjo as Grant laughed so hard the sound would have echoed off the walls if they weren't plastered with dust. Sam snorted and shook her head. He must have been waiting weeks for her to say something that would let him make that joke. Watching him wheezing at his own humor, a small part of Sam enjoyed the fact that the Grant she'd met in front of that building wasn't as stuffy as she'd thought he was. Even better, he was, deep down, a nerd who planned his jokes.

"I deserved that," Sam said when Grant looked up, his body still shaking slightly as he tried to get his giggles under control.

"I mean, I kind of earned it the first time," Grant said, shaking his head.

"Kind of?" Sam reached for a filing cabinet box.

"Hey, I admitted it. That is a big step for me." Grant smirked, then reached for an identical box.

Dropping to the floor, Sam was beginning to lay out pieces of the cabinet when Grant sat next to her. Quietly, he began to take apart his box, setting out the pieces next to hers. He was smiling, and if Sam were a betting woman, she would guess he was still laughing at his joke.

Someone managed to produce a portable speaker and put on Motown hits for the group. Sam hummed along to the Elgins as the pair of them worked in companionable silence. Every so often she or Grant would lean over to look at the other's work, effectively double-checking themselves against each other. Outside of that, they were quiet for a time.

"This was a mistake." Grant's voice shattered Sam's concentration and interrupted Stevie Wonder singing about building a world around someone.

"What was?" Sam looked around, feeling a bit frantic. The basketball team had already taken most of the benches out of the room, and as far as she could tell, Jehan and the emergency team had already swept the floors. Even Duke had managed to make progress on the dreaded walls.

"Nothing is wrong," Grant said, reading her panicked expression. "I meant that we shouldn't have sat so close together, because our supplies have gotten mixed up. I think I have been taking your screws and those little peg things. Do you need an extra peg? Or a screw?"

Sam blanched, then took a deep breath through her nose, her voice shaking as she fought laughter. "Do I need a peg or a screw?"

"Yes." Grant nodded, extending a handful of screws toward her. "I have extra."

The guy was the king of double entendre, and here he was missing a golden opportunity. Sam's eyes went wide with the effort of not yelling a that's-what-she-said joke. Sure, sex jokes weren't exactly appropriate at the office, but technically neither of them was on the clock. Blinking at him once more, she said, "You have an extra peg, and you would like to give me a screw."

For a minute Grant stared at her as if she weren't making sense. Then something clicked, and his face flushed nearly fire-engine red. "I didn't mean—"

"Sure." Sam nodded and drew the vowel out in the word as she spoke.

"No, truly, I do have extra and—"

"I believe you." She did not sound like she believed him.

Grant's eyes grew wide as Sam's shoulders started to shake with the effort of not cracking up. Smiling in spite of himself, he said, "Here. Take these . . . things."

"Can't say what you really mean, huh?" Sam managed to choke out in between laughs.

"Well, no. I can't because you're being prurient."

"Prurient?" Sam's whole body shook with laughter. "Me? Never."

"Here." Grant held out his hand again.

"SAT words won't save you. I know the truth," Sam said, taking a deep breath and reaching for the screws in his palm. She was just about to come up with another joke at his expense when their hands met.

Unlike that day at the Lost Key, this touch was not the warm and comforting feeling of having another body close to hers. This was something altogether different. This felt like a shock of static electricity—unexpected and intoxicating. Like if Sam dropped the screws and touched him again, her hands might be interested in doing something more than just feeling the smooth skin of his palm. Neither one of them was laughing anymore, and Sam wondered if he was quiet because she was quiet or if he felt something too.

Just then, Marvin Gaye's voice started the opening notes of "Ain't No Mountain High Enough." Kaiya's singing voice shot around the room and was quickly joined by the emergency team. Grant cleared his throat at the same time Sam withdrew her hand. Taking more time than was strictly necessary to set the little bits of metal down, Sam was grateful that everyone else's attention was on the song. *No one saw that,* she reassured herself.

Or at least she could convince herself that she was alone in the feeling until she looked over at Grant, who suddenly became very fascinated with tightening a puny little bolt. The air between them grew thick, and Sam began to wonder if they would be doomed to spend the rest of the afternoon in sexual-tension limbo until Grant took an audible breath and said, "So how's Jehan's engagement party planning going?"

"Sorry, what?" Sam felt like her brain had stalled out. Of all the things she had expected him to say, bringing up Jehan's party was somewhere between *What do you think of cubism?* and *Have you ever wondered what it would be like to be a mascot?*

"Jehan's party. She mentioned it the other day. I thought you were part of the group that is doing a tasting for it."

"I am." Sam felt like her voice sounded slow as she tried to process what seemed like a very abrupt subject change. "It's going well. We have the tasting in four days. Once her fiancé arrives."

"And where are you all headed again?" Grant asked so politely that Sam almost wanted to strangle him. Clearly, he thought that whatever had happened between them did not need to be discussed. Meanwhile, Sam was racking her brains trying to remember anything other than what had just happened thirty seconds ago.

"Dorothy's. It's a place that specializes in 'unique, small bites,' according to their website."

"That could be fun."

"Except for the part where Travis is a vegan who hates spicy food," Sam said under her breath.

"Enjoy just eating white bread then." Grant smiled over at her before attaching a set of wheels to his cabinet. "And what about your mom? Has she seen the light and agreed with us that the Lost Key is amazing? Or did she want to go with that restaurant with the mosaic and the fancy bathrooms?"

Sam rolled her eyes. "If by *agreed* you mean, *Did you finally wear her down after an hour and a half of questions about the Lost Key?* then yes. She agreed."

"Well, I think my idea is excellent, so I am just going to believe that she'll be excited once she sees the place," Grant said, looking pleased with himself as he set his finished filing cabinet upright.

"I wouldn't hold your breath," Sam said, fighting to get her own final wheel attached. "With my mom, it is better if you just set your own metric for happiness."

"And what would that be?" Grant said, pulling another cabinet box toward himself.

"I'm gonna vote for 'I ate delicious ice cream while looking for that venue, so even if she has a meltdown about it, I still discovered a place that serves green-chili ice cream,'" Sam said, tilting her filing cabinet upright and rocking it back and forth to be sure she had installed the wheels properly, which of course she hadn't.

"In that case, I'm calling it a success because I got to hang out with you."

Sam stopped fussing with the crooked wheel and found Grant looking directly at her. His gaze scanned her face for any indication that she was picking up what he had laid before her. Sam felt herself soften like room temperature butter, and she smiled. Not fifteen seconds ago she had been irritated by him changing the theoretical subject of their chemistry, and now here he was, bringing it back up in a gentler way.

Something about the softness brought Sam back to the Lost Key. Maybe she was wrong to expect bold declarations from Grant. Just because he seemed to take up a room with his confidence in their day-to-day work lives didn't mean that he shouted his most private thoughts. In fact, at the Lost Key, he hadn't said a word about his experience in the venue until she'd shown an interest in it. Even then, talking about his father and sister was a quiet affair. He didn't run all over the venue. It had been a slow, more intimate sharing.

For so long she had put off thinking about her chemistry with Grant, because it seemed improbable that he was sincere. If she looked at this moment knowing Grant's quiet side, then the decision was hers to make. It might have been for a while, and that scared her. Sam opened her mouth, not entirely sure what words were going to come out. "We did—"

"I need more rags to wipe things down with," Duke announced over Sam's struggling sentence and the sound of the Vandellas.

Both Grant's and Sam's eyes darted toward Duke's lanky frame as he left the room, carrying an armful of dirty rags. The giant room was nearly empty since the basketball team had finished carrying the old furniture out of the space. The only people that remained were Jehan and one of her friends and Kaiya, who was furiously scribbling notes against a wall. Otherwise, she and Grant were alone.

Sam tried to memorize the tender expression on his face, down to the touch of trepidation hanging around the corners of his dark eyes.

"We did have fun, didn't we?" she said, lightly tempting fate. Sam wasn't sure what she wanted from Grant, but she couldn't ignore all the signs the universe seemed to be sending her just now. "I'd do that again."

"Kaiya, we are getting coffee. Do you want to come?" Jehan said, more loudly than her regular speaking voice. Sam suspected that if she took her eyes off Grant, she would see her roommate telegraphing meaningful glances between those remaining in the room, the pair of them, and the door.

"Look for venues again?" Grant sounded unconvinced as he arched an eyebrow. Apparently, he was going to make her spell it out for him.

"I mean hang out with you again." Sam watched him just long enough to see the tension around his eyes ease.

For a moment, Grant was silent, smiling down at the box he was only halfheartedly trying to open. Looking back at her, he said, "You know, you were right about all of this."

"About what? The furniture?" Sam asked.

"About the center. It's a great idea." Grant was quiet as he looked at her. "I doubted you, but I was wrong, and you were right."

"Oh," Sam said, suddenly feeling flustered. After taking a beat to look around the empty room and regain herself, she said, "Well, I wouldn't mind if you said that again."

Grant snorted. "What? That you were right?"

"If you really want to do it for me, you could always throw in the 'I was wrong' part too," Sam laughed, then gently wheeled her fixed filing cabinet next to Grant's finished one.

"I was wrong, and you were right." Grant's smile was indulgent as he watched her.

"Music to my ears. I could listen to it all day," Sam said, scooting a little closer to Grant as she reached across him to pull another box toward herself. She had just gotten her hand around the edge when his voice came again.

"I was wrong." This time, he sounded different. The joke in his voice had been replaced with something hotter. This was dirty talk without any double entendre required.

She was suddenly extremely aware of how close they were, her head just a few inches from his chest, her arms nearly across his lap as she pulled on the filing cabinet box. When he exhaled, she could feel his breath whispering against the back of her neck.

Sam let go of the box and straightened up, just enough to see his face without leaning away from him. All her blood seemed to be rushing away from her brain to other, lower parts of her body, essentially starving her brain of the oxygen she needed to think of anything other than how Grant smelled. If she could have thought, she would have encouraged her brain to look anywhere other than his lips. Instead, she would have the memory of him licking them right along with the sound of his voice, quiet and low, saying, "You were right."

The last thread of common sense snapped, and Sam leaned toward him. She was going to kiss those lips. Hell, if he played his cards right, she would rip that shirt off here and now. As she angled herself closer to him, Grant placed his hand on her hip. God, did she want to be touched like that more. She was so close to him that she could almost taste the very thing she had been trying not to fantasize about for weeks.

"I'm back!"

Duke's voice ricocheted around the room and blew a roughly two-foot wedge between her and Grant so fast that Sam was dizzy from the motion. Or maybe that was just the change in her blood pressure as she worked not to murder Duke with a piece of particleboard shelving. For his part, Grant looked like he had experienced a close brush with an out-of-control car.

"Oh . . ." Duke stopped in the doorway, holding some folded-up surgical cloths. Everyone was silent just long enough for Sam's breathing to return to normal and, with it, the flow of oxygen to her brain.

"Hey, Duke," Sam said, trying to force some nothing-to-see-here cheer into her voice. With the return of her reasonable cognitive capacity, Sam experienced several colliding thoughts, the most prevalent of which was, *What kind of blockhead tries to kiss her coworker?*

While Grant blinked from Sam to Duke and back, her brain started to whir. What had she been thinking? Or better yet, not thinking? She was plenty busy trying to get her life together without the added pressure of even the most casual relationship. And Grant didn't strike her as casual. Perfect people weren't casual people. If anything, that man would be overly complicated. And she absolutely didn't need any more complicated relationships.

If she was looking for a sign about Grant from the universe, Duke interrupting them was a giant, flashing neon one. No matter what tension she felt, she and Grant were, at their core, not compatible. This was a bad idea, a crisis even, that Duke had unintentionally averted for her. She should send him a gift basket. She would shove this moment into the file in her brain labeled *inappropriate relationships* and forget about it in a dusty corner.

Taking a page out of Grant's book, she changed the subject. "Glad you came back, Duke. You want some help with those dustrags?"

Brushing her hands off, she jumped up and smiled apologetically at a still-surprised Grant, careful not to make eye contact with either man. She thanked whatever deity was currently occupying the chaplains' old office for the intervention. At least this was one debacle she wouldn't have to pray about later.

Chapter Fifteen

"See, I choose to engage in capitalism as a mechanism for improving the world," Travis said from the front seat as their rideshare crept along Geary toward Dorothy's. "Jehan, on the other hand, insists that there is no ethical consumption under capitalism. So she keeps working at these little hospitals and NGOs, even though she could make so much more money as a medical concierge. So we'll be stuck paying off her school loans for decades."

It took herculean effort for Sam not to slam her head into the car door as Travis spoke. He smiled over his shoulder at Jehan as if her adherence to public service were the most adorable thing he'd ever condescended to care about.

"What a unique perspective," Duke said, laying on exactly none of his charm. For whatever reason, it hadn't occurred to Travis that the six-foot-four dude might need extra legroom, so her usually easygoing roommate was folded up like a pretzel in the back seat, making him extra cranky.

Jehan wrinkled her nose for a split second, as if deciding whether or not to mention a foul smell, then shrugged at Sam with a nonverbal, he's-so-silly smile fixed to her face. If Sam had to guess, Jehan didn't think he was being silly at all. But then again, her friend wasn't one to make a scene, especially when they were on their way to have a good time. Giving her head a shake, she said, "I think it's the dark-blue building on the right."

"Praise God," Duke whispered as the car stopped. As Travis and Jehan linked hands and walked through the front door, he hung back to throw Sam a warning look.

"What?" Sam whispered under her breath. "Don't look at me like that."

"I can already see your little brain working. Play nice."

"You're one to talk, Mr. Unique Perspective." Sam rolled her eyes.

Duke snorted. "That guy isn't paying close enough attention to catch a southern insult."

"DC is in the south. And even if he isn't, Jehan is," Sam said, half scolding.

"Fine. We both agree to keep each other in line, then?" Duke sighed and held out his pinkie as if they needed to formally promise in order for them to stick to it. In reality, neither would let the other spoil this for Jehan. She'd been looking forward to it for weeks, even declaring it a day off on the chore calendar.

"Deal," Sam said, taking his hand. The two of them blinked at each other, then cracked up. "Come on, let's go inside and eat food that will make us feel hungry."

The pair of them walked arm and arm through the restaurant door into a room that could only be described as dark blue. The paint on the walls was almost midnight blue, while the floor was a blue-and-white pattern that reminded Sam of those vintage Dutch ceramic tiles she sometimes saw in houses from the 1930s. Even the cushions on the furniture were blue. As they rounded the corner, Sam spotted Jehan and Travis seated on one side of a four-person table, speaking in hushed tones. Something about the look on Jehan's face gave Sam pause, and her feet stopped moving. She couldn't put her finger on it, but something in the air was wrong, and Sam wanted to snatch her friend away from the table and take all three of them back outside to try to flag down their ride again.

The act of Sam holding still caused Duke to jerk backward. The sight of a large and extremely conspicuous man flailing brought Jehan's and Travis's attention to them. In an instant, the lines on Jehan's face smoothed, and Travis affixed a smile that hovered somewhere between drop dead and rictus on his face.

"You two ready to grub?" Jehan asked after what felt like a lifetime of silence.

"Yup," Duke said, regaining his footing. Gently tugging on Sam's arm, he added, "I'm super excited about the cauliflower-steak bites."

"You know it." Sam doubted that any food eaten with a man who called ketchup spicy would be grubbable, but Jehan looked like she needed a lifeline, so she said, "I'm most excited about the plant-based brisket."

Reaching the table, the pair of them sat down right as someone from the waitstaff appeared wearing an entirely denim outfit and said, "Hi, I'm Stephanie, and I'll be your server for the tasting. Before we get started, are there any food allergies I should be aware of?"

It took everything in Sam not to grin at Stephanie's stereotypical Valley girl accent as she shook her head no. Before moving to California, she'd assumed everyone there sounded the same way. As it turned out, the accent was literally reserved for the valley outside Los Angeles. It wasn't common to hear it this far north, and it immediately made her feel like she was listening to someone who'd swallowed a reality TV star.

Taking in the shaking heads, Stephanie said, "Okay, then let's get started. I have a series of small plates and pairings featuring local, vegan, organic wines for us to begin with."

As if on cue, a line of servers descended on them with about fifteen tiny plates and a bazillion glasses, and Sam realized that if this was just the passed-apps course, she would be full for three days and need about a week to sober up.

Before Sam could blink, Stephanie proceeded to give them a run-down of how to eat a curry-soup bite, an explanation of the wines, and little note cards with gold pencils. She then pointed to the note cards and said, "I'll leave you to process the experience of our passed apps."

"Shall we try the momos first?" Jehan beamed over at them and scooped up a vegan dumpling, prompting Sam and Duke to do the same.

For his part, Travis reached for a curry-soup bite, and the four of them all nodded and got to work on their respective choices. Sam watched Duke's and Jehan's eyes go wide as they all experienced what could only be described as utter deliciousness.

"Oh, these are—"

Travis barked out a cough, interrupting Jehan, then reached for his first glass of white wine. Downing the glass in a single gulp, he wheezed, "The curry is spicy."

"Do you want some water?" Duke said, pointing to the glass in front of him as Travis reached for the red that was on the table.

Draining half that glass, Travis's face began to turn an uncomfort-able-looking shade of pink as he said, "I'll be fine. But we can't serve those."

Taking in the crestfallen look on her friend's face, Sam said, "Right. Maybe the three of us will try them, and you can have a momo. Then we'll all make notes before we try the other two appetizers. How does that sound?"

"Works for me," Duke said, his gaze darting back and forth between Jehan and Travis. While the three of them grabbed their curry-soup bites, Duke continued, "So, Travis, last time we saw you, you were looking at banking policy. You still working on that?"

Sam tried to focus on not dumping the admittedly awkwardly plated bit of food everywhere while half listening to Travis as he talked about his client, a national bank chain, who was trying to ascertain the effects of a potential new banking law on their business. As far as Sam could tell, it sounded terrible for consumers but good for banks, which, Travis informed them, was actually good for him as well.

"A happy client is a happy analyst," he said, then polished off his second glass of wine.

"Makes sense," Duke said, taking overly careful notes with his pencil.

"Wonder if they'd give us a bit more of the white? I didn't really get to taste it because of the overkill curry," Travis announced, and Sam thought that he seemed like the kind of guy who talked loudly on the phone at work so people would think he was important.

"You can have some of mine," Jehan said, smiling as she handed him her still-half-full glass. "Gotta pace myself if there is a pairing for every course."

"You're so small; it's not like you can hold much liquor," Travis joked, and all of them laughed for possibly the first time since he'd flown in last night.

As if sensing they were ready for the next course, Stephanie and the cadre of servers reappeared with two miniature entrées plus another two glasses of wine.

"First we have a traditional stuffed acorn squash with a brown sugar glaze that has just a hint of black pepper and cloves. Then we have our Better Than Meat filet mignon with a mushroom-based sauce and shishito pepper and cauliflower puree. And of course a red and a white for each. Enjoy."

Duke waited until the staff was gone before eyeing the steak. "And here I thought nothing could top the brisket-bite appetizer."

"I'd be shocked if it didn't," Travis grumbled. So far, he hadn't been a fan of any of their options, which seemed absurd to Sam since he was the vegan at the table.

"Come on, Trav. Will you just try?" Jehan said, rolling her eyes. Sam wasn't sure she had ever seen her roommate truly irritated, and that included the time Duke had accidentally burned popcorn in the microwave and woken them all up at 4:00 a.m. after Jehan had pulled two long shifts in a row.

"I'm only trying for you, babe," Travis said, half grinning through gritted teeth as he reached for the red wine in front of him.

Sam didn't love the tone or the volume of his comment and had opened her mouth to say as much when she caught Duke giving her a microshake of his head and remembered her promise. Duke was right. She wasn't the one marrying Travis. Jehan was smart and grown, and she could speak for herself. Deciding to ignore the comment, Sam said, "Do we want to start with the stuffed squash first?"

"Yes. Let's try that first," Jehan said, her words a little too excited to be sincere. "So Sam is in charge of the doula program I mentioned," she said, trying to move the conversation to safer ground.

"Oh, really? Jehan talks about that thing nonstop," Travis said, looking a little red in the face.

"That's me," Sam said, trying not to gobble down the entire scrumptious acorn squash in one bite. "I have to say, none of this would have been possible without Jehan's grant-writing expertise. She is such a pro."

"Huh. So tell me what it's all about again." Travis's words came out a little fuzzy. Although Sam wasn't sure if that was because of the black pepper in the squash or if it was the wine he had finished. At some point, he had clearly forgotten that he had polished off his red and inadvertently taken Duke's nearly full glass. A mistake her friend didn't bother to correct.

"Really, it's just about putting the person giving birth at the center of our care," Sam said, firing up her elevator pitch. By now, she had given it enough times that she was actually starting to get good at it. While Duke and Jehan threw in bits and pieces about the program, Stephanie and the team reappeared to whisk their plates away. For his part, Travis asked surprisingly thoughtful questions about their work in between writing notes about the food—which were mostly just frowny faces—and finishing off Duke's red wine.

"So that's what the program is all about," Sam said, right as two mini cakes and two dessert wines appeared in front of them.

"Sounds like a lot of work. Is the hospital paying you all extra for this?" Travis asked, gesturing around at the group with his glass.

"Well, no. But ultimately if Sam's theory is correct, her research will lighten our schedules and ensure that we aren't having to see patients for questions that really could, and often should, be answered by someone else," Duke said diplomatically.

"And it isn't that much work when you have such wonderful friends to help," Sam said, picking up her glass and moving it out of Travis's reach before she suffered the same tragedy as Duke.

"Really, it's good to put my skills to use, and you have been such a help with this wedding stuff." Jehan smiled and took a sip of her own sweet wine.

"Did she pick this restaurant, because this cake is dry as—"

"Travis, can you please stop complaining?" Jehan said, her tone quiet but firm.

For a moment everyone at the table was silent as some sort of unspoken showdown between the engaged couple took place. With each passing second, Jehan's eyes seemed to get wider while Travis's face got redder until he finally said, "I don't understand why we can't do this in DC. You say you are going to come back, but when? You're building entire programs at the hospital with your new friends. That doesn't sound like you are coming back. Our whole lives are there, and—"

"Travis, please. I think you have had one too many. Let's talk about this—"

"I don't think you're even serious about us." Travis's voice almost echoed off the blue walls, and Sam was sure the entire staff of Dorothy's could hear their fight.

"Not serious? We are literally in the middle of a catering tasting for an engagement party that is extremely important to my entire family." Jehan gestured to herself but didn't raise her voice. If she weren't in the middle of an argument, Sam would have given her a high five for standing her ground.

"If the party is so important, why haven't you sent out the save-the-dates?" Travis growled. "My mom said she still hasn't gotten hers."

That made Sam's ears perk up. She had sent those out weeks ago, and she knew that for a fact.

"Your mother is so rigid. Are you sure she didn't just receive it on a day that she doesn't check the mail?" Jehan rolled her eyes as Travis's face turned beet red.

"My mother—"

"You know, I think we could all use a walk right now." This came from Duke, who still had a bite of cake sitting on his fork. He didn't yell, but his usually joyful demeanor was dead serious, and he was sitting at his full height. "Travis, why don't you go one way. Jehan, you go another, and once cooler heads have prevailed, you two can talk this out."

Travis glared at the table for a second before standing abruptly. His chair scraped across the tile as he said, "I think that is a good idea. Jehan, I hope you'll give some thought to what I've said." With that, he huffed out of the room. His slightly wobbly walk would have been funny if he hadn't been actively stomping to try to create resonance with his footsteps.

The three of them waited until the restaurant door slammed before making eye contact. For a moment they were all silent, until Jehan exhaled, dropping her head into her hands and mumbling, "I'm so embarrassed."

"Oh, don't be. Lots of couples fight before big things like weddings," Duke said, standing up to come around the table. "You want a hug?"

"Yes, please," Jehan said, her voice pitiful and shaky.

"If you want, I'll take the cards over to Stephanie and the team so they can finalize the menu," Sam said, looking at her small friend as she buried her face in Duke's sweater.

"Thank you both. I don't know what I'd do without you."

"You did just fine, and you'd do just fine," Duke said, nodding at Sam to indicate that he would smooth things over while she handled the caterer.

"All right. Be right back. Then we can all hug while we wait for a car," Sam said, eliciting a weak laugh from her friend. Collecting the cards from the table, she began the walk to where she assumed the kitchen was, trying all the while not to mumble curses at Travis. It was one thing to say she'd lied about sending out the invites. It was another to ruin a perfectly good meal and her friend's day while he did it.

~

Sam's palms felt sweaty as she looked around the new SF Central Community Birthing Center, a mixture of pride and terror working her stomach into the kind of knots sailors would be proud of. The walls had been painted a bright, clean white, and with the combination of the chaplain's encouraging posters, baby charts, and some quilts that Kaiya had brought in, Sam had to admit that it didn't look too shabby.

Any moment now, Kaiya's doulas would come in for their orientation; then she and the rest of the clinical team at the hospital would spend time going over each patient's file so that the doulas knew what concerns each doctor had.

"There," Grant said, lightly placing the last of the tablets on each of the six desks. "These should be all charged and ready for everyone to log in."

The knot in Sam's stomach flipped over as Grant walked toward her. Since the last time they'd been in this room, she hadn't found herself alone with him. Not that she was avoiding him. It had just been an eventful few days. And once she thought about it more, she was almost convinced that nothing truly significant had happened. Otherwise,

Grant would've been acting strange around her. As it was, he was acting no odder than usual.

"Thank you for doing that," Sam said.

"Theo did most of the work. Pretty sure he hogged every plug in the nurses' station and then some," Grant laughed. Taking a deep breath, he rolled his shoulders forward a fraction of an inch and said, "So I wanted to talk to you about—"

"Hello, hello, hello, lovely people! Look who I found in the parking lot." Kaiya's voice boomed down the hall as she walked toward them, a gaggle of people behind her. "It's our prime cohort of doulas."

"Hello," Grant said, giving everyone a short wave, his demeanor shifting as he set aside whatever he'd been about to say to her.

"Welcome," Sam said as the gears in her mind whirled with the details for today.

"Everyone, I'm delighted to introduce Dr. Gao, the center's senior adviser. And this right here is Dr. Holbrook, the architect of our wonderful program," Kaiya said, taking a step back to better see the whole group, then added, "If you each want to pick a desk and grab a tablet, then come back over, Sam and I will run down the day's plan. Also, I have name tags until your badges come in."

With that, a flurry of activity broke out across the room, and whatever Grant wanted to say was officially pushed to the side of Sam's mind to make room for nerves as the program's corresponding physicians began to arrive, including Dr. Franklin. A small piece of Sam wished that he had volunteered to go in a later phase of the program, after they had a chance to work the kinks out and get into a rhythm with the group. Unfortunately, Jehan and Duke had informed her that there was no nice way to tell Dr. Franklin that while everyone appreciated his support, his presence made them nervous, so could he please not try to be supportive.

"Are you ready to start?" Grant said, giving her an encouraging smile as people began to gather around.

"I was born ready," Sam whispered instinctively.

Humor played with the corners of Grant's mouth. His smile had a calming effect on Sam. If nothing else, at least she could count on their inside jokes today.

Nodding to Kaiya, Sam felt her lungs expand as she took a deep breath, then called to the room, "All right, let's get started."

Sam wasn't sure what she had expected, but dead silence and roughly ten sets of eager eyes on her—plus Dr. Franklin's half-skeptical expression—were what she got. Clearing her throat, she said, "So I want to start by thanking you all for coming. I know everyone here is passionate about our community and has a deep sense that we can create an even better way to care for pregnant people. I also want to extend my most sincere and special thanks to Kaiya Owens. Her knowledge has been indispensable."

Sam paused to grin at Kaiya while the gathering clapped. Kaiya smiled, then rearranged the front of her yellow sweater set in an effort to not look too flattered. Finally, she waved her hand at Sam. "Go on."

"As you will have read in the email, we have paired each doula with a doctor or midwife who is in charge of the patients' primary clinical care here at SF Central. Our hope is that we can arrange these twenty-minute meetings once a month where provider pairs can briefly go over the patients' charts and birthing center notes so that each provider can assist the other in meeting the patients' needs. On the tablets the hospital provided, each doula should be able to log in and see their patient list. Just tap the name, and their chart should come up. From there, y'all are off to the races. You'll have about a half hour to speak, and then our patients will arrive so they can get to know our doulas. Any questions?"

"What do we do if we have a patient ask us about joining the program in a couple of weeks? Would that be too late?" Dr. Choi called from the back.

Kaiya glanced over at Sam, confirming that she would field the question, then began to explain the enrollment options. With the sound of Kaiya's voice as a backdrop, Sam felt her nerves start to unwind. The program was officially underway, and even better, the doctors were asking encouraging and even excited questions about the long-term potential of the program. She had been nervous about Dr. Franklin's presence, but maybe it was good for him to see how the other doctors viewed this. Now he knew that it wasn't just Sam on a soapbox. Other people supported this idea too.

"All right, if there are no more questions, let's get going," Kaiya cheered, then whipped out her tablet and marched right toward Dr. Choi, who still had more questions.

"Good work," Grant said, as soon as the pairs had found each other.

"I was a little bit nervous about how all of this would go over, but it seems like people are excited about it."

"You were nervous? What for? It's a good idea," Grant said, looking genuinely surprised by Sam's admission.

"Honestly, Dr. Franklin scares me a bit," Sam laughed. "Plus, what if he was right and everyone was just humoring me or something?"

"One, everyone is scared of Howie." Grant smiled as if using Dr. Franklin's first name would make him any less scary, then added, "Two, did you really think you could get this many medical-care providers to agree to humor you in the middle of their extremely busy workday?"

"Well, when you put it like that," Sam said, shaking her head. "No, really—"

"Sorry, we are having trouble with the sign-in page."

Sam and Grant simultaneously turned their heads to find Dr. Franklin's partner, a green-haired doula whose name tag read *Earnest*, standing near them. Looking nervously between them and Dr. Franklin, he handed Grant the tablet, saying, "I'm sure I've just clicked the wrong thing."

Grant had just started to poke at the tablet, a scowl on his brow, when Kaiya said, "Actually, I'm having trouble too."

"Oh," Sam said, a slow sense of dread taking up the space in her stomach where the knots had previously been.

"I'm getting an *Insufficient Credential* error, if that helps," another doula called from the back, and it took everything in Sam not to yell that it did not, in fact, help. Instead, she swallowed the impulse and tried not to feel Dr. Franklin's eyes on her.

Grant looked at her and frowned. "I don't think their clearance credentials were properly entered into the system." It was a simple sentence, but Sam's brain processed the information as if Grant had just handed her *Grey's Anatomy* and asked her to memorize it in an hour. Mistaking her silence for misunderstanding, he continued, "They can't log in to the portal to see the charts."

"Stupid paper system," Duke said, from somewhere in the back corner. "This happens all the time. You should see what happens when a doctor's office sends over a whole load of charts. Coding errors, lost paper, you—"

"We can just log in to our portal and show them for now," Dr. Choi said, cutting off Duke's rant about the hospital's ancient records system.

"I'm sorry, but you can't." Sam heard herself say the words that made her blood run cold. When they had made the choice to get tablets instead of laptops that were plugged into docking stations, IT wouldn't let them load the full system onto the tablets. They claimed it was a HIPAA violation waiting to happen. Sam could almost hear the IT administrator's smug voice echoing in her head as they asked, *What if someone accidentally walks outa here with one and loses it?* Turned out losing one was the least of their issues.

"Why can't we use them?" Earnest asked, pulling Sam out of her anger spiral. Gazing over at him, Sam almost laughed. While she felt like crawling into a hole, he looked completely relieved that he wasn't the problem with the tablet.

"There were HIPAA-compliance concerns," Grant said, then added, "If you will excuse me, I'm going to call upstairs and see if we can't figure out exactly why our paperwork hasn't been processed." Grabbing his phone from his pocket, Grant dashed out the door, leaving Sam to manage the group.

"Doulas, why don't you give the physicians a rundown on how you usually start working with a client while we get this sorted," Sam rambled. She was fairly certain she had already sweat through her undershirt and began fanning herself. Any minute now, the entire world would see every ounce of what she'd had to drink in the last seven hours on the back of her scrubs. Even the backs of her knees felt sweaty as she looked around the room just in time to see Dr. Franklin striding toward her.

"Dr. Holbrook, if you don't mind, I'd like a word with you." It was phrased politely enough, but his tone left no choice for her in the matter.

"Ah yes. Um. Of course," she stammered, feeling like she was being sent to the office for goofing off in class.

Dr. Franklin launched in without really waiting for her to get close. "Now, I know the old system and the staff shortage for paperwork processing isn't your fault, but someone should have checked this before everybody got here. I understand that setting up this program is an enormous undertaking, but I am concerned that this hiccup is a sign of things to come."

"I understand, sir. And I apologize. We should have had the doulas arrive a bit earlier to check their log-ins. Unfortunately, with the way the system is set up, log-in info is sent directly to the individual, so we had no way of knowing that the doula log-ins weren't active until they tried them on the hospital's secure network." Sam knew her tone was a little prickly. But in a way, she thought this was his fault. While it was true that she didn't control the network, it was also true that he did. If he didn't want these kinds of problems, he only needed to look at his budget and then look in the mirror.

"Be that as it may, I also want you to consider staff time." Dr. Franklin held up his hand, and Sam bit her tongue to keep from arguing as he said, "You and Grant have spent God-knows-how-many hours recruiting doctors and matching doulas, recruiting patients, and arranging this. You don't have a full-time admin budget, and it shows. Administrative and tech needs should have gone into your funding proposal."

"Dr. Franklin, the goal of my fellowship is to learn how to run my own research program. There will be mistakes, but I have three more years at the hospital to figure it out." She had spent countless hours chasing this man, and now he was mad that she didn't know things. Who was supposed to tell her if not the attending?

"You may have three more years here, but you don't have three years' worth of funding. I'm worried about the hospital resources. The staff time isn't being covered by Anjo."

"Actually, the doctors identify good candidates for the program, so that isn't much of a time commitment on the administrative side," Sam said, her veneer of patience beginning to crack. "And really, this is the first wave. This isn't even the formal launch of the program. Our whole goal is to get kinks like this worked out."

If he insisted on being in the first wave of the program, he was bound to get some hiccups. Sam narrowed her eyes at Dr. Franklin as if channeling all her frustration into a single glare would somehow communicate her point.

It didn't. Sighing heavily, Dr. Franklin rubbed his temple with one hand and gestured around the room with the other. "That's just it. Everyone here's time is valuable to the hospital. We have to evaluate research programs on a variety of things, not just novelty."

"Apparently, you aren't considering patient care as part of the evaluation," Sam shot back. "Sir, you say you are trying to help, but I question your dedication to helpfulness when you are trying to scuttle the program five minutes before our clients arrive. I think you are stuck in your ways. You took one look at Earnest and his green hair—"

"I most certainly am not. And I'll have you know that I have been all about progressive care. My entire—"

"All right, good news, everyone!" Grant called, rounding the corner like a professional speed walker. If Sam hadn't been in the middle of an ideological grudge match with Dr. Franklin, she would have laughed at the Olympic-level hip swivel that Grant had employed just to say he wasn't technically running in the hospital. Picking up on whatever weird energy hovered between her and Dr. Franklin, Grant stopped short. Coming to stand between the two of them, he turned to the group and said, "I just got a hold of a few residents on break and some-one on the admin team. They agreed to track down the forms and get the approvals into the system. So if everyone refreshes their browser in about ten minutes, we should be back online with full access."

"Won't the clients be here in ten minutes?" Dr. Choi asked. Her tone was almost apologetic as she pointed out the bad news.

"They will. And I know we promised that all of you would be out of here by now, so Kaiya, how do you think it is best we proceed?"

Kaiya took a deep breath, then smiled at the group. "A first meet-ing with the family is all about building trust. Let's let our doulas do what they do best and get to know the families and their needs. That won't require immediate medical knowledge. Once the portal is up and running, we'll circle back about check-ins and go over how to use the messaging system."

The doctors in the room shrugged and started saying their good-byes. Not for the first time, Sam wished that she had Kaiya's stage pres-ence. Maybe then Dr. Franklin would relax instead of scowling at her like she was a plastic bag blocking a gutter during a rainstorm.

Looking cautiously between the two of them, Grant asked, "You two doing okay?"

While Sam waffled between trying to lie that they were fine and being the petty teenage version of herself and saying no, Dr. Franklin sighed, his shoulders slumping. "You know, I think we are. I was a little short with you, Samantha, and I hope you can forgive me. What you said about this being a pilot makes sense."

"Of course. And again, I apologize for the hiccups. I think we are all a little tired. I know I was not at my best," Sam said, digging deep to be gracious. Sure, she hadn't been nice, but Dr. Franklin wasn't 100 percent wrong either.

"All right then, I'll be on the lookout for an update on how I can message Earnest. Whose hair I do like, by the way." Dr. Franklin smiled at Earnest, whose return smile looked like the nervous grimace of a person who had seen a gator grinning at him.

"Thank you, Dr. Franklin," Sam said, though a small part of her remained heated as she watched Dr. Franklin leave.

Grant waited until the other doctors had emptied out of the room, leaving the birth specialists to futz around with their desk setups until their clients arrived, before he turned to Sam and asked, "What happened?"

"Dr. Franklin sucks is what happened."

Grant snorted in surprise, his shoulders shaking with laughter. "He's just set in his ways."

"His way is just waiting for us to fail so he can kill this off," Sam said, feeling her teeth grind as she remembered his remarks.

"Nah, he's just a principal administrator. He has to be discerning."

"That is such a nice way to say *judgmental*," Sam grumbled and crossed her arms.

"If the two of you let go of your preconceived notions, I bet he would be a good mentor to you. I know he has been really helpful to me in a pinch," Grant said, half smiling as he needled Sam.

"Whose side are you on?"

"The hospital's side. But you are so obstinate that I think you are staying mad right now just to prove a point." This time, Grant didn't even try to hide the fact that he was laughing at her. In fact, Sam was pretty sure he would have stayed in the room slapping his knee if the first client hadn't walked through the door. Giving Sam a long look, he said, "Are you free tonight after the program wraps up?"

"I would've been, but if you are gonna pitch me on the merits of Dr. Franklin—"

Grant shook his head, causing Sam to cut her burgeoning rant short. "I won't do that, I promise. I have a surprise for you. And if you hate it, you can yell at me the whole car ride home about how much I'm not on your side."

"What kind of surprise?"

"Just humor me. I think it will cheer you up. Okay?"

"Okay," Sam said, and Grant smiled that same bright, genuine smile that sent shivers down her spine and made her heartbeat a little too fast.

"See you in a couple hours," he said, turning as one of his patients walked into the room.

Sam watched him walk away and felt herself relax as her own patients started to come in. Whatever else was happening could wait. She had a program to launch and a dream to fulfill.

Chapter Sixteen

Sam closed her eyes, enjoying the feel of the sun on her skin outside the hospital as she waited for Grant. One of the upsides of SF Central was that it was located in one of the city's sunny microclimates. While places like the Richmond got twelve hours of fog a day, here in Mission Bay, there was actually sunshine, and days like today when her shift ended by five o'clock, she could even enjoy a little of it before the fog rolled in.

"Ready?" Grant's voice called from behind, drawing her out of her reverie.

"What are we doing?" Sam asked. She didn't turn to look at him, eager to let a few more rays of vitamin D hit her face.

"That is still a surprise. But we have to get in my car to get there." Grant's voice had pulled even with her now, so she opened her eyes to find him watching her upturned face with curiosity.

"Just enjoying the absence of the fog," Sam said, answering the unasked question on his face.

"You mean Karl," Grant said, readjusting the strap on his bag.

Keeping pace as Grant moved toward the parking lot, Sam pushed her regret about leaving the sun aside to ask, "Who is Karl?"

"Karl Fog Monster," Grant said, his face completely serious.

"You named the fog?"

"No, someone else named it," Grant said, grinning like the story of Karl Fog Monster was his favorite. "I don't think it had a name when I was little. And old San Franciscans get cranky when you call it Karl, but honestly, Karl Fog Monster is a perfect name."

"You're kidding."

"Not at all. There was even a story on NPR about it," Grant said, shifting his bag to the other shoulder as they approached the car. "What, you didn't name the weather in Ohio?"

"Absolutely not. *Oppressive humidity* and *crushing chill* work just fine, thank you very much," Sam laughed as she settled into the passenger seat.

"Well, that's too bad for you, because Karl has come to feel like my friend. Sure, he's cold and kind of unpleasant, but he's always there for you." Grant smiled over his shoulder at her as he buckled his seat belt, then pushed the ignition.

"I'll have to let my friends back home know that naming the next blizzard will help." Sam shook her head playfully as she buckled her own belt. "So can you tell me where we are going now?"

"Kind of. It's located in the Mission."

"Are we getting ice cream again? You want to try the avocado flavor, don't you?" If ice cream was Grant's surprise, Sam had about fifteen places closer that she could direct him to.

"No. I mean, yes, ice cream is involved, but I can't tell you the rest."

"You can't tell me the rest?" Sam eyed him with suspicion.

Meeting her eyes briefly, Grant said, "Just trust me. This won't be murder or anything."

"Well, I hadn't thought murder when I got in the car, but now I'm nervous," Sam said, half laughing as they drove down Sixteenth toward the freeway underpass.

"Don't be. I think you are going to like this."

For a while, they drove in the sort of silence that Sam liked. The kind that meant you were comfortable enough to just be still with someone and that they felt the same about you. Again, Sam thought about their first meeting and how odd it was to be simultaneously so comfortable and so nervous around someone. Part of her wondered if the butterflies would ever go away. The other part wanted to bottle the thrill so she could feel like she was near him even when he wasn't around.

As they approached the Mission, Grant began to look for parking. Scanning the streets, he said, "Do you want to talk about Dr. Franklin at all?"

"Not really. But I know I shouldn't have gotten vexed with him. I can see where he thought he was being helpful. After all, it's not like I chose a lab-based research question that required tracking down funding for data. I could fail at this and never be employable as a clinician again. Not to mention damage the hospital's reputation."

"I wouldn't say timing and delivery are his strong suits. He can be harsh, but he does want the best for his fellow staff and his patients underneath all that grumbling." Throwing the car in park, Grant turned to unbuckle his seat belt, adding, "We have that in common. It's probably why Dr. Franklin and I get along."

"You aren't that rude," Sam said, surreptitiously watching the smile lines on either side of Grant's mouth as she unbuckled her seat belt.

"You don't need to lie. I'll still give you ice cream," Grant laughed as he pushed the driver's side door open and got out of the car.

"I'm not lying. You're prickly, but not like that," Sam called as she slid out of the passenger side and walked around to the back of the car.

"I have one word for you." Grant shook his head, his expression self-deprecating as he said, "Plane."

A beat went by as the two of them just looked at each other, and then they both burst into the kind of graceless laughter that made passersby either wish they were in on the joke or give them extra space on the sidewalk. Grant had doubled over, holding on to the hatch on the trunk to keep himself semiupright, while Sam leaned against the taillight, both of them letting their howls ring out over the sounds of shoppers and traffic.

Finally, Grant managed to pull himself together. Taking two deep breaths, he said, "I really think it was the guy's brocade jacket that did me in. What was he wearing, and why was he wearing it so early?"

"It was the man bun for me. Okay, that and the fact that we had to play twenty-one questions just to get to the fact that he was tripping balls on mushrooms," Sam said, putting a hand to her forehead in an effort to stop laughing, which of course failed as soon as she and Grant looked at each other.

Eventually, Grant straightened up again. Looking at the sinking sun, he said, "We should get going. Just promise me you'll give Dr. Franklin one more chance." Quirking one side of his full lips, he said, "I mean, you got to know me, and I'm not that bad."

"Jury's still out," Sam teased, leaning away from the bumper so that Grant could use the sensor to open the trunk. "I think it depends on what we are doing."

"You'll find out in like seven minutes." Pointing to a fuzzy-looking navy-blue blanket in the back of the car, he said, "Can you grab that? I need to run inside the Bi-Rite real quick."

"A blanket?" Sam said, whipping her head away from the trunk and back to Grant, who was already making his way toward the store. "You said no murder."

"No bodies, no murder. Promise. Just wait there," he called, then dashed through the store's front door, leaving Sam to watch the trunk close with the potential murder blanket held to her chest.

"What do we need you for?" Sam quietly asked the blanket as she waited outside the store. She was fairly certain doctors couldn't eat weed brownies and get the munchies without risking getting their licenses revoked. Even in San Francisco that seemed like the sort of thing that would be strongly frowned upon.

"Ready?" Grant asked, walking out of the store and bouncing on the balls of his feet. The brown paper bag he was holding had the edges stapled shut so she couldn't see what was inside.

"Are you really not going to show me what's in the bag either?" Sam asked, enjoying the excitement radiating off him.

"You already know there is ice cream in here." Grant shrugged and started walking toward the park.

"Yes, but I don't know what flavor," Sam said, nudging him slightly with her shoulder.

"Give me about one hundred yards, and you'll find out." Whatever he had planned, he looked extremely pleased with himself.

Sam opened her mouth to try a different angle as they rounded the corner onto Dolores Street, then stopped. There, at the top of the hill, was a massive screen surrounded by people sitting on blankets just like the one she was carrying.

"Movies in the park?" Her voice sounded more like a whisper as she tried to take everything in. Not two weeks ago she'd mentioned this, and he'd remembered it. Not just remembered it. He'd done it for her. Just like the ice cream or asking questions about her mom's party. Something in her chest squeezed as she looked from him to the park and back.

"Yes. More specifically, *A Goofy Movie*. They don't really do adult-only movies at this kind of thing." Realizing that she was a few paces behind him, Grant stopped and turned to face her, his expression shifting from excitement to apprehension as he watched her. "Is this okay?"

"You pulled together a movie night in the park because Dr. Franklin wasn't nice to me?" Sam felt her lips form the words as her brain tried to process the realization.

Grant shifted uncomfortably and ran a hand down the back of his head. "I mean, I just looked up the show times. And I didn't do it because Dr. Franklin was mean, per se . . . I just knew you wanted to go, and—"

"Wait, so you drove around with a blanket in your car and a plan in your head just in case I had a bad day?"

"Or a good one. Or actually, any type of day at all that seemed like a reason to watch a movie."

"Holy shit," Sam mumbled as it dawned on her. Her friends were right. Grant Gao, sexy doctor of scowling fame, *liked* her. Not the hate-like, have-sex-and-get-you-out-of-my-system kind of like. Not even close. He *liked her* liked her, as in he paid attention to what made her happy.

Sam couldn't remember the last time someone in her life had done something like this. That Grant liked her enough to care if she was happy was . . .

"We don't have to stay if—"

"Are you kidding?" Sam shook her head so hard her ponytail wiggled. Grant blinked at her for a second, and she realized she needed to use her words or risk him having some sort of stress-induced meltdown. "This might be the sweetest thing anyone has ever done for me. Can I hug you?"

"Oh," Grant exhaled, and a metric ton of tension left his shoulders. "Yes."

She closed the gap between them so quickly that Grant barely had time to set his paper bag down. Sam wasn't one of those people who claimed they didn't like hugs. She loved hugs, and she got them all the time. But the second his arms wrapped around her, she was certain she had never gotten a hug like this in her entire life.

Grant gave the kind of hugs that made her want to just stay wrapped up in him. From the way she fit just right in the crook of his neck to the way he held her. Tight enough to feel like he was solid, but not squeezing so hard that the life was crushed out of her. The heat from his body warmed her own, making her light headed. This close, she could enjoy the feel of the muscles in his shoulders. The ones that she pretended not to eye in the gym were now very real beneath her palms. There was something absolutely delicious about the feel of them that sent little bursts of want all through her body.

"Thank you for doing this," Sam said. Turning her head closer into his shoulder, she took a deep breath just to enjoy the smell of him. Everything about being this close to him made her feel like she was experiencing a craving and getting exactly what she wanted at the same time.

"I kept hoping I would run into you so I could tell you about the movie," Grant said into her hair. This close to him, she could feel his voice vibrating in his chest. That feeling was more intoxicating than wine, and Sam had to remind herself that unless she jumped up on him, she literally couldn't get any closer as he said, "But then I didn't see you at all. So I just kinda had to hope you would be free, since this is one of the last movies of the year."

"Had I known, I might have tried to have a bad day sooner."

Music began playing from the massive speakers next to the screen, and Grant let go. Looking as dazed as she felt, he licked his lips and said, "We should go grab our spot."

"All right," Sam said, smiling over at him. She waited until he picked up the paper bag and then wrapped her arm through his.

Grant looked at their arms for a second as if surprised that she was still near him; then his entire demeanor relaxed. As he began steering them toward an open patch of grass, he said, "I wasn't sure what kind of food you would want, so I just got us one of those boards with a bunch of crackers and stuff on it."

"That's perfect. I will always eat cheese and carbohydrates," Sam said, releasing his arm so that she could spread out their blanket. She could deal with not being close to him if it meant snacks.

"I figured. Also, the ice cream is salted pretzel."

"You got a weird flavor?" Sam smiled up at him as she dropped to one side of the blanket. "That feels like a big sacrifice on your end."

"Meh, it's a small price to pay to hang out with you." Grant shrugged and settled in on the other side of the blanket. Sam's heart did a backflip, and she focused on looking at her hands to keep from fully staring at him with doe eyes.

The intensity of how badly she wanted to be near him, not just physically but emotionally, made Sam nervous. She wasn't used to having the people in her life prioritize her, and now she was getting attached. But surely he had sharp edges—everyone who loved her did. Then again, who said anything about love?

Slow down, Sam told herself. She could just enjoy being at a movie and a fantastic hug. That would be enough until she had a better understanding of how all these pieces fit together. No one needed to decide their entire future tonight. Not when she finally had an outdoor movie to enjoy.

While Grant unpacked their snacks and methodically set out their utensils, Sam looked around. The evening could not have been more perfect for this. The golden-hour effect gave everything a tinted glow, and although the sun was setting, the air hadn't started to chill. Streaks of pink and orange were visible behind the screen as Max pretended to be Powerline in the opening scene.

"I love this movie," Sam whispered as Grant passed her a plate.

"Isn't it older than you?" Grant laughed.

"My dad loves it. Whenever we wanted to watch cartoons, this is what he put on." Sam smiled as much at Grant as at the memory of her father howling along to Tevin Campbell / Powerline.

"Guess my timing worked out then." Grant grinned, then picked up a few crackers and a bit of brie for his plate.

Sam let herself fall into the magic of the moment, nomming on charcuterie while happily listening to the campy sound of Goofy trying to reconnect with his son. Eventually, both of them had their fill of crackers and dried fruit, and Grant put the food away and fished out two spoons and the promised salted-pretzel ice cream. Raising one eyebrow at her, he held out one of the spoons. Pushing their plates out of the way, Sam crawled to the center of the blanket so she could sit next to him, then accepted the spoon.

Scooping up her first bite, she made sure to get a big hunk of pretzel wrapped in vanilla ice cream, popped it in her mouth, and moaned. She wasn't sure how they pulled it off, but the ice cream tasted like a sweeter version of a pretzel, complete with the same satisfying crunch. Out of the corner of her eye, Sam caught Grant trying to chew and smile simultaneously. Leaning into him to grab another bite, she whispered, "Have I made you a weird-ice-cream-flavor convert now?"

"Maybe." Grant gently leaned into her arm so their sides were flush. Scooping up some more ice cream, he added, "I need a couple more bites to be sure. But the early results are promising."

Sam snort-laughed in spite of herself, and Grant looked pleased that a joke that even dads should be ashamed of had gotten a laugh. Finishing another bite of ice cream, she said, "That was a pity laugh. You don't deserve it."

Looking into her eyes, Grant held her gaze with a look so hot it could've scorched the grass around them. Like her mouth was just as good as ice cream. He wanted to kiss her; she could feel it.

If the movie hadn't been playing in the background, she would have thought time stopped along with her breathing as her heartbeat sped up. Then he broke the spell with half a smile.

"I'm not too good for pity laughs. I'll take it."

Sam felt like she had just sustained an emotional body slam. Her fellowship was busy, so she was a little rusty on the mechanics of dating, and sure, *A Goofy Movie* wasn't exactly *Love & Basketball* on the sexy scale. Still . . . either Sam had deeply misread this situation, or . . .

"If you want to kiss me, this is your moment."

The words came out of her mouth without thinking. Something about saying what she wanted made her pulse race. There was no coming back from this. Grant was looking at her with his usual inscrutable expression, and Sam thought she might melt into the grass like unwanted ice dumped from a cooler.

What if she had misread the situation? Hadn't she just told herself to slow down? Worse still, she hadn't really thought about the repercussions of what she had just proposed, and now she'd have to work with him every day. The rejection would make staff meetings awkward for at least a week.

Sam opened her mouth to tell Grant to forget about it right as he said, "Okay."

Grant closed the gap between them so quickly that it made Sam dizzy. They were just a few centimeters apart as she reached for him, running a hand up his shoulder and around the back of his neck, enjoying the feeling of the fine hairs at the edge of his haircut. The motion brought them close enough that she could feel his chest rise and fall.

Grant moved a hand to cup her face, tracing a thumb across her lips and along the edge of her jaw. Sam's pulse fluttered with anticipation. Finally, he leaned in. At first, the kiss was a brush, something feather-light, as if he were making sure that her lips were really there. Like all things with Grant, he wasn't rushing through this moment; he gave them both time to feel each other.

The taste of him was heady and sweet, and Sam was sure she couldn't ever get enough of it. When he ran his tongue across the bottom of her lip, it took everything Sam had to stop herself from jumping on top of him to get a better angle. Grant's other arm wrapped around her as his hand moved to the back of her neck, further deepening the kiss. He felt so good against her that she forgot just about everything except for a vague awareness that they were in a park. The intensity was overwhelming. Sam lost herself in the sensation, letting the warmth and the smell of him wash over her.

She wasn't sure how long they had been kissing until Grant pulled away, his face looking as dazed as her mind felt. His chest heaved like he needed to catch his breath, but Sam wasn't interested in a break, and she reached for him again.

"Your phone is ringing."

"What?" Sam blinked at him as if he had started speaking in Klingon. How did he know if her phone was ringing? Better yet, why did he care?

"Your phone is in your jacket pocket, and it's vibrating against my rib cage," Grant said, humor replacing the blissed-out look on his face. Gesturing to her, he said, "Is it the hospital?"

"Oh. Good question," Sam said, shaking the lust fog out of her brain in case she needed to answer and trying to suppress her irritation that anyone would call her in the middle of the world's best makeout session, then reached into her pocket. Both of them looked at the phone, and then Grant burst into a fit of giggles as Mom ran across the screen.

Sam was glad Grant found it funny, because she was furious at her mother for interrupting something so glorious. In fact, she was considering mailing her mother glitter. "Talk about bad timing."

"We were making out in a park like teenagers. It sorta fits that your mom would call."

"I'm gonna send her to voice mail and tell her I ran out of battery later. Just like high school." Sam laughed, tossing the phone onto a corner of the blanket. Turning back to Grant, she leaned into him and said, "Now, where were we?"

"Making out until my dad drives by, I think?" Grant said as he wrapped his arms around her and pulled her close again.

"Let's hope not," Sam laughed, enjoying the look of Grant's smile as he leaned in. The taste of that smile was even better the second time.

Chapter Seventeen

Sam waited until she was far enough inside the apartment hallway that Grant couldn't actually see her, then broke into a happy dance that involved a good number of jumps, fist pumps, and a couple of shimmies. It was not a dignified happy dance. This was the wild tango of a woman who made out with a guy in a park in sight of everyone and their dog and didn't even care because it was hot. Okay, and fun, Sam reminded herself. Then thought, *Okay, but mostly hot.* The only bad part of the evening was the realization that their schedules did not come close to lining up for the next few days, so she would not be seeing him soon. But then again, that was what text messages were for. Maybe she would even get pictures . . .

Running a hand over her hair and down the front of her scrubs to make sure that she didn't look too rumpled, Sam started toward the stairs up to the apartment. As much as she wanted to pretend she could keep a secret from her roommates, she knew there was no way she would be able to hide it for more than three seconds if she showed up looking like she'd tumbled down a hill, which she low-key had, but still.

A little voice in Sam's head reminded her that she and Grant hadn't talked about anything future related in the park. Maybe she should wait to tell her roommates and guard her heart a little longer?

Oh, who was she kidding? She didn't need an engagement ring to tell her friends, the other, happier, louder, and just-kissed voice in Sam's mind said.

With that, Sam ran up the last few stairs and barreled through the front door shouting, "Guess what!"

To Sam's dismay, someone had left the living room light on, but no one was actually there. Turning her head down the hallway, she realized that both Jehan's and Duke's doors were closed, which likely meant that they hadn't gotten home from the hospital yet.

"Guess I'll have to wait to tell someone after all," Sam said to no one as she stood on one foot and then the other to shuck off her sneakers. Grabbing her phone from her pocket, she walked into the living room and flopped on the couch, determined to veg out to whatever *Housewives* franchise was on. Remote in one hand, she flipped on the TV at the same time she unlocked her phone to text her bestie back in Ohio all about her evening.

Sam had almost forgotten about her mother's call until she saw the number of times she'd tried to reach her. Nine missed calls and three voice mails.

"Oh my God." Sam stared down at the phone as dread snaked its way through her veins. Had someone been hurt? Surely if someone had been hurt, more than just her mother would have tried to call. Unless both her father and her brother had been crushed in some sort of freak simultaneous meteor shower that had pummeled both Southern California and Ohio but mysteriously missed the Bay Area.

"Stay calm," Sam said to the only person in the room who was panicking—herself. She hit play on the first voice mail, and her mother's stilted tone came through the line as if she were sucking on a lemon.

"Sammy. It's Mom. I need you to call me back when you can. Thanks."

"That's it?" Sam asked as the line went dead.

Her anxiety increasing, she jumped to the second voice mail, time-stamped forty-three minutes later.

"Sammy, I'm sure you're busy, but this is important. I need you to call me back now. Thank you." This time her mother didn't sound like she had eaten something bitter. She sounded downright pissed that Sam had missed somewhere in the vicinity of a dozen attempts to reach her. Sam hardly thought the volume of calls was reasonable given the amount of time her mother had let pass between voice mails, but then again, what if her granddaddy had fallen and they needed her medical opinion on something?

When she pressed play on the final voice mail, her mother's voice came back through the line. "Samantha, I don't know where you are, but it is clear that you are not interested in returning my call, so I'll just tell you that somehow you botched the invitations to the party. I just talked to Mrs. Blake, and she received a save-the-date to a wedding reception for someone's engagement party that she'd never heard of—Jehan Kazen, if you can believe it."

Sam felt the pit of her stomach drop as her mother began to detail calling her friends and finding out that all of them had received a strange invitation to an engagement party, but none of them had received a notice about her event.

"Holy shit," Sam whispered as her mother wrapped up a message that would have seemed like yelling if the phone hadn't had volume control.

"It seems to me that you somehow managed to swap those lists, and now I venture to guess that Jehan's party is as ruined as mine. So there you have it. No need to call me back. I know you're busy anyway."

"Oh no. No. No. No." Sam repeated the one-word mantra as she dashed from the couch to her room to grab her laptop. Clicking over to the invitation website, she navigated to the *Your Orders* tab and stared in horror as the website confirmed exactly what her mother had accused her of. She had, indeed, mixed up the lists.

Running back into the living room, she grabbed her phone. It was almost one o'clock in the morning in Ohio. Normally, she wouldn't call, but knowing her mother, she was probably doing something dramatic like sitting in their dark living room staring daggers at the phone. Taking a shaky breath, Sam dialed her mother to beg for her forgiveness. The phone rang once, then twice, then went to voice mail.

"Nope." Sam hit the red hang-up button, knowing that whatever voice mail she left would be used against her unless it was perfect.

Clicking over to her contacts, she found her brother's number and tapped it. She was sure Isaiah already knew what had happened, but that didn't mean that she didn't want his advice. The guy had basically mastered the many moods of Diana Holbrook.

The phone rang three times before her brother picked up. "Hey, Sam, it's kinda late for you. Everything okay?"

"Did I wake you up?"

"No. I was just trying to finish up something for work. What's up?" Isaiah asked. His voice always reminded Sam of a weighted blanket. His entire energy could best be described as steady.

"Oh my God, Isaiah, I messed up Mom's invitations. I agreed to help with this ridiculous party just so she'd forgive me for moving to San Francisco, and now she isn't speaking to me, again." Panic spiked through her chest as she imagined a series of worst-case scenarios, including her mother just flat-out refusing to let her in the house for all foreseeable holidays, birthdays, weddings, and funerals.

"That's not great," Isaiah said, pulling her out of her spiral. She could practically hear him taking off his glasses to run a hand over his face.

"Not great at all." Sam felt this was a dramatic understatement, but she was trying to calm down, not sink further into a freak-out hole. "She didn't tell you?"

"Mom called me. It's just that I was in the middle of a project, so I didn't answer. Guess I picked the wrong time to ignore her call," Isaiah joked. Sam knew it was for her benefit more than his own. "You want to tell me what happened?"

Sam took a deep breath and let the whole thing rush out, in the hopes that if she spoke fast, she wouldn't cry. A plan that mostly failed but did mean that she had to repeat salient details a few times, so at least there was that added downside.

"Okay, first, I'm gonna validate that while it's okay to cry, you don't need to. It's ludicrous that Mom expects you to do this while you are trying to adjust to a new job and get this program off the ground. That was bound to cause some issues," Isaiah said, sounding like a TV-show therapist—a trait that might have annoyed Sam on any other day but was particularly helpful to her right now.

"Thanks." Sam sniffed and grabbed the hem of her shirt to wipe her eyes.

"Second, I would say that this isn't really about her having a party for her friends. It was about inserting herself in your life. You know good and well she has already told all of these people about the reunion. The paper invite was a formality." Isaiah's laugh was low and mellow. "If you are going to feel bad for anybody, feel bad for your friend, who is likely going to get some rando wedding gifts from Mom's friends. You know what Aunt Debbie's taste is like. So many unsolicited demitasse tea sets."

Both of them laughed, remembering all the strange gifts that had been sent their way over the years, including the small china cups someone had truly believed Isaiah needed when he'd moved into his own place in LA.

"Well, she found out from Dr. Blake—who she called Mrs. Blake again—so at least the gifts from her will be good." Sam paused so that both she and her brother could roll their eyes. Dr. Blake was the mother of Sam's childhood best friend. It wouldn't have been so egregious except that Dr. Blake was literally one of the world's foremost experts on modern manners.

"So here is what you do. Call Mom back. Leave a simple voice mail with how you plan to correct the mistake. Apologize and say you love her and that she can call you back when she is ready. Then immediately do what you said you would so she can't argue with you about it or lay on extra guilt."

"You're basically the Mom whisperer."

"Clearly she expects some prolonged, dramatic thing. But honestly, who has the time? You'll say sorry, you didn't do it intentionally, and you won't make the mistake again, so she can get over herself."

Sam laughed, feeling her spirits lift as she nodded along with her brother's pep talk. "Thank you, Isaiah. And I'm sorry I interrupted your work."

"It's okay. I wasn't getting much done. I was mostly watching *Housewives*."

"That was my plan, too, before all this stuff went sideways."

"We are related for a reason. Now, go fix this and then get some sleep. You got actual lives that depend on you," Isaiah said, his voice sounding like the aural equivalent of a hug.

"Good night. I love you, brother," Sam said, feeling the knot in her gut start to untwist itself.

"Love you too, sister."

With that, the line went quiet. Sam sighed and looked over at the clock, then at her laptop as her brain clicked something into place. Unpleasant as Travis had been, he was right about his mother not receiving an invitation. Sam shuddered and tried not to gag. She didn't relish the thought of confessing her failure to her friend, but the longer she waited to tell Jehan that Travis was right, the worse she would feel. Assuming Jehan had a midday shift, she should be home in about forty-five minutes.

Picking up her laptop, Sam shuffled into the living room and sank back into the couch. If she was going to wait up for Jehan, she might as well use the time to fix her mom's party. With a heavy sigh, she settled down enough to employ a trick she'd learned in an anxiety-management seminar in her first year of medical school—writing out bad news before you had to say it. The seminar was designed to help future doctors manage the terrible feelings that came with having to tell a patient or their family members difficult diagnoses. However, Sam figured it would work just as well in her own life. After a good twenty minutes of typing and then retyping her apology, she was ready.

Sam picked up her phone and dialed her mother's number again. Just as Isaiah had promised, she was sent straight to voice mail. As she waited for the "You've reached Diana Holbrook; I can't come to the phone" spiel to end, she tried to focus on her breathing. She didn't need to be afraid. This wasn't like in old movies where you'd start leaving a voice mail and then someone would pick up. Her mom had shut her phone off, likely to make a point to Sam, and now she could leave Diana a message without fear.

As soon as the tone beeped, Sam started. "Hi, Mom. Sorry I missed your call. I was with my hospital colleagues." A mild fib for the cause, she thought as she took a breath. "Anyway, I want you to know how sorry I am to have mixed up your and Jehan's invitations. I'm sending out an apology email and a corrected e-vite now, so no need to worry about that. You were wise to send out the Facebook invitation, so at least there is one correct source for the information."

Pausing, she looked down at her script and did her best to not sound robotic as she read, "Again, I truly apologize for the embarrassment this likely caused you. I want to assure you that the other details are being handled with more care. I can understand if you need time to work through all of this, so I won't call again. I'll let you reach out to me. Okay. Love you. Bye.

"Woof," Sam exhaled after the call had been fully disconnected before dropping the phone on the couch next to her. Rolling out her neck, she changed the cross of her legs, set her laptop on a throw pillow, and then got to work on updating the guests.

Finding a sufficiently distressed-looking e-vite template, Sam crafted an "event update" to her mother's guest list. The initial four-sentence email took her all of seven minutes to write. Second-guessing and rearranging those four sentences took a good fifteen minutes. Then she tacked on another five minutes' worth of excessive spelling and grammar checking before finally hitting send.

Setting her laptop to the side, Sam slouched over onto the armrest of the couch. Her night had started off on such a high, and now she was back where she'd begun—an exhausted mess who was out of her depth. Sam massaged one of her shoulders and gently prodded at a thought she'd been avoiding all afternoon. What was she trying to prove? Since coming to San Francisco, she had done nothing but overextend herself. She wanted to be a good doctor, daughter, and friend. Right now, she didn't feel like any of those things.

The sound of the lock on the door turning yanked Sam's attention away from her introspection. She sat upright, a second wave of fear and anxiety flooding her brain as she listened to the seals around the door squelch on the wood floor.

"Hey. What are you still doing up? Don't you have a shift in like six hours?" Jehan smiled as she stuck her head around the corner to see who was still in the living room at almost midnight. Her friend's face faltered when she saw her, and Sam was sure Jehan could tell that she was actually a steaming pile of bad-friend garbage. "Everything okay?"

"I—" Sam's voice cracked. Closing her eyes, she stopped and shook her head before opening them and starting again. "Jehan, I've got something to tell you. And I want you to know how sorry and embarrassed I am."

"What happened?" Jehan asked, tension rolling her shoulders forward as she stopped untying her shoes and walked into the room.

"I promise I will make this up to you, but . . ." Sam looked at her hands as Jehan dropped down on the couch next to her, concern written all over her friend's kind face. Forcing herself to make eye contact, she told Jehan the whole pathetic story. Along the way, Sam watched Jehan's emotions play out from concern to surprise to something that looked oddly like relief.

As she wrapped up with the correction email she was about to send, she watched as Jehan marshaled her expressions into placidity. Taking a deep breath, she asked, "Is your mom's party going to be okay?"

"Does it matter? I'm more worried about your party," Sam said, watching her friend closely. Jehan's reaction was so calm it was eerie. Even for someone as mellow as Jehan, this reaction was understated. Either she was going to explode shortly, or there was something her friend wasn't sharing. Or, Sam reasoned, maybe she was living in a dream sequence, and this wasn't really happening at all. She hoped that wasn't the case, or she would have to throw out the evening with Grant as well. And she wanted that to be real in spite of everything else that had happened tonight.

Jehan shook her head. "My party is a month and a half away. I mean, was your mom planning on inviting people from out of town? Did anyone book a hotel too far from the venue or anything?"

"Not that I know of." Sam wrinkled her nose as she thought through the list of names. "Most of them were local from when we lived around here twenty-five years ago."

"And the party is still like two weeks away, yes?" Jehan asked, her voice calm as a lake.

"Two and a half, really." Sam shrugged.

"Your mom will be fine then. And as for my party, we'll send out an oops email and an updated invite." Jehan threw up a hand as if tossing out some minor hiccup.

"I already drafted one. I just wanted to tell you before I sent it so you weren't caught off guard."

"Even better. See, this is no big deal."

"But Travis was so upset with you because of me." Sam said this part fast. If she didn't acknowledge the trouble she had caused her friend's relationship, the guilt might crush her. Whether or not Sam liked Travis, Jehan didn't deserve that trouble.

"Water under the bridge. As they say, if you don't fight about wedding planning, were you ever actually engaged?" Jehan laughed, but the sound seemed hollow. Sam was about to ask what was really going on and why her friend was so calm when her phone flashed with a text message that she decided to ignore. If it was her mother, she would have called, and nothing else was more important than seeking her friend's forgiveness.

"You aren't upset?" She eyed her friend, who conveniently looked down at Sam's phone blinking with a text message instead of meeting her gaze. "Because I'd understand if you were. I messed up your party and caused a problem between you and Travis. I really apologize."

"I forgive you, and I promise you I'm not mad. In fact, it'll be a funny story for me to tell later," Jehan said, still squinting down at the phone. After a moment, she looked up, her eyes bright. "Do you have anything else you need to get off your chest? Because if you don't, I have a question for you."

"If you don't feel like we need to talk about this more, then I guess not." Her friend's forgiveness felt foreign to her. After all, her mother's party was arguably small potatoes compared to a wedding. At the start of this conversation, Sam would have understood if Jehan had cut her off and thrown a tantrum. Yet instead of dealing with a bridezilla, she just had a friend who managed to forgive her mistakes. The difference between her mother's reaction and her friend's made Sam feel like she was trying to find her balance after spinning in circles for a little too long. One of the two women's responses was off; she just wasn't sure which yet.

Sam watched her friend's face carefully for clues. Whatever was going on with Jehan, she wasn't going to tell Sam now. A fact that was made abundantly clear as the corners of Jehan's mouth turned up and spread into a big grin.

"So," Jehan said, looking at Sam mischievously. "Are you gonna tell me why Grant Gao is texting you at midnight? I heard you left the hospital together."

Momentarily stunned by the conversational turn, Sam felt her mouth fall open. After a beat, she looked her friend squarely in her face, pulled her shoulders back, and said, "Probably because I kissed him."

"What! Finally—wait till Duke finds out. We had a bet, you know." Jehan jumped up and down a little as she rearranged herself on the couch to better face Sam.

"A bet?" The words came out as more of a laugh than a question.

"Yes. But who cares right now?" Jehan patted the pillow in Sam's lap rapidly. Still grinning, she said, "Tell me everything."

"I mean . . ." Sam hesitated, enjoying the sight of her friend getting all hyped up. "Maybe we should wait for Duke since y'all had a bet and everything."

"Don't keep a secret from me now." Jehan lightly shoved Sam.

"Fine. But only on the condition that we tell Duke together. I want to see his face."

"Done." Jehan practically jumped up and down as she agreed.

"So it all started because of Dr. Franklin," Sam began. Jehan's laughter and frequent questions interrupted her and made the story take three times longer than it should have to tell. Sam knew she would be tired tomorrow, but between the sound of her friend giggling and the text waiting for her on her phone, she had to admit that the night wasn't so bad. Not by a long shot.

~

"Earth to Dr. Holbrook." Kaiya's voice interrupted Sam's spinning thoughts, forcing her to stop staring at the poster of a baby in gestation.

"Sorry. I spaced out." Sam gave her head a small shake as she tried to clear the phone call with her mother out of her mind. Logically, she knew there was no way Diana could have known she was headed into the birthing center, let alone that she and Kaiya were going over the early qualitative results from the first month of the program. And yet her timing could not have been worse.

"I know. You've done it twice," Kaiya said, leaning back in her chair and crossing her arms. The gesture wasn't unfriendly, but it didn't exactly read as pleased either.

"Yes. And I'm sorry about that too." Sam winced.

"As I was saying, obviously, we'll want to see the maternal-health and visit-attendance data to corroborate this, but our first client evaluations are overwhelmingly positive . . ."

A not-insignificant part of her wished that she hadn't answered her mother's call. However, it had taken her three days to call back, and Sam had felt like she couldn't miss it. To say the call was jampacked with Olympic levels of passive aggression would have been an understatement. Unlike Jehan, who was way too forgiving and not at all forthcoming about whatever was going on, her mother was not in a place of forgiveness. As much as her mother said she absolved Sam, she managed to pile on twice as many phrases like "I know my party isn't a big deal" and "you kids have lives now." For a call that only lasted fifteen minutes, Sam felt like she had survived forty-eight hours of an emotional blitzkrieg. In fact—

"Sam." This time Kaiya's look left no room for interpretation when she interrupted Sam's thoughts.

"I apologize." Kaiya raised a skeptical eyebrow, and Sam hastened to add, "Again. I apologize. I had a fight with my mother right before I came here, and clearly, my attention is still on that call."

"Well, do you think you can get your attention here? I have started to explain the context for these quotes three times now. But really, this isn't my research initiative; it's your data."

Sam grimaced and nodded. She deserved that. In fact, Kaiya had very few requirements for participating in this program, and one of them was Sam's full attention. Guess she could add *bad pilot-program leader* to her growing résumé of failures, right below *awful daughter* and *questionable friend* but just above *mediocre basketball player*—a title she'd earned by throwing away the ball twice at last night's game. The only good things she could leave on her life résumé were *successful text flirt* and *world-class horny person*. Although she technically couldn't take full credit for either, since Grant had a hand in both.

Eyeing her, Kaiya sighed heavily and pushed the paper in front of her around the desk for a moment before saying, "Look. I don't mean to be unfeeling. What I am trying to say is that both of us have a full caseload. If either of us can't be one hundred percent focused, we may as well call it a day and get back to work until we can. If you need time to concentrate on your outside life, just say so, and I'll give it to you. You can do the same for me. But trying to pretend we are working when we aren't does no one any good."

"You are absolutely right. Your time is valuable—"

"Your time is too."

"Sure. Our time is too valuable to waste," Sam said, pulling her shoulders back in mock importance, then smirked at Kaiya. "We're kind of a big deal. People need us."

"Damn straight they do," Kaiya laughed. "So can you leave that mom of yours outside the door?"

"Yes. You have my full attention for however much longer we have in this meeting."

"Thirty-six minutes," Kaiya said dryly.

"I spent nine minutes floating off?" Sam said, shocked.

"Technically seven minutes. You were two minutes late too."

"Do you know how many seconds I was late as well, or should I even ask?" Sam feigned hurt. Kaiya grinned conspiratorially as if adding a little salt to the exchange was fun for her, and Sam said, "Never mind, just tell me what you learned."

"All right then. As I was saying, our early evaluation forms are really promising. The first-month program surveys for the group who are seven-months-ish pregnant suggest that families are feeling better informed about what to expect in the final term of their pregnancies. Several respondents said that they even reached out to their nurse or physician with questions based on their consultations with their doula, so anecdotally anyway, it looks like patient engagement with the doctors themselves is also improving."

"That is amazing," Sam said. Obviously, she wouldn't have birthing stats for this group for a few more months, but this was promising.

"I thought you'd be happy to hear it. I know that the third-trimester-pregnancy cohort is only fifteen people, but if we see these same results come back from the first- and second-trimester cohort, I think we are onto something really amazing."

"What about the doula evaluations? Are they seeing the same thing the patients are feeling?" Sam asked, her mounting excitement causing the words to tumble out of her. Kaiya opened her mouth, likely to try to slow Sam down, so she added, "I know, I know, it's only a month's worth of data."

"You are stealing my disclaimers," Kaiya said, shaking her hair over her shoulders and smiling at Sam. "I'm still missing Earnest's evals—I'll follow up with him today—but so far, everyone feels like they are starting to build rapport and their clients are getting comfortable. I joke that once people start asking me about their digestive issues, I know I'm building a bond. It seems like we are getting there with all our cohorts. And next week, some of us are starting house calls, not just phone calls or video chats."

"I can't believe how fast this is all moving. I mean, it felt like it took forever to get here, but now we are at house calls. Pretty soon, we will have our first center babies. We should order special onesies for them!" Sam grinned at Kaiya, who didn't even try to bring her back down to earth.

"I will give you credit for this, Sam." A warmth that Kaiya typically reserved for her clients rolled off her as she said, "I always thought I was a lone wolf in this work, but I am really enjoying having a community of practitioners around me. When a client isn't bonding with one of us, we can all meet and discuss if swapping clients might be a good idea or how to work through different ways to grow the relationship. It's actually really nice to be able to share what I know."

"Is it too soon to say I told you so?" Sam asked, fighting the urge to dive across the table and hug her.

"Much too soon." Kaiya rolled her eyes like Sam was the corniest person she'd ever met. "Anyway, I'll finish getting the first-trimester, second-trimester, and doula documentation together and send it over to you and Grant. Do you need anything else from me for the upcoming progress report to Anjo?"

"Nope. Once I have the physician responses and visit-attendance data, I'll summarize everything and send it off by the end of next week. Then we can keep trucking along."

"All right, then, I think we are done here," Kaiya said, picking up her papers and tapping them twice on the desk so they were perfectly aligned before placing them in a purple folder.

Sam looked at her phone, then cocked her head at Kaiya and said, "With three minutes to spare. Despite my staring into space."

"Don't get big in the britches, Miss I Got One Good Month of Results," Kaiya snorted. "Now get outa here so I can reset the room for the first-time-pregnant parents' group and then the chaplains' staff meeting."

"Do you want help?"

"No," Kaiya laughed as Sam's eyebrows shot up. "I want you to go be a doctor and deal with whatever you need to deal with so that you are paying attention next time."

"Fine. I can take a hint," Sam sighed and picked up her bag.

"Not a hint. It's practically a billboard," Kaiya cackled as she started to push filing cabinets around the room.

"Laugh if you want, Kaiya; I still think you're the best, and I know deep down you like me too," Sam said, refusing to let a roasting keep her newfound good mood down.

"It must be buried real deep." Kaiya snorted as she pushed another small cabinet into place.

"It's still there, so I'll take it," Sam called over her shoulder as she reached the door, the sound of Kaiya's chuckles following her out. She made it exactly four feet into the hallway before she whipped out her cell phone. She didn't have much time before she needed to go back to observations, but she had to text Grant the good news.

Just met with Kaiya. 3rd Trimester group loves the program!

Sam tapped the phone in her palm while she waited to see if he was going to reply. Usually, if he was awake and not in the shower, he didn't keep her waiting long. They had been texting back and forth all week. Not so much the steamy stuff Sam had imagined they'd text, although there was some of that. Mostly, Grant texted sweet little personal things like GIFs from *A Goofy Movie* or clips from an opera that Grant promised Sam would enjoy when they watched it together. Admittedly, Sam thought the plot of that one sounded ridiculous—why would a grown woman need permission from an entire army regiment to get married?—but Grant swore that it was his favorite role his mom had ever sung, so Sam guessed she'd learn to like it.

The thought of learning to like something for Grant made her pause. Was she really planning to study an entire genre of music for a guy she'd made out with exactly once? Sure, Grant could be sweet underneath that prickly exterior. And he was funny. Who else appreciated an unintentional sex joke as much as she did? But was that really enough that she was about to just hand over her heart? She should focus on getting her progress report to Anjo. She knew better than to rush into a relationship, especially with someone who had their life so figured out, but—

The feel of the phone vibrating against her palm stopped Sam's thoughts. Looking down at the screen, Grant's name flashed up at her. Quickly unlocking the phone, she read,

That's amazing! Need any help with the Anjo report?

Sam paused. A small corner of her mind pointed out that she had her mom's party, the center's grand opening, and that silly video they needed to film for Anjo all happening in the next week. But it wasn't like Grant didn't have just as much on his plate. When she'd started the center, she'd said none of the work would land back on him. One date with the guy didn't earn her the right to go back on that promise.

I think I got it. But thanks.

She was just about to put her phone away when Grant buzzed again.

In that case, I feel like we both have tonight off.

Want to come over to my place to celebrate?

Sam's heart pounded as she watched the little still-texting bubble disappear. Did Grant mean she should come over so they could order pizza and celebrate with junk TV? Or was this like when someone said, *It's your birthday, I got a present for you, and the present is sex*? More importantly, did she care?

The answer to that was no, absolutely not. She'd run home and put on cute underwear just to be safe. Hell, if she was lucky, she would get pizza and sex. Smiling down at the phone screen, she took a second to think of something she could say just to make sure that Grant knew she would be wearing her good bra and panties.

> I get off at 7. I want to change into something that shouldn't be worn under scrubs. Be at yours around 7:45.

The text silence that followed almost swallowed Sam whole. Maybe he'd really meant a pizza situation, and now she'd just made it awkward. Hadn't she just told herself to slow down? Fingers flying across the keyboard, she added,

> Unless that's too late?

Sam held her breath, her heart sinking and her pulse racing all at once. After what felt like the longest thirteen seconds in her life, his response appeared.

> 7:45 works. See you tonight.

As she felt her pulse plummet back to normal, a grin spread across her face. She could slow herself down and work on that data summary tomorrow. Tonight, she was all about rushing to Grant's place.

Chapter Eighteen

Typically, Sam enjoyed driving by Golden Gate Park, but as the car crossed the 1 and Grant's boxy two-story place came into view, it required heroic levels of willpower for her to not throw herself from the moving car.

Nodding thanks to the driver, Sam jumped out onto the sidewalk and smiled. She wasn't sure what she had expected, but the place was 100 percent Grant in the best way. The building itself was nothing flashy; like a lot of houses in the area, it was squeezed between two houses of the exact same stucco 1940s build, with the paint and window shape being the only serious differentiators. While his neighbors' houses were all sherbet colored, Grant's was the color of a gray sky, with a bright-blue, friendly-looking garage door that screamed, *I don't take myself as seriously as you think I do.* The small square of grass that passed for a standard front yard in this city was packed with neatly arranged succulents and varying shrubs that made Sam wonder if Grant was into gardening as well as basketball.

Reaching into the neck of her scrubs, Sam rearranged the strap of her favorite teal bra. Admittedly, the lace was a little itchy, but the effect was worth it. Giving her shoulders a shake to make sure everything was in place, she started up the path lined with small solar lights toward the front door. All evening, she had imagined candles, wine, and the look on Grant's face when he realized that she'd been serious about putting something sexy on underneath her basic hospital-mandated attire.

Marching up the stairs, Sam took a big breath and knocked twice. She had mentally prepared to admire the landscaping for a minute. Instead, Grant opened the door immediately.

"Hi." He exhaled the word as if he had been waiting to say it for some time.

"Hey," Sam said with a small, dorky wave as if he weren't standing two feet in front of her. She cringed internally at her lack of smooth. Her underwear might be sexy, but her chill level definitely wasn't.

Grant laughed, a combination of nerves and charm that put Sam at ease, then swept his arm out wide and said, "Come in. I'm cooking."

"You're cooking? I figured we'd just be ordering pizza or something. Now I feel spoiled." Sam tossed her hair over her shoulder and put on mock airs as she stepped into the house.

"Oh. This is not . . ." Grant closed the door, then stopped and winced before starting again. "I don't cook. Not really. That statement was misleading." He rubbed the back of his neck and looked sideways. "I mean, I know how to feed myself, and I have specific foods I make on special occasions, but day to day, I have a meal-kit service. I plan to put one of those in the oven."

Sam blinked at him for a second, watching the muscles in his jaw tense as if the difference between a meal kit and him spending hours in a kitchen was a make-or-break issue.

"Well, now I have to leave." Grant's eyebrows shot up, and she started to laugh. "Just kidding. I don't care. In fact, I consume a lot of freezer mac and cheese. What are we eating?"

"Arugula-and-pancetta pizza. But I did have ice cream delivered. And wine. I know you like both those things." Grant started to laugh as he walked them into the living room. "First, I have to confess that I tried to be low key and ask Duke what kind of wine you like. That guy caught on to me immediately. I think I tipped him off about us. Sorry."

"Don't be sorry. I'm pretty sure he figured it out days ago when you texted me late at night," Sam fibbed. She wasn't ready to admit that she and Jehan had shouted the news at him the second he got home. That seemed like she was in way too deep, and this was casual.

"Sorry about that too." Grant shrugged but didn't look the least bit apologetic. "Also, he has no idea what you like to drink. He suggested moscato, which sounded aggressively wrong."

"He is deeply incorrect," Sam laughed. Duke was a beer drinker. Odds were high that he'd just dug around in his head for the only type of wine he could name and come up with a dessert wine that was so sweet it might rot teeth.

"Well, that's a relief," Grant said, steering them toward the living room. "I would have felt terrible if I had denied you your favorite wine when we are supposed to be celebrating. Are you opposed to a red blend?"

"I'm not." Sam fought the urge to make fun of just how Northern California that question was. Grant had lived here his whole life and had likely been forced to learn about wine from age twenty-one on, if for no other reason than he probably had to take out-of-town guests wine tasting no fewer than four times a year.

"Good, because I have that open in the kitchen. Stay here—I'll put the pizza in the oven and bring us a glass." With a smile, Grant sauntered out of the room.

Sam used the moment alone to look around his place. As expected, there was no clutter or mess. What surprised her was that Grant had left a lot of the vintage quirks that came with a place this old. The edge of the room that faced the street had a cozy little window seat, adorned with squishy-looking big pillows and a small stack of books, including a detective paperback. In the center of the room, he had a set of couches and chairs that looked like he'd spent much more than he would ever admit on the perfect 1960s-inspired furniture in the same blue as the front door. Instead of installing overhead lights, he had simply used a number of brass floor lamps of different shapes, heights, and sizes. The light from the lamps cast a soft, low glow around the room.

Wandering over to a long, low sideboard cabinet, Sam touched the cover of a coffee-table book titled *Trolleys: The Radical History of Transportation in San Francisco*. She'd started to open the book to find out exactly what about trolleys was so radical when the sound of two glasses clinking interrupted her. Turning to find Grant standing in the entry, Sam felt her heartbeat stutter.

Memories of the first time she'd seen Grant washed over her and rearranged themselves in front of her eyes. He was still handsome. But when he was standing in his own space, all the hard edges seemed to have been sanded off. The same cheekbones, strong shoulders, and lean build made softer and rounder in the low light of his living room. Even his haircut seemed less stark. Standing there in his typical formfitting navy-blue sweater and basic gray jeans, holding two red wineglasses in one hand and a bottle in the other, he seemed in his element. Everything about the transformation appealed to Sam.

"Food will be ready in fifteen minutes," Grant said as he walked into the room. The entire experience was literally causing all but the most basic want signals in Sam's brain to cease firing. Unaware of what the movement was doing to her, he rearranged the glasses on their own coasters. The muscles in his right arm flexed as he began to pour wine into each glass. The sound alone was like some sort of lust-trigger-ing ASMR experience, sending tingles from her scalp down her spine. Combined with the way the light caught his jaw and traced the line of his neck . . . it was too much.

Lowering himself onto a corner of the couch, Grant looked up at her with curiosity. "Did you want to sit? You're welcome to bring the trolley book with you."

"Ah. Yes." Something about his smirk shook Sam out of the lust corkscrew she was in. Giving her head a shake, she started toward the couch, saying, "Riveting as it is, I think I can have dinner and then come back to it."

"Suit yourself," Grant said, bringing his glass to his lips and taking a long, slow sip that seemed determined to stop Sam's heart.

Forcing herself to focus on something other than how desperate she was to kiss him again, Sam settled into a spot on the couch and picked up her own glass. When she took a sip, her entire body softened as the wine's gentle sting worked its way across her taste buds and down her throat. Sighing heavily, she said, "This is delicious."

"Glad you like it. I know people say don't do red with things like pizza, but I think this wine proves them wrong," Grant said, smiling into his glass. "Plus, it's twenty dollars at the wine shop right now."

Sam laughed. "A good deal for a good day. Who could ask for more?"

"My thoughts exactly." Grant leaned back into his corner of the couch, carefully holding the glass from the base of the stem, then said, "So tell me about the program feedback so far."

"I thought you'd never ask." Sam smiled. There were other things she was dying for him to ask about, but it seemed like they were having dinner first, so she'd just have to be patient. Taking another sip of wine, Sam outlined what Kaiya had told her.

Eventually, Grant stood up and brought back their perfectly cooked, premade meal. Before she'd even had a chance to blow on a bite, he asked her about the feedback they'd received from the doctors so far. Of course, she left out Dr. Franklin's nonanswer and stuck to the positive aspects, of which there was a lot to say. With each sentence, the look on Grant's face grew prouder, as if Sam were telling him how well their baby had done in day care or something . . .

Not that she was thinking about babies with him or anything. Sam had zero idea where that thought had come from. It was just that he talked about how proud his father was of him and his siblings, and she could totally see the same trait in him. He'd probably make a great dad. Again, not that she was thinking about him as a dad or anything. Sam decided to blame her job. She did spend all day thinking about babies, after all.

She refocused her attention, and the two of them slipped into the easy rhythm of conversation. Somewhere in between trading questions and answers, they managed to finish their food. As if watching her gradually melt with desire were his goal, Grant reached for the bottle of wine to pour them a second glass. Bringing the glass toward her very unkissed lips, Sam said, "Thank you."

She was halfway to a first sip when Grant's eyes opened wide and he said, "We didn't say cheers last time."

"That's okay. That's what second glasses are for."

"Cheers," Grant said as he finished filling his glass. Sam raised her glass toward Grant, who was preoccupied with trying to take a sip. Clearing her throat, Sam waited until he looked at her fully before she said, "Careful, we have to make eye contact before saying cheers."

Grant made his eyes wide as if to exaggerate eye contact. After taking a sip, he asked, "What happens if we don't do that?"

"Cursed with bad sex for seven years," Sam said, letting her lips curl into a devious smile.

Grant's expression moved through surprised to pleased to hot in the length of a second. Biting down on his bottom lip, he returned her half smile and said, "That's worse than breaking a mirror. That feels mean."

"I wouldn't level that curse before the end of the evening. I deserve better." Sam couldn't decide if she wanted to punch Grant. Who cared if it was mean? This was an invitation to get busy, not engage in banter. Sam almost said as much, but Grant's face changed again. This time, it seemed like a joke was fighting desperately to make its way off his tongue. Would but jokes were kisses, Sam thought. Instead, she said, "What?"

"Nothing."

"Nothing is always something, so tell me," Sam said, pulling her shoulders back and setting her wineglass down.

"Okay, showing you my hand here, but I low-key thought that's what we were doing tonight." Grant looked at her with his head tilted to one side as if he were trying to solve a puzzle but couldn't touch the pieces until he knew where they went.

Sam felt the corners of her mouth turn up as she said, "Is it not? 'Cause I am wearing my good bra."

"I mean, I thought it was based on your text. But then you were wearing your scrubs, and I thought maybe you were kidding," Grant said, gesturing at her attire with his glass.

"Nope. I was absolutely serious about that." Sam reached for the hem of her shirt, feeling the fabric beneath her fingers for only a moment before she made up her mind. Taking the shirt off in one move, she tossed it away from the couch and said, "If you don't do something about it now, I really will curse you."

The room felt like someone had pressed pause. Like the earth had stopped spinning on its axis. And then something in Grant's face changed. Sam felt held in place by the look, as if she had crossed some invisible barrier and now she was on a course collision with him. The once-playful expression was gone, replaced with sheer desire.

Sam watched his chest rise and fall for one breath. Then two. Then a third. With each of his deep breaths, her breathing became shallower, as if her heartbeat were compensating for his pace. The air felt thick with tension, and her skin tingled as she waited for him to respond.

Finally, Grant moved, methodically setting his wineglass down on a wooden coaster, then turning his full attention back to her. How he had the presence of mind to use a coaster when she was in her most flattering bra waiting for him was beyond her. Forcing herself to take a real breath, she decided she had to move him along. "What are you—"

"Good thing I changed my sheets."

Unlike that night at the park, there was nothing careful about this kiss. All there was, was him. His lips. His face. His neck. He kissed with bold strokes and teasing nibbles as his hands ran over her body, sending cravings shooting through her veins. Slowly, Grant began to work his way down her neck, kissing along her breasts toward her tightening nipples. His hands applying pressure low on her hips, sending heat to gather and throb between her legs.

Sam shimmied, trying to get closer to him as she reached for the hem of his shirt. He leaned off her just long enough for her to pull the sweater over his head and toss it on the floor. Then he was back, trailing lush kisses along the curve of her breast where her skin and her bra met. The feel of him wanting her was enough to drive Sam absolutely out of her mind. She wiggled beneath him, trying to reach either the button of his pants or the drawstring on hers—she didn't really care which as long as they were both naked soon. Grant made a sound in the back of his throat that caused her to shiver as she reached between them.

Working a hand underneath her, Grant pulled her into a seat on top of him in one motion that would have impressed her if it hadn't created more space between them than she wanted. Grant kissed along the edge of her jaw and nipped at her earlobe, causing tingles to run through her. Nuzzling her neck, he panted, "Not here. Condoms. Clean sheets."

"Yes." It wasn't the most eloquent phrase she'd ever said, but it was all she needed to say at this point. Somewhere in the back of her mind, Sam's brain gave her body the command to roll off Grant's lap and onto the couch. For three seconds, Sam felt like ice water had been dumped on her. She missed the feel of Grant. The warmth of his bare chest against hers.

Then he jumped up and reached for her. The force of him pulling her up to stand brought her back in contact with him, and she relaxed once more. Wrapping both hands around her ass, Grant kissed her hard as he walked them backward. Sam heard him knock into the coffee table. Later she'd check to make sure they hadn't spilled wine all over his nice rug. Right now, with Grant's hands moving to the drawstring of her pants, she didn't care if they'd dumped a whole bottle on the ground.

Sam stepped gracelessly out of her scrubs and laughed as they knocked into a wall in the hallway. "We are going to be covered in bruises if we aren't more careful."

"We are going to be sore anyway, with you in that underwear," Grant whispered as he backed her into the bedroom and kissed her again. He tasted like sweat and wine and promises about tonight that he could keep.

Yanking down hard on his pants, Sam paused to watch Grant kick them to the side in a manner that was as silly as it was sexy. As they stood there in their underwear, it was all Sam could do to not leap on him and wrap her legs around his waist. Instead, she waited while Grant pulled her to him, closing the gap between them as he kissed her neck and reached around her back for the clasp of her bra. Pulling back slightly, Sam put a hand on his chest and said, "Before this comes off, I have two questions. First, anywhere you don't want to be touched?"

"What?" Grant said, his eyes glassy with lust as he played with the edge of the fastening on her bra. "Oh. No. You?"

"No choking," Sam said, tracing the tip of her index finger along the waistband of his boxer briefs.

Grant tilted his head to one side. "Feels like that goes without saying."

"You'd be surprised." Sam shook her head. Tracing her other hand along the ridges of his collarbones, she added, "If you don't say it, those are the ones who try without asking."

"Don't have to worry about that with me," Grant said, closing his eyes as his lips tilted into a smile. When he opened them again, the thirsty look had returned. Placing his hand over hers, he brought it up to his lips and kissed the inside of her wrist. The touch of his mouth to the soft skin there sent a tingle down her spine. Pulling her hand away, she leaned in again, this time kissing him in slow, languid turns. They had all night, and she planned to prolong the delicious inevitable until neither of them could take it anymore. She moved to kiss the spot behind his ear, and Grant pulled back a fraction of an inch to look her in the eyes, his lips swollen as he asked, "What's the second question?"

Sam smiled against his lips and whispered, "Anywhere you do want to be touched?"

A lopsided grin crossed his face, and Grant leaned in to kiss the sensitive spot just between her jaw and her throat, then whispered, "Yes. But our underwear needs to come off for that."

Chapter Nineteen

Sam drummed her fingers on the steering wheel of Duke's rust bucket as she crept along the pickup zone at San Francisco International Airport. A small part of her wished she had just told her mom to take a cab or get a rideshare, but Sam knew that if she did that, her mother would knot herself into something resembling emotional chain mail by the time she reached her hotel. It was better for everyone if she just picked her up.

She had almost resigned herself to circling again when she spotted her mother hauling a massive aqua suitcase out of the door toward the end of the terminal. Sam started waving right as her mother started digging through her purse, ostensibly to find her phone so she could call her. Seeing an opening in the traffic, she slid through it and pulled up right beside her mother as her cell phone started to ring. Since the autodescend function on the passenger window had stopped working last week, she answered as she watched her mother clean her sunglasses on the hem of her flowing shirt while holding the phone to her ear with her shoulder.

"Hi, Sammy. I'm outside, but no rush if you're late."

Suppressing a giggle, Sam said, "Look to your right."

Her mother pulled the phone away from her ear and looked at it as if Sam had said something absurd. Then when nothing happened, she looked to her right and jumped about two inches back from the curb.

Shouting at the window and into the receiver, her mom said, "You're here!"

Sam grinned at the familiar face on the other side of the window—which was squeaky clean thanks to Duke's insistence that no one's mom should ride in a dusty car. In spite of all the angst her mother's visit had caused, Sam felt her irritation slipping away at the sight of her. Her hair was longer than the last time Sam had seen her, but she was otherwise unchanged. Diana Holbrook still had the smile creases around her eyes and the lines on either side of a mouth that was just as likely to sing you a bedtime song as it was to mumble under her breath if something didn't go her way. In short, she was still the same mom that Sam loved.

Jumping out of the driver's side door, she called, "Hi, Mom!"

"Hi, baby," Diana said, running around to the trunk of the car and holding her arms out wide for a hug. "I didn't recognize you in that car."

The way she said *car* let Sam know her mother was well aware that it was a clunker but that she was too polite to say something like that within hearing distance of others, lest they think she was an elitist. Which she was, but that was beside the point.

Wrapping her arms around Diana, Sam breathed in deeply, letting the smell of her mom's fabric softener and her grapefruit shampoo envelop her. The combination instantly took her back to when she was a little girl.

"Oh, I am so happy to see you, sweetheart," her mother said into her hair.

"Good to see you, too, Mom." Sam released her mom and fussed with the lock on the trunk. "I can get your suitcase if you want to get settled into the car."

"All right," her mom said, giving her the handle of her roller bag, then walking around the car. Sam tried not to laugh at her mom, who gave the door a dainty tug, which did nothing to make it open.

"You really gotta yank," Sam said after her mom gave the door a few more gentle pulls.

"Right," Diana said, bracing her feet and pulling with two hands. The door popped open with a prodigious groan, and her mom stumbled back a few steps but managed to keep her feet. "Whoo. That one really was stuck."

"Duke's car is a little busted. But it runs." Sam smiled and hoisted the suitcase into the trunk. To her mom's credit, Diana did slam the car door shut. No need to tell her how the doors on a hooptie worked twice.

Jogging back around to the driver's side, Sam ducked into the car, slammed her own door, then buckled in. Half watching as an oblivious Bay Area driver was hustled off by airport security for parking in a crosswalk, Sam glanced at her mom and said, "Okay, so I was thinking we could get you checked in, and then I know a great spot for dinner. It's this amazing French restaurant within walking distance from my place, so we can drop Duke's car off and then go over. It sometimes has a long wait for a table, but—"

"I love that plan, but I think we should go to the venue before dinner if we can."

"Of course, I'll call them and see if they have an event going or if we can stick our heads inside. Make sure all the pictures and hostess gifts were delivered okay. I should have thought of that," Sam said, giving her head a little shake.

"Actually, I had everything sent to the hotel, so we won't have to stay at the venue long. I just want to see it."

"What?" Sam asked, trying to keep her eyes on the road as they neared the end of the freeway and began creeping toward the Financial District, where her mother had booked a ridiculously pricey hotel room because she wanted to earn points on her credit card. "I thought we talked about sending it to the venue."

"Well, yes. But then I tried to call to confirm that they had someone who would be able to sign for everything, and it just seemed so convoluted, so I thought the hotel would be better."

Sam gritted her teeth. She suspected that when her mom said *convoluted*, what she really meant was she hadn't wanted to wait for them to call her back, so she'd done an easier thing and assumed Sam could deal with it. It was too late to do anything about that now.

Sighing, Sam looked for a bright spot. Maybe she'd shipped small pictures and gotten cookies as gifts, so they could just drop a box or two off before Sam needed to hand the car over to Duke. "How many photos did you ship? Will everything fit in Duke's car?"

"I have about twenty-five. A few are pretty big." Her mother looked around the car, as if assessing the space available to them and the viability of her plan for the first time. Frowning slightly, she paused, then fixed her face in an upbeat expression before saying, "We may need to make a few trips, but we have a couple of days. It'll be fun mother-daughter bonding."

"Mom," Sam said, trying to keep a flare of frustration out of her voice. "Remember, I have to work. And this isn't my car. I have to give it back to Duke."

"I don't remember you mentioning work," Diana said, sounding put out as she rearranged her sunglasses on the top of her head. "And I thought we could just rent a car. I'm happy to pay for it."

"We talked about it three weeks ago, at the same time that we talked about Dad starting to volunteer for the community center. Remember?" Sam flexed her fingers on the steering wheel. This was classic Diana; she just wouldn't hear the things she didn't want to know. And she wanted to know absolutely nothing about Sam that contradicted her plan for her daughter, including her work schedule.

"If you say so." Diana's tone implied that she absolutely did not believe her but was too passive aggressive to fight about it. "But what am I supposed to do for the next few days? I planned on spending time with you. Guess that fellowship has you very busy."

"That's why I said you should fly out on the same day as Isaiah," Sam said, pressing her foot down on the gas a little harder than she should have. They were only a few minutes from the hotel, and then her mother would be too preoccupied to pick fights. Sam just had to be patient. She didn't want to ruin this chance to make things right with her mom. "Maybe go to the museums? There is a great K-spa I heard about—"

"Can't you just skip off a little early . . ."

"Not really. Medicine doesn't work like that. Plus, Grant and I have to film a commercial for Anjo. And there's the birthing center grand opening event to finalize. And I still need to submit that progress report to the foundation, which I cannot forget to do, or I will be in big trouble."

"Okay." Her mother clenched her jaw but didn't press.

A small voice in the back of Sam's head reminded her just how much her mother had given up over the years, first for her husband's career and then for Isaiah's and Sam's happiness. If Sam had a different kind of job and stayed close to home, then they could have had lunch every Wednesday just like Diana envisioned. The guilty voice reminded Sam that her mother had to settle for text messages and phone calls. Frustrated as Sam was, she could understand that disappointment. Trying to be gentle, she added, "And it's just a couple days. Isaiah and Dad will be flying in on Friday night, and obviously, I'll be around when I'm not on call—"

"No, no, it's fine," Diana said, turning to look out the window as the freeway ended and they started the slow creep toward the hotel. "Filming a commercial should be fun. Will it be on TV?"

"I hope not. But given the little I know about Duesa, probably." Sam laughed, then took a deep breath. She knew her mom wasn't fine, but there was nothing she could do about it. Hopefully, she'd get over it once she saw just how much planning and work Sam had put into the venue.

Turning into the hotel's passenger-drop-off area, Sam tried to stop worrying about if her mother was happy and make a joke. "I don't think a valet would even know what to do with this car. I'm gonna drop you here and self-park."

"I think that's wise." Her mother laughed halfheartedly, then reached for the door handle.

"You are gonna have to put your shoulder into it," Sam warned with a lopsided grin.

"Ah, all right then." This time her mother's smile was genuine as she leaned back a good six inches, then went at the door with a surprising amount of force. Hoisting herself out of the car, she asked, "You'll bring my suitcase too?"

"Yup. I'll meet you in the lobby once you're checked in."

"See you in a second, Sammy." Diana waved as if she hadn't just been irritated with her, then slammed the door like a hunk-of-junk-riding champ.

Her mother sashayed inside, all smiles at the porters, then disappeared. As soon as she was gone, Sam exhaled and leaned back in her seat. Tonight might not exactly be the meaningful mother-daughter dinner she had planned. But it wasn't the end of the world. There was a really good Thai place near the venue. They could just order takeout and get caught up over dinner while they moved her mother's party stuff.

Sitting up and easing the car back into drive, Sam pulled around to the parking lot and was lucky enough to find a spot near the elevators. At least she wouldn't have to drag her mom's suitcase too far.

Sam had just gotten the suitcase out of the trunk when the telltale buzz of a text coming in rattled her purse. Using one hand to push the suitcase, she fished around in her purse as she walked toward the elevators. Finally locating the phone partially jammed under her oversize wallet, Sam saw Grant's name flash across her screen.

Something about seeing his name made her relax instinctively. Possibly because they'd spent the last three days snuggled in his sheets and relaxing. The time didn't exactly lend itself to getting stuff like the

Anjo progress report done, but it was a hell of a lot more fun. In fact, had her mother not flown in, Sam would likely still be there.

Like Grant was with most things, he'd been secretly prepared with an extra toothbrush and clean towels. All she'd had to do was steal his scrubs when clothes were required to tip the hot-wings delivery person, who'd managed to arrive while Grant was in the shower. Smiling at the phone's sensor, she unlocked the screen and tapped the text.

> Hey! I hope you are having fun with your mom. Just wanted to make sure you saw that Sherilynn emailed over the info for the video shoot tomorrow.

Using a knuckle to press the elevator button, Sam quickly tapped over to her inbox to make sure she had received the email, then flipped back to his text. Sighing as she walked into the surprisingly small elevator, Sam answered,

> Just got the email. I'll give it a read while I'm helping my mom move all her party stuff (she didn't send it to The Lost Key because "reasons")

Sam skipped adding the side-eye emoji. Grant knew her well enough to add the eye roll to the text on this one.

> Ha. Fun is a strong word, then. Maybe I'll just say I hope it ends up being a good time?

> I think it is safe to say we are having "a time."

Sam hit send on the text as the elevator dinged to announce her arrival in the lobby. Her mother was still at the counter, looking irked. Deciding it was better to let her mother sort out whatever was going on,

Sam quietly wheeled the suitcase over to a set of couches and sat down to read Grant's next message.

> If you want a break, you could always come by my place for dinner after the video is done filming tomorrow. I washed your towel . . . and my scrubs if that sways you at all. :-)

Happy little sparks shot through Sam's chest. Part of her had been worried that she had overstayed her welcome, despite Grant's reassurances that she could hog three-quarters of his bed for as long as she liked. Things between them had moved so slowly. Now, suddenly they were speeding by, no matter how hard she tried to slow down. Everything just felt so easy and comfortable.

Now that she thought about it, relationships that were easy didn't come naturally to her. She certainly hadn't been raised with them. Silly as it felt, she hadn't trusted Grant the first time he'd said she could stick around. She just wasn't used to affection without conditions. It still seemed improbable to her that under all those layers of perfection, the only thing Grant seemed truly set on was being fond of her without expectation.

Diana's voice carried across the lobby, pulling Sam out of her head and redirecting her thoughts on the next few days. She needed to focus on the here and now and fixing things with her mom, even if she had a toothbrush at his place. Sighing, she typed out:

> A clean towel very much sways me, but I think that depends on how much of my mom's stuff I can manage to move tonight. Maybe we play it by ear?

> Works for me. Take a picture when everything is set up. I want to know what the party will look like.

Sam could still hear her mom's voice, but something about his text made her pause. Why couldn't Grant see the show in person? It might be nice to have him there. A reassuring presence in the storm that was her mercurial family. In fact, since they were all coming to the grand opening earlier that day, Sam reasoned, this wouldn't even be the first time he met them. Besides, if it was too much, he could always say no.

I could take pictures, or you can always see it for yourself. Party starts at 6:30 if you want to come.

Sam held her breath as she watched the text send, her shoulders creeping toward her ears while the little ... signaled he was typing a response. She wasn't sure why she was so nervous. This was a casual invitation. It wasn't like she was asking him to marry her. And yes, it would be nice to have him there, but she could absolutely survive on her own—

Love to. Do you want me to show up early to help with anything?

Sam's shoulders dropped so fast that she was almost in awe of how quickly the tension left her body. He would be there. She wasn't asking too much. Grinning down at her phone, she texted back.

Nope. Just being there is enough.

"Sammy. Can you come here, please?"

Her mother calling her name jerked Sam out of her happy, hazy bubble and back into reality. Tomorrow she could revel in spending time with someone whose needs were much simpler and, frankly, a lot more fun. Right now, her mother needed all her attention. Tucking the idea of time with Grant away in the back corner of her mind for when she needed some joy, she quickly hit send on a see-you-tomorrow text.

Sam hoped Grant would know her well enough to know that much like the implied eye roll about her mother, there was an implied heart at the end of that text.

~

Yawning as the rideshare pulled up to the Anjo office, Sam fixed a smile on her face. She had spent until well past midnight hauling her mom's stuff around and having her judgment about the low-key cheese-board catering second-guessed, which put her in a mood. Of course, the fact she'd only managed to get four hours of sleep because she was nervous about being on camera didn't help much either. On the upside, while her face might look a little tired, she had used the sleepless extra time to deep condition and style her hair, so at least her curls were poppin'.

After checking in with the security guard, Sam stepped into the elevator and waited for the door to close before she let herself relax against its walls. Not for the first time, she wished she had arranged to meet Grant before this. When she'd finally read Sherilynn's email and the accompanying script last night, she'd realized that (a) someone at Anjo thought she was a professional actor and not a kid who'd gotten kicked out of community theater for forgetting their one line in the second-grade play, and (b) practicing that script with Grant—even in the car on the way over here—would have been helpful. Instead, she was just going to have to hope for the best and pray that the fifteen minutes of choppy practice running her lines while she was also trying to fix her mascara would be enough.

Leaning away from the wall as the elevator dinged, Sam was greeted by a flurry of activity. Sherilynn stood in the hallway, pointing one direction and giving instructions to two people in cargo pants with a large pushcart piled with camera gear. Spotting Sam, they waved and gave the work crew a firm nod. As soon as the people wheeled the cart away, Sherilynn rushed around the corner and rolled her eyes.

"The second camera crew apparently didn't understand the difference between a loading dock and a loading zone." Giving her head a shake, they sighed heavily and then looked Sam over, frowning. "We brought makeup in, so we can take care of the bags under your eyes. Rough night?"

"I . . . ," Sam stammered as she tried to process both the insult and the fact that they had a proper makeup person for a three-minute promo video. Blinking rapidly, she pulled herself together and said, "There is a makeup person?"

She had only been in one promo video before—advertising for the tragic high school state playoffs game—and there definitely hadn't been a makeup person for that.

"Oh, of course. You know, this is gonna go out to Anjo partners and companies around the globe. Not to mention Duesa plans to play it as part of her talk at Mykonos," Sherilynn said, gently nudging Sam's arm to get her to follow them.

"Mykonos?"

"You know, that venture summit that all those big billionaire hedge fund tech types attend. She is obsessed with it. I'm sure she mentioned it to you in the interview. Every year she does a profile piece on Anjo's latest philanthropic investment."

"Sorta . . . ," Sam said, noncommittal as she tried to remember the details about it. She'd known that the summit existed and that the *New York Times* loved to hate it. She just hadn't realized she might be attending it in video format.

"It's like Coachella for boring people," Sherilynn said breezily. Turning a corner into a door marked PRIVATE, she said, "Here we go. Grant's already in the conference room. He wanted to watch the crew set up. Bless him."

Sam rounded the corner into a private bathroom, where a makeup artist with an undercut and a deadly dull expression on their face stood waiting. "Bebe. This is Samantha. As you can see, the bones are there, but she looks tired, and you know Duesa's feelings on that."

Bebe pressed their lips into a very flat line and tilted their head. After a few moments, they said, "It's salvageable. Have a seat. We need to get you going."

"I'll leave you to it. Sam, when you are done, Bebe can show you where you are headed."

"Okay, thank you," Sam said as she was hustled into a chair.

"Right. We have a lot to do here and not a lot of time. Duesa likes a very specific look for this, so tilt your face back for me," Bebe said as they dug through a giant case on the counter.

Sam's heart started to pound as they began running some sort of wipe all over her carefully placed bronzer.

"Are you a doctor too?"

"Yes." This was not at all what she'd been expecting, and now the nerves were starting to make her sweat. What if she sweat through her blouse? Would there be wardrobe for that too? Worse, what if she was so awful on camera that they revoked her funding? How would she explain that to Kaiya? Dr. Franklin would be so smug.

"Cute!" Bebe shrieked as they went back to digging through their makeup case. Sam tried to calm herself down. She would be fine. She would remember her lines. In fact, she could mentally run them right now.

"What kind of doctor are you?" Bebe asked, interrupting her as she tried to recall the first thing she was supposed to say.

"I'm a—"

"Oops. Hold still," Bebe interrupted. "I just love . . ."

Sam realized that it was likely that Bebe would talk to her the entire time she was in the chair, just like she was at the dentist with the hygienist asking her questions while polishing her teeth. She wouldn't be able to think about her lines or answer Bebe like this—an idea that made a lump in her throat rise. Then again, Sam thought as she tried to take deep, calming breaths without moving, given the amount of money Duesa was spending on this, they could probably just photoshop a supermodel next to Grant or something. Somehow the idea that she could fail and be replaced with a model didn't make her feel any better.

~

"Bryce, can we slow the teleprompter down please?" The producer's voice was patient, even if his face read like he was about to scream *REDRUM.* "Whenever you are ready, Sam."

This is an actual disaster. It was all Sam could think as she watched the words on the iPad mounted under the camera scroll backward for the fifth time. Next to her, she felt Grant go completely still for a moment, as if he were trying to swallow his frustration as well. Of course he was good at this. And of course he had managed to find time to memorize the last-minute script they'd sent because unlike Sam, he seemed to meet everyone's expectations just by breathing in his oh-so-charming and camera-ready way.

Doing her best not to smile in a forced way—a mistake she'd made on her third take, or was that the fourth take?—Sam started again. "Hello, I'm Dr. Samantha Holbrook, a research fellow at San Francisco Central Hospital and cofounder of the hospital's birthing center."

"And I'm Dr. Grant Gao, senior clinical fellow and adviser for the birthing center." As if it hadn't been in the script, Grant gestured between the two of them and said, "We're so excited to tell you all about this one-of-a-kind center, the seed funding for which was generously provided by the Anjo Foundation, which is the philanthropic arm of the Anjo Group. The birthing center started out as Sam's brainchild, but it has—"

"Wait, Grant!" Sam placed a hand on Grant's forearm and tried to sound as if she frequently interrupted Grant with excited exclamation points to add details about a tangentially related website. "Before we tell them about the center, we should say that if you want to know more about the Anjo's Group's—" Sam paused, realizing that she had just made both *Anjo's* and *Group's* possessive, a mistake that was definitely not in the script. Blinking, she tried the line again, adding an extra smile for good measure. ". . . if you want to know more about the Anjo Group's work, you can visit their website, listed below. It's Anjo Group dot com. That's—"

"Sorry, Sam. You're doing great. Just one minor fix—it's Anjo Group dot co."

"Oh. Sorry. What did I say?" Sam felt like her makeup was going to start melting under the hot lights the camera crew had brought in.

"'Dot com.' Not a big deal. Just a small correction. When you are ready." The producer gestured in a way that implied that he had worked with temperamental Hollywood stars before moving to the Bay Area in the hopes of working on easy corporate commercials. Poor guy clearly hadn't seen her coming when he'd made that jump.

Out of the corner of her eye, Sam watched as one of the second camera people slumped over in their chair with frustration. Sam couldn't say she blamed them, but knowing they were irritated didn't help her nerves any.

"Just relax. You'll be fine," Grant said, giving her hand a squeeze and pulling her out of her thoughts.

"Sorry," Sam said, guilt piling on her. Trying to lighten everyone's mood, she added, "I should have had an extra coffee."

"I'll have one delivered," Sherilynn said matter-of-factly from their perch by the door. Sam suspected she was keeping an eye out for Duesa in case they needed to intercept her before she saw Sam breaking down and pitched a fit.

Sighing, Sam shook out her shoulders and then smiled at the camera again. "If you want to learn more, visit Anjo Group dot co. That's Anjo Group dot co. Okay, now you can tell 'em, Grant."

She nodded at Grant in her best scripted playful manner, then mentally sighed with relief. Only a few more lines to go, and then she could get the hell away from all these cameras and the bright lights that were definitely going to make her sweat through the pits of her blouse. Thank God she hadn't chosen to wear silk—

"Sam. Do you need another minute?" the producer asked through gritted teeth. Sam felt her face flush when she realized that she had been so happy to be done with her line that she'd completely missed the handoff for her next one.

"So sorry," Sam said, pointedly avoiding the looks from the sound guy, whose gray hair was poking out in tufts under his headphones.

"Coffee's here," Sherilynn announced. "Why don't we take a ten-minute break to get caffeinated?"

"I think that would be wise." The producer sighed and walked away from camera one.

Sam's eyes burned as she slunk out of the chair and over to the table in the corner, where something that was thankfully not boxed coffee had been placed. If Bebe hadn't worked so hard on her makeup, she would have started to cry. As it was, she had a feeling that the ten-minute break being extended because one of the actors had a meltdown would only make things worse for her.

Reaching for the creamer, Sam tried not to think about how badly she was tanking. Sure, it would have been nice if she'd had more time with the script. But she also should have put her foot down with her mom long before 12:30 a.m. If she'd just stood up for herself—

"Hey," Grant said, coming to stand beside her. "How you doing?"

Sam knew his tone was meant to be supportive, but she wished he wouldn't ask right now. After all, the only answer to that question was somewhere between *terrible* and *do you know if there is a nearby manhole I can jump in?* Letting her shoulders sag, she turned to answer him. "Been better."

Grant snorted and shook his head. "Don't worry. This stuff is hard."

"Not for you." Sam glared at her coffee and wished she could just make a break for the door without anyone noticing. With her luck, Sherilynn probably had someone watching for just such a thing.

"Oh no. It was hard for me too. Since you were busy, I actually forced my mom to run lines with me. Let me tell you, she had a lot of notes." Grant laughed.

"Sorry I couldn't be there," Sam said, trying to laugh.

"What time did you finish up with your mom anyway?"

"Twelve forty-five."

"In the morning? Sam, that's ridiculous." Grant sounded incredulous as he watched her sip her coffee. "No wonder you are tired. Why didn't you just leave?"

"It's not that simple with my mom." Sam frowned at Grant as she blew on her coffee, creating miniature waves in the beverage as she tried to cool it down. She knew her mother's expectations were unreasonable, but it wasn't like she had much of a choice. She only had Duke's car for the night. What was she supposed to do? Just leave her mom throwing a tantrum in the hotel for the next three days with no way to move her party stuff around? She couldn't do that. Every moment she stalled was another minute for her mother to get more worked up. Trying to stop her would only make Sam's life more difficult down the road. All she had to do was keep it together and stick to the plan. Short-term suffering for long-term peace.

"I feel like midnight when you have a big day in the morning crosses into the 'simple' territory," Grant said, using one hand to put air quotes around the word *simple*.

"You try telling her that." Sam took a step back from Grant and reached for her purse sitting on the next table with all the crew members' bags. She didn't want to argue with Grant right now. She'd had enough of that with her mother correcting every little step she'd taken last night. Besides, she couldn't fix the fact that she wasn't perfect at this.

Or that her mother wasn't a professional entertainer. He had to believe that she was trying, didn't he?

"I mean, I know she isn't my mom, but it sounds like you need to set a boundary with her," Grant said softly as he stepped closer.

"Yeah. You've said that before," Sam said, hoping her uninterested tone would dissuade him from pushing the matter.

"It's just . . . you don't have to help everyone all the time. You could say no and let someone else figure it out." Sam looked up sharply, causing Grant to close his mouth, his jaw tense. Sighing, he put his free hand in the pocket of his slacks and said, "What I mean is—"

"Are you really criticizing me for trying to help?" Sam cut in. If anyone should get family pressure and her mother, it was Grant. But clearly he didn't, and now he was piling on more guilt. The one thing she had plenty of in her life. Of course, Mr. Practically Perfect would think there was a neat little solution to her problems because there always seemed to be one for his. Grant didn't juggle complex and conflicting commitments. He just solved a problem or said no to someone and moved on because he was lovable. He probably thought that anyone he was with had the same easy-breezy experience—otherwise, why would he be with them? He wouldn't knowingly invite a mess into his life.

Sam recoiled from the thought. Sure, he could be hard to read, but did one criticism make his feelings fickle? The muscles in her neck bunched, and Sam said, "Look, Grant, I—"

She stopped as the phone in her hand buzzed with a text. When she looked down, Kaiya's name and one word scrolled across the screen.

SOS

"Sam. I didn't mean—" Grant started, but Sam held her hand up to stop him as she unlocked the phone and read the rest of Kaiya's message.

I know you're not working today. But I have Sheila here and something seems off. Are you available to come into the birthing center?

Taking a deep breath, Sam furrowed her brow. She could feel Grant trying to be discreet as he read her message upside down.

I'll be there as soon as I can.

For a tortured minute, Sam waited as the little dots that implied Kaiya was still texting blinked in front of her.

Alright. I'm gonna take her up and see if I can get a nurse or someone to look at her. Who's most likely to listen to a doula? Is Duke here?

"Shit," Sam muttered. Duke was likely napping after twenty-four hours on call. She could wake him up, but he wouldn't be able to get to the hospital any faster than she could. Maybe Dr. Choi, or . . .

"Isn't Dr. Franklin in today? He can help," Grant said, watching Sam closely.

"I mean, probably, but . . ." Sam bit down, considering her options. She hoped Dr. Franklin would take Kaiya's concerns seriously, but he wouldn't have been her first choice, naturally.

As if reading her thoughts, Grant said, "He's never ignored a red flag from even the most junior surgery tech as long as I have known him."

The recommendation was as good as she was going to get. Looking down at her phone, she typed the answer she was reticent to give.

Ask for Dr. Franklin. Don't let her leave the hospital until you see him.

"I think I've got to go," Sam said, looking around at the crew. Frankly, they'd be better off with just Grant in the video anyway.

"Dr. Franklin and Kaiya can handle this," Grant said, his tone firm but gentle. "Different doctors handle emergencies and deliveries all the time. You can finish without Sheila thinking you're a monster or something."

"I know, but it's Sheila. She is basically the reason this program even exists." Sam watched Grant closely, willing him to connect the dots. All the sacrifices, all the stupid fights with her mom, the lost sleep, the mix-up with Jehan's party? Disappointing Sheila wasn't just letting a patient down; it was letting herself down too. "Her baby and my time at the hospital are inextricably linked with one another. I can't just not be there for her."

"I'm not saying it's easy to walk away from a patient you care about. But think about all the other people we let down if we walk away from this. Our funding is tied to this video and our reports." Grant's voice sounded as if he was speaking through a clenched jaw, trying very hard not to lose his temper. "If the funding dries up, all those people won't have access to the program. We'll be done. Simple as that."

Sam had to admit he had a point. If she hadn't made such a mess of filming this morning, she might be able to claim a medical emergency and dash off. As it was, the crew didn't look like they were dying to cut her some slack. Glancing down at the phone, Sam read Kaiya's next message.

Get here when you can. I'll raise hell if I need to.

And I was helping people before you were born. I was never gonna let Sheila go anywhere :-)

Sam's shoulders started to relax. Holding her breath, she let herself smile faintly as she typed back a reply.

I knew you wouldn't. That's why you are the kind of professional
I want to be. :-) Keep me posted.

Looking up from her phone, Sam glanced at the crew. They had
mostly reassembled and were likely waiting for another hour of torture.
An hour that Sam didn't have. She needed to finish this, and quickly.
Looking back at Grant, she sighed, "You're right. I'll wrap this up and
then head over."

"Makes sense." Grant nodded, his voice less strained than before.
"Sam, about what I said earlier—"

The irritation she felt had been pushed out of her mind when Kaiya
had texted, but now it washed over her in waves. This was not the time
for Grant to try to convince her that a simple chat with her mom would
yield magical boundaries without any cognitive bloodshed. Better for
him to realize that her life didn't work that way now than for him to
waste his time trying to pretend she was also perfect only for him to
realize she was a wreck three months later. Sam dropped her phone in
her purse before narrowing her eyes and glaring at him. "I don't have
time to debate handling my mother with you right now. I need to wrap
this up and get to the hospital."

"I meant about the other doctors pitching in if you want to rest.
No one will be mad if you don't help."

"Look, I get that there are other people who are capable. But this
is the program's first real test. I need to be there for that. I need to be
there for Sheila and Kaiya. I am not failing this one."

Grant's face shifted to surprise. "Failing? How is relying on the
hospital's coverage system failing? It's literally designed for this."

Sam raised an eyebrow and tilted her head in an unmistakable
warning gesture that made Grant change course.

"Never mind. I don't feel like arguing right now either. I'm ready
to start again if you are." Dropping his shoulders in resignation, he set

his coffee cup down and said, "Do you want me to drive you to the hospital after we're done? I could pick you up too."

"I'm perfectly capable of calling a car. But thanks," Sam said, emphasizing *capable*. Whatever help Grant thought he was offering, she was certain that she could do just fine without the awkward weight of judgment that came with riding in a car with his disappointment.

Turning, she marched over to the producer and did her best to mask the anxiety and frustration that had settled just beneath her skin. "I think we are ready to start when you are."

The producer blinked twice, then looked down at his watch and said, "All right, let's get going. And remember, just relax. As long as we get the script down, we can cover the rest with B-roll."

Sam didn't know what B-roll was, but she smiled anyway. They wouldn't need to cover anything. She was going to nail this and then get out of this hellhole. She might not be an actor, but she was a damn fine doctor, and she was going to prove it to Grant, Dr. Franklin, her mother, and anyone else who doubted what she could do.

Chapter Twenty

Sam looked at the numbers on Sheila's test results and felt her heart drop. She had arrived shortly after Kaiya got a hold of Dr. Franklin. Apparently, the doula had stood at the nurses' station and, true to her word, raised actual hell about Sheila's stress levels and swollen fingers. The nurse at the desk thought she was nuts, but Kaiya was so persistent that they finally gave in and called Dr. Franklin. Just as Grant promised, Dr. Franklin took a look at Sheila's hands, and while he thought it was likely normal swelling, her blood pressure had been higher than he liked, so he'd asked her to take a urine test and ordered blood work to check her liver and kidney functions.

And thank God he had. If Sam was reading these numbers correctly, then Sheila was very likely dealing with severe preeclampsia. Realistically, Sam thought she was lucky the woman could still see given her platelet count. She'd consult with Dr. Franklin to be sure, but if she was right, Sheila needed to deliver like yesterday.

Taking a deep breath, she marched toward the nurses' station and asked them to page Dr. Franklin. While she waited, she looked back down at the results, hoping to see anything other than what she was seeing. Unfortunately, the numbers didn't change. She'd delivered babies early, but thirty-three weeks was so small. Sheila and the baby would need to be in the hospital for a while. A thing no new parent wanted to hear. The poor woman's blood pressure was already—

"What's up?" Dr. Franklin called, his sneakers slapping against the beige linoleum floors.

"I think she needs to be induced or we need to schedule a C-section. Like, now," Sam said, not bothering to mince words. If time was short, she might as well cut to the chase. "Taking all the other factors into account, I don't think we can wait to see if her blood pressure comes down."

"Huh," Dr. Franklin grumbled as he felt around his head for his glasses. When he didn't immediately find them, he grabbed the chart and squinted at it for a second. Adopting a tone as if they were talking about the weather, he said, "I think you might be right. We've got to watch this one like a hawk, you and me. You let the patient know. I'll let the team know to be on standby."

"That's it?" Sam asked before her brain could stop her.

"What's it?" Dr. Franklin said, setting the chart down and patting his pockets, evidently still hoping to find his glasses.

"You don't need any more information?" Realizing her mouth was slightly open, she closed it, and Dr. Franklin started to smile.

"No. You read the results correctly. You have good instincts. I don't need to second-guess that," Dr. Franklin said, giving up on the search and turning to go get himself ready for what Sam assumed could be Sheila's delivery. Right before he turned the corner, he stopped and added, "By the way, I gotta tell you, that doula of yours is a real crackerjack. She knows her stuff."

With that, Dr. Franklin was gone, leaving Sam alone with nothing but his confidence in her and the program. She had been fighting to earn his trust for months. Knowing that she'd finally managed to prove herself to him was enough to make her float away with joy.

At least until she spotted the chart in front of her. As amazing as earning Dr. Franklin's respect was, the comedown was twice as hard. No doctor wanted to tell a patient bad news. This was the part of the job that Sam knew was coming. At the same time, she hoped she'd magically be the exception to the bad-news rule. Pulling her shoulders back, she walked toward the room Sheila and Kaiya were settled in. As she walked, Sam tried to remember every tiny thing she had ever learned in medical school about hard conversations. She didn't have time to write this one out, but she could at least listen with compassion and try to be as gentle as she was direct.

Opening the door, Sam thanked her stars that no one else was in the shared room with them, so at least they had some privacy. Sheila was propped up on a bed, still in her street clothes. Next to her, Kaiya had pulled a chair up and was holding her hand. In the other hand, she held a small battery-powered fan, which gently blew Sheila's hair away from her face. Kaiya had also taken out her phone and put on a relaxing playlist to cover up the sounds of the hospital outside their door and the machine that was monitoring Sheila's vitals.

"Hi, Dr. Holbrook," Sheila said, sounding tired but trying to smile just the same. "So what's the verdict?"

"Well, I'm afraid it's not great news. I can go over your numbers if you would like, but the short version is, Dr. Franklin and I think you need to deliver as soon as possible. We can try and induce you, which may take a day or so, with the caveat that if your blood pressure increases or the baby's heartbeat changes, we may need to get you in for a C-section as soon as possible."

"Oh." Sheila's face fell flat. "Is the baby okay?"

"Baby is okay for now, and that is good news. Unfortunately, you won't be able to leave the hospital. With preeclampsia like this, we need to watch you and the baby very closely."

Sheila's eyebrows shot up as panic crossed her face. "That is bad, right? I watched this show where a woman—"

"While it isn't good, TV is probably not the best source of information on this one," Kaiya said softly as she switched off the fan and set it in her lap. Giving Sheila's hand a squeeze, she said, "As Dr. Holbrook will tell you, most people with severe preeclampsia deliver, and the vast majority of them are fine."

"We were coming up with a whole plan." Sheila's lower lip trembled for a second. "I don't have the crib built. And C-sections scare me . . ."

"No one will force you to have a C-section; I'm only letting you know what your options are. As for the plan, you can revise it. It can take a while to get the OR set up or for the drugs to send you into labor, so we still have time. Kaiya can help you develop a whole new way of thinking about your first few weeks as a parent," Sam said, praying that Sheila didn't refuse to deliver at all. She didn't want to explain all the profoundly scary things that could happen if she tried to walk out of here in her state.

Kaiya looked at Sam, then turned her full attention to Sheila. "I know this isn't the birth we planned for. But I do trust Dr. Holbrook. And we have time. Ulysses is on their way, and the three of us can think about how to process and celebrate the baby's early arrival. And I'll be around after the baby arrives to walk you through each phase."

Sheila closed her eyes for a moment, then took a deep breath and opened them. "Okay, I can do this. Can we try to induce first? Or does it need to be a C-section? I just want the best for my family."

Sam made eye contact with Kaiya for a split second, hoping her eyes communicated a massive thank-you for her help, and then she returned her focus to Sheila. Smiling, she said, "We can try to induce first. I'll have the team come get you ready. A few nurses will come in with paperwork. Then the baby will be here before you know it. In the meantime, hang in there. I know this is scary stuff, but Kaiya and I got you."

"Thank you, Dr. Holbrook. For everything. Not just this but getting me connected to Kaiya. I don't know that I could do this without you two."

Sam tried to think of something to say as a lump formed in her throat. No matter what else the day held, this moment—the hard moment that she'd been afraid of—made it all well worth it. Blinking a few times, Sam cleared her throat. "I . . . you could . . ."

"You could do it without us. But you don't have to," Kaiya said, flashing a kind smile between Sam and her patient before adding, "You're stronger than you know."

Sam took a deep breath, then tried again. "Thank you, Sheila. I'll see you soon."

~

What no one tells you, Sam thought as she slumped onto the couch in the lounge, *is how long it takes to actually deliver in an emergency labor. On TV they make it look like patients just turn up, and BAM, someone sprints them into a magically prepped operating room and screams* Scalpel, *and then there is a happy crying baby.*

In real life, you induce someone, and roughly fifteen different hospital personnel watch every blip on a giant vitals monitor for both the baby and the person delivering. Then a light in the delivery room needs to be changed, and that takes two hours. Plus, the person delivering has about fifty pounds of paperwork to do. Eventually there is local anesthesia administered, and someone is gently wheeled into a new delivery room—where the light is working—while wide awake and chatting about knowing they have legs but not really feeling them. Then the doctor and everyone else in the room goes on high alert for thirty-five minutes. Only then does a baby start crying.

Then the parents start crying. And then everyone around them also wants to cry because everything about a premature birth is overwhelming, even when you know what you are doing. Plus, there is the relief that the baby is small but, in this case, wonderful and fine.

And that was how Sam found herself in the staff lounge twelve hours after she'd walked into the hospital, dangerously close to crying. It had been a roller coaster of a day, but somehow she had managed to push all the Anjo stuff aside and pull off a lifesaving delivery. She was exhausted and exhilarated and . . . simply too tired and overstimulated to deal with anything other than the cup of coffee sitting in front of her.

Smiling to herself, she decided to do a little mindless scrolling through social media until the caffeine kicked in. This time of night, Muni didn't run frequently, so she had a few extra minutes to waste. Taking her phone out of Do Not Disturb, she'd flipped over to a video about a French bulldog who jumped around like a frog when the phone in her hand started to buzz with missed calls and text messages. For a moment, Sam considered ignoring the messages, but then she thought better of it. What if Jehan had locked herself out of the apartment or Duke needed her to settle a basketball-based dispute?

Deciding to start with the texts, Sam clicked on a message from Duke that said:

I was super hungry and I ate your balsamic vinegar and coffee ice cream

(you were right. It sounds gross but is delicious).

I tried to buy more of it just now, but Melvin's was out. I just got a gallon of regular coffee almond to replace it.

Sorry and you're welcome.

Sam snorted and shook her head at the phone. Of course Duke would eat her ice cream and replace it with the wrong ice cream. At least he had tried to replace it. How was he to know that he needed to go to Carver's, the other corner store, to get it? Really, that was Sam's job in their little threesome. Duke had a car and charm, Jehan had ChapStick and a plan, and Sam had dessert and big ideas. It was better for the dynamic if he never figured out how the ice cream got there. Smiling at the phone, Sam typed her response:

Thanks for trying.

And don't doubt my superior ice cream taste again!

Sighing, she clicked over to her missed calls and saw that all three were from her mother. Sam debated whether or not she wanted to listen to the voice mails. There was more than a 50 percent chance that she'd been calling to complain. Then Sam stopped.

Her mom's party was just a few days away. If it was a problem, Sam would hear about it eventually. If it was a rave review about the show she was supposed to see at SFMOMA, then Sam could be pleasantly surprised.

She bounced her knee up and down a few times as the phone rang. She had just started to think that maybe her mom wouldn't pick up when Diana's voice came over the line.

"Sammy. I left you three voice mails."

"Sorry, Mom. I had an emergency delivery."

"Oh," Diana said flatly as if Sam being busy saving a life was a bit of an unwelcome surprise.

"Baby is fine. A little smaller than I would have liked, but the family will be fine." Sam finished the story as her blood pressure began to rise. What did her mother think she was doing when she didn't answer her calls? Laughing like an evil villain while she pressed "Ignore Call" and flipped through a magazine?

"Right." Her mother let a beat of uncomfortable silence hang in the air, then plowed ahead. "Well, the reason that I was trying to get a hold of you is that I realized we really can't just have cheese boards for the catering. The more I think about the venue, the more I believe we need to up our game."

"What?" Sam said, her tone sharper than she meant it to be.

"Plus, your brother is doing something more robust."

"We already went over this," Sam said flatly. Had her mother seriously called her three times in order to get her way after Sam said no last night?

"I mean, what if our friends from San Diego talk to our friends from Monterey? Our Monterey friends will feel shortchanged."

"That's not going to happen," Sam said bluntly.

"Why wouldn't that happen?"

"Because, Mom, no one is going to talk about the food. They'll reminisce about the pictures you took and how good it is to see you." Sam stood up and paced the empty lounge, trying to shake off the excess jitters the call had reignited.

"No, Sammy. It's the entire ambience that matters. And the Lost Key, while—"

Sam couldn't hear her mother speak over the sound of her teeth grinding themselves to dust. Was her mother really picking apart the venue now? After everything else Sam had done?

"Mom. The venue is fine. The food is fine."

Was there anything she could do to make her mother happy? Or was she going to spend the rest of her life trying to earn love and being taken apart for it?

"I just want it to be equal. I want my friends to see you putting in your best effort, Sammy."

"My best effort?" Sam let out an exasperated squawk. Since when had she ever given her mother less than her best?

Her own stupidity crashed into her like a wave. Sam's eyes started to sting as her thoughts collided, each more painful than the last. She'd thought that if she did just one more thing for her mother, then she would love her without strings or guilt trips or outrageous expectations. But no amount of acquiescence was going to make her mom happy. At each turn, the goalposts moved.

"You know what I mean, Sammy." Her mother's voice was low and hurt, as if she were the one being asked for a miracle at the last minute.

"I know you just want me to stay in my little corner and forget about me. First with the invites and then—"

The aging tape that was holding Sam's relationship to her mother in place snapped. There was no party she could throw, no award she could win. It didn't matter if she lived next door to her family or in a remote corner of the Andes. No amount of sacrifice or availability would ever be enough because there was no enough for her mother. Sam couldn't make her mother happy, because she wasn't actually unhappy with her daughter; she was unhappy with her own past. And Sam couldn't fix that.

"You know what, Mom?" Sam felt her breathing come in sharp, short bursts. "I'm sorry, but I have too much going on right now. You need to work this out without me."

"If you didn't want to be a part of this, you could have said so. I would have handled it myself."

"Would you? Because I tried to do that months ago, but you're so self-centered you couldn't hear it." She knew she had more or less shouted at the phone, but honestly, in trying to please her mom, she'd been awake for nearly twenty-four hours, had gotten in a fight with Grant, and very possibly still had camera makeup caked to her face. She was tired, hungry, and in need of a soak in a tub with a serious scrub brush.

For a moment, there was silence, and then her mother's flat voice came over the phone. "Well, you know what? I don't have to have the party. We can cancel since it's such a burden to you."

"Oh, grow up," Sam spit out, rage clawing at every word she tried to say. "No one is saying you can't have a party. You literally just have to go to the store or call a catering company yourself . . ."

Sam paused. Somewhere in the back of her mind, something clicked into place. There was no amount of reasoning she could apply that would make her mom back down. As long as Diana thought there was a chance that she could get Sam to put her life on hold for her, she would continue the cancel-the-event charade. Either Sam would do this and then get suckered into the next thing, or she would have to put her foot down and risk her mother cutting her off again as punishment.

Was living like this worth the relentless struggle to maintain the relationship? Sam knew the answer as soon as she thought the question, but it still broke her heart to say it out loud. "I'm setting a boundary. I love you, but you'll have to figure this situation out on your own. You can text me what you decide."

Sam sighed, then pressed the red end-call button. Standing in the dead silence of the lounge, she looked at the dark screen. She'd never in her life imagined she would hang up on her mother. This was not something Sam had ever done to a living soul, not even a telemarketer.

Stunned, Sam dropped back down to the couch and threw her elbow over her eyes, creating a little cocoon for her to try to get her thoughts around what had happened. She just had to focus on pulling herself together. If she could do that, she could order a car and get herself home without being one of the crying messes that rideshare-driver Reddit threads mocked.

Eventually, Sam peeled her arm away from her eyes, then snorted. Almost nothing about feeling this bad was funny, except that the heat of her skin and her watery eyes had combined to melt some of the mascara and eyeliner off her face and onto her elbow crease. Two black eye shapes stared up at her from the crook of her arm, like some sort of all-knowing, rough-day-watching parody.

Gathering up her now-cold coffee and her phone, Sam had taken two steps toward the door when it opened, and she froze.

Grant stood in front of her, looking as surprised as she felt. After a tense second, he relaxed and said, "I've been meaning to text you. How is Sheila?"

"Emergency delivery." Sam looked at her cup as she said this. For whatever reason, looking at Grant's face felt more difficult right now. "Everyone is okay. Baby is in the NICU, but they're all doing great."

"That's good." Grant spaced the words out as if he wasn't entirely sure what else to say.

Sam wished she'd just stayed sealed off on the couch. She had been naked in front of this man, yet with her shot nerves and their fight hovering over them, she felt more exposed now than she had at any point in the last week. Part of her wanted nothing more than to hug him. To feel the security of his arms wrapped around her.

The rest of her wanted to dump her coffee on him. Just because the day had been long didn't mean that she had forgotten what he'd said. How he'd just defaulted to assuming that she couldn't handle her own life.

Grant pursed his lips together and looked at the floor, then looked back at her as if he was debating saying something. Sam considered warning him that the only thing she wanted to hear was an apology, but before she could figure out exactly how to phrase that, Grant started speaking.

"So listen. I know now isn't ideal, but we have a problem."

"Grant, I don't want to fight about my mom. Can you just let it go?" Sam closed her eyes and dropped her head to her chest. She wished she'd come up with a plan for this. It wasn't like she couldn't have predicted running into him. This was basically the workplace-dating scenario that every TV show warned her against.

"I'm not talking about earlier," Grant said, sounding irritated. "I'm talking about the progress report for Anjo." He waited for a second to see if she would jump in. Sam's mind spun as she tried to sift through the fog of the last twenty-four hours.

Oh shit. Those were the only two words that came to Sam's mind, and they raced through her brain like a mantra, slowly burning away whatever good feelings the delivery had left behind.

Grant watched her like a teacher waiting for a group of second graders to get quiet, the I'll-wait expression plain as day on his face.

Finally, Sam took a deep breath. "I'm so sorry. I got busy and I just . . ." Sam looked around and shrugged as she tried to find a word that felt more accurate than *forgot*.

"The thing is, when I asked you if you needed any help, you said you were on it. And I took you at your word. But I just got an email saying the progress report hasn't been submitted. Since I'm the administrative adviser for the program, I'm at fault if we lose our funding. This program could get shut down."

"I know, and I can't stress enough that I'm sorry," Sam said, feeling her shoulders sinking with each word. "I just got busy, but I'll—"

"Sam, this isn't the kind of thing you can just forget and have it be okay. Being a researcher means being responsible for your own funding." Grant ran a hand down the back of his neck, his voice tight with frustration.

"I didn't 'just forget' it. With the exception of a few days at your house, I've spent the last week jumping from emergency to emergency." Sam clenched her jaw. She knew she'd let him down, but it wasn't like Anjo was the NIH. They were a few hours late, not six weeks.

"Why didn't you just say you needed help at my place?" Grant said, his hands falling to his sides with a noisy thud. "We could have written it together."

"Because I wanted to avoid this," Sam said, gesturing between the two of them. "I feel like I'm constantly swimming around with sharks just waiting for me to fail. Between you, Dr. Franklin, and my mother, I'm basically drowning in other people's doubts and expectations—"

"What expectations? I'm not being unreasonable here." Grant cut her off, the volume of his voice rising. Gesturing at her with both hands, he added, "You said you could do it. Is believing you were capable of something an outrageous concept?"

For a moment, Sam struggled to find words to explain herself. Someone like him never overextended himself. He could just glide through life with all the right words and charisma to match. He'd never overcommit just to prove himself. It was the perk of being perfect.

"I'm not saying you are unreasonable." Trying her best to find the words she needed to explain herself, Sam gritted her teeth and said, "What I'm saying is that it isn't easy to ask for help. I know that has to be hard for you to understand."

"Why wouldn't I get it?" Grant narrowed his eyes. "No one likes asking for help, but we do it when things like our funding are on the line. When you came to me with this idea, I told you this was going to happen, that you were taking on too much. I literally said you don't have time for this, and I was right."

"Look. I am tired and I am dirty. Can you please let this go?" Sam asked, the tension in her voice palpable as she glared at Grant. By his own admission, he knew now was a bad time, so maybe he could just cut her an ounce of slack and drop it.

"This is something that has to get fixed, like, twelve hours ago. So no. I can't let it go," Grant said, each of his words sounding clipped. "Moreover, this is your reality, so even if I did, are we going to have this conversation every month?"

Frustration welled up in Sam's chest. There was no way that she could make Grant understand this. She'd walked enough tightropes to recognize that getting involved with someone whose experience with imperfection was losing a sock in the laundry was bound to end this way. "I get it. You were right. I failed. But does it really seem like an I-told-you-so is helpful right now?"

Grant's eyebrows shot toward his hairline. "When would be a helpful time? Because it seems like that would have been a few months ago, when I said it originally."

"Maybe your stupid I-told-you-so is the reason I didn't ask you for help in the first place. Did it ever even occur to you that I might have asked for help if I didn't have to constantly second-guess whether talking to you was going to come back to bite me in the ass?" Grant's jaw dropped open, but Sam was riled up now. If she was going to burn a bridge, she was going to do it so thoroughly and completely that even the ashes would be unrecognizable.

"I'll call and offer a groveling apology tomorrow so your precious reputation isn't dinged. As for us, I think we can acknowledge that our relationship was an unmitigated disaster. Surprise! I can't meet your standards of perfection. And I don't even want to try. Living with judgment and an I-told-you-so hanging over my head just isn't going to work for me."

Sam's heartbeat felt like a kick drum in her chest, slowly keeping track of the silence between them. Even the ancient coffee machine seemed to have stopped wheezing just in time for her to vent at Grant. From where she stood, Sam was close enough that she could see Grant's otherwise lovely face contort with something that looked suspiciously like hurt. The less spiteful part of Sam's brain tried to suggest that maybe she had gone too far, but Sam was determined not to hear it. Whatever it had to say could be said at home, where she could cry off the rest of Bebe's stupid makeup.

She watched as Grant schooled his features and took a shallow breath. "Listen, Sam—"

"Nope." Something inside her snapped. Whatever was coming, she had no intention of sticking around to hear it. He could send her a nasty email or leave a bunch of shitty voice mails like her mother for all she cared. "You know what? I'm taking your advice for the second time today." Sam looked at him squarely and gestured to herself, then to him and said, "Boundary."

With that, she went for the door, letting a combination of her rage and exhaustion carry her to the elevators and down to the lobby. That anger kept her company while she waited for her rideshare and all the way to her front door. It was only as she got out of the car that she let herself think about the day. Somehow she had gone from the extreme high of saving two lives to having fought with her boyfriend and her mother, both of whom she still had to see at some point in her future and neither of whom she knew what to do with. Worse still, her favorite ice cream was gone.

Chapter Twenty-One

Sam felt like dirt. But, she reasoned, that could be because she was probably sitting on some dirt. When she had come home, she'd spent a good hour on the couch crying every single moment of the last twenty-six hours out of her system. At some point, she'd cried herself to sleep only to wake up hungry and ready to cry again. In an effort to find some spot of happiness, she had pulled it together long enough for her to make it to the freezer for Duke's replacement ice cream and a spoon. Afraid that she would cry-sleep again, she decided to sit on the floor crisscross applesauce, where she hoped the hardwood would prevent her from repeating her own history.

Swallowing back a sob, she stabbed at the block of still-very-frozen ice cream, which didn't budge. "Can't you just help me out here?"

The sound of a key in the door stopped her cold in the early stages of another catastrophic meltdown. For the span of one breath, she considered trying to dive onto the couch to save face, until Jehan's head popped around the corner.

"Sam. Did you get my text?" Jehan asked, looking down as she tried to slip off her shiny silver tennis shoes.

Sam glanced over her shoulder to where her phone was stuffed between the couch cushions, just to be sure that neither her mother nor Grant could reach her, even if they tried. Which, as far as she knew, they hadn't.

"No. I put away my phone. What happened?"

"Well . . ." Jehan fiddled with the laces of her shoe for far longer than someone with three master's degrees, a PhD, and some of the best fine motor skills in the medical world needed to untie a simple knot, then said, "Trav and I broke up."

"What?" Sam said, her voice lurching dangerously close to shrieking territory.

"We called off the wedding," Jehan said, finally slipping her shoe off and giving Sam a good look for the first time. "Are you—"

"Don't try and distract me. What do you mean, you called off the wedding?"

"You're sitting on the floor," Jehan said, eyeing Sam with concern. Sam shook her spoon at her friend, warning her not to dig into anything. For a moment, the two remained locked in a stalemate, until finally, Jehan sighed. "After the mess at Dorothy's, Travis and I needed to take a step back. He thought it would be a week or two. But it wasn't that way for me."

Jehan was silent for a moment, and Sam began poking at her ice cream. Managing to dig out a chocolate-covered almond, she looked up at her friend and said, "Go on."

"Can I have some of that first?" Jehan said, nodding to the container in Sam's hand.

"It's still very frozen, but yes."

"Fair enough." Jehan shrugged and walked into the kitchen. The sound of her roommate rummaging through the silverware drawer cracked around the apartment until she returned with a large dinner spoon. Plopping down on the floor next to Sam, she tried to dig at the ice cream for a second before giving up. Leaving her spoon lodged in the ice cream, she started again. "The funny thing about space is that while one person asks for it, the other person can choose to maintain it. I think Travis thought of space as some kind of punishment. In the end, I decided it needed to be permanent."

"Oh, so you decided this then?" Sam tried to keep her surprise under wraps. She'd always felt like Jehan intended to stay loyal to Travis, no matter how obviously absurd that commitment became. It seemed like in some ways it was one of the things she and her roommate had in common. Unwavering loyalty to their loved ones even as their relationships became increasingly temperamental. Apparently, she was wrong about that too.

"I went a whole day without wondering what he was up to or wanting to tell him anything, and then a few days went by, and I honestly—this sounds bad." Jehan stopped and scowled at her spoon for a moment as if she needed to marshal her strength before she admitted to something shameful. Pulling her spoon out of the container, she said, "I don't think I've been so relaxed in years. Then I started asking myself, *Who would I be if I were alone?*"

"Good question."

Jehan smiled. "The wild part was, once I asked the question, I found that I liked me when I was alone. Nothing about Travis helped me be better or dream bigger. At best, Travis discouraged me from watching movies that gave me weird dreams."

Sam laughed until she realized that her friend was serious. Clearing her throat, she said, "So you just said, *Let's take space forever?*"

"God, no." Now it was Jehan's turn to laugh. "I did what any self-respecting newly single person would do. I drug it out for another week and a half. Tried to pretend I hadn't learned anything about myself. Wallowed over wasting money on a deposit at Dorothy's, then broke it off when I couldn't emotionally handle avoiding him anymore."

"Reasonable." Sam shrugged and watched as Jehan found a soft edge of ice cream and loaded up her spoon. "How'd Travis take it? What about your family?"

"My family took it like champs—except my uncle, who is upset about the logistics of me wasting my youth with a bozo more than anything." Jehan snickered, then popped the spoon in her mouth. In between chews, she said, "Trav took it poorly, but you know what?"

"What?"

"I don't really care. That is for him and the therapist I hope he invests in to work through." With that, Jehan burst into giggles and went back for a second bite. "So you ready to tell me why you are on the floor now? Or do I need to stall a bit more?"

"I don't think asking a friend how they are doing after calling off an engagement counts as stalling." Sam rolled her eyes. "If anything, you're avoiding."

"And now you are deflecting. Spill." Jehan smiled sweetly as she stabbed at a frozen almond.

"Ugh," Sam said, closing her eyes. Deep down, she'd known she would have to eventually tell someone what had happened. She'd just hoped that she could put it off for a day or two, until either Anjo refused to accept her groveling apology or some other calamity struck. Sam had just started to reach into her shallow reservoir of ice-cream-induced emotional stamina when a key in the front door's dead bolt stopped her.

"Hey," Duke called as the door cracked open.

"In here," Jehan answered, eyeing Sam as if she expected her to try to sprint away before she had to confess what had happened. Actually, now that Sam thought about it . . .

"What are y'all doing on the floor?" Duke said, his gym bag in one hand and a random bag of frozen fruit in the other.

"Sam is having a day," Jehan said, still watching her closely.

"Ah. All right. Lemme get a spoon." Duke turned toward the kitchen, then called over his shoulder, "Sam, don't start until I get there." After another second of rattling around in the silverware drawer, Duke reappeared with a soup spoon and dropped down on the other side of Sam. "All right. I think we're ready. What's up?"

Sam crammed a spoonful of ice cream into her mouth to buy herself time until she couldn't take the feeling of Jehan's and Duke's eyes on her, then started talking.

Once she got going, Sam couldn't stop. Nor did her friends try to stop her. In fact, outside of a few raised eyebrows and occasionally dipping a spoon into the ice cream she was holding, they didn't do much at all.

"Anyway, that's why I'm on the floor with this ice cream that has lived at the back of a freezer for about twenty-seven years."

"Hey. It's not the ice cream's fault you had a bad day," Duke said, shaking his head and watching Sam as she wiped her tears on the hem of her scrubs.

Looking at her spoon, Sam noticed chocolate on her hands and wanted to cry all over again. Sniffing as she tried to keep it together, she said, "My hands are sticky."

"It's okay. We've all been there," Duke said, patting her shoulder and looking at Jehan for support. "We can fix this."

"And I thought I had a day," Jehan said as she scooped up a particularly chocolaty bite of almond. Duke narrowed his eyes at Jehan as Sam leaned back against the couch and groaned. Picking up on the missed cue as she stood up and walked toward the kitchen, Jehan said, "Of course we can fix this. Or at least part of this, anyway."

"It's okay. I'll figure it out. I dug this grave, after all."

"Sam," Duke said over the sound of Jehan opening cupboards. "Don't take this the wrong way. But not everyone is your mom. Jehan and I don't expect anything in return if we help you."

"I don't think . . ." Sam faltered. She was going to say that she didn't think everyone was like her mother, but that wasn't true. At least, not entirely. Somewhere along the way, she'd started behaving like everyone was her mother. Like if she couldn't handle her own needs plus anticipate every whim and expectation of any friend, partner, or mentor, she wasn't worthy of a relationship with them. According to her mother, if Sam failed, the only relationship she was worthy of was one with shame. Without noticing it, she'd started to believe it too.

"You what? Don't think that you approach everyone like you need to play defense? Because Jehan and I have seen it firsthand for months now."

"I mean, I don't think you two are like that . . . ," Sam said, trying to ignore her sticky fingers.

"It's true," Jehan said over the sound of the sink. "You didn't know the first thing about party planning, but there you were sending out invites because I helped with your grant applications."

"But I wanted to help you, Jehan. My mother is different. She lives for a constant sense of obligation and stark repercussions for failure."

"Both can be true. You can feel obligated and want to help at the same time. The question is how you feel after you help someone," Duke said, hunching to catch Sam's eye. "You can deny it if you want, but there are people in your life who love you and aren't keeping score. Your mom just may not be one of them."

Sam sniffed as Duke's words wrapped around her. She was grateful to have her roommates' unconditional love, even if she didn't always have her mom's. Holding back tears, her voice sounding small, she said, "I'm so lucky you two love me."

"We are all lucky we love each other." Duke straightened and picked up his spoon again.

"The thing is"—Sam sighed and rubbed a spot on her forehead with the back of her hand—"my mom's not evil. I know my mom loves me. She just needs to back off and let me be my own person. Imperfect and separate from her as that may be. I think I need to apologize."

"I know you didn't ask, but I think you should be honest with your mom. You were wrong for the way you said what you said, not the sentiment behind it," Jehan said, offering Sam a damp paper napkin from the drawer of take-out silverware they were saving for God only knew what event.

"I felt like I was honest." Sam intentionally kept her focus on wiping her hands so she wouldn't have to watch Jehan's facial expressions.

"Were you, though?" Duke's tone was gentle, but Sam didn't dare look up. Her eyes had started to water again, and she couldn't bear the thought that Duke might be looking at her with pity.

"I mean. I tried to manage her expectations with the catering and the venue."

"Okay, but why do all of that when the best choice would have been to just tell her you couldn't put the party together?"

"I was struggling with the idea of saying no. I mean, what if I actually hurt her and she stops speaking to me for good this time? In theory, I could live with the space. But never seeing my mother again? Over a party? Is that really worth cutting out our relationship forever?" Sam paused. Even voicing the idea made her feel like she was chewing on tinfoil, the words only half as uncomfortable as the painful sensation that came with the memory of having lived through a version of them. "I mean, sure, I don't have unconditional love, but she does love me in her own way. And I wouldn't just be losing my mother. Sneaking around to talk to my dad and being snubbed on family vacations . . . that was awful."

"So instead you hurt you?" Jehan ducked her head so she could look Sam in the eyes.

Sam let Jehan's words turn over in her mind. She prodded them, then backed away with a shudder. Since she was little, she'd walked on eggshells lest she damage what little relationship she and her mother had. Looking back, she realized the more she tiptoed, the more the cracks grew. In this light, she wasn't sure that avoiding a break was ever possible. No matter how much her mother said she loved her unconditionally, the truth was Sam was behaving as if her mother's love was conditional, because it was.

"I just . . ." Sam sniffed and ran her chocolate-stained napkin under her eyes. "I get where my mom is coming from. We all want to be loved and have our needs met. She just goes about it in a weird way. Growing up with someone self-centered, you just start to think it's normal. I guess I let it go too far."

"You did." Duke nodded, then stopped to add, "But who doesn't have something like that from their childhood? God knows I have stuff I need to work out with everyone from my little brother to my great-aunt."

Her laugh sounded watery, but Sam was grateful for the joke. And really, Duke wasn't wrong. In a way, part of getting older was making peace with the strange and unintentional scars family members gave each other.

"Guess I better try to talk to my mom." The thought of her mom refusing to talk to her made Sam's lip tremble. She'd started to dab at the remnants of her makeup when Jehan threw her arms around her.

"Don't cry. We're in the same place with our relationships. Only you can't call off an engagement, so you'll figure this out."

Sam laughed, feeling her friend's humor in her bones.

"I have faith in you two," Duke said, grinning at them as if this were exactly where he wanted to be at roughly 7:00 a.m. on a Friday morning. "You want to talk about Grant now, or . . ."

"Not really." The warmth Sam felt for her friends faded as the two of them looked at her expectantly—Jehan with catlike intensity and Duke with a level of laid-backness that was so mellow it was obviously fake. After another tense breath of silence, Sam caved. "Fine. Say what you want to say."

Looking pleased with himself, Duke took his time sticking his spoon in the ice cream before laying out the truth with his characteristic smile. "No one wants to hear their boyfriend was right, but . . ."

Duke blinked at her as if the eye movement alone could finish the sentence.

Sighing, she mustered her best big-girl behavior and finished the sentence she didn't want to say. "Grant was right . . ."

"Yup."

"About the boundary-for-my-mom thing or being mad about Anjo?" As soon as she asked the question, Sam wished she hadn't. Jehan became suddenly very interested in a throw pillow on the couch behind them.

Duke shrugged and wrinkled his nose like the answer tasted sour. "Both. You didn't need to entertain your mom's projects. As we've discussed, you needed to establish a boundary for them."

"And you clearly didn't have the headspace for the progress report. As previously stated, getting you to admit you need help is like pulling teeth," Jehan blurted. Then, catching Sam's miserable look, she dropped her head on Sam's sagging shoulder and said, "We still love you, though."

"Speaking of Grant, still loving you, and headspace . . . ," Duke said, moving the conversation along as he crunched an almond, "what are you gonna do about all this? You can't totally ignore him unless you want Dr. Franklin to be your new adviser."

"Just sort of hope that an asteroid hits the planet so I don't have to figure it out." Sam laughed halfheartedly.

A stitch in the corner of her heart where she stored the happy memories of herself and Grant twinged, and she caught her breath. The way he watched her when he thought she wouldn't notice. Standing in his kitchen watching him make a coffee filter out of a paper towel after the first night she'd slept over. He'd run out of them, but they were too happy snuggled in bed to run to the store. Even the cut of his silly sweaters.

And those were the small things. The things she could stand to think about. Not the big things, like him walking her through how to work with Dr. Franklin. Or the way he'd rallied interns when the doulas couldn't get on the intranet. The ways he supported her . . .

But she couldn't be with him and be flawed. The two of them just didn't fit. It was better not to think about those big things. Drifting too near to those memories felt like singeing her heart.

Sam blinked, pulling herself out of her thoughts while her friends waited for a real answer to the question. Clearing her throat, she said, "Obviously, I'll call Anjo, apologize, and then speed write the progress report."

"Is that before or after you talk things out with your mom and put the final touches on the center's grand opening?" Jehan asked.

Sam frowned. She was starting to develop a headache, which she blamed on this conversation and not the excessive amount of sugar and dairy she had decided to eat for breakfast. "I'll call them from the car on the way to my mom's—"

"I know this is gonna sound terrible, but could this be a place where you need—wait for it"—Duke grinned, then stopped smiling after Sam leveled a murderous gaze at him—"help? Like, would you let Jehan and I help you?"

"I don't even know where you two would start. I've made such a mess," Sam deflected.

"If you can work it out with your mom," Jehan said, her tone patient as she put a hand on Sam's, "I think I have a catering solution. I can't get my initial deposit back from Dorothy's. Since I'm not getting married, maybe they'd be willing to let us use my deposit to cater your mom's event?"

"And no one can resist my southern charm," Duke added, layering on a near-cartoonish amount of drawl, then said, "Let me call Anjo while you sort things out with your mom and you kiss and make up with Grant."

"I'll apologize to Grant, but I'm not making up." Sam said the words with enough bite that Duke held up the hand that wasn't holding his ice cream spoon in a calming gesture.

"Are you—" Jehan started, then closed her mouth when Sam shook her head with the force of a toddler on the verge of a meltdown.

"Trust me. He may have been right. But ultimately, we just aren't compatible. I overpromise and run late. I can't get along with my mother or Dr. Franklin. I constantly have to check my shirt to see if I spilled food on it. That's just not Grant's world. He is always the guy with the right answers at the right time. He wears a watch and sticks to what it says. His relationships are figured out—he even gets along great with Dr. Franklin."

"Okay," Duke said, making wide eyes between her and Jehan. "So you are breaking up with him because he likes Dr. Franklin?"

"No. I'm breaking up with him because we aren't a match," Sam said resolutely. "Grant gets boundaries, not boyfriend material."

"Maybe this is just your first fight with him?" Jehan said, gently nudging Sam with her shoulder. "First fights always feel like the end of the world."

"Not the end of the world. Just the end of us as a couple," Sam said, feeling exhaustion creep back into her bones.

"But—"

"Please, I really don't want to talk about him anymore," Sam cut in over whatever Duke was going to try to say on Grant's behalf. She just didn't have it in her to relive any more memories of him right now. Or anytime soon, really.

"So no making up with Grant, then." Jehan sounded skeptical and opened her mouth to say something more, but Duke gave her a look that basically begged her not to make the situation worse. "All right. It sounds like we all have the start of a plan, so maybe we'll just work from there. Assuming you will accept our help, Sam."

The words *no* and *thanks* were halfway out of her mouth when Sam stopped. While she could probably find a solution on her own, did she have to? Her friends had been with her the whole way; she'd simply been too caught up in all her plans to appreciate them fully before. Leaning her head on Duke's shoulder and taking Jehan's hand, she said, "I'd love your help."

"That's our girl," Jehan said, giving her hand a squeeze. For a heartbeat, the three of them stayed put, just enjoying the warm, fuzzy feeling that came with seeing friends after a long, hard day.

Eventually, Duke cleared his throat, forcing Sam to sit up to look at him. He took the nearly empty ice cream container out of her hands as he spoke. "I know we aren't talking about him right now, but I do have one question for you, Sam."

She was just starting to feel happy again, and she might strangle Duke if he killed the vibe. Sighing, she said, "Okay."

Smiling mischievously, he said, "You do know yelling 'boundary!' at someone isn't how boundaries work, right?"

"Duke!" Sam's shoulders shook with laughter as what felt like the first real smile she had smiled in days spread across her face. "Yes. I know."

"Just checking," Duke chuckled.

~

Sam wiped her palms on her pants as she stepped into the hotel bar. Part of her was shocked that her mom had even agreed to meet her for a drink after everything that had happened yesterday. Once she and her roommates had finished coming up with a plan, Sam got some sleep and a hot shower before writing down everything she wanted to say. Originally, the words were hard and angry, but as she reread them, she found herself softening the language until they were the kindest version of the truth. After she'd settled on the words she hoped would allow the two of them to reset their relationship, she'd texted her mom.

She spotted Diana tucked away in a quiet table by a big picture window. Her mother had already ordered what looked like a half carafe of wine and two glasses, which Sam decided to take as a good sign.

Throwing a prayer in the air, she took a deep breath and started a slow but deliberate walk toward the table.

"Hi, Mom." The words came out breathy and smaller than Sam would have liked, but they got her mother's attention just the same.

"Sammy, I ordered some wine. I hope that's okay." Her mother tried to say all of this with a casual air, but her words felt just as shaky as Sam's sounded. Knowing they were both unsure made the knot in Sam's throat relax.

"It's fine. Great, in fact," Sam said, dropping into the cushy designer chair across from her mother. It was oddly low to the ground, and it made her feel even more off balance.

"Here you are." Her mother passed her a glass, then tried to lean all the way back in her chair in the same silly way Sam had just tried. Something about it reminded her of how much they did have in common. Hopefully, her mom could see that too. Playing off the weird seating as if it were natural, her mom said, "So you wanted to speak with me?"

"I did." This was it, Sam thought. Forcing her shoulders to relax, she said, "We need to talk about yesterday."

"Sammy. Let's call it water under the bridge. I've spoken with your father and—"

"I don't think we should ignore it. Mom, I love you, and it's time for us to work some things out." Sam rotated the wineglass in her hands and waited while her mom worked to wipe the shocked look off her face. Clearly, she hadn't expected pushback. "I don't want to fight like that again."

"All right . . ." Her mother drew the words out as her skin went so pale that Sam could see even the faintest of her freckles.

"First, I owe you an apology. It was clear to me that I didn't have time to commit to helping with your party in the way you needed. I should have been honest and said no from the start, but I wanted to make you happy and be a good daughter, so I didn't. So first and foremost, I'm sorry for not being honest."

Sam paused just in case her mother wanted to say anything. She knew it was unrealistic, but in the darkest and most personal corners of her mind, she'd hoped that her mother would jump to accept her apology and admit to being too wrapped up in herself to see Sam's limitations. But all Diana did was straighten her posture, so she took it as a sign to continue.

"I also should have been more assertive about my time constraints. That was unfair to you, and it resulted in the invitation mix-up and you not getting the kind of food that you wanted at your party. It wasn't fair of me to get that angry when I hadn't been crystal clear with you about my needs and boundaries."

At the word *boundary*, Diana became so still that Sam was a little worried she had stopped breathing. On the upside, she was a doctor, but as the plane up from Los Angeles with Grant had taught her, she was clearly no emergency medicine specialist.

"Mom, I know you love me, and I hope you know how much I love you, but we can't keep going on like this. I know it's hard to have both Isaiah and I go away. You have given up so much for us. You constantly had to control so much of our lives to keep us safe as we moved around. But I need you to let me go now. I didn't leave home to hurt you."

"Sam, I don't think you and Isaiah left home to hurt me. When did I give you that impression?" Diana said, managing to look both affronted and shocked, as if Sam were in the midst of a complete fabrication.

"Mom, when I told you that I was accepted to this fellowship, you said, 'But why would you go so far away from me? Don't you love me?'" Sam quoted her mother but didn't use the voice she and Isaiah typically adopted when mimicking her.

"Well, that was a joke," Diana said with a dismissive wave.

"Was it, though? Because you didn't act like it was," Sam said, losing herself in her mother's defensive argument for a moment. Remembering her goal was to settle a fight, not start a new one, she shook her head. "But what you said matters less than the fact that I don't make decisions with punishing you as the goal. And when I say no, I'm not saying it to make you feel bad. I'm saying no because it's time for me to make my own decisions. I know I'm not always the daughter you hope for, and that can be disappointing, but I hope you can accept this and we can find a path to a better relationship."

By the time Sam finished speaking, her heart was pounding so hard that she thought it would give out at any moment. The pit of her stomach began to sink as her mother took a sip of wine, frown lines creasing on either side of her mouth. This was a classic unhappy-Diana expression, and it took everything in Sam not to try to bend over backward to fix her mom's hurt feelings before she could even give voice to them.

Finally, Diana exhaled and her entire posture changed, her spine no longer rigid as her shoulders rolled forward. "Sam. I don't want to control you, and you've never been a disappointment to me. I know I have never said that. Where on earth did you get that idea?"

"You didn't have to say it. Your actions speak much louder than you think they do."

"I . . ." Diana slumped and looked out the window as if she might find the words she needed somewhere on the gray rooftops of the other high-rises. Finally, her mother looked back at her, her eyes shot through with pain. "Could you tell me what I did? I won't do it again."

Sam looked at her mother and wondered if she was genuinely surprised by the accusation. The kind part of her wanted to believe she was, but the part of her that had lived through years of emotional manipulation said otherwise. Sighing, Sam took a sip of her wine, then decided that she might as well try. If she gave up now, then she wasn't really giving her mom the chance to grow into the kind of parent Sam needed.

"It's hard to narrow it down. I don't say that to be mean, but you've been trying to redirect my decisions for a long time."

"Well, pick a few then." The phrase was blithe, but Diana looked stricken.

"Here's a great example. Remember when I was six and you desperately wanted me to be a girlie girl? Lace dresses, the whole nine."

"You were darling." Diana nodded and smiled fondly down at her drink.

"I was." Sam shook her head. The memory didn't have the same fond ring for her. "But I also had a big brother, and I loved playing in the dirt. You would get so worked up about me tearing my stockings and destroying a dress every week. I asked to wear jeans, but you said no. Do you know what I did instead?"

The smile on Diana's face fell slightly as she remembered what came next. "You started wearing camisoles and leggings under your dresses to school."

"The dresses went in my cubby. I didn't wear them at school. I'd have Isaiah or a friend help me in and out of them. You wouldn't let me be me, and I didn't want to let you down, so I lied."

"I didn't know that."

"I know. Dad figured it out. He was in charge of laundry, and there was always sand in my leggings. When he asked why my pants were dirty but not my dress, I told him the wind did it." Sam chuckled at the memory of her father eyeing her with his most stern Naval Dad Look. Inside, he was probably cracking up.

"Your father would find that kind of thing funny." One corner of her mother's mouth lifted ever so slightly at baby Sam's attempted trickery. "I wish he would have told me, though. I would have softened if I knew."

"Would you have heard him if he did?" Sam meant the question to be gentle, but it still made her mother flinch. Diana took another sip of her wine, so Sam hurried to make her point. "Anyway, that is sort of like what happened with the party. I didn't have time, but you were so angry with me for leaving Ohio, and the party seemed like a way to make you happy. I knew my arm was being twisted, but this also felt like a way to prove myself as a daughter. With each added element for your party, I tried to slow you down. But when I couldn't, I tried to rush or cut corners to fit my time constraints. Hence the invitation mix-up."

Diana looked down at her lap, and Sam used it as an opportunity to sip her wine, just in case her mother wanted to argue. "I just wanted a baby girl. Your father and I were married so young, and Isaiah and your dad were such cookie-cutter father-son types, baseball in the yard and the whole bit, you know?" Her mother looked up then, and Sam nodded along cautiously, unsure of where Diana was going. "Anyway, after years of being by myself, we finally had you, and I thought, *This is my chance. I'm gonna have a friend too. She'll like art and dolls and piano, and we'll be thick as thieves.* But that just wasn't who you are."

Sam hadn't really thought about how lonely her mother must have been when she was young. It was true that Isaiah was basically a mini version of their father: good natured and nonconfrontational unless you cornered him. It must have been hard to feel so isolated even in her own home.

"I guess I still hope that. A small corner of me thought that if I manufactured enough pressure, you'd see things my way and stick around," Diana said, her voice weak, as if admitting that took something out of her that she hadn't wanted to give.

"But I need to be my own person." Sam tentatively reached out to squeeze her mother's hand. Her sadness washed over her, and Sam felt her heart soften. It didn't make the way she'd treated Sam okay, but the context was helpful for healing her heart.

"You do. And I should've known. Isaiah did everything your father did. But you did the opposite of the things I wanted. The only thing you got from me was my hardheadedness." Diana laughed wistfully and looked back out the window as a seagull perched on the top of a parking garage outside. "Even at six, you were going to find a way to make something happen. Even if it meant being sweaty in two layers of clothes. If anything, I'm not disappointed in you. I am disappointed in myself, and I let you feel that. I was never going to be your idol, no matter how hard I pushed for you to engage."

Suddenly, Sam understood. Diana just wanted to be seen, much like Sam wanted her mother to see her now. With tears welling, her mother looked at her square in the eyes as if that alone could convey three decades' worth of apologies—and in a way, it did.

"The good news is I don't need an idol, and I don't want to be a clone. But I do want a mom, and I want to be a daughter. Luckily, I think the mom I have is very impressive, even when she is far away." Sam's throat felt thick with emotion.

"You don't have to say that." Diana sniffed and ran a finger under her eye to try to stave off tears. "I'm sorry I hurt you. That was never the kind of relationship I wanted for us."

"I'm sorry for letting my frustration build up for so long," Sam said, her own eyes starting to water as her mother smiled. Laughing, she added, "And that my playing the piano meant that much to you. Had I known, I wouldn't have switched to playing basketball seven nights a week."

"You weren't very good at the piano, so it was for the best," Diana laughed. After a moment, she reached her hand out and grabbed Sam's. "I guess what I want to say is that I've tried very hard for a very long time to make you into the kind of daughter-friend I wanted, not the kind of daughter-friend I had."

"Maybe now that this is out in the open, we could work toward that instead? Because I think we could be friends. Especially if you still have updates on the neighbors' cats and like ice cream."

"I'd like to try that. The friendship part. Not all those weird flavors you eat." Sam wrinkled her nose at the minor criticism, and Diana jumped in to add, "But I can ignore what you choose and get an orange sorbet."

"We could start by you coming to my program launch Saturday morning. Maybe you could meet my friends? If you aren't too busy prepping for your party." Sam laughed at her mom's kind-of recovery. Baby steps.

"I wouldn't miss it for the world." Diana smiled, then added, "And don't worry about the catering for the event. Your Aunt Marilyn can live with cheese cubes."

Sam laughed as the bits of tension in her heart shook loose. She knew that her mother wasn't going to become less controlling overnight. But now they had a foundation for an honest relationship that they could build on. Really, that was all Sam needed for today. The rest would come later.

Sighing, she turned her attention back to her mom and said, "Funny thing about the cheese cubes. Turns out I have a solution for you. And I gotta tell ya, I'm so glad we talked this out, because boy, do I have a whopper of a story to go along with your new caterer."

"Oh, really. Well, now I'm dying to know how this came about." Diana's face sparkled as she lit up with curiosity. "Let me order another carafe. I have a feeling catching up will take some time."

Chapter Twenty-Two

Sam looked around the birthing center as it started to come alive with guests. The desks and filing cabinets had all been pushed to the edges of the room to make space for folding chairs. Anjo's film crew was roving around the room, getting footage of community members smiling and chatting with each other or the physicians. Duesa even seemed to have her own photographer following her around, with Sherilynn behind them pointing out other shots she would like the crew to take. Duke had a shift, so she hadn't had a chance to ask him for the details; however, his text had said that they would talk and that everything was worked out, so she guessed his charm must have bought them an extension on the report. Sam was just considering how she could say hello to Duesa and hide from the camera when she spotted her family coming down the hallway.

"I gotta tell you, Sam, this is incredible." Isaiah spread his arms wide as soon as he walked into the birthing center, smiling at the photos of families they had propped up on easels around the room. Behind him, her mother and father were grinning as if they had won the lotto.

"You made it," Sam said, holding her arms out wide as her brother wrapped her in a big familiar hug.

"Wouldn't miss this for the world, little sister," Isaiah called loudly, rocking her back and forth. Then, whispering, he added, "I heard you and Mom talked. Good for you."

"Thanks," Sam said, using the telepathic meaningful glances that siblings used to communicate an hour's worth of words in one split second.

Is she mad?

No, Mom's not upset.

Thank God. I was afraid.

Proud of you. Love you. Good job. Ahh, here they come!

"Samantha, this is really something," her father said, pulling up even with the two of them and cutting the siblings' nonconversation short. "I should've known you'd come out to California and do something like this. Look at you, a grown doctor in your white coat."

"Thanks, Dad," Sam said, shaking her head as she reached in to give him a hug.

Once he released her, Diana said, "I'm so impressed, sweetheart," before crushing her in another hug. When she finally let go, she said, "And those are beautiful portraits."

"Earnest, the doula with the green hair, took them. Turns out he has a real knack for photography. You two should chat."

"You'll have to introduce me." Diana smiled.

The corner of Sam's heart that was still tender from their discussion twinged, and she smiled back. It was a small gesture, but it reminded Sam of how far they had come in just a short time and how much further they could still go if they made an effort.

"He shouldn't be too hard to find," Sam said, leaning around the shield her brother's height and broad shoulders provided so that she could see the rest of the room. She spotted Earnest easily, then flinched. Standing right next to him, smiling as if the sight of him hadn't just knocked her world off its axis, was Grant.

In theory, nothing about him should have been special. The problem was that he'd had the nerve to show up looking handsome as ever. Objectively, Sam knew he looked the same as he always had—that same jawline with his brow gently furrowed in concentration as he tried to listen to whatever Earnest was saying over the din of the crowded room. In fact, compared to the first time she'd seen him, the white coat and basic black pants and button-up did almost nothing to show off his body. He didn't even look tired or the least bit sad. Meanwhile, she was still recovering from an ice cream overdose and the kind of puffy eyes that were still sensitive to the touch because she'd cried them into oblivion.

Sam bit down on her bottom lip as anger curled around her, making her face hot and her palms sweaty. If he wasn't even the slightest bit socially crushed over losing her, then he shouldn't have ever had her in the first place. In fact—

Oh shit. Sam jerked her gaze around the room and prayed Grant hadn't caught her staring. Taking a deep breath, she plastered a massive smile on her face as she spotted Kaiya and waved. Nodding to the person she was talking to, Kaiya started to walk over, unknowingly bailing Sam out of yet another jam. If Sam were Catholic, she would have single-handedly begun the process of trying to canonize Kaiya as a saint.

Turning back to her family, she said, "I can't find Earnest, but there is someone else I want you to meet. Family, this is Kaiya Owens, one of the most incredible doulas I have ever had the pleasure of knowing. Kaiya, this is my family."

"Pleasure to meet you all," Kaiya said, smiling at three people who seemed as awestruck by her as Sam was.

"Such an honor. Sam basically spammed the family text chain with articles about you," Isaiah said, half grinning as he ribbed Sam. "It's incredible what you've built here."

"Your sister deserves just as much credit. I've never met someone more determined in my life. You should have seen the way she went after Dr. Franklin for this thing. I was scared she was gonna lose her job." Kaiya smiled over at Sam. "Instead, she got this."

"*Determined* is such a nice way of saying *pigheaded*," her dad teased.

"Don't give me that much credit. I think Dr. Franklin was just too busy to fire me." Sam shook her head and chuckled. Catching sight of her watch, she gestured to her family and said, "Anyway, y'all should go grab a drink. The event is about to start, and I want to make sure you have something to toast with."

"She just doesn't want us to embarrass her anymore." Her father held out his hand. "Thanks for watching over her. I know she really looks up to you."

"It's been my pleasure," Kaiya said, shaking his hand, then turning to take her mother's.

"So nice to meet you," Diana said, giving Kaiya's hand a squeeze. "I'm just so impressed with this."

"Nice to meet you," Isaiah said, nodding at Kaiya as he wrapped his arms around his parents and began steering them away with his typical big-brother affability.

"Your family is darling," Kaiya said as soon as they were out of earshot. "Y'all are just cute. The Holbrooks are like an insurance commercial. All midwestern sincerity, fresh haircuts, and straight teeth."

"I'm pretty sure that is just my dad's naval experience rubbing off on the rest of us." Sam giggled. "I don't think any of us would iron our clothes if he weren't around."

"I'll bet you still make your bed, though," Kaiya said, a tell-me-I'm-wrong expression on her face.

"Every day before I leave the house." Sam wrinkled her nose as her friend snort-laughed. "But not first thing when I get up, so I'm slowly unlearning the habit."

"Right," Kaiya said as if she didn't believe a word of it. Which was fair, since Sam had no intention of giving up the habit.

"Anyway, before the event starts, I just want to say thanks. Thank you for being my partner in building this. I know I came to you with nothing but enthusiasm and the promise of building something that could maybe help others someday." Sam stretched out *maybe* to drive the point home.

"That's not true," Kaiya said, reaching out to squeeze Sam's shoulder. "You also came to me with grit—I mean, I dead tried to scare you away with that coffee rag, and you weren't having it. And you brought an understanding of my work. I've had plenty of people offer me partnerships or shares in their business before. But you"—Kaiya let go of her shoulder and pointed at her—"you were the first one who I thought, *She might actually do something,* and look. You did!"

Sam smiled at her shoes, unsure of what to do with the flattery. In truth, she had done a lot of this, but she'd also had a ton of help, not just from her roommates and the other doctors in the pilot program but from Grant too. She remembered him driving her home from the interview with Anjo, pretending to be casual despite his carefully studied application materials. The thought of him made Sam's eyes sting. Looking back up at Kaiya, she said, "I had a lot of help building this, especially from you."

The two women stood there blinking at each other, both looking like they might cry. Instead, they burst into giggles as Kaiya held her arms out. "Come here and give me a hug before you make me smear my makeup."

Wrapping her arms around her friend, Sam marveled at how lucky she had been. In medical school, people talked about the profession as lonely, but so far, it had been anything but, because of people like Kaiya. Sam released her friend and smiled.

She was just about to suggest they grab a drink when Dr. Franklin's voice interrupted them. "Oh, good. You two are together."

"Hello, Dr. Franklin," Kaiya said, clearly less startled than Sam was by his sudden appearance.

"Hello. I wanted to give you both a heads-up that a couple of reporters are here from the *San Francisco Tribune* and the Channel

Eighteen news. The hospital's media team contacted them, and it looks like they will want to talk to both of you at some point." Dr. Franklin nodded toward two people talking to Duesa and the hospital employee hovering nearby.

"Thanks, Dr. Franklin." Sam thought it was generous to call the hospital's media personnel a team, since she was pretty sure it was just one overworked admin, but she let it slide. "Are you enjoying the party?"

"I sure am. And I have to say, Samantha, when you came to me with this idea, I thought it was nuts and it wouldn't go anywhere—sorry to be so candid," Dr. Franklin said as if the truth might surprise Sam or Kaiya, which it most certainly did not. When he continued, his expression was stone-cold serious. "After looking at the patient-retention and response numbers from your early assessment and then hearing from my own patients, about how they have come to lean on Earnest, plus seeing you and Kaiya in action, making a call that saved lives . . ."

Dr. Franklin stopped and shook his head, and Sam realized that the traditional hospital administrator that she had come to think of as her knowledgeable nemesis was getting emotional. Under his hardened exterior was a man as squishy as a stuffed panda toy. Something about it made Sam's heart soften, and she found herself smiling at him.

Clearing his throat, he tried again. "Anyway, I have to say, I feel truly lucky to have this program at our hospital. SF Central may not have the big dollars or a fancy name, but we have practitioners like you two, and I'm damn proud of that."

And now Sam wanted to cry too. Dr. Franklin had dedicated his career to a hospital and a community that the city frequently tried to forget. He'd probably seen thousands of short-lived programs designed to help him and his clients come and go over the years. Sure, he was cranky and at times paternalistic, but deep down, he cared. Drawing a shaky breath, Sam held out her hand and said, "Thanks, Dr. Franklin. That means a lot coming from you."

Smiling, Dr. Franklin shook her hand as Kaiya watched with a mixture of disbelief and *this is adorable* on her face. When Dr. Franklin let go of Sam's hand, he extended his to Kaiya, who looked at Sam's watery eyes and then back at the administrator and shook his hand before saying, "Since I have you here, I'd love to talk to you about what Sam and I could do for the community classes with just a smidge extra budget."

"Oh boy. I'm in trouble with you two around, aren't I?" Dr. Franklin rolled his eyes.

"You sure are. Shall we grab our drinks and talk before the program gets going?" Kaiya winked back at Sam as she steered Dr. Franklin toward the beverage table, leaving Sam to compose herself before the event started.

Taking three deep breaths, Sam fanned her face with her hand, hoping to dry her makeup before her tears did any real damage. She was just thinking about grabbing her notes from the desk drawer she had hidden them in so she didn't forget to thank anyone, when she spotted Duke and Jehan making their way toward her. While Duke maintained his usual relaxed stride, Jehan's eyes were wide, so Sam knew something was up.

Walking quickly to close the gap between herself and her friends, she whispered, "What's wrong?"

"Nothing's wrong," Jehan squeaked. "Why would you say that?"

"You look like you just saw a poltergeist or something."

"Man, I knew you couldn't keep a secret. I shouldn't have told you." Duke shook his head and ducked a little so his height wouldn't have him broadcasting what he was about to say to the whole room. "It's about the Anjo report."

"Did they reject the extension?" Terror seized Sam's heart. She had seen Duesa enjoying the party, and Duke had said everything was okay. She kicked herself for not forcing Duke to text the details or at least going over to grovel at Duesa's feet. If she hadn't been avoiding the cameras—

"What? No." Duke shook his head, putting a stop to her panic spiral.

"Then what's the problem?" Sam's whisper had more bite to it than she intended, but Duke had scared the hell out of her.

"We didn't need one at all." Jehan's eyes were wide, as if the look alone could communicate something.

"Like Anjo doesn't require progress reports?" Sam wasn't understanding something that both Duke and Jehan did not want to say.

Duke looked over his shoulder, as if checking to make sure there wasn't even the slightest chance they could be overheard. The gesture was so obvious that Sam was sure it would catch the attention of whoever they didn't want to hear. Finally, he turned his attention back to the group and huddled forward a few inches more before saying, "Sherilynn said she wasn't supposed to tell me this, but someone turned it in for you."

"Who would do that? Is there some kind of fairy that just goes around writing out data-driven progress reports for fun? I don't get it."

Her roommates exchanged heavy glances, then turned back to her. Jehan winced, then broke down and finally mouthed, "Grant."

Her friend's voice was barely a whisper, but she might as well have screamed in Sam's face. Heat washed over her as roughly one million conflicting thoughts collided and tried to override the circuitry in her brain. "I don't . . . that doesn't make sense. Are you sure?"

"Sherilynn was very clear. I even asked if they meant that Grant had received an email about the report. But no. He turned it in."

"But why?" Sam said, her voice going hoarse with panic. She had been so rude to him. But of course he'd still managed to fix all this. Why on earth would someone with so much going for him waste his time doing something like that for her? Surely his reputation could have waited forty-eight hours for her to solve the problem.

"Sherilynn didn't say. But if I had to guess . . ." Duke paused and shrugged his shoulders forward. When Sam didn't respond to the gesture, he opened both palms toward her and said, "You know."

"You think I guilted him into it? That was not the intention of that speech," Sam hissed.

"Not guilt," Jehan said, gently reaching up to set her hand on Sam's shoulder. "Grant's love language isn't words. It's service. Think about it."

Bits and pieces of Grant's actions slowly began to click into place. Agreeing to be the birthing center's adviser even when she'd lost the game, driving her around to look at venues, remembering her ice cream preferences. Those weren't the kind of things someone did when they were casually interested. Friends didn't put energy into talking their way into a building for her. Certainly, someone who needed her to be perfect wouldn't write a report for her. Only someone who cared about her would do that . . .

"Oh God. I'm such a fool." Sam's skin felt clammy, even though she was too warm.

"I think *impulsive* sounds nicer than *foolish*," Duke said, as if the semantics would soften the blow. He'd told her to apologize to Grant and hadn't even had to wait two full days to be proved right. She should have apologized. Instead, she was stubborn. And now she had this glaring chasm of an error in judgment standing in front of her. Anjo hadn't shown up because Duke had made promises. They'd shown up because Grant had given them everything they needed.

Sam glanced up just in time to see Grant smiling at Dr. Franklin and Kaiya, who were walking toward the podium. The realization that any second now the event could start and she would be stuck sitting just a few chairs away from Grant, looking like a coldhearted jerk, hit her like a truck speeding down an empty street. "I have to say something."

"Better make it quick. The event starts soon," Jehan said, nodding at the podium, where Duesa, Dr. Franklin, and Kaiya were already standing. "Good luck."

"Right. Thank you both," Sam said, wiping her palms on her pants as she glanced in Grant's direction again.

"Go get 'em," Duke said.

Sam was almost positive she was going to need more than luck to fix this. Even if Grant's love language was service, it was very possible to love someone and let them go. For all she knew, turning in the report was his way of saying he'd never let go before prying her off the edge of a nice big door so she could sink to the bottom of the ocean like Jack in *Titanic*.

Grant had every right to let her go. After all, she'd behaved horrifically. Made all kinds of terrible assumptions based on her own trauma and not what was standing steady before her. She hadn't even tried to think of things from his perspective. The poor guy had basically gone out on a limb for her, carted her around town, backed her up at every turn, and then committed the unconscionable sin of bad timing.

That was it. That was all it had taken for Sam to throw everything she knew about his character out the window and start them back at square one. How dense was she? And would Grant even want to give someone that stupid a second chance? She clearly wasn't about to make room on the door for him when the tables were turned and—

Grant finished his conversation with a very pregnant person and looked up, knocking Sam out of her spiral. Without thinking, she closed the remaining ten-foot gap between them before he had time to slip off. Reaching a hand out, she touched his forearm and said the first thing she could think to say. "If you are letting go, can we talk first?"

"What?" Grant said, his eyebrows shooting up as if he thought Sam might have had one glass of Martinelli's too many.

"I . . ." Sam gave her head a shake, hoping to rattle more useful words loose. "What I mean—"

"Hello! Hello!"

Kaiya's voice rang out from the podium, causing both of them to jump with surprise. In Sam's mind, she'd thought she'd at least get the words *I was wrong* out of her mouth. Instead, all she had managed was a contextless *Titanic* reference and mounting regret. The room began to shift toward their seats, and she felt her hand tighten around Grant's forearm. She needed to speak fast. "I know about the report. You were just trying to be helpful, not judgy. You have every right to be mad, and I can understand if you need to—"

"If you can all take your seats, we'll get started," Kaiya said, her gaze landing pointedly on the two of them. Sam felt her panic spike sky-high as she belatedly remembered that she had labeled their chairs on opposite sides of the podium to avoid having to sit near him. The act was so petty it was almost comical now.

Releasing Grant's arm, she said, "Maybe we can talk about it later? I'll let you decide. Okay, bye."

"Yeah—" Grant's expression was inscrutable as the lights in the room dimmed and the video the two of them had shot only days before began playing on the wall above the podium. Grant looked at Sam hard, his lips pressed together in a thin line, then turned and hustled over to his chair without another word.

For a moment, Sam simply stood there, the absence of Grant's words ringing in her ears as a giant version of herself started to speak. Something about seeing her own face on camera, even with Bebe's excellent makeup job, forced her to move to her chair.

Sam tried to pay attention to the event. After all, this was a celebration of the hard work that she had put into the birthing center. At some point, she would need to get up and thank everyone. But it was almost impossible to focus, knowing that Grant was all of ten feet away and she still had no idea what he was thinking.

And she might never know, she reminded herself. Grant had every right to keep his thoughts to himself. She had said as much when she'd launched her mess of an apology at him. Looking back on it, she wasn't even sure the words *I'm sorry* had come out of her mouth. Hopefully, he wanted to speak to her. If it ended like this, Sam wasn't sure she could ever get over letting him go.

Chapter Twenty-Three

Sam sipped her glass of champagne and tried to smile as one of her mother's oldest friends began showing her a patch of skin. This was one of the hazards of being a doctor. Suddenly everyone wanted her to look at their moles and tell them if they were going to die. No amount of *I'm not a dermatologist* could preempt it, so Sam had taken to letting people finish before saying, "Aunt Marilyn, you're likely fine, but you should go to your dermatologist, just to be safe."

"I just wanted to be sure I wasn't nuts. I don't want my doctor to think I'm making this up."

Sam nodded in a noncommittal but kind way. Aunt Marilyn most definitely was making this up, and Sam had the various pictures of "areas of concern" she had emailed her since her first year of medical school to prove it, but she didn't say that. As far as Sam was concerned, her aunt's dermatologist could break it to her when she went in for a visit.

Catching sight of her mother, Aunt Marilyn paused, then said, "There's your mother; let me go say hi. Thank you, sweetie."

"Good to see you," Sam called as her aunt scurried away. Sighing, she took another sip of her champagne and looked around the room. If possible, the Lost Key looked even more incredible with her mother's photographs spread around the venue. Out of the corner of her eye, she could see her brother chatting with her dad and one of his retired naval buddies. As her father and his friend laughed, Isaiah stopped one of the Dorothy's staff to grab a spicy momo. Making eye contact with her, he smiled, his joy radiating around the room. Sam felt her heart melt.

Her family might not be perfect, but the one thing she would be forever grateful for was their sibling relationship. Sam wanted to find the event photographer so she could be sure she and her brother got a picture of the two of them together, looking cleaned up. Her mom would want to print it out and bring it around town so she could brag. Meanwhile, her dad would pretend not to care but make it his phone background. In short, her parents would love it.

Spotting the photographer, Sam almost laughed. She was sure that to them, it looked like they were taking a picture of two people engaged in joyful conversation and holding hands. In real life, her Aunt Marilyn had managed to corner Duke and was showing him the same spot of skin on her arm. Catching her eye, Duke half grinned, half grimaced at her before returning his full attention to Aunt Marilyn's made-up maladies.

"You look pretty," Jehan said, pulling Sam's attention away from her other roommate as she stepped out from the buffet room. "I'm loving the yellow."

"Thank you," Sam said, running a hand down the front of her sunshine-yellow fit and flare dress. It had cost more than she was willing to admit, but now that she was wearing it, she didn't regret a penny of the purchase. It made her feel like a queen. And it had pockets. Taking in Jehan's dark-blue off-the-shoulder cocktail dress with her signature silver shoes—in sling-back-heel form—she said, "You look amazing."

"Thanks. I figured if I wasn't going to wear this to my engagement party, I may as well wear it here." Jehan did a small turn so Sam could get the full effect.

"Glad you got an opportunity to show off." Sam chuckled as her friend finished spinning. "Thank you, again, for using your credit with Dorothy's on my mom's event. I know the last few days have been extra hectic, and I genuinely don't know how I would have survived them without you and Duke."

"Aw, you are most welcome, my friend," Jehan said, holding her arms out wide for a hug. As Sam bent down and wrapped her arms around her petite friend, Jehan continued, "It's been embarrassing to have to call off a wedding, then listen to your siblings say 'I told you so.' You and Duke have been little islands of positivity in an otherwise dreadful storm. Dorothy's feels like the least I could do."

Releasing her friend and taking a step back, Sam said, "I feel like I'm getting the better end of the friendship. Seriously, the birthing center never would have happened without your grant-writing skills."

Jehan wrinkled her nose. "Maybe we just agree that we are both lucky?"

"Only if you let me buy you ice cream tomorrow."

"Deal," Jehan laughed.

"There you girls are." Diana appeared in front of them. "Jehan, I wanted to say thank you."

Sam let her mind wander as her roommate and her mother chatted. Diana was almost incandescent while being the center of attention tonight. As much as it hurt Sam's heart to think about it, Grant had been right about how special the venue would make her mom feel. In fact, before the guests arrived, Diana had gotten choked up at the sound of the fountain and how perfectly the natural elements of the space tied in to her photos and party favors. So much of the way her mother was feeling was due to Grant, and he wasn't there to see it.

Sam forced herself to smile at her mother as she thought about how Grant had just disappeared after the center's event ended. It felt like in the time that it took her to shake Duesa's hand, he managed to fly out of the room. Of course, Sam had sworn to herself that she would leave him alone, and she had. Until she was in the car on the way to the Lost Key. The idea of him missing the event was killing her, and in a moment of weakness, she had texted him. Luckily, it was just a short apology, which included the words *I'm sorry*, and not the novel-length grovel she'd been rehearsing. He still hadn't answered her.

"Are you enjoying the food, Sam?"

Jehan and her mother were both looking up at her expectantly.

"Oh, very much. This might sound weird, but I think it's even better than when we did the tasting." Sam nodded, then took a sip of her drink.

"Well, it's my pleasure to do it. Congratulations on a lovely party, Mrs. Holbrook. Now, if you'll excuse me, I'm gonna grab another curry bite before Duke eats them all." Jehan grinned as they all looked over to see their third roommate grabbing two bites from a passing server.

"Poor girl. Her mother must have been furious with her calling off the wedding," Diana said as Jehan made a beeline for the curry bites.

"Not as furious as she would have been if Jehan had married the wrong man." Sam fought the urge to roll her eyes. Since their conversation, her mother had been careful not to criticize Sam at the expense of everyone from Jehan to the unfortunate server with a crooked tie. But Rome hadn't been built in a day. For now, Sam would settle for her mom not haranguing her about every fault.

"True." Diana shrugged, trying to look as if Sam's gentle correction didn't irritate her. "Sammy, this is lovely. Honestly, I know we struggled to get here, but I couldn't have imagined something this beautiful if I tried."

"Thanks, Mom." Sam looked around the room as family and friends milled from picture to picture, admiring her mother's work and laughing at the much-younger versions of themselves in the photos.

"During the center's grand opening, I think it really hit me just how much you were taking on while launching a program that is actually improving people's lives. I'm proud of you."

"I'm proud of you, too, Mom," Sam said without so much as a trace of irony.

"You don't have to say that; I know I was a pain in the ass." Diana waved her hand in front of her face as if pushing Sam's words aside.

"No. I mean, yes. You were a pain, but this party is beautiful. And your photographs? Everyone loves them. The nature pictures, plus the family photos—they really show off what you've learned to do," Sam said, looking just behind her mom, where a picture had caught her eye. A photo of the little ribs of a mushroom all lit up with dewdrops and the first rays of daybreak sunshine. It was God's tea. The very mushroom the man on the plane had consumed the day she'd met Grant. The thought made Sam's heart squeeze, and she pushed it away, focusing all her attention back on her mother.

"Come here, kiddo." Diana threw her arms open and wrapped them around Sam. Surrounded by her mother's hug, she felt another piece of the hard shell she had put around her heart crack and float away. It wasn't as if she wouldn't need to spend some time and possibly many therapy sessions unlearning some of the unhealthy patterns they had established, but in this moment, she felt like they could get to a place of okay.

"I love you, Mom."

"I love you too." Diana released her and then fanned her eyes with the hand that wasn't holding her empty champagne glass. "I guess I shouldn't call you *kiddo* anymore. You are fully someone's doctor who delivered an emergency baby, according to Kaiya."

"Dr. Franklin helped," Sam laughed. "Don't give me that adult badge just yet."

"So sorry to interrupt." Duke appeared, his smile all apologies.

"Oh, Duke, honey, don't be sorry. Thank you again for the use of your car."

"My pleasure." Of course Duke was laying on the charm extra thick as he spoke to her mother, and of course Diana was lapping it up. "I actually came to see if you would like to get another glass of champagne with me. I noticed yours is empty."

"Aren't you sweet," Diana said, throwing a hand over her heart as Duke held out an elbow for her to grab on to.

Sam wrinkled her nose. Duke didn't need to take her mother to get a glass. If he really wanted to be helpful, he could have brought them both a fresh one. Something was up. Sam had opened her mouth to call out her friend when he cut her off, his eyes going wide. "Sam, I think there's a guest over by the door that you wanted to say hello to."

"Who?" Sam asked, whipping her head around. When she spotted the red curtain that hid the entryway to the venue, her heart stopped. There, in all his perfectly tailored splendor, stood Grant. Turning away as fast as she could to avoid eye contact, Sam widened her eyes at Duke in the universal look for *help me.*

"I'll just take your glass too." The joke in Duke's voice was almost palpable as he reached for her empty glass. Grinning like a dog with a bone, he began leading her mother toward the bar as he said, "If you need a refill, come find us."

"So much for being a gentleman," Sam whispered at Duke's back.

Taking a steeling breath, Sam ran a hand over her hair to make sure her curls were still in place. Next, she looked down to make sure that she hadn't gotten any momo on her dress and then checked that her shoes weren't scuffed. Finally running out of things to look at that weren't him, Sam tried to look casual as she turned to face him.

Grant was still standing at the entrance, looking around the room and squinting at the different guests. He was wearing a burgundy-colored suit that was so dark it looked almost black in the venue's soft lighting. Watching him made Sam's face flush. That suit had to have been made for him. It was the only way he could have found something that highlighted every one of his features, from the broad line of his shoulders to the muscular quads she used to secretly appreciate during basketball games. She had just finished admiring the way the cut of his white dress shirt complemented the angles of his face when he turned and saw her.

Sam wanted to jump behind a picture and hide until she could get her heartbeat to slow down, but then she noticed he was holding flowers. Flowers had to be a good sign, didn't they?

Twisting the bracelet around her wrist, she took a step forward, excitement and anxiety coursing through her as she watched his face for any sign of what he was thinking. As she got closer, she could see him fidgeting with the edge of the flower wrapping. He was nervous, which made her nervous all over again.

It dawned on her that the flowers might be for her mother. Grant was a gestures guy. Maybe this was the ultimate rot-in-hell gesture. Something to really drive home the congrats-Mrs.-Holbrook-your-daughter-is-a-judgmental-monster message. Dread washed over her, and she slowed her pace down, reminding herself that not everyone was waiting to trip her. Grant had been nothing but consistently there for her; one mistake on her part didn't mean he would change now.

Before she could fully calm down, Grant closed the last five feet of distance between them. For a second the two of them just sort of blinked at each other. The fine lines between his eyebrows appeared. Sam's thoughts bounced off one another. One of them needed to say something, or this would turn into an hour-long uncomfortable stare.

Taking a deep breath, Sam said, "You came."

Right as Grant exhaled the word "Hi."

The two of them both laughed in that awkward way that indicated that the experience was new for both of them. Sam's anxiety eased as she watched Grant's shoulders relax. Even if he hadn't come to talk and was simply honoring his RSVP, he was still the man who listened to her friends just to find out what she liked. He was kind and thoughtful in his own way, and Sam realized she wasn't scared of what he might do or say. She was afraid that she might have inadvertently broken her own heart by pushing him away.

"So I—"

"Actually, can I say something first?" Sam reached her hand out to gently silence him by touching his lapel, then remembered her situation and pulled her hand back.

"Okay." Grant tilted his head to one side and watched her closely.

Sam put her hands in her dress pockets so she wouldn't be tempted to touch him again. "I know I sort of babbled a somewhat incoherent apology at you earlier today, and I'm not sure that was fair. You deserved to hear thoughtful words, not panicked ones. So here it goes. Grant, I'm sorry."

Sam paused to collect the rest of her thoughts, and Grant's brow furrowed as he said, "It's—"

"Don't say *it's all right*, because it wasn't." Sam shook her head. Listing all the ways it wasn't okay was the hard part, but if she was ever going to have a shot at rebuilding their relationship, she needed to learn to admit when she was wrong. It was unfair of her to expect him to become a mind reader.

"My behavior was egregious and unfair. I took my frustration with my mom out on you, and I jumped to conclusions about the way you were behaving based on a single negative interaction." Grant raised an eyebrow and pursed his lips as if he was biting down on a response, and Sam hastily said, "I should add that I did this in spite of myriad evidence that you are not *that* guy. Instead of simply asking you why you were doing what you were doing and being clear about what was really going on with me, I lashed out. Anyway, it was wrong, and I apologize."

Grant's eyebrow had returned to its usual place as she wrapped up, but his lips remained pursed as the silence stretched between them. Sam felt her heartbeat pick up, and she was suddenly aware of how warm her palms were inside her dress. She had said the words *I'm sorry* this time, but Grant wasn't responding, and that made her mind start to spin. She must have missed a detail . . .

"Thank you—"

"Also, I'm sorry I yelled 'boundary' at you," Sam blurted out over the top of whatever Grant was finally going to say. Exhaling the last of her thoughts, she said, "I know that is not how a boundary works or should be communicated. Okay, I'm done now. I won't interrupt you again."

Grant looked at her hard for a second, and Sam wondered if the stress might make her pass out. Maybe she should also apologize for talking over him? But she'd promised she'd stop speaking, so that apology would have to wait.

"You sure you're done?" Grant asked, looking at her with detached skepticism.

Sam's stomach plummeted as she nodded while Grant continued to watch her, his head slightly tilted to one side. After three more excruciating heartbeats, Grant's face relaxed and spread into a slow smile. "You sure you're sure? Because every time I think you're done, you have more."

"I promise." Sam nodded. Being in the presence of his smile made her relax. It hadn't been long since she'd last seen it, but she had missed it. When Grant smiled at her, she felt like she was standing in warm sunlight.

"In that case, I have some things that I would like to say as well." Grant's expression was neutral, but he pulled his shoulders back a fraction of an inch and fidgeted with the flower wrapping again. "First, thank you for your apology. I accept." Grant nodded, as if he had finished ordering a meal, and Sam wasn't entirely sure what to say or do. Somehow, she had envisioned him accepting her apology in a much more kiss-and-make-up kind of way. She took her hands out of her pockets and twisted the bracelet around her wrist while she waited for Grant to say more or give her any indication of where he was headed.

After four and a half seconds that felt like five minutes, he said, "Also, I owe you an apology, I think—"

"Why? I was clearly wrong." Sam burst in without thinking, then closed her mouth as Grant's face twitched into a smile. "Okay, but you knew I had to interrupt you one more time. Now I really will be quiet."

"You're lucky I like you." Grant laughed and shook his head. "I owe you an apology because clearly, you were having a hard day, and I knew my timing was bad, but I put my agenda in front of yours. It wouldn't have killed me or my reputation to wait until you'd had a chance to decompress."

"It really wouldn't have," Sam said, echoing his laughter.

"I know. I thought about it later, and I'm fairly certain that was your first emergency delivery at SF Central. It took me like a day and two phone calls to my grandma to burn off that level of anxiety when it happened to me."

"I ate like a quart of ice cream and cried to my roommates. I think your coping mechanism was better." Sam shrugged and turned her bracelet over on her wrist again as Grant smiled.

"Anyway, I am sorry for that. We still needed to have the discussion, but you were right about us not needing to have it then."

"Thank you. I accept your apology." Sam nodded in the same manner, suppressing the urge to hug him. She was ready to get this show on the road and get down to brass tacks. Were they breaking up, heading inside to get a drink, or both? If she didn't get the answer soon, she might twist her bracelet clean off her wrist and into the stratosphere.

"Well, that's good, but I'm not done," Grant said, the serious expression returning to his face. "I also realized that part of the reason you were upset is because I've made you guess in the past. Will I be your adviser? Did I read the materials? Is this a date or am I really just showing you a venue for your mom's party? The thing is, I like you—so much it's a little scary, actually." Grant paused to laugh at himself, then said, "You said we wouldn't work because I couldn't understand how hard it is for you to ask for help. While I can't know your exact experience, I can empathize. You have big dreams, and those get messy.

That stubborn ambition is one of the things I adore most about you. I just want you to know that I'll always help you. I don't always let you see what I'm thinking or feeling. Sometimes because I don't know, but sometimes because I prefer to let my actions speak for themselves. But you can't know that I have your back unless I say it. So I'm sorry I kept you guessing. It was a recipe for disaster, and I won't do that again."

For a moment, Sam just looked at him, too stunned to say much of anything as her mind turned his words over. Her messy ambition wasn't a hurdle to him. It was something he loved. Grant didn't want her to be perfect or even close to it. He just wanted her to be herself, convoluted, chaotic big dreams and all.

Sam had started the evening just hoping he might return a text. She hadn't expected an apology, let alone for him to see her side of things. Sam was the one who'd acted poorly, yet he was willing to meet her halfway and learn along with her. The more she thought about her previous behavior, the more humiliated she was. If there were ever an award for sterling character in the face of stupidity, Grant deserved it. Sam let go of her bracelet and looked Grant over. "You are—"

"Or I'll try not to make you guess again. And you can call me out if I do," Grant jumped in, grinning as if he had been waiting for her to respond just so he could cut her off. Sam wrinkled her nose in an attempt not to laugh, which she failed miserably at. Once she was done, he said, "Okay, now you can speak."

"You are sweet." Taking a step closer to him so there were just a few centimeters and a bouquet between them, Sam smirked. Batting her eyelashes, she tapped the flowers and said, "Are those for me?"

Grant's face faltered, and his eyes darted around the room as if he were working through a serious conundrum and needed a place to hide. When none appeared, he sighed and said, "Actually, they're for your mom."

"Seriously?" Sam asked, trying to maintain a straight face as she realized she'd been half-right about the flowers.

"I mean, yeah. If I'm gonna meet my girlfriend's family, I want to make a good first impression," Grant said, like this was obvious, and another little piece of Sam's heart melted. Not only did he think she was his girlfriend, but he wanted to make a good impression on her family, disastrous as she made them sound. Mistaking her silence for concern, Grant furrowed his brow as he sputtered, "But yours are at home . . . with the ice cream . . . assuming you want to be my girlfriend and I'm not stuck in the friend zone."

Something about the way he said the words reminded Sam of the first time they'd met, only now she saw him in an entirely different light. He wasn't the cold man she'd believed him to be. Somewhere along the way, she'd started to see him for who he truly was, a thoughtful man with an occasionally surly exterior. He was softer than his pride implied and kinder than she'd understood that day.

Sam smiled up at him and felt her heart flutter as the small crease that had appeared between his brows relaxed. "Since neither of us wants each other to guess, I'll just tell you now. I accepted your apology the second you offered it, and I became your girlfriend the minute you said the magic words . . ."

"'I'm sorry' really does it for you then, huh?" Grant smirked as he shifted the flowers out of the way and reached for her.

"Not those words," Sam said, enjoying the feel of being so close that she could see the way the soft lighting played with his lovely dark eyes as he watched her.

"What words then?"

Sam ran one hand along his lapel and around the back of his neck, leaning into him until she could almost feel his lips, then said, "Ice cream."

Grant was still laughing when he kissed her. The kiss was sweeter than any dessert she could have imagined and more intimate than any single embrace. It was a kiss that held forgiveness and their future. Most importantly, it was a kiss that promised that no matter what happened next, they knew they had each other.

ACKNOWLEDGMENTS

The first acknowledgment of this book goes to everyone who manages our health generally and our reproductive health specifically. I don't think any of us made it through the last few years without developing an increased awareness of and gratitude for the individuals that make medical care available to us. From public policy and medical researchers and frontline health workers to paraprofessionals, administrators, and equipment suppliers, our systems simply don't run without the people behind them. Thank you.

My second thank-you goes to my readers. You are what I love most about being a writer. Thank you for your encouraging emails and posts, for coming to conferences with dog-eared copies and homemade candies, and for just being kick-ass. I am grateful for each of you.

Writing a book is one of those things that seems to evolve its trickiness level no matter how many times you do it. Thank you to my editors, Maria Gomez and Lindsey Faber, for being the perfect partners in crime. Thank you both for getting my humor and Post-it speak and generally knowing what words my sound effects are standing in for when I'm squawking with excitement. Similarly, thank you to the team at Montlake: Jillian Cline for always being ready with the answer to a question, Patricia Callahan and Karah Nichols for your fantastic organizational and production skills, Riam Griswold (again) and Alicia Lea for the outstanding copyediting, and Kelsea Reeves for your cultural and sensitivity edits and excellent taste in movies.

I also want to thank my agent, Nalini Akolekar. The more I think about it, the more I am convinced that I lucked out when you decided to represent me. Similarly, thank you to the team at Spencer Hill. I am grateful for all you do to support me and my agency siblings.

Thanks to the medical professionals who let me interview them for this book, including Naomi, Sarah, and others who shared your anecdotes and experiences with me. Your knowledge of the profession, from hospital administration to nursing, midwifery, doula work, research, and complex medicine, was indispensable in writing this book.

While I technically wrote this book alone, I had a whole crew behind me—Struggle Bus friends, thank you! Thank you for helping me brainstorm and talking me out of spirals. Thank you for your energy, enthusiasm, and dedication to the ever-important panda. Thank you for being there on the hard days and for breaking out the champagne on the good ones. This book wouldn't have happened without you all.

I also owe a big thank-you to my Day Ones, Ang and Ashley. You two are Beyoncé in my eyes. Similarly, thank you to GAP (Great-Aunt Patty), who at ninety-seven continues to be the best early reader and cheerleader I could ask for. Also, thank you to a whole host of friends from near and far who cheered, reassured, encouraged, and occasionally cajoled me into taking a break and having some fun. You all listened to me be stuck on plot points, deep dive into the mechanics of tropes, and talk about so much more inside baseball than anyone outside of publishing should have to listen to. If I ranted at you about my nonsense, just know that I love you and I appreciate you.

Finally, thank you to my family. I love you.

ABOUT THE AUTHOR

Photo © 2020 Natasha Beale

Born and raised just outside Seattle, Washington, Addie Woolridge has spent her life cultivating the experiences that make her characters so richly developed, relatable, and real. Though her love for knowledge, diversity, and different cultures has honed her writing, Woolridge is also a classically trained opera singer with a degree in music from the University of Southern California, and she holds a master's degree in public administration from Indiana University.

When she isn't writing or singing, Woolridge can be found in her Northern California home, baking, training for her sixth race in the Seven Continents Marathon Challenge, or taking advantage of the region's signature beverage—a good glass of wine.

To learn more about her books, upcoming releases, and other news, visit www.addiewoolridge.com.